The Basel Account

Being Part 3 of The Basel Trilogy

Best Wishes

Ian H. Lane

This is a work of fiction. Names, characters, organisations, places, events and incidents are either products of the author's imagination or are used fictitiously.

ISBN-13: 978-1540514981

ISBN-10: 1540514986

Printed by CreateSpace. An Amazon.com Company

Dedication

For my Daughter and my Son:
Kathryn Fiona Cowdry and Timothy Hamilton Lane

Contents

Acknowledgements

With grateful thanks to:

Times Newspapers Ltd for permission to quote Elie Hobeika's Obituary of 25th January 2002 in Chapter 39.

The Basel Trilogy - The Story So Far

The Basel Formula (Part 1)

Elizabeth Fielder, born Lizaveta Feldman, Moscow, 12th June 1964, an agent of the SVR the successor to Russia's KGB, is in prison in Basel, Switzerland. She is charged with the murder, on the night before the city's annual *Fasnacht* carnival, of a colleague Eugene Preston, also known as Vladimir. She had come to Basel with Peter Lewis her boss, the director of a small north-London scientific glassware company, to make a delivery to a research laboratory there. Lewis' company had been targeted by the SVR, who had been led to think that it provided the *entrée* to the laboratory which they believed was developing a drug which they planned to steal. Elizabeth and Peter are lovers but the affair is fast unravelling as Peter's son is suffering psychologically from the absence of his father, for which situation the boy blames Elizabeth.

Keeping the Russians under surveillance both in London and in Basel is Israel's Mossad in the person of Sam Kagan, also known as Sam Charles. The SVR had been set up by Mossad but the project took a turn that affronted Sam who resigned at the debriefing in Tel Aviv. He has fallen for Elizabeth almost from his first sight of her - though he has only spent one day in her company, the day of the shooting - and is determined to secure her liberty, though how he will do so is very far from clear to him.

***

The Basel Exodus (Part 2)

Sam has returned to Basel and is at his wits end trying to find a way of securing Elizabeth's release. He visits Poland to research family roots and the Holocaust, in which many of his family perished, and while there realises that he must give evidence at Elizabeth's trial. The evidence will be based on his bugging of Elizabeth's hotel room and he knows that he has broken Swiss law and that he himself will face arrest. A further complication is that Elizabeth's defence lawyer is in therapy and her therapist has planted false memories of childhood abuse. Sam has to ensure that she is in a fit state emotionally to conduct an effective defence. There are various twists and turns to Elizabeth's trial and the story ends with both Elizabeth and Sam regaining their liberty and with their eventual marriage.

***

The Basel Account (Part 3)

A serious threat to the State of Israel is uncovered and Sam is persuaded to serve with Mossad once more.

Now read on!

PART 1

Recalled to Duty

Secret services are psychologically unstable places and their internal mind-set is quickly reflected in performance.

Markus Wolf, Memoirs of a Spymaster

Chapter 1

Wednesday 30th May 2001

He stood looking down on the Rhein, watching the ferry, secured by a pulley to its cable high above the river, being carried by the force of the stream from the boarding point below him to *Klein Basel* on the other side of the river. The geraniums decorating the ferry were now in bloom, adding their splash of scarlet to the brown painted vessel with its white roof. A clock chimed three, drawing his attention to the red sandstone bulk which rose behind him - the *Münster*, the Protestant Cathedral - with its twin spires and patterned roof of tiles in varied colours. Somewhere within its austere interior lay buried the great Erasmus of Rotterdam who had died on a visit to Basel in 1536, either on 11th or 12th July - the ambiguity, so characteristic of the life of the great scholar, arose from the difference of one hour between Basel time and that then kept in the suburbs of the city. It was a calm afternoon with hazy sun and a touch of warmth. Tourists and sightseers came and went but the man in the dark, well cut business suit remained there lost in thought.

Balthasar Feuerbach was usually, indeed almost always, back from lunch and seated at his desk by 2 p.m. but this afternoon was different: he had a problem that had to be resolved quickly and to his satisfaction. It was a problem that had arisen that morning and which demanded his immediate attention. He had thought about it over lunch and at 2 p.m. he had called his secretary on his mobile telling her that he had been detained and would be out for part of the afternoon. The good woman, knowing that he had no visits to clients booked for then, had shown her customary concern for his well-being, he wasn't unwell or anything like that? No, a business matter had come up over lunch and he needed to deal with it immediately. He'd be back at his desk later on and would attend to the documentation for tomorrow's meeting of the trustees of the new arts foundation. She had known that there was no business lunch appointment booked in his diary for that day and her concern had remained unabated.

The ferry was now on its way back across the river and he was no nearer to a decision on the right course of action, so once again he turned his mind to what had happened earlier. He had spent the first part of the morning dealing with some investment decisions for a client with whom he had dined at *Die Drei Könige am Rhein* the previous evening. An American from Denver, a bit brash, but, nevertheless, a discerning connoisseur of the graphic arts with a shrewd nose for both commercial value and artistic merit. Over the years Feuerbach had taken his advice on which works to buy and he had certainly not been disappointed with the subsequent performance of the artists' work in the international auction houses. And besides there was considerable satisfaction in seeing the canvases on his office walls and in his comfortable house on the fashionable and tranquil *Gellertstrasse*. He had pleasure admiring his paintings - they brought with them the pride of possession - and it was even more pleasant to hear the admiration of others, especially those best qualified to judge. He considered that the ownership of such things enhanced his standing in the city as a man of substance and culture. He returned to the events of the morning: while he had been having coffee, his personal assistant, Herr Rosenau, had asked for a very confidential word. Rosenau was, among a number of things, responsible for the bank's internal security - though the amounts of money it handled were substantial the bank itself was a small organisation, almost a family, albeit one which maintained formality and hierarchy in its staff relationships, first names were for signatures and not for daily use between the members of its staff. It was regrettable, but outside his control, that many of the present generation of the bank's clients expected to be on first name terms with him. In his mind he now replayed their conversation:

'There is a problem, Herr Feuerbach, and a very embarrassing one at that. When I reviewed a selection of yesterday's security tapes I heard a telephone conversation, or at any rate one side of a conversation, involving one of your clients, Herr Jakob Schmidt.'

The security system, monitoring telephone calls as well as conversations in the staff and directors' rest rooms, had been installed quietly and at considerable expense one Sunday six months earlier on the advice of Captain Erik Blum, an old colleague of Feuerbach's from his days with the Swiss Security Service. Initially Feuerbach had not wished to include the directors' rest room in the system, but Blum had pointed out that if the staff ever came to know that their facilities were bugged, while the directors were excused such indignity, there would be much aggravation and, possibly, legal action against the bank. The system was there to detect any breaches of security: the preservation of total secrecy and confidentiality was a *sine qua non* of Swiss banking, and especially of Swiss private banking. A spy within was an enemy of the bank and its customers as well as an enemy of the Swiss State.

'And you would like me to drop what I'm doing and listen to the tape, Herr Rosenau?'

'Exactly that Herr Feuerbach. As you know there has been nothing of consequence over the last six months but *now* there is something you should most certainly hear.'

'But, Herr Rosenau, Herr Jakob Schmidt is a customer not a member of our staff. He only knows about his own affairs and what we have arranged for him, he has no knowledge of anything else that is done within these walls.'

'That is true, but you *must* hear what the tape records of the telephone call he made from the rest room yesterday morning.' Feuerbach wondered to himself whether it was thoroughness or curiosity that had made Rosenau choose to review the directors' rest room tape.

'Very well, Herr Rosenau, I'll come.'

They had proceeded to Rosenau's room two doors

down the corridor, Rosenau unlocking the door with his security card to regain entry. Feuerbach's secretary had the next room, but Feuerbach disliked interconnecting rooms which gave direct access to one another and so the way from one room to another was via the corridor. Rosenau had previously rewound the tape and had it ready to play to Feuerbach, to whom he had handed a typed transcript that he had made.

'If you would like to take a seat at my desk, Herr Feuerbach, you will be able to follow the tape more comfortably.' He depressed the key on the player and the recording began to play:

> "Karl, I'm at our Swiss bank. You'll be pleased to know the finance is all in order, we've $9.2M available and more on the way. You've seen Alyosha? .... He wants twelve million Dollars? *Twelve million!* Tell him he can have ten, then we might get it for eleven and that includes packing and delivery to the port. After all Alyosha's anxious for us to use the thing. His father was a guard at Treblinka and the Poles hanged him in 1946. .... You didn't know that, well don't let Alyosha know that I've told you - he'll mention it if he wants to. .... You're not sure whether it's a clean or a dirty device? If it's ex-USSR stock it will be clean and powerful. That really doesn't matter, though, it's for the Jews. What's important is that it works - that, when we want it to, it goes off with one hell of a bang. You can tell him from me that if it malfunctions he'll have the fury of the16th September Unit after him and that we won't leave off until we've got him crying for mercy and not even then!"

Rosenau had waited for him to respond and Feuerbach had mentally given his PA high marks for this:

any comment would have been superfluous and Feuerbach had no time for people who chattered needlessly. There could be no doubt whatsoever about the intent of Schmidt and his friends.

'Well, Herr Rosenau, as the bank's security officer you don't need to be told to keep your lips sealed about what we've just heard.' He indicated the transcript, 'Is this on your PC?'

'It's on a floppy disc not the hard drive.' He handed over the floppy disc in an envelope with the date and time written on it: 10.47 a.m. 29th May 2001.

Feuerbach opened the envelope, 'And the tape, please.'

'You would like me to run it back to the start?'

'The start?'

'Of Herr Schmidt's telephone call, Herr Feuerbach.'

'What else is there?'

'Before the call Herr Schmidt is using the facilities of the rest room.'

'Bodily functions?'

'Yes, bodily functions, Herr Feuerbach.'

'It will be enough to start with the telephone conversation, Herr Rosenau.'

The tape had been rerun and handed over, joining the floppy disc in the envelope. 'I'm most grateful to you, Herr Rosenau. Now you must forget about all you've heard. It's not your problem, it's mine.'

'And for that I'm grateful ... not that I'm trying to avoid responsibility, Herr Feuerbach ... '

'Of course not, I'd never accuse you of that.' He turned to leave.

'One thing, Herr Feuerbach, *perhaps* you would be agreeable to signing for the tape. There's a register of tapes and if at any future date ... '

'Someone should come looking for this one and find it missing ... "

'Just so, Herr Feuerbach.' Rosenau had opened the register which was already on his desk and Feuerbach had signed for the tape.

Well that was it. Feuerbach noticed that the ferry had set off from the near shore once more and he wondered whether he had seen it arrive there. He took his pocket watch, an antique English Hunter on a heavy gold chain, from his waistcoat and checked the time, twenty five after three. He'd probably missed the ferry leaving and returning, his thoughts had been elsewhere. He tried to analyse his reluctance to act. Was it really that he was anti-Semitic or was it simply that he was pro-Palestinian? True, some of his best clients were Jews, but then he never turned away good business. But, in truth, there was no choice, he'd known that all along, Rosenau knew what had been said and if an atom bomb - or was it a hydrogen bomb? - went off in Israel he would have to face Rosenau's, probably unspoken, accusations for years to come. And, in any case, common humanity demanded that he should act. He gave himself a little pat on the back for his grave concern that the veil of banking secrecy should not be drawn aside too readily. His earlier years in the Security Service had made him slower, rather than swifter, to inform. And so, after a final glance at the river and a heavy barge making its way with the stream to the sea at Rotterdam, he set off back to his office.

He walked along the side of the *Münster*, on his right the trees of the *Münsterplatz* were beginning to come into leaf. The sight lifted his spirits, he responded readily to the changing seasons and particularly to the arrival of spring and early summer. At the front door of the *Münster* he paused for a moment and then entered. He had always wanted to locate Erasmus' burial place. For a couple of minutes he stood at the back of the cathedral, taking in its cool dignity, before leaving again. Perhaps he should donate some money from the next sale of surplus paintings to fund the search - there was the small van Gogh of a battered boot that he didn't really like but which he had bought for the name - yes, that would be appropriate, using profit from the sale of one Dutchman's work to track down the resting place of another. Erasmus, scholar in the ancient tongues, who though proficient in Latin and Greek, had given up trying to master Hebrew but who had, nevertheless, striven to encourage the scholarly study of that tongue. Well, Balthasar Feuerbach had an important message for today's Hebrews, or at any rate, for someone to pass on to them.

The bank was just a little way along the *Münsterplatz*, partly screened from gaze by the trees, the only thing that distinguished it from a private house being the brass plate beside the front door, "Feuerbach et Cie". The plate had been so well polished for so many years that the wording took a little deciphering and testified to a long established and very respectable concern. He called in momentarily to make a telephone call and collect the tape and the transcript from his wall safe. He knew that he had better set his secretary's mind at rest and he told her that he had an appointment in central Basel and would be returning later, though there was no need for her to wait for his return. Frau Wieland sensed an excitement about him and wondered to herself whether he had an assignation at some hotel with a woman he had met at lunch. She sighed to herself, perhaps if she were to drop a hint and let him know that she had at last separated from her husband he would then show some interest in her. She touched up her lipstick and applied a little perfume to her neck, she would be there for his return to the office.

***

Feuerbach made his way to the appointment on foot. He passed between the museums in *St Alban-Graben*, perhaps it was time for him to donate a suitable painting to the *Kunstmuseum*, past the *Elizabethen-Kirche*, with it's hollow trellis-like steeple, and then past the back of the *Stadt-Theater* before descending, by way of the *Klosterberg* and *Steinentorstrasse*, to the *Heuwaage*. Fifteen minutes after leaving the bank he was standing at a window looking down from the Public Prosecutor's

Office onto the red and yellow trams making their way along the *Binningerstrasse* below.

'An unexpected visit, Balthasar, but a welcome one. It's seven years, I think, since you inherited the bank and left the service. I suppose this place looks a bit Spartan compared to what you're used to.'

'True there's a degree of luxury at the bank, Erik, but, of course, that's because it's what our customers expect to find when they visit an institution of our distinction.'

'Of course, Balthasar, whyever else? You were fortunate to find me in Basel today, lately I've been spending a lot of my time in Bern. You said you had some information that needed to be passed on urgently.'

A knock at the door heralded the arrival of a tray with a couple of mugs of coffee, a bowl of sugar and a plate of biscuits.

'It appears I'm an especially honoured visitor, Erik, they didn't run to biscuits in my time!'

'But you were staff in those days, Balthasar, today you are the bringer of information and we must make you feel wanted - in the most pleasant sense of that word - and welcome!' They both laughed and the visitor was reminded by the use of his first name that in leaving here for the formal, dignified life as chairman of the bank he had lost something of the comradeship of working in a team of superiors, equals and juniors where you were valued according to the contribution you made to the team effort. But then he couldn't have refused the call to head the family firm when his father's premature death had created a crisis.

'There's a tape recording for you to hear Erik, from our security monitoring system. You don't need telling about that, after all you advised me on the subject last year and pointed me in the direction of some discrete installation engineers.'

'Yes, you mentioned the tape on the telephone and there's a machine on the desk ready for you to play it. Have a seat.' They turned away from the window and sat facing one another at Erik Blum's desk. Feuerbach remembered that when he had left the service Lieutenant Erik Blum had occupied this room. Now he was still here, the same room, one rank higher as Captain. Perhaps there was little movement out of the service and few opportunities for promotion; Blum deserved better, he was a good investigator, or he had been in the time they had served together. He took the envelope from his pocket, removed the cassette and handed it to Blum.

Blum inserted it in the player. 'First coffee. If I remember rightly it's no sugar, isn't it?' Feuerbach nodded and Blum extracted a beer mat from a drawer and passed it in his direction before handing him the mug. 'Biscuit?' Feuerbach took one and placed it next to his coffee. 'Shall I start the player? Though first of all who are the speakers?'

'There's only one on the tape, a client from Frankfurt, one Jakob Schmidt, supposedly a property developer, though he looks more like an academic *manqué*. It's one end of a telephone conversation, the call was made from the directors' rest room. The tape is, I think, self explanatory.'

Blum started the machine:

> "Karl, I'm at our Swiss bank. You'll be pleased to know the finance is all in order, we've $9.2M available and more on the way .... You can tell him from me that if it malfunctions he'll have the fury of the16th September Unit after him and that we won't leave off until we've got him crying for mercy and not even then!"

Feuerbach indicated that there was no more to hear and there followed a silence which remained unbroken for the next minute or so. For some reason Feuerbach found himself reflecting on the furnishings of the room, the metal desk and furniture. Even the lowliest of his staff had a wooden desk and chair, either antiques or very good reproductions. He wondered if he was wasting the bank's money. No, it was buying an ethos, his staff felt they were superior employees of a very superior bank and made that little bit extra effort: it was money well spent. He was brought back to the afternoon's agenda by Blum's voice.

'And you believe this is genuine, not some sort of send up, a hoax?'

'For there to be a send up Herr Schmidt would have had to know that we recorded events in the rest room. He couldn't have known, you'll have to treat it as a genuine threat and the only place where you would want, or rather a terrorist would want, to use a *nuclear* weapon,' - that solved the problem of whether it was an atomic bomb or hydrogen bomb - 'against Jews would be in Israel itself.'

'That's my own conclusion too, Balthasar. I'm glad I persuaded you to wire the directors' rest room as well as that used by lesser mortals! I'll keep the tape and report to my masters. I've no doubt we'll be back asking for more help, information on Jakob Schmidt, his address and full details of all his financial dealings.'

'You'll be asking for this officially?'

'Yes, though as you know it's not likely to be in writing.' Feuerbach nodded, that was the way with matters of this kind.

'That's it for now then?'

'As you say, Balthasar, I know you're a busy man. Expect to hear from me tomorrow morning.'

'There's just one thing ... '

'You aren't anxious to have me crossing the threshold of your very private bank in my big police boots, lowering the tone of the establishment and putting the frighteners on your clients?'

'Well, I wouldn't have put it precisely like that, Erik.'

'But that's the general drift of your concern?'

'Well, yes, generally.'

'Don't worry, you can count on our discretion. If we need to visit you I'll send Lieutenant Peter Gruenweiler, he's a law graduate and a recent recruit who hasn't had time even to begin looking seedy like the rest of us.' Feuerbach threw up his hands in protest and they both laughed before Blum showed him to the lift.

'And how's your daughter, Erik?'

'Clara's growing fast with expensive tastes in clothes but she's doing well at the *Gymnasium*, so I can't complain.' His wife had died ten years before and he'd had to be father and mother to the girl. Colleagues said he hadn't married again because he was already married to the Security Service. Somehow he'd always managed to balance his duties: he was a good father and a good investigator. Whenever he was tempted to envy the wealth and good fortune of the likes of Balthasar Feuerbach he consoled himself with the knowledge that he was fortunate in having a daughter like Clara, a thought that both reassured him and reminded him of his vulnerability should anything untoward ever happen to her. And he was also well aware of his good fortune in having a job which he regarded as worthwhile and which used his abilities to the full.

On Blum's metal desk the visitor's coffee was undrunk and the biscuit untouched. Well, they'd have to bring out the bone china the next time Balthasar Feuerbach called. Blum made a few notes and then called HQ in Bern. While he was waiting for his Head of Section to come to the 'phone he thought of Sam Kagan. His first meeting with him had been in this building shortly after Sam's arrest at the *Strafgericht* - the Basel Criminal Court - and Sam had been more than happy to drink their coffee and eat their biscuits! He was the first Israeli security man he'd met, though apparently he had since quit Mossad's employ - immediately after the fiasco of their Basel Formula operation. He smiled to himself at the way Sam's colleague had negotiated Sam's early release from prison, using copies of bank accounts of some of the Swiss Council of Ministers as a bargaining counter. Sam Kagan had - what was the Jewish word? - yes, *chutzpah*, that was it! Blum's superiors had been furious but the early release had been welcomed by the Baslers in general and Blum himself had been well pleased with the outcome. If he could deal with Kagan on this case he would be very happy. His thoughts were interrupted by the Head of Section's voice, 'Captain Blum, I understand you have something interesting to report ... '

Chapter 2

Tuesday 5th June 2001.

Sam Kagan was indeed now ex-Mossad. Since his marriage in 1998 to Elizabeth Feldman, herself a former Russian spy - of the commercial variety and in the employ of the SVR, the current designation of what had once been the KGB - he had worked for the Golan Heights Winery. From the Israeli point of view the Golan was in the north of Israel, having been annexed as part of the country 20 years before. In the eyes of the Syrians, who had lost the territory in 1967, as well as the UN and the USA among others, it was occupied territory. Comprising around 500 square miles of strategic terrain it had, prior to 1967, provided a base for Syrian sniper and artillery fire directed against the *kibbutzim* of the Galilee. Israeli enthusiasm for the Golan ebbed and flowed: at times there was a general willingness to return it as part of a peace settlement with Syria while at other times its strategic significance was uppermost in people's minds and its retention was demanded. But the matter was largely academic as Damascus was unwilling to talk peace on any acceptable basis.

That morning Sam had made an inspection tour of some of the vineyards that supplied the winery. In all there were eleven, ten in the Golan Heights, one of which was in any case tended by him, and one in the Upper Galilee - a compact group of sites to visit with an interesting mix of folk to meet. They belonged to a number of *kibbutzim* and *moshavim* - collectives and co-operatives - with their different political outlooks.

Apart from one visit to a vineyard, the afternoon was his and he had planned to make the most of the available time, visiting places that were significant to him. He felt the need for a stocktaking, a return to his roots to reappraise the direction life had taken. He began with a visit to his parents' grave on a small kibbutz in the Upper Galilee. There he spent time alone with his memories of them, particularly of the old man: before World War II a baker in the small Polish community of Brok to the east of Warsaw; later one of the few survivors from among the men who escaped on 2nd August 1943 from the death camp at Treblinka; from the late 1940's a taxi driver in Crown Heights, Brooklyn and later owning his own taxi business; after *aliya* to Israel, a *kibbutznik* here in the north of the country keeping the tractors and farm machinery in working order until the day in 1985 when a *Hizballah Katyusha* rocket from over the border in southern Lebanon snuffed out his life. His demise could easily have led to bitterness in Sam's heart but his father's outlook and attitudes had been his most important legacy to his children: for he had been an open and welcoming man, on good terms with all humanity whatever their origins. In Brooklyn his business partner had been an Afro-American who had been killed on a Civil Rights march. At the *kibbutz* he had numbered among his friends Palestinian and Druze workers who came daily to work there, friends whose mourning of his death had been as heartfelt as that of his fellow *kibbutzniks*.

From the *kibbutz* Sam drove north to Metulla continuing the short distance beyond to the fence marking the Lebanese border. Once he would have met IDF soldiers there waiting their turn to head north into bandit country in their armoured personnel carriers, but now the Israeli presence in southern Lebanon was over. At 6.40 a.m. on 24th May 2000 an IDF officer had locked the Fatma gate in the border fence and brought to a welcome end 22 years of the Israeli army's presence in the Lebanon. Their occupation had sought to protect the northern Galilee from rocket attack but without complete success, as the inhabitants of Kiryat Shmona had too often experienced. And the occupation had been at the cost of the slow but relentless loss of the lives of young IDF soldiers. This process of slow attrition had lowered the morale of both the men in the combat units and their families.

Sam's time there in the Golani Brigade during the early years of the occupation had been another factor in making him what he was. The comradeship of army life, especially in the face of the constant fear of attack by militias hiding in the rocky landscape and the actual experience of such encounters when comrades had been terribly and sometimes mortally wounded, had left its stamp on him. He didn't have any wish to be back over "The Good Fence" but nevertheless he missed the comradeship of the soldiers he had led. Army life had knocked the corners off an earlier excess of individualism and had made him into a good team member.

He greeted an IDF patrol who were keeping a wary eye on the other side of the border, 'It's as well you're this side of the fence these days!'

Their sergeant agreed enthusiastically, 'You're right there. I was with the troops when we pulled out last year and we weren't sad to see the last of the place. We lost too many good men there for sure.'

'You hail from the States?'

'Yea, Atlantic City, New Jersey, got fed up working for one of the casinos and thought it was about time I came here and gave a hand. And you're not from very far from New Jersey, I reckon. I'm Daniel Krieger, by the way.'

'And I'm Sam Kagan.' They shook hands. 'I hail from Crown Heights, Brooklyn - I've been here for quite a while now but I still have a soft spot for New York, I've a lot of good memories of the place.'

Sam noticed that throughout their conversation the sergeant had been on the alert, keeping an eye open for any threat from over the fence, and he approved the man's professionalism. He too was wary of what might be hidden out of sight there.

'Can't say I miss Atlantic City, hardly the cultural capital of the USA! But this is different, it's given me a genuine sense of purpose - and the comradeship's something I've not come across before.'

'Yes, danger welds a good unit together and makes you reliant on one another. It's some years since I served on the other side of the fence there in southern Lebanon but I know it was one of the formative experiences in my life. Mind you, like you I'm glad we pulled out. It was too high a price to pay for little or no benefit. But it took some courage for Barak to give the order to clear out - that's one legacy he's left, even if his negotiations with Arafat came to nothing.'

'Soldering I love, but keeping the Palestinians in order is something I can do without, we're not really trained for it - it's a job for the police - and the men aren't happy. But like good soldiers we get on with the job, there's no one else to do it.'

'It wasn't a job I had in my time in the Golanis. I'd finished full time service by '78 and while I was a reservist we didn't have this unrest. Though we did have hair raising times north of here in the Lebanon. It's strange, we were always mighty pleased to be back out of the place, but I often come here to stand, and look, and remember.'

A stillness took hold of the two men as they gave free rein to their varied memories. There was a deep comradeship in their common sense of shared, though unexpressed, experience. They stood looking towards the mountains in the north, across the fields, some showing freshly tilled rich brown earth - reminding Sam of his brown beret of the Golani Brigade - others green with the promise of the year's harvest. In the distance and to their right were the snowy peaks of Mt. Hermon. The scene breathed tranquillity though both knew full well just how deceptive appearances could be and how easy and dangerous it was to be lulled into a sense of false security.

The sergeant broke the silence, 'I expect like me you were remembering them, the ones who didn't come back alive from over the fence.'

'Yes, them as well as the ones who still carry the marks of the conflict in their hurting bodies. Holding our ground hasn't been easy or cheap in terms of courage and casualties. Seeing that rich soil reminded me of the blood that our men spilt on the earth of Lebanon.'

'But that's all behind you. What are you doing now, presumably you live here in the north?'

'Yes, my wife and I live in Katzrin in the Golan? D'you know the place?'

'That's where there's a winery, isn't it?'

'Just so, that's the outfit I work for. My job is to go round the vineyards keeping in touch with the growers and making sure that all is well, that the grapes are coming on properly. We're jealous of our reputation, we make a quality product and need to keep it that way.'

'Good for you, keep up the good work. Time for us to be going, we've got a stretch of the fence to patrol and check, hope to see you again some time.'

They shook hands and then the sergeant got his men together and set off. Sam gave them a wave and continued his contemplation of the scene. How long ago was it that he'd come out of the Lebanon with two dead comrades in his armoured personnel carrier after they'd been ambushed five km or so from here? Could it really be all of 17 years? Yes it must be - it had been a couple of years after the IDF's push north to Beirut. But it seemed like yesterday. As fresh and detailed were his memories of his visits to the men's families to break the news, attend the funerals and share their mourning. He remembered Arieh's widowed mother and his sister in her mid-teens and the look of uncomprehending disbelief on their faces - they had only been in the country for twelve months, having come from France to find security and a new life. The background of Shimon's family had been different, their forebears had been among the original *kibbutzniks* at Degania Aleph at the southern end of Kinneret, the Sea of Galilee. They had known plenty about strife and loss throughout their time in Israel; members of the family had distinguished themselves in the War of Independence in 1948 and in later conflicts. But that hadn't made it any easier to face the loss of the 20 year old Shimon, their youngest son, the pain of loss was exactly the same.

Was coming here and remembering them in this way an indulgence? No, he told himself, it was what he owed them, young men of potential and promise whose lives had been cut short by a conflict which, showing no signs of reaching any conclusion, continued to drag on inexorably. Young men with whom he'd been proud to serve and who'd looked to him for leadership. An intense time and one for him now long past, though there were plenty of IDF personnel like those he'd just met facing similar risks and having now to face Palestinian unrest in the West Bank and Gaza. A restlessness rose up within him, stirred by memories of sharing military life as a close knit team with the men of his platoon. He shrugged his shoulders, it had been a phase of his life, a significant one but not the whole of life. No good trying to re-live it or to wish it had gone on for longer, had it done so he would probably have been one of those afforded the trappings of a military funeral. He made his way back to the car - one more vineyard and then home.

His journey was southwards from Metulla on Highway 90. He passed through Kiryat Shmona, the past target of many *Katyusha* rocket attacks though fortunately there had been none recently. At Ko'ah Junction he took a winding road up to Ramot Naftali, the only one of his vineyards outside the Golan - if the Syrians were ever given back the Golan this vineyard, in the Upper Galilee would still be able to supply the winery, always supposing the winery itself was shifted out of the Golan. At 420 metres elevation this was one of the lower vineyards. He was due to make a call at 3.00 p.m. and found he had nearly an hour to spare. He took his map from the car door and got his bearings. For a while he'd wanted to see the view from here and he felt in need of exercise. He parked the car by some small buildings and a watchtower, evocative of the early watchtower and stockade *kibbutzim*, and set off up the hill to the top of Keren Naftali. The exertion was worth while for, at the top, he stood and drank in the view of the watery Hula Valley of the Jordan. The Golan Heights, with Hermon on his left, formed a dramatic backdrop as a storm cloud rolled away. From here the strategic necessity for controlling the Golan was patently clear.

He returned to the road before heading north along a path beside a pine wood until he reached a domed building with a courtyard and a tomb in the abandoned Arab village of Nabi Yusha. A note on his map had said that it was claimed by some to be the tomb of Joshua the son of Nun, Moses successor, the leader of the conquest of the Land of Canaan. And the tomb was revered by the members of a Shi'ite Moslem sect! This was indeed a land of strange contrasts and the most unlikely associations of people and places. A land with more prayer and more war than anywhere on earth and with a greater readiness to venerate the dead than to respect the living, whether they were your own people or outsiders. To the south, in Tiberias, were three tombs of eminent rabbis, Akiva, who had endorsed Shimon bar Kochba in his ill fated revolt against the Romans of CE 135; Meir, healer and revealer; and the great Maimonides, rabbi, philosopher and physician, who had died in 1204 and whose remains had been brought from Egypt. Nearer still was Safed - the third of the holy cities of Israel - the home of Jewish mysticism and the cabalistic thought of the ancient rabbis like Isaac Luria, the Holy Lion. Today the town had an interesting intermingling of ultra-orthodox and artistic communities. And it was near the Horns of Hittin where the Muslim warrior Salah al-Din - Saladin - finally defeated the Christian Crusaders. And Hittin was the location of the supposed tomb of Moses father-in-law Jethro, a holy place to the Druze, who gathered there for their annual festival. And of course the Galilee, where Jesus had lived and taught, had throngs of Christian pilgrims - at any rate in better and more peaceful times. What a mix! History and faith thick on the ground with layer upon layer to be unpeeled like the skins of an onion! He checked the time, 2.40. He'd better be on his way back to the car, he didn't want to be late for his visit to the vineyard at *Moshav Ramot Nafthali*.

'Early, Sam, by one minute I reckon!'

'I always try to be precise, Yossi.'

They shook hands, men who had known one another for two or three years but who were still somewhat wary of one another.

'All's well with the vines, Yossi?'

'How else might it be? We care for them properly, we don't dodge work or cut any corners here.'

'Far be it from me to suggest otherwise, Yossi, but despite our best efforts at caring things can come along to upset them. Let's take a stroll and have a look.'

They set off together, inspecting the vines which had been pruned some months before and which were displaying healthy shoots. Their talk was of viniculture and the success of the co-operative project between the *kibbutzim* and the *moshavim*, the owners of the vineyards supplying the winery.

'We've a good location here, Sam, with the hills on three sides to shade the vines from the morning sun, it gives us the effect of a slightly cooler climate, we want to grow grapes not cook them on the vines. I'm looking forward to a good crop this year but as always it all depends on the weather we're sent ... and provided the present unrest stays away from the Galilee and the Golan. What do you think?'

'My guess is that the worst that might come your way is a stray *Katyusha*. They're talking about a *super-Katyusha* which could reach Haifa from over the border.'

'Over the border from here's only 3 km, Sam. That's uncomfortably close! You're rather safer at Katzrin.'

Yossi Schwartz like Sam was ex-Mossad but, while Sam had resigned from the service, Yossi had come to the end of his time and his contract had not been renewed. A thorough, indeed fastidious, man he had lacked the imagination that made for an effective contribution to the Security effort. This difference in their departures from the service made for a tension between the two men that time had not been able to lessen. When they had first met they had exchanged comments on old colleagues but this had soon come to an end and now their conversation was always of the vines or of generalities.

'You never know what might come up over the top of the hill from the direction of Damascus, Yossi.'

'It's a long time since anything did. It's not since '73 that Syrian tanks have come that way. We're far more likely to be on the receiving end of something unpleasant here in Ramot Naftali.'

'But you are happy to remain?'

'Happy is the wrong word. Willing, no, *determined* is more like it! I was born here and I'm not going to trot away with my tail between my legs because there's some risk in being here. I owe it to people like Eitan Balahsan who lies buried in the *moshav* graveyard. You remember his death I expect, with two other Paratrooper

Reconnaissance Unit officers at the hands of *Hizballah* in the Lebanon a couple of years ago? Yes, of course, you were at the funeral. I might think differently if I had a wife and kids.' That was another thing, Yossi was single, none of his many liaisons had come to anything permanent, and he showed resentment at the fact. But he was good at caring for his vines and Sam knew that keeping him talking on that subject would make for a more pleasant and relaxed visit.

'So you're hopeful of a good crop this year?'

'I'm always hopeful but, yes, you can see they're shooting well this year, come and have a look at the far side of the vineyard where they're doing particularly well.' And so their business continued.

As Sam drove away from Ramot Naftali he reflected that this was a small country. Both he and Yossi had memories of those who had died in the continuing conflict. And his thoughts turned to what they had not discussed, their time with Mossad. Sam had two or three close ex-colleagues with whom he discussed the Institute past and present. Others seemed to have decided that it was dangerous, so far as their career prospects were concerned, to be seen in the company of Sam Kagan. And in a way that was welcome. Sam had known ex-Mossad people whose whole talk was of what they had done in the past, men who not only had lived their past career to the full but persisted in reliving it to the detriment of the present. That wasn't a temptation for him: he had Elizabeth and the two children as well as a job with the winery that he enjoyed and which enabled him to get out and about and meet any number of people. And yet ... and yet he looked back with longing and affection to his time with Mossad, at any rate until he had been involved in the Basel operation and discovered that it wasn't what he had thought but something far nastier over which his conscience had demanded that he protest.

He thought of the good times he had spent in the service. It was always the same when he visited Yossi, almost as though their avoidance of discussion of the "old times" forced memories to the surface. He asked himself whether his was the nostalgia of an ageing man looking back to the excitement of more youthful days of action. No, he knew it went far beyond a nostalgic longing for the past: his work had been vital for national security and he was proud of what he'd achieved, or rather with what he and his colleagues had done, for it had almost always been a team effort. He knew that had he stayed he would have had much to contribute and that was what brought pain and regret. But he knew that quitting had been necessary, otherwise he couldn't have lived with himself. There really had been no choice for him in the matter. So he set himself to shake off the longing for the past. He told himself that his present job was one that he enjoyed and it was good to be living in the Golan with Elizabeth and the kids, no great distance from the *kibbutz* where he and his family had lived on first coming from the USA. But, despite his efforts, there remained as always a lingering, longing wish that the Basel business hadn't turned out in the way it had. But, when he reminded himself that the decision to quit had left him free to return to Basel and secure Elizabeth's release, all feelings of regret fled away.

As he turned into his road he saw the car parked outside his house, a metallic blue BMW Z3. They had visitors, not anyone he could identify from the car - none of their friends owned anything so exotic. Well he would soon know who was calling. He parked behind the BMW and walked to the familiar and welcoming front door. Another day's work was over and he was home.

Elizabeth greeted him at the door. 'You've got a visitor. By the name of David Goldberg, seems he used to work with you. He's been here for a couple of hours. I tried to call you on your mobile but you'd switched it off.'

'I sometimes do that. Sorry, but there are times when I can do without interruption, times when I'm conversing with myself, like today. Goldberg? Ah yes, I remember him. What does he want?'

'He didn't say, though from his manner and the fact that he's sat here for the last two hours it's probably urgent.'

'Well we'll see, Elizabeth.'

Goldberg was in the back garden under a lemon tree which was in full fruit. He was sitting with his back to them drinking tea and reading a file of papers. He heard them come out of the house and rose to meet them.

'Glad you're back, Sam. I need to be in Jerusalem for a meeting at the PM's office at 20.00 hours.'

'You're obviously a very busy and important man, David.' There was a touch of mockery in Sam's voice but his visitor didn't notice it or, if he did, then he chose not to react.

'It's not me that's important it's the matter that's brought me here to see you.'

'Indeed we'd better hear about it. But before you get going I need a drink. Elizabeth, seeing the vineyards at Odem this morning has given me a hankering for some Gewürztraminer. There's a bottle in the fridge. If you could bring it with a corkscrew and some glasses I'd be grateful.'

Elizabeth departed for the kitchen.

'It's of the highest importance, Sam, we need your services again.' Goldberg began but was stopped before he could get any further.

'Not until Elizabeth is back, David. What you have to tell me you can tell her and I'll vouch for her silence. We have no unnecessary secrets. I somehow think that our present lifestyle is under threat. If that is so Elizabeth will have a substantial say in how I respond to you and she should hear it from your mouth.'

Goldberg seemed about to object but evidently had second thoughts as he responded, 'OK we'll wait for your wife.'

There was silence for a couple minutes until Elizabeth returned with the wine. Sam removed the cork and looked at Goldberg, 'A glass of wine David?'

'I'm on duty and driving but, just to keep you company, pour me a small one.'

Elizabeth poured the wine and looked at Sam who indicated the chair next to him, 'Our friend has an important message, Elizabeth and I want you to hear it. If I'm not mistaken it could affect our lifestyle. I told David that he'd have to wait until you were here. Right David, let's hear what it's all about.'

David Goldberg looked around to make sure that there were no other listeners. They were at the foot of the garden with a field of cut grass beyond. He was satisfied but nevertheless he lowered his voice. 'We need to have you back working for us again, Sam. We have intelligence that suggests drug monies are being used to buy nuclear material from some part of the old USSR. The buyers are thought to be a terrorist group but we don't know whether they're the end user or whether they're agents for some government. We've been getting some assistance from the Swiss who have been prepared to lift the edge of the veil from their banking system but we want some more co-operation. Their man is Erik Blum, Captain Erik Blum. You know him I think?'

'I knew him when he was a lowly Lieutenant. So he's a Captain now. A good fellow. He interrogated me and he was the one who negotiated my release with Noam Cantor. He also interrogated Elizabeth, so she knows him as well.' Elizabeth nodded.

'The regard is mutual, Sam. In fact he won't deal with anyone else but you. Says you're the only Mossad agent for whom he'd give a character reference. Goes even further in fact, says you're the only one who's *kosher*! The top brass weren't too flattered at that!'

'I don't expect they were, David. I appreciate the compliment though. And what are you asking me to do?'

'If the operation is approved, go to Europe, act as the link man between Blum and some of our people who will be operating around Marseilles, which is where the drug smuggling seems to be organised.'

'For how long?'

'Could be three months, perhaps less. It depends how fast the thing moves.'

Elizabeth broke in, 'We've only been here three years, Sam. Are we on the move already?'

'Not unless you agree, Elizabeth.' He noticed the expression on Goldberg's face. 'David, you must appreciate that this is a serious turn of events so far as Elizabeth and I are concerned. OK, I appreciate that the situation may be critical, perilous even. But you've had plenty of service from me and you won't have forgotten that I was not best pleased when I left the Institute. I detested the way the Basel operation turned out and the attitudes of some of my masters. Surely there is someone else that could work satisfactorily with Erik Blum?'

'Not according to Erik Blum. If we're going to get full co-operation from the Swiss it seems that it has to be you. You can ask him yourself if you like, one of my colleagues is keeping him amused as his guide to Jerusalem at the moment. No amused isn't the word, they're at Yad Vashem. Blum asked to go there and wanted to make a full day of it. He's certainly not ticking it off as just another tourist attraction to be done.'

'I'm unable to give you an answer yet, David. Elizabeth and I will have to consider it together in principle and then, assuming we're prepared to take it further, we'll have to have the full details of what the assignment involves. We will see you at the Institute on Thursday.'

'But that's two days time.'

'Well done, David. Yes, Elizabeth and I need adequate

time to reflect and decide - to decide whether to take it further, you understand. I can say no more than that for the moment. And Erik Blum? He'll be around?'

'We'll have to keep him amused tomorrow.'

'I'm sure that's possible, David. There's quite a lot to see in Jerusalem.'

'Sam, we could entertain him here. Bring him back north with us on Thursday for a couple of days.' Elizabeth was enthusiastic.

'Do what you like with him, Sam, but we really would appreciate it if you would come back on board - for a while at any rate.'

'And if I said I had aspirations for a management rôle at the Institute. Having a hand in reshaping the organisation, putting some professionalism back into it?'

'I'll pass the message on to them. There are some of us who would welcome that, after the wounds we've inflicted on ourselves recently, we need to be seen to be getting a firm grip on things. We could do with a steady pair of hands around the place.'

'Good, David. That's as far as we can go until Thursday. 10 a.m. at the Institute and Elizabeth will attend with me. Now you must be on your way, you mustn't keep the PM waiting. Wouldn't help your own promotion prospects, would it!'

'Arik won't be around when it matters, Sam. It's just that punctuality is important to me.'

Goldberg shook hands with Elizabeth who stayed in the garden as Sam showed him to his car.

'Well Elizabeth, so I'm wanted back at the Institute! What time are Olga and Ya'akov due back from the *crèche*? In ten to fifteen minutes? Then refill our glasses and I'll tell you about my day. Once we've got the youngsters to bed we'll eat and then, after that, we can start to think about Goldberg's rather unwelcome offer of employment.' In his mind however he asked himself just how unwelcome the invitation really was. Was he being selfish in reacting with quiet excitement? - it would all depend on what the job entailed.

'You always stay so calm, Sam!' She fought back tears, 'That's not meant to be sarcastic. I admire you for it. But when we're so happy here ... I never thought I would be sitting with a husband like you under our own lemon tree and surrounded by this glorious countryside. Have you seen the wild flowers by the roads today? I love the Golan, I love our home, I love Israel.' She paused and looked at him, 'And I love my husband, Sam Kagan, and our children. Thanks for telling Goldberg that we would decide together. But Sam I want you to know that I will respect your judgment. If you feel that you must say yes to them ... then that is what you will do.' She had driven her tears away, proud that they had come cap in hand to him and asked for his help. She drank the Gewürztraminer, how good it was just sitting there together .

Sam seemed to read her mind and said, 'One vision of the blessing of peace and contentment for our people during Solomon's reign was of everyone sitting under their vine and their fig tree. Here we are with the fruit of the vine and sitting under a lemon tree instead of a fig tree.'

'Peace you said, Sam. For how long if some madmen have nuclear weapons as their playthings?'

'That Elizabeth is a factor in our consideration. So is the increasingly uncertain future of the Golan, one day the politicians may decide to hand it back and cause us to look for somewhere else to live. We'll get your mother to come up this evening to look after the children. Someone may be able to drive her up. Then tomorrow we'll spend the day out in the Golan and the Galilee as we make up our minds.' He raised his glass, uttered the blessing over it, paused and added, '*L'Haim* - To Life - and to the destruction of all that would endanger it!' They sat there, comfortable in the quietness. Sam broke the silence, 'I've been up near Mt Hermon today and being there brought to mind a Psalm, one our people used to sing as they went up to Jerusalem on the three great annual pilgrimages:

> "Behold, how good and pleasant it is
> when brothers dwell together in unity!
> It is like the precious oil upon the head,
> running down upon the beard,
> upon the beard of Aaron,
> running down upon the collar of his robes!
> It is like the dew of Hermon,
> which falls on the mountains of Zion!
> For there the Lord has commanded the blessing,
> life for evermore." '

Their silence returned, the silence which, nevertheless, is communication and which those who are close to one another can share with enjoyment. How good it was to sit there, feeling the residual warmth of a glorious day in early summer, the pair of them together with a bottle of excellent wine, the fruit of the Golan's soil, to share. The words of the Psalm permeated their thoughts. Sam was particularly struck by the idea that brotherly unity was a holy thing - the oil running down from Aaron's head had been the fragrant oil of his consecration. If only the Israeli people could find that kind of unity! And if only the offspring of Abraham - Jew, Arab and Christian - could agree just to get on together! At the moment they were very far from it both within and outside the borders of Israel. He and Elizabeth lived here in Zion, and Hermon was visible from a little distance along the road. The Psalm's setting wasn't somewhere remote, there was for them both satisfaction and deep fulfilment in living here. The sound of children's voices reached them. Sam smiled, 'Time for our little ones, Elizabeth. They too will have to figure in our calculations as we turn our thoughts to David Goldberg's kind invitation.'

Both Sam and Elizabeth knew that the decision they faced was a hard one and that it could, once more, turn their lives upside down.

Chapter 3

Thursday 7th June 2001

They drew up at the gate of Mossad Headquarters in Tel Aviv. 'Sam my friend, my comrade in arms, I saw your name on the list of visitors when I came on duty. It's good to see you again, it's been much too long since we met.' Elizabeth watched while Sam got out of the car and embraced a great hulk of a man in uniform.

'Elizabeth, come and meet Dov!' She joined the two of them by the gatehouse. 'Dov and I were together in the Golani Brigade, Elizabeth. We had some fine times there.'

'Hikes and picnics in the sunny south of the Lebanon, hide and seek with *Hizballah.* That sort of thing. Good to meet you, Elizabeth.' He looked like a bear, albeit a friendly one, and his handshake was appropriately firm.

'Dov would have been a near neighbour of ours in West Hampstead, that is if he hadn't made *aliyah* years ago.'

'I've never regretted coming here. I gave up fighting to get on Underground Trains for service in the IDF. Such friendships! When you've faced death and shed blood together you bond as a group of soldiers - there's nothing, absolutely nothing, like it anywhere else.' He turned to Elizabeth, 'I owe my life to your husband, not once but twice over and he's got medals to prove it.'

Sam looked uncomfortable, 'And you'd have done the same for me if I'd been wounded. You were the one who suffered bad wounds and yet you went back into the Lebanon for more!' He wrote on a page in his diary and tore it out, 'Here's our address and 'phone number, Dov. In any case I'll call you in the next couple of days, we must have a good long chat. How long is it since we did? A year? That's far too long!'

'Good, I'll look forward to that. And it's good to see you here, improves the quality of the personnel by about

100% to have you back again. It's certainly gone to the dogs since you left, too many own goals for anyone's comfort, except the enemy's, of course. Look after him, Elizabeth, we need him.'

'That's what I'm afraid of, Dov.'

'No need to be afraid, Elizabeth. We always looked on him as bringing us good luck, protection from the enemy, that sort of thing. Sam's unit suffered much lower casualties than other units. Sam's are a safe pair of hands all right!' It was the second time she had heard the phrase used of Sam in less than forty eight hours.

Again Sam showed mild embarrassment, 'You exaggerate Dov ... '

'Only a little, there was never a shortage of soldiers keen to serve with you ... '

'We were experienced and alert, Dov, that helped to limit casualties.'

'Helped, yes, but it wasn't the whole story, not by any means.'

'I'm afraid our reminiscences will have to wait until we next meet, Dov. Elizabeth and I have an appointment at 10.00 hours.'

The men gave each other another comradely hug and then Dov had a gentler one for Elizabeth during which he once more charged her, 'Look after Sam, he's special!'

'I know that, Dov, and don't worry I'll look after him.'

***

They sat round a table in the conference area at the end of the Deputy Director's room. With introductions over and coffee served they turned to business. Anticipating some official resistance Sam had made it clear on their arrival that Elizabeth was part of the team and that Mossad's secrets were as secure with her as they were with him. Erik Blum had needed no introduction to either of them and he had greeted them with warmth, a warmth they reciprocated. In addition to the Deputy Director himself there were three other Mossad personnel; Ehud from the World Terrorism Section; Moshe, whom Sam hadn't met before, a lecturer at the Weizmann Institute and an expert from the Nuclear Desk; and Zvi from Admin.

The Deputy Director called the meeting to order and said that business would be conducted in English (a tongue he regularly used in his liaison meetings with the CIA). Then, having formally welcomed "the visitors", as he termed them, particularly Elizabeth Kagan and Captain Erik Blum of Swiss Security, he asked Blum to tell them what had brought him to Israel.

Blum glanced down at the single sheet that comprised his notes and began, 'Firstly I'm grateful to you for your welcome and also for the opportunity of renewing my acquaintance with Sam and Elizabeth Kagan whom I last saw on their wedding day.' He smiled in their direction and they read in his face a look of real affection and esteem. 'Before I go any further I must make it clear - as I have already done in previous meetings a couple of days ago - that, if my service is to work smoothly with Mossad in this matter, then I must deal directly with your Mr Kagan. In that matter I have the firm backing of my masters in Bern. The recent surveillance activities of Mossad on Swiss soil haven't exactly endeared you to my colleagues or to their political bosses but, on the other hand, the way in which Sam Kagan conducted himself and his selfless readiness to give evidence in Elizabeth Feldman's trial impressed our nation. Impressed them to the extent that, when he avoided a stiff prison sentence, the court's decision was met with only a minimal dissent from the usual ultra-nationalists and grumblers.

'I am here because of information that has come to us from one of the Basel banks. As you know Swiss banking is a closed world, that and our stable society are what make our banking facilities so attractive to customers world-wide.' He stopped and looked around the table, 'And before anyone raises the question of the treatment by Switzerland of refugee Jews during the conflict with Hitler ... '

'May his name be eternally blotted out!' it was Elizabeth who had spoken and her vehemence surprised the assembly.

'With which I entirely concur. On Tuesday I spent the day at *Yad Vashem* and was deeply moved by what I saw there.' He looked across the table to Zvi who nodded back in acknowledgement. Then he continued, 'You can take it that I am as sympathetic to the safety of Israel and its people as a Swiss can be and, that being so, I hope you will not object too strongly to my saying to you that Israel would be well advised to think carefully how it handles its internal security problems ... '

The Deputy Director broke in, 'Arab *intifadas* you mean ... '

'Yes, problems of that sort. I raise the matter as a friend and not a foe, the best friend is an honest one who tells you the truth. I'm not suggesting you should be soft in the face of violence, lumps of rock can and do kill and maim, but I'm suggesting you make a greater effort to counter the way you're seen on the world's TV screens. It's a question of training and method and you shouldn't expect young conscript soldiers, trained for warfare, to be on that account skilled in containing civil disturbances. And in the matter of assassinating guerrilla leaders ... '

The Deputy Director broke in, 'The practice is known as the "targeted interception of terrorists." '

'I'll not argue over what it's called - if you're on the receiving end it probably makes very little difference - but it doesn't do Israel any good internationally when innocent bystanders, especially children, are harmed as well.'

'I'll pass it on to the GSS, Captain. But just consider for a moment the additional atrocities that a terrorist like

The Engineer would have perpetrated if we had left him alone and not given him an exploding telephone as a present: the world needs to see it that way and follow our example. Perhaps in time softer nations will learn from us and act.' The Deputy Director kept most of his irritation from view. Sam had been watching his face, seeing there vestiges of annoyance and tiredness. He could only guess at the man's weariness with the politics of the job, internal wrangling within Mossad as well as having to do the impossible for the various Government ministers with an interest in security.

'Thank you, I note what you say.' Blum had delivered the message on behalf of the Swiss Foreign Minister, now he looked down at the single sheet of paper before him and took up the immediate issue. 'I return to the subject of Swiss banking. We offer a whole range of private and highly confidential facilities. People generally think of Zurich as *the* centre of Swiss banking but there is also Basel, a city well known to some of our company.' He looked in the direction of Sam and Elizabeth. 'While you wait for your luggage at the carousel at the airport - Basel-Mulhouse-Freiburg Airport as it is now known - you will see the advertisements of some of our private banks seeking customers, private customers, that is, with substantial sums of money to be managed. The bank's absolute discretion is an important part of what the customer buys. Some advertise and there are others who disdain to do anything so demeaning, they operate on the basis of professional advisers - lawyers, accountants and the like, introducing them to their clients or of old customers recommending them to their friends. Now it happens that one such bank has a director, its Chairman indeed, who spent a while working for Swiss Security. On occasions - rare occasions - he comes across something which looks dubious, and then he has a quiet word with us. A week ago something happened that brought him to my door with information that seems to be of immediate concern to Israel.

'I'll go back to the beginning of his story. Last autumn, almost nine months ago, an account was opened at the bank by Jakob Schmidt, a German, apparently from Frankfurt. He was a property developer, it seemed, and had come on the recommendation of a lawyer in that city. There was nothing strange about that. Money began to flow into and out of the account most of it coming from Jersey banks. Some of it was used to buy investments in the name of a Liechtenstein Anstalt - a cross between a trust and a company - but most stayed with the bank. There were considerable cash flows, something like $11M came in and about $1.8M went to buy the Anstalt's investments, $9.2M remained at the bank in Basel and eventually moved onwards to a bank in Monaco. The Jersey accounts were no doubt simply conduits and probably there were other foreign banks involved along the way.'

'A money laundering operation?'

'In all likelihood, yes. And if that was all I knew I would be at my desk in Bern this morning attending to other matters. The reason for my friend, the banker's, concern was something that happened a week ago. How it happened is a rather amusing story. The bank's Chairman had been concerned about the possible leakage of commercially sensitive information. As I've already said, among the essentials in Swiss banking, and particularly in the sort of business carried on by my friend's bank, are absolute discretion and total secrecy. As he had once worked for our Security Service he had spoken to me off the record about the problem. I suggested the clandestine recording of all telephone calls into and out of the office. In addition I advised the bugging of the restrooms so that, if anyone slipped off with a mobile, their conversation, or at any rate one side of it, would be picked up. Somehow tapping the office telephone didn't bother him but he was quite concerned about bugging the restrooms: for some reason or other it didn't seem to him to be right and proper. Bodily functions, he seemed to think, should be afforded a greater degree of privacy than business conversation! I stressed that all the restrooms - that for the directors as well as the staff ones - should be dealt with: then if the bugging ever came to light he would be able to point out that it was a case of the same sauce being served for the goose as for the gander!' This adage however conveyed little to the Israeli contingent. 'In the end he agreed and the equipment was installed. Though it hasn't brought to light any lapses by the bank's staff, it has led to the discovery of an interesting 'phone call made from the directors' restroom by one of the bank's customers, by Jakob Schmidt in fact. My friend was most embarrassed that this should have happened but, with his security background, he felt compelled to contact me. The discovery may prove providential so far as you are concerned. Here's the transcript, he passed copies round the table:

> "Karl, I'm at our Swiss bank. You'll be pleased to know the finance is all in order, we've $9.2M available there and elsewhere and more on the way. You've seen Alyosha? .... He wants twelve million Dollars? *Twelve million!* Tell him he can have ten, then we might get it for eleven and that includes packing and delivery to the port. After all Alyosha's anxious for us to use the thing. His father was a guard at Treblinka and the Poles hanged him in 1946. .... You didn't know that, well don't let Alyosha know that I've told you - he'll mention it if he wants to. .... You're not sure whether it's a clean or a dirty device? If it's ex-USSR stock it will be clean and powerful. That really

> doesn't matter, though, it's for the Jews. What's important is that it works - that, when we want it to, it goes off with one hell of a bang. You can tell him from me that if it malfunctions he'll have the fury of the 16th September Unit after him and that we won't leave off until we've got him crying for mercy and not even then!"

It hadn't taken them long to read the note and Blum began again, 'So that's it. The call certainly didn't throw any light on banking leaks but it did, it does, indicate that Jakob Schmidt's dirty money - and there can be little doubt that it was dirty money - has been accumulated for something very unpleasant indeed.'

'There was no way that Schmidt could have known that his 'phone call was being overheard?'

'No way that I can think of. You don't expect the restrooms at discrete Swiss private banks to be bugged and neither do you expect your discrete and urbane Swiss banker to have a Security background and to be listening in to your restroom activities! No, I think you can accept that the conversation was genuine and that Schmidt had no idea he was overheard.'

Ehud nodded, 'Twelve Million Dollars for *a* device, not a number of items but *a* device, which might be clean or dirty - there's little doubt that the thing's a nuclear bomb.'

The room was quiet until Sam broke the silence, 'Money being laundered to buy a weapon for delivery from Russia. A weapon not weapons and costing $10 or $12M. Yes, it would have to be nuclear wouldn't it? Elizabeth what do you think, it would have to be a weapon from the old USSR? Can you get them by mail order like this?' He wanted both to call on her expertise and ensure that she had a full part in the discussion and its consequences.

'What I know is that things were falling apart at the

end. As the Communist regime weakened, so life and organisation became more and more chaotic. I can imagine that their records, even for nuclear bombs and warheads, weren't very good and that some records might have been lost and weapons with them. No, it doesn't surprise me to hear that something like that can be bought for $10 or 12M cif. It horrifies me though.'

'Cif?'

'Cost, insurance and freight - I dealt with a lot of exports while I was working for Peter Lewis in London. They're unlikely to find an insurer though, *if* it's a bomb that they're buying! Alyosha might be a Russian, but the reference to his father being a guard at Treblinka, that would more likely make him a Ukrainian. The Ukraine might well have nuclear weapons left over by the old USSR. And it could leave the country from a Black Sea port, somewhere like Odessa'

'Moshe?', the Deputy Director called on the nuclear expert. 'Our nuclear friend has a contribution here, either that or he's wasted our coffee. Moshe, we would be *delighted* to have your contribution.' It was clear that the Deputy Director hadn't a lot of time for boffins.

Moshe wasn't deterred, he had been called on to contribute and he was going to make sure that they listened. He was in his early thirties and had a substantial black beard that led some to identify him as an Ultra-Orthodox religious Jew, something that, to a committed secularist like him, was a source of frequent amusement. 'Yes, we've known for some time that there is material available in the Ukraine - available at a price - and clearly these people have more than enough money to make the purchase. So, yes, it's a distinct possibility. Whether the ex-USSR surplus nuclear weapons lying round in the Ukraine are in good working order is another matter. It's unlikely that they've been given many regular checks since 1991 to ensure that they're in prime condition but that doesn't mean that they wouldn't work. In 1994 *part* of the Ukraine's nuclear arsenal was transferred to the Russians in return for nuclear fuel for power generation and the USA has been giving aid in an effort to encourage them to get rid of nuclear weapons and co-operate with the West. But that hasn't rid the country of nuclear weapons, certainly not of those that have somehow or other been lost.' Sam was held by the delivery in a rich deep baritone voice, which suggested more of the professional cantor rather than the scientist.

'But surely someone in the USSR's military and their successors from 1991 kept a strict tally of the things?' Zvi's tidy mind couldn't comprehend a lack of order in such matters.

Sam broke in, 'Elizabeth has already spoken of the chaotic situation as the Communist regime came to an end. It's a mistake to overestimate the efficiency of the old enemy. *Any* large organisation will have some weaknesses in its stores records. I remember, when I was serving in the Golani Brigade, that I damaged a radio transmitter/receiver, it was carelessness - I'd put it on a wall and it rolled off. Well, when I went to the stores to replace it they'd got one on the books but two on the shelf. The storeman just handed the new one over, no need to make a report on the damage, and the servicing people were glad to have the smashed one to cannibalise for spares. That was simply by chance and I'm sure that with a little bit of Ukrainian cunning they could have contrived to achieve an unrecorded nuclear surplus. Add the element of corruption, with many on the make at all levels, and I'm sure the goods can be bought if you've enough cash.'

The Deputy Director summarised, 'So they've got in place their source of finance and means of procurement. How about delivery?'

Ehud responded, 'Air or sea are the only real possibilities, they wouldn't want to risk a lorry being searched at a border check-point here in Israel or along the way. I'd guess at a delivery by sea from a Black Sea port, possibly Odessa.'

'When might all this be?' The question was asked by the Deputy Director.

Captain Blum replied, 'They've taken six months to accumulate $9.2M. At that rate it would take them two months to get the rest, even if its $12M that they have to pay.'

'And do you, Erik, know for sure that it's dirty money they're using?'

'With the way its routed it's not going to be from cleaning people's windows or selling Swiss army knives ... '

'Or from cuckoo clocks ... ' Erik Blum's icy facial response told the Deputy Director that their guest had heard too many jibes about this aspect of the benefits conferred on the world by the Swiss and he wished he'd kept the thought to himself.

'Or *even* from those. The likelihood is that it's drug money. There is one other helpful piece of information that we have: the bank was asked to deal with the purchase of a 10 metre ocean-going yacht for someone living near Marseille. The man's name is Mustafa Malik and we have an address for him in Cassis, a small port to the east of Marseille. Here's a copy of the invoice from a boatyard in Toulon for the yacht which rejoices in the name *Viagra*.'

There were some smiles as people heard the name of the yacht but a woman's presence held them back from making the ribald comments that were in their minds. it was Elizabeth however who was unable to refrain from asking, 'Are you sure its *Viagra* and not *Niagara*? One rises and the other falls, just like a yacht in fact!'

Ehud concurred, 'That would seem to be a likely place for the drugs operation, we could keep Malik under surveillance. What about Jakob Schmidt?'

'Nothing apart from the probability that he's from

Frankfurt. All correspondence is via a Liechtenstein *Anstalt* and his telephone number is that of a prepaid mobile. His visits to the bank are infrequent, he's been there four times in all and there's no real pattern to go by apart from the visits all having been on Tuesdays: 19 September 2000, 10 October 2000, 9 January 2001 and the visit which brought me here was on 29 May. He usually arranges his visits to the bank a week in advance so there would be adequate warning to enable him to be tailed.'

'We could have a team in place at short notice ... '

Blum stopped the Deputy Director in his tracks, 'But you won't! Anything of that kind will be done by our people, you will not intrude on Swiss soil, though we'll be more than happy to liaise with your people at the Bern embassy. If you want our help and co-operation - and I assume you do - then it will be on our terms.'

'Understood and accepted.' The Deputy Director had been put firmly in his place by their visitor, though he did his best to keep from his face the annoyance he felt. This man was dictating to them how the case should run and choosing the Mossad personnel with whom he would deal! And whose country was it that these people were targeting? 'And what about the 16th September Unit? Ehud, have you heard of them?'

'Not in years, one of those outfits that starts up, runs for a short while and disappears.'

'Only now it's back again, either that or some other lot have taken the same title.'

Elizabeth queried, '16th September? When, what year?'

Ehud brought enlightenment, '1982, I expect. It was then that the massacres in the Sabra and Shatila refugee camps took place. Our *Phalangist* allies slaughtered four hundred - some say eight hundred - Palestinian civilians, men, women and children. Arik, that's Ariel Sharon, carried the can for letting them into the camps, he resigned as Defence Minister, thrown to the wolves by the rest of the cabinet.' The identification of Arik had been added for Erik Blum's benefit.

Blum took the point, 'And now Sharon's your PM. As I remember it, Raful Eitan your Chief of Staff was quoted as saying, "The *Phalangists* went overboard this time." It seems you've now reached payback time then?' Blum had clearly done his homework.

'Payback indeed and with a vengeance! Their name might well indicate just when they plan to strike. It would be quite some way of marking the anniversary of the bloodshed.'

Blum asked, 'You've got nothing recent on the 16th September Unit then? Nothing on members or where they operate?'

Ehud forced a smile, 'Nothing and they're not likely to be in the Jerusalem telephone directory. We have something from ten years back but we haven't anything more recent.'

Once more Blum was on the ball, 'Here again I think I can help, or at any rate point you in the right direction. I had a word with a contact in British intelligence. They've come across the Unit in the last couple of years in connection with a dissident Irish terrorist group. There's a contact in France, a British ex-pat who served in the military in the North of Ireland, who can give you more information to help you with your problem.'

"*If* it's a problem. We're grateful to Captain Blum for bringing this to our notice but what if it's a hoax, we don't want to be made to look like a bunch of amateur fools.' The Deputy Director's weariness was showing through more strongly now. He had more than enough on his plate already without this.

Elizabeth was grateful to Sam that he had brought her into the discussion and resolved to make a further contribution, 'Better to look a fool when there's nothing there than to ignore the threat and find that Haifa's a radio-active hole in the ground, that things are even worse there than they are now - at least a nuclear explosion would vaporise the poisons in the Kishon river.' She turned to the Deputy Director, she would be blunt with him, 'Your organisation hasn't too much kudos to lose at the moment so perhaps its time to take necessary risks and trust to instinct. We're Jews so let's show a bit of *Arik's impetuosity*, a *considered* impetuosity, of course.'

Sam felt that some explanation was needed, 'We were at Gamla in the Golan yesterday and we were reading Josephus' account of Vespasian taking the citadel. He derided Jewish impetuosity but we decided that the occasional flash of impetuosity, like Arik's in the Sinai in 1967 was no bad thing.' He held the Deputy Director's gaze and there was a moment's silence. Sam wondered about the relations between the Deputy Director and the PM.

'OK let's say that it's likely to be a genuine threat, what then? Back to you again Moshe, you had some experience with US nuclear weapons manufacture before you came to the Weizmann, didn't you? Couldn't these people have built one of these things in a garden shed and saved some of their $10M?'

'You would need to have a substantial garden shed and some large quantities of precision equipment to make a nuclear weapon and you would need to obtain the radioactive material itself. You might like to find out what it's all about from this. Take it away and enjoy the read.' He passed round sets of A4 sheets, 15 pages of text and diagrams headed, *"Documentation and Diagrams of the Atomic Bomb"*. 'This is the sort of thing you can find on the Internet and it's the sort of thing that the *unscientific* might understand. You might like to read the disclaimer at the top, particularly the last couple of sentences:

> "Should a layperson attempt to build a device such as this, chances are s/he would probably kill him/herself not by a nuclear

> detonation, but rather through radiation exposure. We at Outlaw Labs do not recommend using this document beyond the realms of casual or academic curiosity."

'No, their only option if they want that sort of weaponry is to buy it on the military surplus market. As you should be aware there were plenty warheads and bombs in various parts of the old USSR and there are certainly still some of them in the Ukraine, Mrs Kagan is right. Do they still work? As I said earlier the answer is that some probably do. It could be that the vendors have expertise in this field and have kept up to date with checking on the effectiveness of the goods they're selling.'

Moshe paused to observe the effect of his words on the Deputy Director who, gave the appearance of being convinced, this wasn't a matter that would be resolved in a morning, it was going to take his time and energy for perhaps months to come. Moshe continued, 'So it has to be taken seriously as a *possibility*. If they loaded it on board a ship in one of the Black Sea ports, say Odessa, it wouldn't take long to deliver it to our coast - the ultimate suicide bombers, perhaps! It would make everything that has gone before look like flea-bites by comparison. An explosion at sea level ... making a large hole in our coast and creating tidal waves. There would be any amount of fall-out and where that went would depend on the way the wind was blowing at the time and for a while afterwards. If you look at page 5, in front of you, there are tables of the destruction caused by airbursts - take the 20 megaton bomb at 5,000 metres, there's a vaporisation area with a radius of 15 km - that's big hole!'

Zvi from human Resources broke in, 'You say that it's the vaporisation zone but the notes show 98% fatalities, who are the lucky 2%?'

'Worried about having to continue to pay their pensions?' Sam couldn't resist the quip.

Moshe too wanted to tweak someone's tail but he was

looking in Sam's direction, 'Probably they're those of our religious community who *really* believe that souls are immortal!' Pleased with this repartee and with having established his credentials as a thoroughly secular scientist, Moshe continued his seminar, 'Also there's the Electro-Magnetic Pulse generated by a nuclear explosion, a high level explosion is capable of disrupting electronic devices for a radius of 80 km or so. A ground level one would affect a smaller radius, perhaps 20 km, I'm not sure on the precise distance - I could find out for you if it were relevant. But no doubt someone here or with the GSS has a contingency plan for this sort of thing?'

The Deputy Director responded, 'Thank you Moshe. Of course we've always known that one day someone might go for something of this kind but we've hoped firstly that the technology would be beyond any likely perpetrators of such an atrocity and secondly that no one would be so irresponsible as to sell a nuclear bomb to terrorists. We seem to be agreed that this isn't a hoax, something to waste our time and energy while other kinds of attack are launched against us or the USA?' Evidently he still had difficulty in shaking off the idea that it might all be a well contrived red herring.

'I haven't the slightest idea whether this is a genuine threat or not, that's your area of expertise not mine, all I can say is that - as a possibility - it's not far fetched. Technically It could be done and the material is certainly there for those who can pay the suppliers.'

The Deputy Director turned to the Swiss, 'Captain Blum are you completely sure that we aren't being taken for a ride?'

'As sure as I can be. Our informant served in Swiss Security for a number of years and is completely reliable. It might be that he was fed false information, that the 'phone call was bogus but I don't think so. Schmidt wouldn't have known of his Security background and contacts. And I can assure you that *I'm* not up to any sort of tricks, if that's what you might be hinting!'

'Not in the least, Captain Blum, not at all! I was suggesting no such thing! Clearly we do have to take this seriously. As Mrs Kagan has already pointed out it's far better for us all to be made to look foolish than to be vaporised or to die of radiation sickness!' He looked around the table, 'Our first priority is to identify the enemy and attempt to fill in the detail of their plans. Sam, are you willing to help us in this? It seems you would need to go to Marseille initially.'

'Of course we're willing!' It was Elizabeth who replied, 'Knowing what's being planned we could hardly remain enjoying an idyllic life in the Golan! You can take it that we will both join your payroll.'

'But in the past you ... '

'Have had other employers? Yes? Well, having served with the KGB and the SVR might even be an advantage - you never know - though most of my work with them was in commercial areas.'

'I'm grateful to my wife for volunteering our combined services! But there are one or two conditions.'

"I had expected as much!'

'First, I want to be assured that nothing about the project will be withheld from us. You must keep us fully briefed on every aspect. As you know I resigned from here because that didn't happen with the Basel Formula operation.' Sam noticed Erik Blum raise his eyebrows. 'And, two, once this is over I want a desk job here, as Director of a Department in fact. When are you due to retire, Dan?'

'Next year, would that it were tomorrow. You're welcome to it Sam, *if* you can deliver on this project. There won't be anything in writing, just the Minister's word when I can get his attention.'

'If we can't deliver it won't matter very much will it? There isn't likely to be much of this place left.'

'Very true if Moshe is correct.'

'I think you can count on that. Science deals with fact, not opinions or prejudices!'

The Deputy Director looked at his notes, 'We need a name for the project. *Operation Basel Account*, perhaps?'

'Perhaps *Operation Account* would suffice, my masters in Bern would prefer not to run the risk of the origins of the project becoming public.'

'*Operation Account* it is then. I will need to see the PM now and appraise him of the situation but in the meantime perhaps you gentlemen - and Mrs Kagan - can begin to put down some ideas on paper about how to proceed. I will see you again later in the day.' It was more an order than a mere statement of fact. The Deputy Director's ready access to his political masters, though he found them wearisome in the extreme with their concentration on how everything would play with the electorate, gave him the added aura of authority that those with an *entrée* to the seats of power so quickly acquire and use with relish.

Chapter 4

Thursday 7th June 2001 (continued)

With the departure of the Deputy Director they relaxed and moved to the easy chairs at the other end of the conference area. After a break for coffee they returned to work. Sam took over as chairman and got the meeting under way again. 'Any plans we come up with today will, of course, be tentative and subject to confirmation by our masters and to constant revision as we progress. To summarise: we know of a stratagem, which appears to be real, to buy a nuclear bomb and ship it to somewhere on our coast. Presumably it would then be detonated or perhaps the idea is to use it as a means of blackmailing us in some way. We don't know who these people are, though their name - the 16th September Unit - has given us some guidance and a possible date for an attack. We suspect that the weapon is to come from the Ukraine and it seems that the money for the purchase of the bomb is coming from drug running and that they don't need much more cash before they have the asking price for the bomb. So how do we get a clearer idea of who is involved? Erik, what chance is there of getting onto their tail at your end, in Basel?'

'My banker friend's customer is somewhat shadowy but not entirely invisible. The banker is a most hospitable host and to be entertained by him is quite an experience. The German who operates the account is in fact due to dine with him in a month's time, well in about four or five weeks. As I've told you his name is Jakob Schmidt, though no doubt it and the papers on which he travels aren't genuine. My people will be tailing him from the restaurant at *Die Drei Könige*, or rather, if possible, from his departure from the airport at, probably, Warsaw until he leaves Switzerland.'

Elizabeth broke in, 'Sam and I dined there the evening before Vladimir was killed ... before I shot him.'

'And if I remember rightly neither of you were on

genuine papers! Evidently *Die Drei Könige* attracts a certain type of clientele!' Blum laughed, 'Which brings me to the point I made earlier and which I make again with as much force as I can command. *All* action on Swiss soil will be undertaken by Swiss Security personnel, if you attempt to involve yourselves you will be arrested and you must not expect the short sentences that were - quite rightly in those particular circumstances - handed down by the Basel and Bern Courts after your last intrusion into our territory. We want no embarrassing events - we are well able to handle things in our own way. I know that your country appears to be the target but you must trust us to do the job properly, after all in our country we know the places and we have the contacts and the clout. Am I fully understood?'

'Completely, Erik. But you will allow us liaison personnel to make sure that our lines of communication are always open and operating?'

'Certainly, Sam. No problem there but their role will be liaison pure and simple. They will not be operating independently as Mossad agents, at any rate not on Swiss soil. And we would prefer that, if as is likely, you are going to use your people in other countries, you do not compromise us.' He turned to Ehud, 'You might care to have a look in your archives for the consequences of the activities of your Dr Otto Joklik and Joseph Ben-Gal at *Die Drei Könige* on 2nd March 1963!' Ehud nodded and made a note.

'That too presents no problem ... ' Sam took up Blum's point on ensuring Swiss Security were not compromised.

'However the need for economy ... '

Sam cut Zvi short, 'The need for economy goes out the window in the face of a threat of this kind. Whatever Erik asks we will provide, whatever he tells us to refrain from doing on Swiss soil we will avoid.'

Erik Blum nodded his grateful acknowledgement to Sam and continued, 'You Israelis seem to be the target but let me assure you that we Swiss are utterly committed to ensuring that any attack will be thwarted.'

'Erik, lets go back to considering this German, Jakob Schmidt'

'He has a post box address in Frankfurt am Main and messages can be left at a telephone number, but that turns out to be a prepay mobile telephone which can't be tracked down - there are arrangements for monitoring calls on that telephone number but its only use, so far, has been to take messages from the Basel bank - so that gets us nowhere. There's also the Liechtenstein Anstalt at a lawyer's office in that country. What we do know is that in a month or so's time Schmidt is due to make another visit to Basel on a flight from Warsaw and to remain overnight at *Die Drei Könige*, but whether he will return to Warsaw is anyone's guess. But we will find that out in good time.'

'And the 16th September Unit?' Sam looked towards Ehud, 'You're our resident expert on terrorism. Did you turn up anything more while we were relaxing over coffee?'

'The first time we heard of them was 10 years ago as I said earlier. There was a Syrian connection then and talk of arms purchases. Then nothing further. We wrote them off as a joke. There's nothing in our records for any Jakob Schmidt.' Ehud was clearly displeased at having nothing much to contribute on the subject. 'Perhaps it's a one off group for this operation. Research Section will help us there, no doubt, if you can pick up some more names.'

Blum broke in, 'You'll remember that I told you of my discussion with British Intelligence who *had* come across the Unit. They put me in touch with a Briton whom they authorised to speak to me. Now he's a *négociant*, that's a wine dealer, in the French Rhône Valley but he served for four years with the British Army in Northern Ireland. It seems the 16th September Unit were involved in some sort of failed arms deal with a dissident Irish Republican group. I've got some notes which you can see but it would be a good idea for one of your people to speak with him direct. A pleasant individual, very British, but an efficient operator - you would probably need to be to come out unscathed from under cover work in Ireland.' Blum was pleased that he had more information on the Unit than Mossad did and his pleasure showed.

'So our leads are, firstly Schmidt, secondly the 16th September Unit and thirdly Mustafa Malik with his yacht and decorative ladies in Cassis on the French Mediterranean coast. What about Mustafa? Your people have him under observation still? And French Security?'

'Yes, we are still keeping an eye on him and, no, we haven't involved the French. Our suspicion is that the French have a somewhat ambiguous attitude to you Israelis and that France and its trading interests with the Arab world always come first.'

Sam nodded, 'In any case it's just as well to limit the number of players in the game. Too many and the whole thing will seize up. We'll look after the Cassis end of things, if you like, and release your people, Erik.'

'That would be completely acceptable to us. One idea occurs, Sam, you're involved in the wine industry here - up in the Golan - aren't you? Yes, I thought I had it right. Well Cassis is a wine growing area and one of our people has a brother, who was once a Swiss diplomat and is fully trustworthy, who owns a vineyard there. If you like the idea of running it as cover while you keep Mr Malik under observation I think it could be arranged. There's the added advantage that, if it is necessary to establish links with the British, then visits to you by Mark Gould, the *négociant* from Valence, would fit in with what you were doing - though I suppose that's not essential, it's not as if the French or anyone else is going to keep *you* under surveillance.'

'That sounds interesting, Erik. Thanks for setting that up, we'll certainly be in touch with him. OK, let's look at the programme of events:

'In a month or so Schmidt arrives in Basel, possibly from Warsaw, at least that's where he says he'll be coming from. Your people will keep him under observation from the airport or earlier if possible and certainly from dinner at *Die Drei Könige* onwards until he leaves, presumably by air?'

'Presumably, and we plan to put one of our people on the flight out with him when he leaves. On the assumption that he's going to Warsaw, Berlin or Frankfurt, can you have some of your people at his return destination to take over on arrival? You can? Good! Then between our combined efforts we might succeed in running him to earth. I'll be here for the next few days as liaison between my people and the Institute. Right, back to you Sam.'

'So that leaves the 16th September Unit and Mustafa Malik. Let's work on the basis of Elizabeth and myself going to Cassis - by the way isn't that a blackcurrant liqueur of some sort?'

'It is, but they don't make it where you're going, rather it's the name of the town. A pleasant fishing and holiday port with vineyards just inland, to the back as well as to the east of it. Presumably it was once famous for currants as well as wine. I suspect we'll find that Schmidt is the efficient professional and that Malik is the weak link in their organisation - his womanising and his love of *la dolce vita* certainly suggests so - our people didn't take long to find that out.' The censorious streak in Blum was showing through. Sam liked the man but was aware of a certain priggishness in his make-up. Of course, none of Blum's men would ever think of behaving in such a way! Or, if they did they, certainly wouldn't let their chief know.

'And you will handle the introduction to the Brit, what's he called, Mark ... ah yes, Mark Gould isn't it?'

'If your people get approval from London then I'll be pleased to introduce you. Also I can set in motion your appointment as manager at the Cassis vineyard.'

Sam looked in Elizabeth's direction. She replied, 'If we can take the children, after all it's probably going to be safer there than it is here - if we don't sort this out properly!'

'Ehud, you can square the Brits? Good! OK Erik, once Ehud's done that can you speak to them and set up a meeting with Gould? Yes and if you can arrange the job at the vineyard as well as some sort of back up, just in case that when the grapes should be receiving attention, Moshe and I are sweating it out trying to defuse a nuclear device with screwdrivers, pliers and a prayer.'

'I'd leave you to do the praying my friend and, as for me, I would need rather more than a screwdriver and pliers - a manual on the workings of the device would be handy and I believe I know where I can get hold of one.'

'And the costs of the vineyard?' Zvi evidently felt the need to intervene.

'We might even be paid for our labour, Zvi. I wouldn't worry about it. The number of personnel involved will probably grow as we progress but for a start I want someone who welcomed Elizabeth and myself this morning, Dov Levin who was on gate duty. I know he's IDF rather than Mossad but we served together and we'll need someone to help out in Cassis whenever either Elizabeth or I are away.'

'That's rather irregular, he's untrained.'

'He's had enough training for what he'll be doing. I've served with him in the Golani Brigade and I know. Besides he's also served in *Sayeret Maktal* in the Lebanon.' This announcement of Dov's time in the IDF's élite General Staff Deep Reconnaissance Unit killed any further objections stone dead. Sam knew that Dov would welcome the chance of some action and the overseas allowances he would receive. He was looking forward to Dov's companionship, if he could do himself a good turn at the same time as doing one for an old friend he certainly wasn't going to miss it.

They took a comfort break and then, with the return of the Deputy Director, went back to the conference table for more coffee and sandwiches and a final rounding up of the day's discussions.

'Of course the PM's horrified and you will be pleased to hear that he's authorised *any*, repeat *any*, action that may be needed. And,' he turned to Zvi, '*any* money needed will be found. I spent twenty minutes with him and then had to give place to Rabbi Yehuda.' He looked towards Erik Blum, 'He's an eminent kabbalist, a Jewish mystic ... '

'Some of us would describe him differently, if ever there was ignorance and superstition it's to be found among that lot ... '

'You see, Captain Blum, we Israelis are a varied and interesting people! Our very secular scientist thinks one thing and our Prime Minister another.'

Moshe hadn't finished, 'I doubt it, I very much doubt it! I bet the PM and I both think the same about the old fellow. The real difference is that the PM is after votes from religious electors and will put up with any undignified photo-call to get them, as well as squandering public money bribing the *Chassidim* for the upkeep of schools that aren't worthy of the name.'

'That's as may be Moshe, you're lucky not to need the approval of the electorate to continue your work at the Weizmann. Just think about it that way.' The Deputy Director had cultivated the smooth ways of the diplomat.

Moshe warmed to his theme and turned to Sam, 'What do you think of these rabbis, Sam?'

'Can I state a personal interest in the question, Moshe? Well, I happen to be one! But then there are rabbis and rabbis, just as there are scientists and scientists. I'm not taken with some manifestations of religion and I wouldn't be surprised to find that you don't endorse everything done by your scientific colleagues - but I expect we'll have plenty of time to discuss it in the weeks ahead.'

Elizabeth was surprised to see some embarrassment in Moshe's face, 'I'm sorry if I've offended you, Sam, only ... '

'Don't let that worry you Moshe, some of my best friends are sceptical scientists - you've said what you think and I prefer that to dissimulation.'

The Deputy Director called the meeting to order, 'I'm sure that Captain Blum doesn't want to have his time taken up with a discussion of our religious/secular divide and, in any case we all have other calls on our time. What stage have we reached in our discussion and planning, Sam?'

Sam outlined the discussion and what had been decided.

'Fine, keep me fully up to date and don't hesitate to come back to me for any resources you need or authorisation for contact with other Security services. You've got that Zvi? Ehud, you've made a record of the day's proceedings? Good. Let me have a copy as soon as it's typed up, won't you. So then, I'll leave it to you to work out any additional detail over the next few days. Sam, when can you and Elizabeth be on your way to Marseille?'

Elizabeth replied for them both, 'We can be on our way within four or five days. The sooner we're on Mr Malik's trail the better.'

The Deputy Director nodded, 'That makes good sense. Well, thank you all of you and our particular thanks to you Captain Blum.' He led the way to the door and Sam noticed that his shoulders were far more rounded than when they had first met ten years before. The Deputy Director certainly was a tired man. Was this the sort of job Sam had asked for as a *quid pro quo* for returning to the colours? Was he wise, was he sensible to want it? He probably wasn't, but he felt an obligation to be involved in restoring Mossad to its former standing as a security service with few equals: alert, informed, disciplined and capable, when the occasion called for it, of considered impetuosity.

Chapter 5

Friday 8th June 2001

Sam and Elizabeth had arrived back home in Kazrin with Erik Blum the previous evening. Now, breakfast over, their guest balanced one of the children on his knee and sang a nursery rhyme in his Basler Swiss/German, a language Elizabeth had mastered during her time in the Basel remand prison and which brought back mixed memories for her. Since leaving Mossad HQ Elizabeth and Sam had seen a very different side of Erik Blum. The rather starchy persona of the Swiss Security official had been left behind in the conference room - he had put it aside with his tie - and he had proved delightful company, both interested and interesting.

On their journey north to Kazrin the previous day they had stopped at Megiddo to see the excavations and enjoy the view looking down from the great mound onto the Jezreel Valley. Blum had stood there fascinated, 'Armageddon! I've always wanted to see this place! I hope and pray this operation won't prove to be our Armageddon. We've got to make sure that they don't succeed. How far away is Haifa? 40 km? And the coast south of Haifa is even nearer? Well it would reach here, not much of these excavations would remain. But we won't let them!' He turned to Elizabeth and Sam, taking their hands in his. 'Whatever the price, you can count on me doing all in my power to help you to prevent them.' There were tears in his eyes. 'My grandfather was a Swiss border policeman who turned away a family of Jews who sought refuge in 1942. Afterwards, when he had discovered how dire the consequences of his action would have been for them, he bitterly regretted having obeyed orders. I want to do something in return ... I can't remedy what was done then but I can try to ensure that the present threat is thwarted.'

Sam took up his thought, 'Armageddon. Yes, it's a name full of drama. A place of past battles and, in Christian thinking, the future final conflict. Your apocalyptic has something in common with the thinking of the Essenes - our Dead Sea Scrolls People. The forces of light and darkness in conflict and the eventual triumph of the Sons of Light.'

'Well, there's a certain comfort in the idea of a final resolution of conflict and the defeat of evil. So often in history evil has seemed to prevail, for a while at any rate ... sometimes for a very long while ... it's unnecessary for me to remind the two of you of that, of course. But the idea of a final calling to account, of justice being done once and for all, and being seen to be done, that somehow provides the present with meaning. Your Law and Prophets are relevant for Christians as well as for Jews. We share the same roots, Sam.'

'Indeed we do Erik, more people in both our communities need to appreciate that. Perhaps, when this is all over, you would care to come back for a proper tour of Israel? We could show you Qumran and Masada as well as the Christian sites.'

'I will be more than delighted to take you up on that, Sam, but for the moment I'm looking forward to seeing the Galilee, the hills and the lake.'

'You'll catch a glimpse tonight but we'll have a longer look tomorrow.'

On Friday morning after breakfast Mrs Feldman took charge of the children and the others prepared for their journey to Tel Aviv.

'A few hours tranquillity in the Galilee, Sam, before we turn to making the detailed arrangements to take on our adversaries!'

'It's nearly nine, we'll have to be on our way within the next twenty minutes if we're going to see much. Let's hear what you've got on the list.'

Erik Blum took a piece of paper from his wallet and unfolded it. Yes, here we are: the old boat, Capernaum and the Church of the Loaves and Fishes and the Church of the Primacy of Peter.'

'Good, that's all on our way. The old boat's at *Kibbutz Nof Ginnosar*, which was set up between the world wars by Czech Jews. But first we'll go to *Kfar Nahum* - Capernaum, that is - then to Tabgha where your two churches are. At Peter's church you can stand on the shore and enjoy the view of Kinneret and the Golan beyond. Elizabeth hasn't been there so she'll enjoy the sightseeing too.'

Elizabeth was fussing round, making sure that food and clothes were ready for her mother to cope with looking after the children. Mrs Feldman was chattering away to her daughter in Russian as the men sorted out the day's itinerary. She said something to Elizabeth who turned to Erik Blum and said, 'My mother says I've got to tell you that she's extremely grateful that you didn't keep Sam locked up in Basel. She's very satisfied with her son-in-law and with being a grandmother!' Mrs Feldman embraced Sam in a great hug while Blum hoped that he would be spared such a show of affection, a hope that was swiftly dashed as Mrs Feldman proceeded to knock the breath out of him with her display of gratitude.

By the afternoon they had reached Tiberias and were sitting by the lakeside at a fish restaurant enjoying a late lunch of Peter's fish. 'They're bony things, Erik but if you eat here you have to have one, I fear!'

'Bones or no, they're not at all bad - though there's rather more flesh on a Swiss trout. Thanks for managing to fit in the visit to Bethsaida. This lake must have been much bigger when that village was on the shoreline - it's about two kilometres back now isn't it?'

'Yes, all manner of things change over the years, over

the millennia indeed! There was once the "jungle of the Jordan" so it must have been hotter, wetter and more humid in the river valley than it is now. And we could certainly do with some more water in the lake, if the rainfall declines any further we'll be in real trouble - and not just Israelis, the Jordanians and the Palestinians too, all of us in fact! Without water none of us can exist here, *none* at all. It would be one way of achieving peace here!'

'What about desalination?'

'They're still experimenting, probably they'll succeed in time, but it's not viable yet, I fear, not even with all the sunshine we get.'

Erik looked at his watch, '14.45. When do we meet up with your HQ people?'

'Our transport and an escort vehicle are due here at 15.00 hours and we leave our car at a hotel down the road - but that doesn't mean to say we've got to head straight to HQ. We can eat in Netanya on the Med and still get to HQ with time in hand. When the Deputy Director telephoned this morning he insisted on providing transport in case we broke down or had an accident ... or ran into bad company.'

'Very wise, I wouldn't be pleased to be shot in an ambush or have the pair of you shot.'

Elizabeth broke in, 'And what do you have in mind, Sam, for the next couple of hours. What do you want to show us here? Tiberias isn't exactly full of Christian shrines.'

'I'll keep my tour of the rabbis' tombs until another day. How about a visit to the Golani Brigade Museum? Once our transport has come we can head off up the hill out of Tiberias and take a photo of Erik next to the sea level sign. Then we can run south past Tabor - the Mount of the Transfiguration - to the road for Hadera and then south again to Netanya for an early meal.'

At Netanya they felt in need of no more than a snack,

so they had coffee and falafel with salad in pitta bread. Blum had viewed it all with intense fascination but for Sam, much as he had enjoyed his rôle as tour guide, he had felt that he was treading water, filling in time before the action began. Now he just wanted to get to HQ and prepare for their departure for France in a few days time. So, after a short stroll to get a view of the Mediterranean, they set off again. At HQ the same personnel were gathered round the table as had been present the previous day, with the addition of Dov Levin who looked well pleased to be inside rather than on the gate. Clocks on the wall showed the time in Israel and also Swiss time, one hour behind local time.

'How did you get on with your research on Joklik and Ben-Gal, Ehud?' Blum had been waiting for this opportunity.

'A lot of publicity in the Basel Court that we could have done without, though we did our best to use it to publicise the German scientists' work in Egypt, and two months in jail for each of the accused. Point taken!'

'I just wanted you to remember. You will have seen from your files that there were discussions between Mossad and my people in Bern during the trial that persuaded the prosecution to tone down its accusations? Yes? An agreement not to make a nuisance of yourselves on Swiss soil.' Blum smiled, 'Something that you have been a little slack in holding to recently! But you will behave this time, I'm sure!' He was enjoying it here, glad to be involved in something more substantial than the commercial espionage that was his bread and butter fare back in Bern. It occurred to him that he should have a chat with Elizabeth Kagan about the commercial side of spying. There might be something she could tell him that would be useful to him in the future, especially with the large pharmaceutical companies in Basel with their secret research as a target.

They got down to finalising the arrangements for Sam

and Elizabeth, together with Dov, to set up home in the substantial house at the *Domaine du Cheval Rouge*, the Cassis vineyard. Accompanying them, to keep house and cook, would be Mrs Feldman and Esty Levin, Elizabeth's and Dov's mothers. Dov would be setting off as the advance party with his mother on Sunday. That pleased him, he was a soldier who travelled light and relished getting on with things rather than talking about them.

Chapter 6

Friday 15th June 2001

Dov Levin had reached Cassis earlier that week and was there to meet them at Marseille-Marignane Aéroport. He had acquired a Renault Espace and fitted it with child seats. He was waiting with a broad smile on his face to welcome them off the Paris flight that had connected with their El Al flight from Tel Aviv. Sam, pushing the heavily loaded luggage trolley, and Elizabeth, holding a very lively Olga's hand, were followed closely by the bulkier Mrs Feldman and a sleeping Ya'akov in the pushchair.

'This is more like living, Sam! Out and about, getting busy and enjoying things. Far better than gate duties. Welcome Elizabeth, you'll like it here.' He bent down and picked up Olga, 'You're going to enjoy the sand and the sea. It'll be non-stop holiday for you.'

'For the children but not for the rest of us, Dov! You haven't met my mother, have you? Dov Levin, Mrs Feldman. Mum, this is Dov.'

'An old and trusted comrade in arms, Mrs Feldman.'

'You keep him out of trouble, Dov! That's your job now. I want to take him back to Israel in one piece.'

'Dov's here to help and cover for me when I'm away from Cassis, that's his job.'

'And he's to keep the two of you out of trouble, I've just given him that job as well.' Her energetic bear hug served to invest him with the required authority and remind him that he would be answerable to a formidable woman.

'Never worry Mrs Feldman, we've kept one another out of trouble in the past, in some pretty dangerous places, and I'm more than happy to take responsibility for your daughter as well - indeed I'll keep a watchful eye on all of you. But, unless you want a drink before we go, we're wasting our time here. You'll all be wanting to see your new home and the vineyard before it gets dark. I swear you'll be delighted with the place. Your advance luggage has arrived and it's waiting at the *Domaine*, so you'll be able to sort it out and have your own things handy. This way, we're in the short term parking not too far away.'

'We can either go under Marseille or through the city, you may like to drive past the *Vieux Port* and get some idea of the place - that's *Notre Dame de la Garde* way up there in the distance, the church with the shining gold statue on the top. Quite a landmark and they say there's a good view of the city and the islands off the coast from in front of the church.'

'Through the city, Dov. We're probably going to get to know it well following Mustafa, but I'd like to get an idea now of what it's like.'

They dropped down off the long elevated section of the A 7 *Autoroute Nord*, with its view of the modern port with cruise ships and container vessels, passed the cathedral and then, in heavy traffic, worked their way round the three sides of the basin of the *Vieux Port* with its multitude of small craft.

'No shortage of restaurants or hotels here, Dov. There should be fresh fish in quantity.'

'I know we're not on a gastronomic trip and French cooking's hardly likely to be kosher, Sam, but you'll probably be OK with the fish.'

'So long as they don't add crab or lobster or some shellfish concoction! Where are you taking us now?'

'The map's in the door. Got it? Right, you can see where we are at the back of the fort at the east of the harbour entrance? Good. We go along the *Corniche* President Kennedy, hugging the coast, then when we get to Georges Pompidou we take a left onto Prado. Got that? Then north to the *Rond-Point du Prado* where we take the first exit, passing the *Vélodrome* - if one can mention the word - and head for Cassis.'

'*Vélodrome*? What's unmentionable about that?' Elizabeth was puzzled.

'The *Vélodrome d'Hiver* - an indoor cycle stadium in Paris; 16th July 1942, eight thousand of our people rounded up by the Nazis and held at the *Vél d'Hiv* until they can be moved to Drancy on the edge of Paris; the first train for Auschwitz is delayed; Adolf Eichman declares the delay a "disgrace", but then the Nazi machine gets going again and on 21st July the first thousand Jewish men and women reach Auschwitz; of that thousand only 17 survive the war. *That's* why the word *Vélodrome* is pregnant with meaning for a Jew! That's why we're here! Haman didn't succeed in Hadassa's (Esther's) time, Vespasian didn't succeed, Hitler, Eichman and the rest didn't succeed - neither will Jakob Schmidt and the16th September Unit!'

Elizabeth had never heard Sam speak quite like this, the detail memorised and brought forth with fluency on the spur of the moment, together with the confidence of his declaration had made a profound impression on her. They were the words of an informed and dedicated warrior, it wasn't only Talmudic studies that furnished his capacious mind. Once again, pride in her husband brought tears to her eyes.

There was silence as they pondered his words and watched the streets of Marseille pass by. Their stillness was broken by Sam, 'Look the Recruiting Office of *La Légion étrangère* is down that road on the right. Any volunteers for the Foreign Legion? They're being pressed to recruit women, so we could all join and become French citizens in ten years time!' Characteristically, he couldn't stay serious for very long.

'I somehow don't think the children would fit in. Do they issue diapers as part of the kit?'

A growl came from Dov, 'And I don't want to become a Frenchman. Being an Israeli/American or an American/Israeli, whichever it is, will do me for the rest of my days!'

So he navigated them through the eastern side of Marseille and then over the hilly coastal route and its summit at the *Col de Gineste*. At last they began the descent to Cassis and before them on the far side of the bay was *Cap Canaille*, its redness heightened by the evening sunlight.

'What a wonderful spot, Mum!'

'It's certainly different from Moscow, I give you that, Elizabeth. But, yes, it looks wonderful, it's just as though the setting sun has waited for our arrival. I pray that we will have a safe and healthy time here, especially the little ones, now that you've decided they aren't going to join the Legion or whatever its called.'

'Amen to all that, Mother. How much longer Dov?'

'Ten minutes or so Sam. Make sure your seat-belts are fastened, extinguish all cigarettes and prepare for landing!'

And so they came to the *Domaine du Cheval Rouge*, situated behind and to the east of the little town of Cassis, nestled against the mountains that run southwards to *Cap Canaille* itself. This would be their home for the next few weeks or months. They were glad to have got the journey over, it had been tiring for the children in particular. And they all wondered, as they got out of the Renault Espace, what kind of memories they would take away with them from the *Domaine*.

The sun was nearly down as they entered the house for the first time. The hallway had the aroma of lavender scented polish but more powerful was the appetising smell of food from the kitchen. Dov called out that they had arrived and an elderly woman emerged from the kitchen. He introduced his mother Esty to the others - Dov had had no difficulty at all in enrolling her as one of the team.

'Just time to light the *Shabbat* candles, Elizabeth, if we can find them.'

'No problem, Sam. They're on the table. If we light them now you'll have half an hour to wash and freshen up before you eat.' Esty had taken charge of the domestic arrangements.

They gathered round the end of the table with the candles. Sam held Ya'akov who was just beginning to wake up and Mrs Feldman held Olga's hand. Elizabeth lit the candles and said the prayer. Then Sam prayed:

> 'May it be Thy will, O Lord our God, to grant us long life, a life of peace, a life of good, a life of blessing, a life of sustenance, a life of bodily vigour, a life in which there is fear of sin, a life free from shame and confusion, a life of riches and honour, a life in which we may be filled with the love of Torah and the fear of heaven, a life in which Thou shalt fulfil all the desires of our heart for good! Amen.'

The others added hearty *Amens* and then they were shown to their rooms by Dov and his mother. Sam and Dov carried the cases up the stairs and distributed them.

***

'Well here we are, Elizabeth. First impressions are of a good feel about the place. Dov tells me that Mustafa's away at the moment so we'll have a quiet *Shabbat* and then on Sunday we can get to grips with the vineyard and have a look at Cassis as well as Mustafa's place.'

'Fine, I'm ready for a meal and then bed. It's been tiring keeping the children occupied through the journey. And thanks Sam for that prayer - long life with peace, good, blessing, sustenance and bodily vigour - for us and our friends, above all for the children!'

'But not without the fear of sin, the love of Torah and the fear of heaven! Only then will we truly find the desires of our hearts fulfilled. We need, in the Yiddish words of one of the *Chassidic* masters, *an stark kelp be-ems fun shine* - a strong attachment in truth from the very soul. Our desires need to be shaped by truth if they are to be fulfilled for good.' He took hold of the children's hands, 'Yes, may it be especially so for them!'

***

The children were asleep upstairs and the adults sat around the big kitchen table. The dishes had been stowed in the dishwasher and they had only their glasses and coffee cups before them. The oil fired stove in the corner purred quietly, warming the kitchen pleasantly and the atmosphere was one of peaceful somnolence. Esty was clearly a good cook and organiser and already a member of the family. Sam had insisted that she should leave it to the men to clear the table and wash the pans and she had allowed them to but with a show of reluctance.

'So this is what we produce, Dov!' He held up the glass to let the light shine through and admired the ruby hue of the wine.

'So it seems, there's plenty of it in stock but even more white. Don't ask me about the details. The previous manager's calling in on Monday to brief you on the technicalities. All I know is that we have about 50 hectares of vines to tend.'

'That will occupy you and myself, Dov. The ladies can look after the office, visitors and the house - not forgetting the children. And that's a reminder that it's time for Elizabeth and me to join them. Goodnight everyone!' He moved Elizabeth's chair to enable her to stand. 'Any complaints about accommodation or the facilities to Dov, please. Mrs Feldman, you're happy with your room?'

'Very happy, Sam. And don't worry I'll let Dov know if anything is less than completely satisfactory and comes below the standard I was accustomed to in Moscow. My word, how long ago that all seems. It's thanks to you Sam that I got out of there. I wasn't sad to leave, especially as the KGB and their friends were making a nuisance of themselves!'

'It's not the KGB any longer, Mother!'

'Isn't it? Well you can call a stinking fish by another name but it's still a stinking fish! I'll be happy here with my grandchildren and I hope there's plenty to keep me busy. You're not to do all the work Esty, I want to help.'

'Don't worry, we'll sort out a routine to keep us both busy. We'll share the cooking, you can give us Russian, I'll give you Moroccan ... '

'And I'll give you American, English or French.' Elizabeth was anxious not to be excluded from the cooking arrangements by the other formidable women.

'And Sam and I will give you the best of army cooking, if that appeals!' Dov's suggestion was laughed out of court and they all made their way up to bed.

Chapter 7

Saturday 16th June 2001

Saturday morning was slightly overcast, though when they ventured out of doors they found it pleasantly warm. Breakfast was leisurely and unhurried as people gradually emerged from their rooms, served themselves and then went off on trips of discovery. Sam and his family were recovering from their journey while Dov and his mother had spent long hours the previous two days getting the house into good order. The scent of lavender that permeated the ground floor was due to the furniture polish that they had applied plentifully to the heavy oak furniture. Dov had organised the equivalent of a barrack block "domestic night" to ensure that all dust and cobwebs had been banished from the large, ancient house. Windows had been thrown wide open to let in the air.

It was clear that the kitchen would be the room where they would all meet and eat. It had abundant space, with a large, well-scrubbed pine table in the middle. The longer of the outer walls had the deep stone sinks, cooker and preparation surfaces, while the external door, another sink and the dishwasher were on the shorter outer wall. Cupboards and a dresser were along the third wall, while the door from the hallway was in the remaining wall and to one side of it was a small table which could be used for office purposes, though in fact, there was a proper office next door. The flooring was of warm red quarry tiles.

Sam was in the kitchen feeding the children so Elizabeth was free to explore the remaining rooms. The immense salon stretched from the front to the rear of the house, and was furnished with a couple of sofas and assorted armchairs, it had plain cream walls and a heavy oak sideboard. The morning room was much smaller and lighter with whitewashed walls and lighter furniture altogether, it would be a good place for the children to play and let off steam. A small library/smoking room, "wallpapered" with floor to ceiling books, many with leather bindings, faced the main door and beside the kitchen was the office. There was plenty of space to prevent them from falling over one another, though she was still pretty sure that the kitchen would serve as their main meeting place. She returned to the hallway, admiring its dark oak panelling and the stairway which rose three steps to a small landing from a point to the left of the main door, and then turned through 90 degrees and ran as a single flight of steps to the next floor. It was all solid and substantial but it was also comfortable and it had the feel of being more than a house - a home indeed - and that pleased her.

Outside, the walls were rendered stone, painted white, and the windows were fitted with brown wooden shutters. Like almost all the local properties the house was roofed with orange clay tiles. On either side of the porch were wisteria plants which had been trained on wires to cover the front of the house. To each side of the door was a terracotta pot of scarlet geraniums. The surrounding pine trees kept a discrete distance. The house faced south east and, beyond the main road from Cassis to Roquefort-la-Bédoule, was *La Couronne de Charlemagne*, a pine clad hill topped by limestone cliffs, with its crest sloping down in the general direction of the sea which was to the right.

***

Sam and Dov strolled among the vines enjoying being out of doors. The sun was struggling to break through the thin cloud, it would be a hot day shortly.

'So what have we here Sam? What sort of grapes are we going to be looking after?'

'Different varieties from those I've been looking after in

the Golan. As grapes I think our varieties are probably better but it's as much the soil – the *terroir* is the French expression - as the grape and we'll see how this lot turn out - if we're here long enough to discover.' He consulted the notes left by the departed manager, 'The reds are *Grenache* and *Mourvèdre*, I believe *Grenache* is happy in dry conditions and pretty wind resistant, though the local literature claims that the *Mistral* is a spent force by the time it reaches here and meets the hills that encircle the vineyards. Last night's bottle was very palatable, Dov. What did you think of it?'

'Bottles, Sam. We got through two, almost. Esty will use what's left in her cooking, I expect. Yes, it was fine, I've no grumbles especially when it comes for free!'

'We'll have to go carefully, Dov. Limit ourselves to a couple of glasses a day. This is active service after all, even though it seems more like a holiday at the moment. That won't continue. We don't want to be the worse for drink if we have to set off in pursuit of Monsieur Mustafa Malik. You said he was out of town, how did you find that out?'

'Talking to one of his fellow yachtsman. No I haven't drawn attention to our interest in him. I just asked what sort of yachtsman named his boat *Viagra* and I was told plenty about him. It needed hardly any prompting at all. A colourful character indeed, an oversexed playboy was how he put it, though he conceded that Mustafa's generous with his hospitality. Always a pretty girl to adorn the yacht and Mustafa's cabin, it seems. Sometimes more than one. They marvel at his energy and predict for him a short life but a merry one. Seemingly he's away in Paris until Wednesday, so that gives us time to look at his house before he gets back. There's a couple who look after the house but they're going to take the boat out for a couple of days on Sunday so the place should be safe for an inspection visit then. We can look at the *Viagra* when they bring it back in on Tuesday.'

'I'd like to know what he's doing in Paris. If we can get the place bugged we'll have a good idea of what's going on and, perhaps, a lead into the command structure of the 16th September Unit. I wish we knew something more about them, as you know there's a Brit locally with a security background who's going to get in touch.'

'Sorry, I hadn't told you - I took a 'phone call yesterday from your Brit, Mark Gould. I think he's a wine dealer from somewhere on the Rhône. He said he'd drop in on Tuesday morning unless we called back to change it.'

'Good, Erik Blum arranged that for us with the Brits. It seems *they* know something about the Unit - it's more than our people do. Well, let's have a look at our vines - I bet you never expected to be running a vineyard when you signed on in the IDF, Dov!'

'I can think of more unpleasant ways of serving our people, though you're right in what you said, we'll have to go easy with drinking the stuff. You never know when you're going to need all your wits about you. The enemy won't operate for our convenience, that's certain. Lets make a recce of our territory and see what we can find out. It's just as well you know something about vines, Sam, even if these varieties are new to you. That hill over there, across the road's pretty distinctive isn't it?'

'Yes we'll have to study the map to find out what it's called and get the lie of the land. Besides this vineyard we've got some terraced vines on the hillside near the headland, *Cap Canaille*, I know what *that's* called anyway. We'll have a look out there tomorrow. The pruning and training's been done but I'll have to keep an eagle eye open for diseases, keep the weeds down and make sure the vines have enough water, though it's from deep down that the older vines draw their moisture. It's only four years since French law was changed to allow watering from 15th June, but it's only allowed for a couple of months. At any rate the manager's deputy will be working for us and that should keep us on the rails, or at least keep us from making too many mistakes – the rules about watering are quite complex, you've to apply to the authorities for permission. Let's have a look at the buildings and plant, whether we'll be here in the autumn for wine making is an open question.'

'So where are we Sam? What do we know and what do we need to know to stop it?'

'We know of money laundering, a target of $10 M or so for something from the old USSR to be used against Israel and a link with our friend Mustafa Malik - which of course is why we're here at the back of Cassis - presumably he's involved in drug smuggling. So there's *finance* - drug monies and their laundering - *procurement* of what's likely to be a nuclear weapon, though it might just be biological, and lastly *delivery*. I expect it's all kept separate without those responsible for one area knowing anything about the other areas. But there must be someone who holds all the strings, co-ordinating operations. My guess is that he's the one who holds the purse strings, if I were running it I'd certainly want to make sure the cash was safe, and that points to Jakob Schmidt. Now whether Mustafa's directly in touch with the boss of the operation or there's someone else interposed as a buffer is an open question. I suspect it's direct but you don't know how they've arranged things for security.

'So, Dov, we've got to find out to whom Mustafa reports and then we've got to get on *his* trail. But there's the possibility that Mustafa may have some other or additional rôle in the organisation or that he might lead us to some other part of the operation, so we've got to hang in here as long as necessary. In a way it's going to seem frustrating, stuck here in this tranquil and beautiful spot with our own vineyard to look after, waiting for crumbs of evidence from Mustafa. But it's a vital part of the task - Blum and his folk may pick up something more from their banker in Basel, it was a bit of luck that he got the indication of their plans and the lead to Mustafa. And there's always the slight chance that we're being set up by someone, possibly even the SVR getting its own back for the Basel Formula Operation. So we'll have to watch our backs, Mustafa may not be so harmless as he appears!'

'Our weapons were delivered yesterday, a courier from the Paris Station. The bugs and the other equipment came as well. You'll want to check it all over some time.'

'Yes, it's as well to be equipped for any eventuality. Now lets have a look at the buildings and plant, then an early lunch and a siesta - if the children permit - they seem particularly lively today, probably after being cooped up on the flights yesterday.'

Chapter 8

Sunday 17th June 2001

Sunday morning, a perfect summer's day, saw the beginning of their action. Sam and Dov paid a visit to the *Viagra's* berth to ensure that Mustafa's housekeeper and her partner really were going to be out of the way. The conditions for taking the craft to sea were ideal, a strong sun shone from an unclouded sky and a moderate breeze was blowing. The boat was kept at one of the outer berths of *Port-Miou*, the *calanque*, or inlet immediately to the west of Cassis. Sam had read his guide book on the flight from Tel Aviv and discovered that this was one of a series of deep limestone inlets along the coast between Cassis and Marseille, of which, at 1 km in length, it was the longest and formed a safe haven for yachts and other craft. Between the inlet and the *Baie de Cassis* was the *presqu'île* or peninsula on which Mustafa's villa was situated, well placed for access to his pleasure craft.

They parked the Jeep at the small unsurfaced car park at the landward end of the inlet and walked along the western side of the *calanque* whose height had been reduced by past quarrying. The other side was unquarried, a steep slope clothed with pines and bushes and in places having bare limestone outcrops and small cliffs. Through the pines some of the houses on the *presqu'île* could be seen, though they didn't know if Mustafa's was one of them. Below them on the deep blue water were a variety of craft tied up at their berths, many of them expensive playthings - public statements of wealth rather than craft sailed with enthusiasm by real yachtsmen out on the blue Mediterranean beyond the mouth of the *calanque*. The *Viagra* was tied up towards the middle of the waterway, at the seaward end of the *calanque* with only a handful of craft nearer the sea. It was a smart looking 10 metre yacht, as much a floating suntrap as a sailing vessel, it had a white hull with dark blue from the keel to a little above the waterline. The teak deck was well scrubbed and to the stern there was adequate space for a number of passengers to laze under a canvas awning. An energetic couple in their 20's had evidently just reached the *Viagra* and were unloading supplies and fishing rods from an inflatable dinghy which was tied up to the yacht and which they then winched up at the stern. They next set to getting the sails sorted out and it was clear that they knew what they were doing. They had probably been hired by Mustafa as much for their seamanship as for their housekeeping skills.

'Let's walk on towards the sea, Sam. We can see them go from there, we're in no hurry. Once they're out of the way we can have a preliminary look at the house and then attend to the serious business tonight.'

They took the footpath towards the mouth of the *calanque*, the breeze was in their faces but the warmth of the morning sun took away any chill. It was a good morning to be out of doors and Mustafa's people were set for a fine couple of days on the water. Across the inlet and over the top of the narrow peninsula they could see the water of the bay and beyond the bare brown cliffs topping the headland leading southward to *Cap Canaille*. Sam and Dov stopped near the mouth of the *calanque* and sat on a rock. The first of the pleasure boats from Cassis was making its way into the inlet, its passengers poised with their still and video cameras to record the scene. 'That's something we can do, Dov, when Mustafa gets back, make some trips with the tourists and photograph Mustafa on the boat, then see whether anyone back at HQ recognises him. You got a shot then of his crew on the boat, didn't you? Good, but whether they're part of all this or merely hired domestics is anyone's guess at this stage.'

The *Viagra* came into view, running on its motor. The woman, clad in a turquoise bikini, reclined in the stern smoking while her companion stood at the wheel. Sam watched them through the binoculars. 'He's rolling a cigarette, I think. Yes, that's it. I wonder if it's tobacco or cannabis?'

'Cannabis more likely if he's rolling the stuff. They could well be part of the drug set up without knowing what the Unit's collecting its money to do. That would fit in with your idea of everything being in separate watertight compartments.'

'It could well be but I don't expect *they'll* give us our lead to the boss. Still, you never know.'

The *Viagra* cleared *Cap Cable* and began to ride the waves of the open sea, taking an easterly course along the coast towards Toulon. The mainsail was hoisted and then a blue and white spinnaker was unfurled and ballooned out, filled by the moderate south westerly breeze. The yacht appeared a perfect sight even to those as un-nautical as Sam and Dov. Wispy clouds decorated the sky.

'Lucky them! Not a care in the world! I'd like to be out on the waves in that boat. What about you Sam?'

'I'm not a seaman but I wonder whether we shouldn't get ourselves a boat. Nothing like the *Viagra*, of course! And in any case something with a less striking and less memorable name! You never know when we might need one. If we suddenly found we had to put to sea to discover where they were going in the *Viagra* we might have trouble finding a boat quickly and then we might have to put up with a helmsman who would get in the way. No, we must have our own boat. Not a sailing craft, I should think a fast cabin cruiser is what we need.'

'HQ are going to wonder what we're doing here. Our own vineyard and crate upon crate of wine. And then we want a cabin cruiser! It sounds like we're setting up a holiday company just for ourselves!'

'Let them think what they like, we're going to be properly equipped for *any* eventuality, Dov. The risks, if we get it wrong are unthinkable. So your next job is to look around for the right sort of boat, nothing too showy but nonetheless one with a fair turn of speed. Something we can keep in Cassis harbour, always handy if we have to put to sea in a hurry. Now that couple have gone we'll have a first look at Mustafa's villa and then after lunch you can make for the harbour to look at boats. Elizabeth and I are going to look round the town this afternoon and get the feel of the place.

***

They drove past the house, parked a quarter of a mile away and then strolled back along the road. The house was set a hundred metres back from the road and screened from view by a fence and trees. Beside the gate was its name, *Villa des Pins.* The gate was locked and the wooden fence rose to a height of two metres. It was only through the gate that the house could be seen, a moderately sized white villa with a detached garage capable of taking three or four cars and with a second storey which appeared to be living accommodation, possibly the staff quarters.

'I don't think we're going to be able to approach it from here, Dov.'

'It had better be accessible from the other side, we saw houses from across the *calanque*, lets drive to the end of the peninsula and park, then we can try to find our way along behind the house.'

'And hope we've got the right one!'

'It should be OK, it's the fourth house counting from the seaward end of the road.'

They continued their stroll for perhaps half a mile before turning and making their way back to the car which they drove down to a car park near the sea. There they parked and made their way on foot through the pine woods towards the back of the house.

'This is it Sam. House number four and with the same sort of fence that we saw at the front. There's a gate but I suppose it's locked. No it's not! Do we have a look?'

'Better here than at the front. There's no one around and I think there are enough trees to screen us from being seen by Mustafa's neighbours. Yes, let's have a look but watch out for guard dogs! I have no wish to be bitten by one of the Unit's canine members.'

They opened the gate and went into the garden. As Sam had thought they weren't visible from the neighbouring properties, Mustafa evidently liked his privacy, which was to their benefit as intruders. There was a well watered lawn in the middle of the garden and at its centre was a sundial surrounded by a small circular bed of French marigolds. A large seat/swing stood near the house. A flight of seven or eight steps led up from the garden to a paved patio in front of the house with a French window giving access to the house itself. On this was a gas fired barbecue under a cover and a teak garden table and chairs. A bikini top was draped over the back of one of the chairs.

'So this is where Mustafa's nymphs report for duty, Dov.'

'Or where the staff take it easy when their master's away.'

They continued to examine the exterior of the house for a point of access. At the corner was a window that didn't lock closely: the window fittings weren't new and it would be easy to ease them open with a piece of flexible plastic. They had seen a burglar alarm box on the front and there was another at the back. A streak of rust ran down from each, Mustafa clearly was more interested in his comforts than in security, though the bells might be loud enough to attract attention.

'You'd expected an alarm system Sam?'

'Yes, of course. If there hadn't been one that would have been a big bonus and if this isn't too effective that will be a bonus as well. We'll muffle the sound of the alarm bells and cover the flashing light before we break in, we have a lightweight extendible ladder we can bring but there may be a ladder around the place to save us the trouble. The garage is the likely place, let's see if we can get in or look through a window. It might be that the alarm also sounds at a security company but somehow I doubt it; Mustafa's not going to want too many visitors, and certainly not the police, if he's using this place as a base for smuggling, is he?'

They made their way cautiously towards the garage. A dog barked loudly next door and a gray cat fairly flew over the top of the fence. A useful warning, they would have to keep away from that fence at night. The cat seemed an affectionate creature, following them round the garden. Dov's luck held, the garage door opened readily and they were in. Two gleaming vehicles were on the far side, a Range Rover and an open top Mercedes. Along the wall with the door were several ladders including a light aluminium extending ladder.

'That's what we need, Dov. Good to have it on site and so convenient. We'll get it out of here and to hand for tonight, I think the back of the house is the place. But rubber gloves first, we don't want to leave any evidence. We could have a go at the staff flat now, did you see that open dormer window? I'll go in and you can keep a weather eye open for anyone.'

They moved the ladder carefully through the door and quietly placed it upright against the side of the building. Sam climbed up, pulled the window open and swung himself through into the flat. Cramped accommodation, a bedroom with a double bed and a small shower room off, a small lounge, a kitchen and a lavatory. He would concentrate his efforts on the kitchen and the area around the 'phone in the lounge. He found, pinned to the kitchen wall, a list of numbers of what appeared to be local suppliers and shops, together with a note in another hand giving dates of absence and a number to call in emergencies. He suspected that it had been written by Mustafa. He noted down all the details in a small pocket book. Beside the 'phone was a blank message pad and he took the top sheet - the pressure of a ball point pen usually revealed on the blank page the last note made on a pad. He fitted a bug to the 'phone, probably a waste of time but then you never could tell. Better one too many than one too few. The place had a slightly odd smell, confirming his guess that the *Viagra's* crew had been smoking cannabis. He decided he'd seen enough and returned to the window, made a neat exit onto the ladder, returned the window to its almost closed position and climbed down to join Dov.

'A few 'phone numbers, including Mustafa's contact number while he's away, and I've bugged the 'phone. That's the flat dealt with. Not much of a place and they smoke pot in there. I wonder if they're into anything harder, it might limit their usefulness and alertness. Right, we'll get this thing out of sight among the shrubs near the back fence. Then it will be handy when we make tonight's visit.' Sam turned and almost stepped on the cat. An idea struck him. 'That cat may be useful Dov, even if we muffle the alarm Mustafa will know someone's been in the house when he returns. We've got the benefit of an open window in the house through which a cat could enter, so we'll take this cat in with us tonight and leave it there. We'll give it a good feed and a drink first: they're due back the day after tomorrow so it shouldn't be too hungry by then.' Sam made for the garage and the cat followed him hopefully. There he made a quick circuit of the cars, noticing for the first time a bowl of water and another of cat food in a corner of the garage. So this was Mustafa's cat, so much the better. Before he left he locked the cat flap in the door and slipped out before the creature could follow. It was ready for the evening's visit to the house. He would need to bring a bag to transport it from the garage and through the window.

They hid the ladder and then ensured that they had taken in the layout of the garden, it might be very dark and they wanted to be able to move safely, but quickly if necessary. The price of Mustafa's privacy was vulnerability to the likes of Sam and Dov. Then it was out the back gate and a stroll in the late morning sun back through the pines and cypresses to the Jeep.

***

Despite Sam's instructions to Mrs Feldman and Esty, their light lunch had turned out to be a substantial meal. A half hour's siesta was therefore called for before the afternoon's activities commenced. Then Dov set off to look at Cassis harbour and local boatyards. Mrs Feldman was to look after the children, while Esty prepared dinner so leaving Sam and Elizabeth free to make their first visit to Cassis. They drove the Renault Espace the two miles into town and found a multi-storey car park about 300 metres back from the sea. Then they strolled down the narrow *Rue Mistral*, turning left at the church into the *Rue du Saint Icard* before taking a right turn into another narrow street which led them straight to the harbourside.

'It's pleasant here, Sam. Mustafa's chosen well for us, hasn't he?'

'It's the sort of place where you could get into a fine lazy routine, getting up late in the morning and coming down here to the harbour for a newspaper and a morning coffee, then a light lunch before taking your boat out for a few hours sunbathing and fishing. After that back to harbour before drinks at a bar and fresh fish and fine wine for dinner. But for how long that would satisfy us, I don't know. Somehow I don't think we would enjoy it for very long. We both need to be doing something genuine, not living a life of pampered leisure.'

'But we will enjoy our time here, it'll be good for the

children. And my Mum's happy looking after them and running the house along with Esty. They get on well together.'

'That's a relief, I really wondered how they would get along. It's a plus to have harmony, let's hope it continues!'

They strolled to the western end of the harbour before turning around and working their way back past their starting point to the far side where the fishing boats were tied up. Across the harbour, where they had just walked, were the pastel and terracotta coloured houses, shops and restaurants, mainly the latter. Beyond and climbing up the hillside were the orange tiled roofs of the houses, while beyond them were modern apartment blocks. They stopped at the *Quai St-Pierre* to watch the *vedettes*, tourist boats, filling up with eager trippers off to see the coast and its *calanques.* Besides the fishing boats a variety of sailing and motorised craft thronged the harbour. It was a lively place where leisure and commerce happily rubbed shoulders.

'How about a coffee or a cold drink, Sam?'

'A good idea, Elizabeth. I'll leave you to order, you spoke French when you were working in Canada, I expect.'

'I speak it with a Canadian accent, I hope they'll understand.'

'I'm sure they will, in any case they must have them as tourists. Canadians should be more welcome than Americans who are much less likely to speak any French.'

'OK let's try the *Bar de la Marine* over there, it looks the sort of place we're in need of.' They left the tourists and the *vedettes* and made for the bar on the *Quai des Baux.* Its tables were set out on the pavement under a blue and white fronted awning and the four storey building's cream painted windows above were fitted with light green metal shutters. Or rather buildings, for it comprised two houses, with slightly differently roof lines, which had been turned into one, at any rate at ground level, to accommodate the bar with its long pavement frontage.

***

The night was dark and windy, so they would be hidden from sight and hearing. Elizabeth dropped them near the end of the road and then returned to a point near the front gate: she would warn them on her mobile if anyone arrived to disturb them. The rain earlier in the evening had cleared and the route to the rear gate proved less troublesome than they had expected. For a moment it seemed as though the gate had been locked but with a harder push Dov succeeded on opening it, most likely the rain had caused the timber to swell. Their acquaintance with the layout of the garden paid off and they quickly located the ladder and placed muffles over the burglar alarm bells on the front and rear of the house. The cat was to be left to its own devices in the garage until their work in the house was over; they didn't want the animal getting under their feet while they were busy indoors. A further factor was their need to avoid disturbing the guard dog next door beyond the fence near the garage. They would remove the muffles and return the ladder to the garage when they collected the cat for delivery to the house immediately before their departure for the rear gate and safety.

The window at the rear corner opened easily and they slipped plastic bags over their shoes before climbing in; after all cats don't wear muddy boots. Their torches swept the salon. It was expensively furnished with heavy French furniture and the wood block floor was covered with matching Oriental carpets. A large plate of fruit sat on a table by the main window whose curtains were closed. Mustafa had either paid out a considerable sum to furnish the place or he was paying a sizeable rent for the house.

They worked their way around the ground floor, locating the study and deciding to inspect the other downstairs rooms first.

The kitchen had a telephone and they checked for notes and numbers, finding only a further copy of those that Sam had found in the staff apartment in the morning. He noticed that this kitchen was tidier than the one in the apartment. There was nothing of interest in the other rooms or in their waste paper baskets. Their attention now turned to the office and here they found a list of provisional arrival dates for shipping at Marseille with the number of containers on each. Sam extracted the details into his pocket book. The waste paper bucket yielded information; a Post-it note torn into four pieces was easy to reassemble and read, "Jakob next seven days" and a French telephone number with a 3 prefix for the North East. Sam copied the details and returned the pieces to the bucket. They now had something for their efforts. Apart from a telephone directory and some bank statements in Mustafa's name showing considerable sums going through the account, there was little in the office.

'Not much here for us Dov, our man doesn't put much on paper, it seems.'

'Too busy with other matters, I expect!'

'Upstairs then and see what's there.'

They climbed an impressive stairway to a wide landing that looked down into the hallway. This was a spacious house designed to impress its owner as well as his visitors. The main bedroom was in the south west corner of the house. Sam drew the curtains closed and put on the light, 'Might as well do this with some visibility, Dov.' It was a large room, perhaps twenty four feet by thirty feet and around twelve feet high. A huge circular bed with a dark blue spread faced a mirror-lined wall. The other walls were papered with a wine coloured wall paper with a flock design of large roses. A mahogany dressing table was in front of the west facing window while a large sofa was placed in front of the French window that faced south. Beyond the French window Sam had noticed, as he drew the curtains, a substantial balcony. The curtains too were of the same wine colour as the wall paper.

Dov looked around, 'French brothel decor, I suppose.'

'From experience or from reading Dov?'

'I did say, "I suppose", Sam! It's no more than a guess, but from what we already know of Mustafa it's probably a well enough informed guess.'

'I wonder whether it was like this when he took over the house or whether he's had it done since.'

'Ask him when you meet, Sam! I'm sure he'd love to tell you.'

They checked out the dressing room - well stocked with expensive shirts and suits - and the en-suite bathroom. They went through the pockets of the suits but there was nothing of any significance. Then they returned to the bedroom itself. The dressing table yielded nothing and neither did the drinks cabinet or the video unit, except to confirm that Mustafa's taste in video entertainment was exactly as they had expected. Only the bed-side cabinets remained to be checked. The one to the left of the bed had the telephone and suggested that was Mustafa's preferred side of the bed, if a circular bed could be said to have a side, but then the bed head and the cabinets created such a geometry. Once more Sam removed the top sheet from the note pad beside the telephone. The bottom drawer of the cabinet had a telephone directory. The upper one was more interesting: it contained a list of women's names and their telephone numbers, some struck through and others underlined; a plentiful supply of French currency and a well thumbed sex manual. Sam had taken a good look at the arrangement of the drawer's contents before moving anything, 'We need to make sure it all goes back precisely as Mustafa left it, Dov, it's all too easy to jump in and then forget how things were before you touched them.'

'A bit like a game we played as kids where you had to look at twenty items on a tray for a minute and then, when they'd been covered, write down as many as you could remember.'

'But now, in addition, we've got to put them back just as we found them. It may be that he keeps the things in a particular way to check that his staff don't interfere, though if he were *that* suspicious of them I suppose he'd lock the drawer.' He removed the money and leafed carefully through the bundles; nothing there but money and a lot of it - Mustafa must be keeping the local tarts busy or perhaps he also used cash for travel and the like to avoid leaving the computerised trails that credit cards generated. He replaced the money and picked up the list of what were evidently Mustafa's women. He began to copy the list into his pocket book, counting the number of entries first, fifteen of them. Mustafa evidently had considerably more than his proper share of energy!

'Elizabeth won't be too pleased if she finds you with that Sam!'

'Oh, don't worry, you're the one who will be getting to know these girls, Dov. In the national interest of course!'

'Of course, why ever else?'

'There's a girl here - Yvonne Charpentier - who merits not just one underlining but two as well as a tick against her name and *then* a striking through ... now I wonder what all that signifies?'

'I wonder. I suppose my next job is to find out.'

'Not your next but it's high on your list of priorities, Dov.'

'And all in the national interest ... '

'Just so my friend, just so!' He turned the list over and read out a pencilled note, "Last Unit cargo due 15 July." Useful information, perhaps vital - that would provide the remaining funds for the operation and they would be ready for the procurement of the weapon ...

That left Mustafa's sex manual. Sam noted that it was written in French as he searched it for any note that might have been pressed into service as a bookmark. He succeeded, finding a half sheet of dog eared A4 paper with the note: "Ring Anatoli Kyrienko, Kiev" followed by a telephone number. Perhaps it was to do with the procurement of the weapon, as distinct from the other sort of procurement that Mustafa's longer list evidenced.

Dov leafed through the manual with obvious amusement, 'Our friend Mustafa must have energy and agility in abundance if he manages even half these positions, Sam! He must be a regular contortionist!'

'Twister, more likely than not, Dov. Right lets put that back where we found it.' Sam scrutinised the drawer's contents, all was back in proper order. He bugged the telephone, 'Good, we've finished with the master suite. There probably won't be much in the other bedrooms.' And he was right, though their search was as thorough as before. It didn't appear that the other rooms were much used; probably most of Mustafa's guests were invited for the purpose of sharing his bed with him and for no other reason. Sam switched off the bedroom lights and opened the curtains. He was pleased that the cloud was still obscuring the moon.

They had dealt with the telephone in the master bedroom, or as Dov termed it the master and mistress bedroom - though Sam wondered whether any of the women really qualified for the title of mistress - that left them to bug the telephone in the study. Sam ensured that all the doors were as they had found them. It then remained to get the cat from the garage and let it loose in the house. Their final task was to climb the ladder to remove the muffles from the burglar alarm bell boxes. Fortunately the bells had rung for their prescribed duration and stopped so they didn't unleash a clamour to disturb Mustafa's wealthy neighbours. The ladder had stood on firm ground and so needed no wiping before they stowed it away back in the garage - the moisture collected while lying in the shrubs had drained off while it stood against the house and the warm interior of the garage would dry it completely before anyone returned. As they made their way across the garden the guard dog next door began to bark, but that didn't disturb the departing intruders, though an hour and a half earlier it would have been a matter of concern. Now all that remained was to install an electronic device to pick up the transmission from the bugs and send it on at greater strength to *the Domaine du Cheval Rouge*. When this had been hidden among the dense branches of a cypress they called Elizabeth on the mobile and waited for her to pick them up in the car at the end of the road.

'Glad you're safely out of there. I didn't really enjoy it very much sitting here keeping an eye on the front gate. Successful?'

'Yes we got some useful telephone numbers, bugged the 'phones and Dov's going to make himself acquainted with some of Mustafa's friends.' Dov sat on the rear seat and winced - the things you were called on to do for your country. Still, some of Joshua's spies had once been given hospitality by someone of that sort in Jericho. Jericho, he mused to himself, home of a new mosque, a besieged synagogue and - to the ire of some of the more militant Palestinians - Arafat's new casino! And all a long way off from Cassis.

PART 2

Time of Hope

Whether we be young or old,
Our destiny, our being's heart and home,
Is with infinitude, and only there;
With hope it is, hope that can never die,
Effort and expectation, and desire,
And something evermore about to be.

William Wordsworth, The Prelude

Chapter 9

Monday 18th June 2001

Jakob Schmidt stood waiting in a short queue for the Immigration Control at Basel-Mulhouse-Freiburg Airport. Behind him was Lieutenant Peter Gruenweiler from Eric Blum's staff in Basel. Gruenweiler had sat near Schmidt on the Crossair flight from Zurich and now to his surprise he found himself in the queue for the *French* Immigration Control and not the *Swiss* one that he had expected Schmidt to take. It was indeed an international airport, situated on French territory but with a corridor that ran directly into Switzerland, so that once cleared by Swiss Immigration and Customs you drove straight into Basel. That was if you chose the Swiss exit.

Contrary to expectations Schmidt hadn't done so and therefore this was going to be more complicated than the young officer had anticipated. He had, of course, called Bern on his mobile and cryptically explained his problem. Use your initiative, they had responded and be grateful you're not a French investigator faced with your quarry going into Basel. The message was some consolation, but not very much help. OK, he would do what he could. It wasn't vital, Schmidt was due at *Die Drei Könige* at 8.00 that evening, they would have no trouble tailing him from there. Still they needed to find out why he was now heading for France. Gruenweiler looked at his watch, 2.30 p.m. - five and a half hours to go until Schmidt was due in Basel. Schmidt had been dealt with and Gruenweiler's passport was given a cursory examination by the French Immigration official. It was a good thing he'd put the passport in his case the previous day, though he hadn't given much thought to it at the time.

Outside the terminal Schmidt was about to get into a taxi. Gruenweiler engaged the next cab, took a deep breath, and half instructed and half besought the woman driver, 'Would you please follow the taxi in front, but not so closely as to attract attention?' The expression on the driver's face compelled further comment, 'Look, I'm a private detective with a lady client who suspects her husband of infidelity.' If the driver had been a man he would have most probably given a Gallic shrug of the shoulders, raised his eyebrows and muttered, *'Zut alors!'* - 'You be blowed!' But Gruenweiler's good fortune had been to find a cab with a woman driver who was happy to assist him.

They worked their way out of the airport before heading eastward through Blotzheim, Ranspach-le-Bas and then along the D419, passing houses festooned with geraniums and other flowers. The road ran through undulating countryside and there was little other traffic. At last they turned left off the main road and headed into Altkirch, on their right was the hospital while on their left were houses with tidy gardens. Gruenweiler noted their route. Next they took another left in the middle of the town, passing a fountain with its taps dripping water, and into the *rue de Ferrette*. There was a school on the left and what Gruenweiler later discovered to be an old synagogue on the right. Then on the left came a row of plane trees and at the end of the row the leading taxi slowed down, pulled over to the left and turned back on itself into a slip road that paralleled the main thoroughfare. Without having to be told Gruenweiler's driver turned her taxi round and came back down the road on the other side of the row, keeping an eye on the other cab through the trees. Schmidt's taxi drew up in front of cream painted house with metal roller shutters on the windows. Gruenweiler's driver pulled up fifty metres behind and they watched Schmidt get out and climb the steps to the front door of a house, 'It seems that your client's husband's infidelities are causing him some stress! That's Dr Garnier's house, she's a psychotherapist. Though she's also a very attractive woman! He might be calling on her as a patient or a lover ... or even both!'

'Thanks for the efficient pursuit and for that information.' He paid her handsomely in Swiss currency, explaining that it was all he had, he hadn't expected the man to enter France. The taxi drove off leaving Gruenweiler to wait on the pavement. He had kept in touch with Bern by telephone throughout the journey and now confirmed his location and waited for the car that was on its way from Basel. Then they would keep the house under surveillance until Schmidt emerged from his session of therapy or whatever else it might be. It didn't look the sort of road where they would get a parking ticket but if they did that was a minor problem. The main thing was to remain unnoticed by the residents of the area and particularly by Dr Garnier and her visitor.

He had a spy thriller in his raincoat pocket and was glad to have something to read to pass the time, but first he set off to stroll past Dr Garnier's house. He wondered who might be on the couch and then told himself to get a grip on reality, he was beginning to believe the taxi driver's suggestion of Schmidt's supposed dalliances - but that had been his invention in the first place as part of his assumed rôle as a private detective. Well if he didn't pass his probation in the service, that was what he might be doing for a living! He took in the details of the house, *rue de Ferrette 17A,* a two storey building with a semi-basement in addition. Part of the basement was occupied by a garage, to the left of the front door, accessed by a short slope from the pavement. The house was well maintained and had a prosperous and substantial appearance. He counted six windows on the second floor, one of which was a door onto a small balcony which formed a porch over the front door. The roof had a small dormer window indicating full use of the available space. The front door itself was approached by a flight of steps and troughs of orange geraniums lined the walls beside the steps. Dr Garnier's psychotherapy practice evidently wasn't doing too badly.

***

'Ishmael, I love to call you by that name, it says so much about you and your commitment to the cause.' Dominique Garnier looked up at him as they lay together in the small bedroom at the top of the house.

'It's a few years now since I took Ishmael as my *nom-de-guerre*, when I vowed to avenge the Palestinian people for what's been done to them. But perhaps it's the name I ought to have been given, my mother came from Hebron though she became very Westernised.'

'And no thought of anti-Semitism? I only ask in my rôle as your therapist and not, of course, as your lover!'

'Anti-Semitism? Never! After all, the Arabs are Semites too. It's Zionist imperialism that I'm, that *we're*, fighting. Some of ... '

'Some of your best friends are Jews?'

'Well, yes, that's what was on my tongue ... but it happens to be true, trite as it may sound. But you've seen what's been done to the Palestinians - you've been in Gaza City, and in the refugee camps in the Lebanon and Jordan. And now the man who shared complicity for the massacres in Sabra and Shatila is the Zionist's Prime Minister! We've got to act ... we are acting already, it's in hand as you know.'

'I just hope it achieves what you intend and no more, Ishmael! It's dangerous to say the very least!'

'But the so called peace talks are going nowhere, can go nowhere. Camp David, Madrid, Oslo ... it's all a load of nonsense to suit the Jews and their American friends. And the latest *Intifada* is not achieving anything either except provoking Jewish assassinations with exploding car headrests and attacks by their helicopter gunships. Just imagine what the Americans would do if *we* sent in aircraft to attack the Israelis in that way! Our people, the Palestinian people, need to be able to hold their heads up in the world, which includes the Arab world. And that's what we, you and I and our friends are working for. Don't think that the other Arabs nations regard us with much esteem or love, they've used us as a pawn in their own struggle against the Zionists. We've got to do it ourselves and regain our own self respect and the admiration of others.'

For a while they lay together quiet and content with the warmth and softness of one another's bodies. She broke the silence, 'Ishmael ... I want you to rape me at gunpoint. I know you keep a gun here in the wardrobe. Take me by force, that's what I want now!'

He sighed inwardly, 'If that's really what you want Dr Garnier!' He got out of bed and went to the wardrobe to take out a small automatic, wrapped in a silk scarf, from a pile of underwear. He looked at it and shook his head, she was becoming more and more obsessed with fantasies of this kind.

'Now dress and pretend you've broken into the house ... your shirt, underpants and trousers will do. Right, now go out onto the landing, make a lot of noise as though you're breaking in and come back into here. The gun's loaded? No? Then load it! Do as I say or it will be the end of today's session and possibly tomorrow's as well.'

'OK, Dr Garnier, if it's really going to help.' He found the clip of ammunition and slipped it into the pistol then left the room and did as she had instructed him. He burst into the room and brandished the pistol.

'The safety catch is off?'

'No, of course it isn't.'

'Then do it?'

'That's dangerous, Doctor!'

'I like danger, do as I tell you. Now point it at me and take me by force.'

He stood there sweating, she was mad. But she was

an accomplished lover and he needed the release of tension their love making usually brought him. Though there was no release of tension this afternoon: he found himself shaking.

She interpreted his reaction as one of rising excitement, the rapist about to achieve satisfaction. 'Come on get it over with, don't kill me and I'll give you what you're after. And remember no condoms, you're a rapist!'

'I can't undress while I'm holding this thing!'

'Then put it down for a moment and strip, you're allowed to use some initiative. Good, I can see you're ready, take me and don't be gentle about it! Put the gun under the pillow and tell me you're not afraid to use it. No, don't apply the safety catch.'

He did as he was told, climaxed quickly and powerfully and was surprised to find that she too was climaxing before his was over.

He lay there for a while before removing the pistol from under his pillow, applying the safety catch and removing the ammunition. It was the first time she had wanted this, though they had acted out the rape scenario before. Was she crazy? Could a psychotherapist catch madness from her clients? Was she safe to be entrusted with the secrets of the operation? Not much choice now, she was deeply into it. He wondered if he would be able to use the pistol on her if she ever endangered the operation. No, he mustn't think about it. And his mind turned to the effect on himself of the game they had just played. It had scared him but, he admitted to himself, he had enjoyed it. It had certainly raised the level of his excitement. Was there a latent rapist there under his skin? He didn't want there to be, but you just didn't know. He was conscious that his genitals were aching.

'Are you comfortable, Dr Garnier?' She insisted that, in bed, he should address her formally. Presumably more fantasy, irregular intimacy between therapist and patient or something of that sort. Perhaps it was about time she stood in front of a mirror and talked to herself and then billed herself with the fees for her professional services.

'Fine, Ishmael, that was good. I'm probably a bit bruised but it's the only way I climax. No bleeding so you're safe.'

'And how did you discover the benefits of rape?'

'By being raped, of course!'

'Raped, where?

'Oh by a man I picked up in a Basel club. I suppose it wasn't really rape, I egged him on but then made it difficult so that he had to force me. He enjoyed it and so did I, so that was OK.'

'Except that you may have turned him and myself into rapists.'

'Oh, I suspect all men are latent rapists. Don't you really think that you might be? I'd be very interested to hear how you reacted to this afternoon's fantasy. Be honest did you enjoy it?'

'Yes, I'm afraid I did.'

'In spite of yourself?'

'In spite of myself, yes.'

'So there you are, the conventions that inhibit you didn't stop you from enjoying raping me.'

'But I didn't rape you, I responded to your invitation.'

'No you didn't, you raped me. Don't spoil it. You raped me at gunpoint ... I don't know which excited me more, your pistol or your penis. You raped me ... I enjoyed it, you enjoyed it, we both did. But now you can be gentle with me, fondle my breasts and I'll rub some cream onto your aching penis.'

He responded to her invitation wondering where it would all end. 'Yes, Doctor, I'd like that.' He too was gripped by the fantasies in their relationship, she had introduced the doctor/client motif into their lovemaking, and he had found that it heightened his own enjoyment as well. Would she want, one day, to reverse their rôles and rape him at gunpoint? He certainly wouldn't be happy about being at the other end of a loaded pistol. He reflected that he might have chosen more carefully than this for his lover and, more importantly, for his companion in arms. But there was no going back and he needed her emotionally. It was a lonely business undertaking an operation as big as this one, very, very lonely, and he needed to be able to unburden himself to someone with whom he was close, both physically and ideologically.

'Dominique.'

'Dr Garnier in bed, please!'

'No, Dominique, I'm speaking to you as a friend and soldier in the cause.' She had pulled away from him and was studying him closely. 'I saw my oncologist this week and he gives me six months at the most. It's a race to get the project over before I go.'

There were tears in her eyes, 'No, Jakob, it can't be! You're so lively and alert, he must be mistaken.'

'I don't think so. Time will tell. The point is this, the money's almost in at last. I'm seeing our banker in Basel this evening to authorise the next transfer, though I'm not going to tell him that it's the last. The money has been off on its world tour, Jersey, Nauru, the Cayman Islands and a few other places beside. Then in a couple of months time it will be a simple matter to transfer it to our vendor friends and have them send the goods on their way. So, it's all in hand and I wonder if I might come here and spend my last days with you in Altkirch? I'll need someone to care for me at the end as I become more and more incapable of looking after myself. Besides I think I might have been followed today when I was at Frankfurt airport. I relish the chase but can't run the risk of being caught and for it all to come to nothing. If I stay here and don't venture out they won't be able to track me down. No one in the organisation knows about you and your part in all this.'

She gulped back her tears, his illness had not been a

secret between them but she had always hoped ... well she had hoped what everyone did in such circumstances. To hear from his lips that the oncologist had ... passed sentence wasn't quite appropriate but it seemed like that. 'Of course Jakob. I'll be honoured to have you here and to nurse you if necessary.' She pulled him to her and wept quietly.

'And I look forward to intelligent conversation and discussion. On my way here I came across this in Wittgenstein ... '

He sought the paperback in his bag while she laughed, 'Wittgenstein again! What wisdom is it this time?'

'What he says is this:

> *"It is impossible to speak about the will in so far as it is the subject of ethical attributes.*
> *"And the will as a phenomenon is of interest only to psychology."*

What do you think Dominique?'

'Jakob, does it really mean anything? For that matter does life itself mean anything?' His news had made her despondent. Her tears had stopped but once he was on his way into Basel they would flow again. She didn't know how she would get by without him. 'OK, I'll give it thought, we're going to have plenty of time to debate and discuss in the weeks ahead, Jakob.'

They kissed before he opened the door to leave. 'No don't come outside into the street, Dominique. There's always a risk in being seen with me, though it's probably OK here in Alsace. We must never forget what we saw in those refugee camps in Gaza, Jordan and the Lebanon. The taxi's waiting. I hate leaving you but I'll be back tomorrow if I can't make it tonight. Sometimes I think I'm too old for all this cloak and dagger stuff. Never at home, more like the wandering Jew, though in the circumstances that's an inappropriate comparison. No perhaps not, I've no objection to them wandering - it's just when they think they can come back to the Promised Land and take it over again without so much as by your leave! Thanks for agreeing that from now on this can be my home.'

'Perhaps the Flying Dutchman's more apt, Jakob, especially as it's by Wagner - but it's not as if you're looking for a woman to die for you, is it? I would though, if I had to. Perhaps, once we've defeated them we can settle down together like any other couple. That will be a triumph! How many of us in the Unit? An inner core of six and not more than a dozen in all. And against us, *if* only they knew, the might of the IDF, Mossad and their General Security Service. Hurry back, I'll be waiting.'

He asked himself whether she was ignoring his medical condition to encourage him or whether she was in denial, defending herself from the grim reality of his prognosis.

***

As the taxi carried him towards Basel he wondered how long their relationship would have held together if he had been fit and well, especially now that her fantasies had taken such a dangerous turn. He would have to keep things on the rails until the Unit's operation was over. And then? Well it wouldn't matter. He was the only one she knew in the Unit and he would shortly be dead. She was showing every sign of needing to undergo therapy herself and they certainly couldn't have her blabbing out all she knew to another shrink. If she showed signs of being a security risk he would have to use the gun, not for fantasies acted out in bed but for real. It would be a pity, but there it was: the safety of himself and the Unit depended on maintaining tight security. She was the only living human being for whom he really cared as an individual. Certainly he was absolutely committed to this work for the Palestinian people. But in truth they were an abstract, connected to him by birth - and not by real human relationships. They were a *cause* that possessed him. That cause and avenging his fiancée, who had died all those years ago in the Lebanese massacre, were all that mattered. It was true that he had Jewish friends and it was an interesting fact that there were more of them than he could number as friends from the Palestinians. With only a few months to go to 16th September Dominique ought not to be a risk. This operation was anything but a game: for years now it had been his life. He would see it through in Altkirch, he would relish some easing of the pressures and respite from the constant travelling the task entailed and which had lately become so tiring.

***

Lieutenant Peter Gruenweiler sat in the car waiting. He had been there for over three hours feeling increasingly conspicuous. He thought they should have brought another car along to take over after a couple of hours. He supposed it was a matter of economy. One woman had passed them a couple of times and looked very suspiciously at the car on the second occasion. Or had he imagined her reaction? Possibly he had, for in truth the location was about as good as you could get for a surveillance operation: the row of trees had enabled the car to remain generally unobtrusive and out of sight from number 17A. At last a taxi stopped outside the house. 'OK get ready to follow.' His driver muttered something about stating the obvious and they were ready to go. He couldn't see who opened the door of the house for Schmidt to leave but he watched him cross the pavement and get into the taxi. He had clearly had a long session with his psychotherapist, presumably therapy plus quite a lot more. 'OK, follow with caution.'

'And how else might we proceed?' The driver's

contempt for this new recruit was barely hidden.

'Just as you're used to doing, my friend, and then we'll see whether it's good enough!' It would probably be no more than a run straight to Basel via the border crossing at Allschwil. And he proved to be correct in this surmise. They stopped near the entrance to *Die Drei Könige* and watched Schmidt enter the hotel. 'OK, driver, off to *Binningerstrasse*.' He would report at the Public Prosecutor's Office and go home. The others would now be taking care of Schmidt. The thought occurred to Gruenweiler that he might volunteer to visit Dr Garnier as a prospective patient - he could tell her that he appreciated the services of a shrink who wasn't living in the same town as himself and he could hint that he couldn't afford Swiss fees. Yes, it seemed a good idea. He'd keep quiet, of course, about the taxi driver's comments on the Doctor's good looks. The lady could be interesting and he'd always wondered what a therapist might dredge up from his subconscious. Perhaps, when Erik Blum got back from his jaunt to Provence, he would take the bait and send him off for treatment over the border in Alsace. It would certainly be a way of finding out something more about Schmidt's French therapist. And it might give an opportunity to place some bugs in Dr Garnier's house.

***

They had the first report, received at 18.15 hours from Bern. 'So he's gone to see his shrink - or is it a lover or an accomplice - in Alsace. Thanks Erik, that gives us something to go on. I wonder how often he goes to her for therapy or whatever else he receives there.'

'I'll see what I can do about that when I get back there tomorrow, Sam. It would be irregular to break in or to bug the house but in the circumstances ... well, I'll see what can be managed. If *I* can't get approval ... '

'Then *we* will have to look after it, Erik, but nevertheless your local knowledge of people and places would be very helpful ... '

Blum was looking forward to dinner by the harbour in Cassis with Sam and Elizabeth before flying back to Basel the next day.

***

Schmidt had become more and more wary as the day progressed, he knew that he might be imagining that he was being watched but he preferred to err on the side of caution rather than have his long laid plans thwarted. He had arrived an hour ahead of his Swiss banker and established the geography of *Die Drei Könige*. In the corridor to his room he had picked up a wedge that the cleaners evidently used to hold doors open. Around the corner from the dining room and on the way to the restrooms was a fire escape door opening outwards. That was what he needed. Then he went for a stroll round the outside of the hotel and found where the fire escape reached the ground. He was probably being over suspicious but better safe than sorry.

Dinner with Balthasar Feuerbach followed the signature of the paperwork for the transfer of monies out of the Basel account and he insisted that Feuerbach action the payment immediately. Good, he would have his first course and then vanish on his way to the restroom – he had identified two men on the far side of the dining room who had looked in his direction rather too often. He reckoned that he could reach the fire escape door before anyone could catch up with him and so he excused himself to Feuerbach - he would only be a couple of minutes – and set off, speeding up as soon as he was out of the dining room. On the way he collected a small briefcase which contained his medication from behind a curtain, opened the fire door and stepped outside. He used the wedge to prevent the door from being opened by a pursuer, quickly but safely he descended to ground level and climbed onboard a tram at *Schifflände* and headed over the Rhein on the *Mittlere Rheinbrücke* for *Klein Basel* where he found a small hotel for the night, paying in cash.

He telephoned Dr Garnier apologising for being unable to return as planned as he was being followed. Tomorrow he would head for the *Badischer Bahnhof*, the German railway station in *Klein Basel*, and begin his journey back to Frankfurt. He didn't doubt that his pursuers would be keeping a look out for him at the airport.

Chapter 10

Tuesday 19th June 2001

They stood at the window of Peter Gruenweiler's room in the Basel Public Prosecutor's Office looking down at a tram heading out of town along *Binningerstrasse*. Erik Blum wasn't in the best of moods. 'So we lost Schmidt at *Die Drei Könige* last night. Two of our people wasted a small fortune on dinner and then let him walk out and disappear! And I've had to tell the Israelis ... hardly a triumph for Swiss Security is it? Especially when I'd warned the Israelis off from operating on our territory. We're watching the airport of course and we placed that French psychiatrist's place under observation immediately Schmidt disappeared but she's had no callers. He's probably a long way from Basel by now and the last lot of money was sent on electronicaly before he started dinner, evidently he'd planned it all carefully.'

Peter explained the idea that had come to him the previous day.

'So, Peter, you're offering to become one of Dr Garnier's patients to try to find out what's going on and possibly bug the place. And, of course, it has nothing to do with her being a good looking woman!' Despite it all Erik Blum smiled at the indications of the younger man's embarrassment.

'If you don't think it a good idea ... '

'Oh, I'm sure it's an excellent one, Peter. It will need thorough preparation though. To me you seem pretty balanced, hardly the sort of a person to need the help of a shrink, to undergo analysis, therapy and whatever. I may be wrong but if you really are normal, whatever that might mean, wouldn't she realise that too and be suspicious? This isn't New York in the era when everyone had a shrink and tried to keep up with Woody Allen!'

'That had occurred to me too, Erik. I would need two

shrinks: Dr Dominique Garnier herself and one working with us in an advisory capacity, guiding me about what to tell her, how to bring the past to the surface bit by bit in a convincing way.'

'Yes, perhaps it's worth a go, even if it does no more than allow you to bug the house, though a break-in might give better access than your visits as a client - unless you have in mind going beyond the client/shrink relationship. They can get struck off for that sort, of thing of course.'

'I was intending to play it professionally.'

'I'm glad to hear it, after all we'll be paying your fees for the treatment and I wouldn't like to find that the sessions had been misdescribed on Dr Garnier's bills. False claims are a disciplinary matter as you know.' He kept a straight face but the younger man knew his boss was joking. 'But, first, you're sure it's all over between you and Julia? You were together for five years after all. I don't want you getting into a tangle that you'll regret later.'

'Stop trying to father me, Erik. I'm old enough and experienced enough to look after myself.'

'And we don't want an emotional entanglement which mucks up our operation! It's too important and dangerous for that.'

'No problem, I'm not looking for any deep emotional entanglement for the time being. First of all I've got to get over Julia walking out.'

'Just so long as it's not a case of a new relationship formed on the rebound. I'm not completely sure we should get *you* mixed up in this.'

'And then who would you send. Are *you* volunteering to become her patient, Erik?'

'Heaven forbid! No, it's not for me, I couldn't carry it off. I'll approve your idea provided you keep me fully informed on progress, particularly any emotional attachment to your therapists. Because it seems to me that it may be better to have a woman briefing you at this end. I don't know whether male and female shrinks see things exactly the same way - I suppose in theory they ought - but having a consultant of the same sex and background might well help.' And it would be far safer, if Peter were going to form an attachment with anyone, for it to be with their own tame shrink rather than with Dr Garnier - that could endanger everything and risk warning them that their plans had been detected. 'I'll make enquiries with a contact at the University and see who we can find to probe into the murky depths of your mind. I just hope you end up as well adjusted and well balanced as you now seem to be. After all we'll be consigning you into the hands of not one shrink but two!'

Thursday 21st June 2001

Two days later, on a wet afternoon, Peter Gruenweiler walked through the Basel *Fischmarkt* and turned left into the *Kellergässlein*, a long flight of steps leading upwards towards the University. Beyond the top of the steps he turned into a narrow street of old houses, the *Petersgasse*, and soon found himself in front of the door of a very old house, the *Offenburger-hof, Petersgasse 40*. A water trough and fountain stood opposite, unusually plain for a Basel fountain. Before he rang the bell he studied the plate to the right of the doorway, it gave a history of the early, distinguished Baslers who had lived there. In 1501, exactly 500 years before it had been the home of Peter Offenburg, *Oberzunftmeister und spätere Burgermeister* - Chief Guild Master and later Mayor. An ancient and distinguished place indeed! Now it seemed to be the home of a number of academics.

He rang the bell marked "Dr Maria Bertorelli", announced his name to the entryphone and entered the hallway. He climbed the stairs to the fourth floor and, as he stood looking for apartment 403, heard a door open and a woman call, 'Mr Gruenweiler?'

He turned and saw a woman of a little above medium

height whom he guessed to be in her early thirties waiting for him, 'Dr Bertorelli, I presume?'

She responded with a light, easy laugh, 'Indeed it is. Come in, let me take your coat. Goodness it must be wet out there, it's dripping - I'll hang it in the bathroom. Take a seat while I do that.' She indicated a sofa to one side of a bay window, 'Make yourself comfortable. Coffee? What sort? I can cater for most tastes: Espresso, Turkish, decaffeinated, just name it and I'll try to find it.'

'Espresso, I run on the stuff.'

'OK, just make yourself at home, it seems you're going to be here quite a lot over the next few weeks.'

He stood at the bay window and looked out at the rainy scene. Over the top of the *Fischmarkt* he could see the tower of the *Martinskirch*, set on the hill next to the Rhein. Its clock showed 2.25. Basel wasn't a bad place to live. There was a lot going on in the city. It was a pity that Julia had quit. He was lonely without her, it wasn't much fun going out on your own and certainly not pleasant coming back to an empty apartment at the end of the day. And she was probably working now, over there in the University Mathematics Department not far from the *Martinskirch*. He had often collected her from work but now he made an effort to stay away from the area.

He sat down on the sofa and took in the furnishing of the room. It was light and airy with modern furniture in light wood. It contrasted with the antiquity of the house. A small hi-fi was playing what he took to be a Mozart Symphony but it was very much background music. Another sofa was set at right angles to his and faced the window, while a small desk, probably used for taking notes, was to the other side of the window. The walls were adorned with a couple of almost abstract Impressionist paintings. He guessed they were from Monet's London period. He picked up a book from the sofa table; photographs of the Alps and Alpine flowers. He worked his way through, checking his identification of the locations against the captions at the back of the book. Apart from one or two in the *Grissons* he had got them all right, but then he knew the Alps pretty well. He loved them, both in summer and winter. Indeed he loved them in all seasons.

He was finishing his perusal of the book when she arrived with two cups of Espresso coffee, 'Sugar, Mr Gruenweiler.'

'No thanks and I'd rather you called me Peter.'

'Good, I prefer to be on first name terms. As you know I'm Maria - the gift of devout parents!'

It was then that his eye caught the name of the photographer on the cover of the book, 'You're a fine photographer, Maria. You've really got the feel of the mountains and their flowers.'

'I don't usually leave my books around but it was published last week and I have to admit I'm rather pleased with it. The publishers have made an extremely good job of it. The photos are sharp and the colours are pretty well spot on. And as a book it's good, decent heavy quality art paper and a good binding, a fitting tribute ... a nice book, yes.' He noticed that she had stopped herself from continuing.

'Your publishers obviously had the very best material to be working on.'

'Thanks, I've got to admit there's a special pleasure in having something published which isn't work-related. As you know I teach in the University and I'm expected to keep a spate of papers and research material flowing. But this is me expressing myself ... giving, I hope, pleasure to people. Not that the psychiatry projects aren't for the public good, but you quickly lose the magic of seeing your name on a publication, knowing that you're working on the next one and beginning to think about the one after that - the usual academic treadmill.'

'You don't look very much like a shrink, Maria.'

'And what should a shrink, a female one, look like?

What sort of caricature do you have in your mind, Peter? A prematurely elderly woman with a sack-like skirt down to the ankles, a knitted twin set and beads? Oh yes, and her hair in a bun?' Again he heard her light, relaxed laugh as he looked at her, taking in a smartly turned out woman whose camel coloured Jaeger skirt revealed legs and knees to be admired and whose matching blouse emphasised, rather than hid, an attractive figure. Far from being in a bun her black shoulder length hair testified, by its style and sheen, to a good and probably expensive hairdresser.

'Exactly that and, of course, I'm bitterly disappointed to find you so *very* different.' He joined in her laughter, this wasn't going to be as bad as he had thought. He could relate to her.

'And you don't look very much like my idea of a policeman. From what Erik Blum told me this morning that's going to be useful for what you have in mind. OK, he's put me in the picture, at any rate so far as your part of it is concerned. He didn't tell me absolutely everything but he did say that the people you're after could be dangerous both to you and to a very, very large number of people somewhere.' In fact Erik, whom she had known for years and with whom she had worked on several cases, had told her the whole story. If she was going to be involved in something that might pose ethical problems for her, he had felt he owed it to her to explain why he was asking her to take it on.

'Good, that makes it a lot easier.'

'This afternoon we'll go through what it is that you're trying to achieve and I'll tell you how I intend to go about my task. By the way do you want the hi-fi left on? Some people find it helpful, particularly on a first visit like this, others can't stand it?'

'Leave it on, I'm perfectly happy with it. Indeed, at home I live with the radio or the hi-fi as a constant background.'

'And companion?'

"Yes, and companion. Erik's been giving you some of my background then?'

'A little. He did tell me that your fiancée had walked out on you three months ago.'

'Yes, Julia's gone. But, of course, that on its own wouldn't make me material for a shrink would it?'

'Of course it wouldn't, but it's the sort of thing that we could build on for you to off-load on Dr Garnier, a trigger for the things that have gone wrong since then. But that's only a suggestion at the moment. What we'll work on at first is seeing whether there's any inherent disorder, however slight. Incidentally I won't be reporting on anything of that sort to your bosses. If there's any abnormality there we might build on that, otherwise we'll have to create a fictitious disorder. So, we're going to chat over the next few afternoons, I want to find out about you and your childhood and development since then. Erik has stressed to me the urgency of all this and we'll probably have to work through next weekend to get it all done. A crash course of analysis then, and paid for by the Security Service, you're a lucky policeman, Peter Gruenweiler.' More laughter.

'I just hope I don't come out of this more disordered than when I started!'

'That's a good point and an important one, Peter. We're going to be talking about psychiatric problems and you might begin to have doubts as to whether you're sane, you might begin to think you've got some of the symptoms I talk about. When that happens we call it an *iatrogenic illness*, but you're not going to need to know what the label says. And it will be the same with your sessions with Dr Garnier. We're very suggestible and it's easy to imagine that we're suffering from the disorder being discussed - I know it happens regularly with my students. So, if at any time you start feeling like that, tell me and we'll sort it out. I'm not here to turn you into another psychiatric case to become the subject of yet another of my scholarly little monographs.'

'Thanks for the warning, I'll do as you say.'

'Oh, by the way, I know Dominique Garnier. She's highly regarded, very competent in treating childhood trauma. She's worked among refugee children in Kosovo and before that in refugee camps in the Lebanon and probably other places. She's lectured at the Faculty here.' Peter Gruenweiler guessed that the link between Dr Garnier and the 16th September Unit would turn out to be her experiences in the Palestinian Refugee Camps. Maria continued, 'Well, that's our programme. Perhaps we could start with something recent and significant in your life ... it was three months ago that Julia walked out on you. Perhaps you'd like to tell me about her. How long had you known her? When did you first meet? And how long had you been together? ... '

A telephone call from the University Faculty had interrupted their session. She had gone off to her study to consult her diary. Peter Gruenweiler looked at his watch, 17.55, he'd been there for three and a half hours. It didn't matter, he was in no hurry to get back to his apartment and in any case it would take less than ten minutes for him to walk there. His attention returned to the book on the sofa table, *"Mountains and Flowers - a Tribute"*. A *Tribute*, that was the word she had used when they had talked about the book earlier, *a fitting tribute*, had been the expression. He opened the book to find the dedication. There it was:

> *"An inadequate tribute to the evergreen*
> *memory of Klaus Bonner (1960 to 1997)*
> *psychotherapist and mountaineer, who lived*
> *for people and the mountains and who died*
> *alone on the Matterhorn."*

He closed the book and then reopened it. He needed to know more. The telephone conversation had finished and she returned to the room.'

'Sorry for that interruption but we were due for a break. Another coffee? Same as the last? OK, perhaps you would like to give a hand making it? Join me in the kitchen? Follow me then.'

As the machine spluttered and dribbled coffee into their cups he asked her, 'Who was Klaus Bonner? I've just seen your book's dedication, I hope you don't mind me asking.'

For a moment the only sound was the final spluttering of the coffee machine. Then she said, 'Of course, I don't mind. We were lovers. We'd been lovers for six years.' She seemed glad to have Peter as an audience, to have someone to address and her words were declaimed almost as though they were a creed. 'Klaus was married with two children and couldn't leave his wife. You see, he came from a broken home and knew the hurt it had brought him. He couldn't bear to inflict hurt on his wife or the children. And he couldn't bring himself to break our relationship any more than I could. It had begun back in 1991 when we were attending a conference in Berlin. The place was heady with reunification and I suppose we both caught something of the atmosphere and the excitement, so we were less careful together than we ought to have been. We both thought it was something we could simply switch off when we got back to Basel. And when we did get back we found we couldn't. Somehow he managed to live at home with his family and to live ... here in my apartment. I've found the place empty since he went ... since he went to his early grave. I'm like you there in being alone. Klaus is buried at Zermatt in that little graveyard in the town, in the company of so many ... of so many other climbers.' Her voice had thickened. Four years had passed but loss and pain were clearly still her regular companions.

For a moment his hand touched hers, 'I'm sorry to have stirred up memories. But your book ... it's a lovely tribute.'

'It says something I hadn't been able to say at the time. You see, at the funeral I had no status. I mean how do you incorporate the mistress into such a ceremony? OK I know Mitterand did but that was unusual and it doesn't happen here, especially when you're both colleagues in the same academic faculty. To those who know, the book says it all, to those not in the know it says enough. Lets take the coffee through into the sitting room.'

He returned to his sofa while she changed the CD on the hi-fi, 'I sometimes play this when I think about him, about Klaus. It's the Allegri *Miserere*, something deeply penitential. And ... it was the last thing we sang together in the University Choral Society. Yes, I feel guilt at what I did, he should have spent more time with his family not with me, certainly not in my bed ... but despite all that I'm still glad we were lovers. It was a deeply satisfying experience. I wouldn't have missed it for anything.'

He didn't interrupt but allowed the music to play. He knew the piece and was aware that it would last for around fifteen minutes.

'Thanks for being patient with me, Peter. It's not often that I can bring myself to listen as intently to it. Not often that I can speak about him and my sense of loss. That wasn't part of *your* programme, of course. Perhaps we ought to call it a day and resume tomorrow afternoon at two?'

'Yes and no to that. Yes, let's call a halt to the shrinking process, if you don't mind my calling it that! But, unwittingly, I've led you along paths of memory that hurt, while you've led me there because that's what you're supposed to be doing. For you this place has been empty for the last four years. Am I right? I thought so. For me the apartment has been empty for the last three months but it seems a lifetime. If you're not doing anything else I suggest we go out for a meal. I haven't much enthusiasm for cooking for one these days. And then I'll return you to the outer door of your apartment. Unless, of course, it would constitute unprofessional conduct on your part to accept such an invitation!'

'Unprofessional? No, I don't think the Association would be worried. It's a brilliant idea but we both pay our way. Agreed? Fine! Now, if you'll give me five minutes to get ready, we can be on our way. If you want to use the telephone to reserve a table somewhere it's over on the desk.'

He looked again at the book's dedication. For those who knew what emotional weight those few words carried! And he felt grateful that she had been able to take him into her confidence. He would buy himself a copy tomorrow from Bider und Tanner's bookshop at *Bankverein*.

***

He shook his umbrella as he entered the lobby of his apartment block in the *Lohnhof*, the heavy rain had returned as he walked back from Maria Bertorelli's apartment in the *Petersgasse*. Strange to think this had once been the Basel Remand Prison, though the solidity of the walls was evidence enough. Lately he had felt imprisoned by the place, three months ago he had been moved to solitary confinement! Or so it had begun to feel. It was just as well that he often worked late and then came back here to fall into bed and sleep. He opened the apartment door and switched on the light. A drink was called for before bed. He made a milky coffee in the small galley kitchen and took it to the lounge. He was glad not to have spent the evening alone. It had been a good meal at the *Restaurant zur Harmonie* in the *Petersgraben*. He had been intending for a while to try the place and he hadn't been disappointed. They had had well cooked food and pretty good wine. She had been excellent company, able to converse intelligently on a wide range of subjects. He had paid on the basis that she would pay next time, which gave him something to which he could look forward. He had begun the day looking forward to seeing the French shrink now he saw that as the call of duty, Maria was a much more interesting prospect ... almost on his doorstep and much safer.

Far below a tram rumbled down *Kohlenberg*. He looked at the photograph of Julia and himself in its silver frame. It had been taken at a friend's wedding last year, when he hoped she would be ready to fix a date for their own nuptials. But she had continued to put it off and then made her sudden exit from his life. His exaltation diminished. The hurt was real, it wasn't going to be removed by an evening spent with another clever and attractive young woman.

Tomorrow morning he would go to his room at the Public Prosecutor's Office and make a short note of the afternoon's proceedings. The evening was another matter, it was nothing to do with his masters - he had paid for the meal out of his own pocket.

***

Dr Maria Bertorelli closed the book and placed it in the middle of the sofa table. She was glad that Peter Gruenweiler had, like so many of her friends, shown appreciation of it. She had put a lot of time and effort into the photography and the planning - and negotiations with the publishers had also taken much valuable time. But it was so little really. Klaus had meant so much to so many people - colleagues and patients, especially his patients, his wife and family ... and to her. He would never be replaced, she knew that. And such was the nature of her grief that she didn't want him to be replaced. Perhaps in time she might find happiness with someone else, but he would never be quite like Klaus, never have that indefinable something that had made him such a joy to be with, such a complete human being.

But it had been a good evening, Peter was pretty bright for a policeman, but then the work he did certainly called for sharpness and mental agility as well as for more macho qualities - at any rate she assumed that there must be considerable complexity in the cases that crossed his desk. She admitted to herself that, just as Peter had had his stereotype of therapists, so she had had hers of the police.

Her notebook was on the table and she sat down to make a short note of the ground covered in the afternoon's session. Erik Blum had warned her to be careful about what she recorded and not to put anything on her PC. So in her notes she made no reference to Dr Dominique Garnier but, as she wrote, she wondered how Peter would get on in his sessions with her. Dominique was no fool, an able therapist and a very attractive woman. She hoped Peter would avoid becoming emotionally entangled with her, it wouldn't do to have the Security operation compromised in that way. He was very vulnerable in his present state. She was tempted to advise Erik Blum to find another officer but she decided against. She would make sure Peter was properly briefed for the task and its dangers and, she was forced to admit to herself, she was looking forward to seeing Peter over the next few weeks. She had already decided where they would eat the next time they dined out.

Yet, even as she savoured her elation, the mood began to drain away as quickly as it had come. Once more loneliness was her companion and *that* was how she wanted it to be. It would have been better for her if she hadn't been so very tough emotionally, then there would have been crisis followed by resolution and recovery. Dr Maria Bertorelli was so very far from applying her professional knowledge to her own situation. She told herself that to feel differently would be treason to Klaus and disloyalty to all their shared memories. If she had asked herself whether the dead retained their memories in any meaningful way she might have dismissed the question as having no meaning.

She removed the Allegri CD from the player and replaced it with Schubert's *Winterreise*. It had been kind of Peter Gruenweiler to listen to the *Misere* with her, she knew he had listened intently, just as she had and it had helped to share the music with him. The Schubert began and she latched on to the familiar words:

"Muss selbst den Weg mir weisen
In dieser dunkelheit."
("I must find my own way in this darkness.")

Yes, emotionally, four years on, it was still darkness.

"Love loves to rove-
God made us so-
from one to another;
Dear love, good night."

Not so for her, she still belonged to Klaus. Though he was dead she wouldn't rove. A pleasant evening with Peter Gruenweiler couldn't change that. And those last words were on her lips:

"Fein Liebchen, gute Nacht."
("Dear love, good night.")

And she could see no morning in prospect to end the night.

After a few minutes she got up from the sofa and switched the player off. Enough of this! Schubert's song cycle was a tale of unrequited love, of love spurned - that was Peter's experience not hers. She had work to do to prepare for tomorrow's lecture. Immersion in work was balm to her. She stood for a moment at the window, the clock of the *Martinskirche* showed 11.45. She would make a coffee and then spend half an hour on the next day's notes before heading for bed.

As she stood in the kitchen waiting for the kettle to boil she thought of that afternoon when she had opened up to Peter. She hadn't done that before with anyone. And now she had told a stranger, a policeman at that, of her inner hurts and sorrows. But she was glad she had shared her grief with him. She remembered the soft, momentary touch of Peter's hand on hers and his compliment on the book, his words came back, " ... its a lovely tribute." That had been just right, she couldn't have taken a sentimental expression of sympathy. Yes, she knew that he had shared her grief. He knew what it was to lose a lover. And she asked herself whether it was worse for the loss to be occasioned by death or by a conscious and deliberate decision of one whose continued, but separate, life was part of the sorrow - loss compounded by rejection.

Chapter 11

Thursday 21st June 2001

A movement outside the morning room window caught Sam's eye as a green sports car came gently down the drive, turned in a half circle and backed into place to the left of the front door of the house, so that it faced back the way it had come. He reached the front door just before the caller had the chance to ring the bell.

'Mark Gould, I presume.'

'Your presumption is entirely correct and you must be Sam Kagan.'

They shook hands each making his first appraisal of the other. Sam's assessment was that here was a typical Brit belonging to or at any rate aspiring to membership of a certain superior class. Gould's car and his clothes - sports coat, check shirt with a woolen tie in autumn colours and his brown brogues, all evidently expensive, particularly the shoes - projected an image of costly, but unshowy, good taste. A slight excess of flesh suggested a measure of indulgence in good food and drink. In Sam, Gould saw someone who kept himself in good trim and who was dressed for the work he had to do on the vineyard - jeans and a shirt of a much bolder check than Gould's were clearly Sam's working clothes and his face was that of a man who enjoyed being in the open air rather than behind a desk.

'Sam it is. Shall we start with coffee Mr Gould.'

'Mark, please. And a coffee later would be in order - I got to Cassis early and had a cup down by the harbour. Sorry I had to postpone the visit from Tuesday.'

'That's no problem, we've been busy here getting to grips with the place and its vines. You're in the wine trade, Mark, I believe?'

'Yes, I'm a *négotiant*, a dealer and I also have a small vineyard of my own in the North Rhône producing St

Joseph, a fairly heavy red from the Syrah grape. So a visit to Cassis is of interest from a business angle, as well as the matter that's brought me to the *Domaine du Cheval Rouge*. Mind you the accepted wisdom, among Brits who know, is that Cassis wines are rather ordinary and overpriced and that it's the visual qualities of the location that sell the product. But I'm always ready to be persuaded otherwise, there's plenty of nonsense written about wine as you will know. I believe you have experience of wine production in Israel.'

'In the Golan, let me say, where we produce a number of good quality wines with the best grape varieties: Cabernet Sauvignon, Merlot, your Syrah, Riesling and even Gewürztraminer!'

'Gewürztraminer! That I would like to try. Perhaps you could be my host some time and introduce me to the Golan's wines - my business partner usually looks after foreign sources, by that I mean those outside France, but I'm sure she wouldn't mind my visiting Israel. Though as you must know Israeli wines aren't generally regarded as world beaters.'

'That's true but in the Golan we're doing our level best to change all that. Our techniques are rather like those in California, pneumatic membrane presses, computer controlled steel tanks and so on. Everything for a consistent product. Yes, I think you'd enjoy our Gewürztraminer. The vineyard has quite an elevation, at 1,200 metres, up near Mount Hermon. Though I wonder whether it won't all be given back to the Syrians one day. We could move the winery, of course, but establishing new vineyards to replace the ones lost would be another matter. In the Golan our vines grow on well drained, volcanic basalt soils. And as to hosting you, Elizabeth and I would be delighted. You'll meet her when we have coffee. Now would you like to come indoors to talk business or would you prefer to stroll around the vineyard? It's such a glorious morning.'

'Why not. I'd like to see how the vines are. What varieties do you grow here?

'The reds are Grenache and Mourvèdre, the whites Clairette and Marsanne. Not varieties we would consider for the Golan but they seem to be successful in this location. It would be interesting to see how Cabernet Sauvignon, Merlot and Syrah would fare here. But then there's a lot to be said for variety, it wouldn't do to have the same product everywhere.'

'That's true, Sam. We need the inferior - or shall I say the second division - to show just how good the best really are. And of course there's the subjective element, our variable palates. I remember drinking one of the local reds in a restaurant near Arles, at Fontvieille, a place more famous for Monsieur Daudet's windmill than for its wines, it was brilliant with just the merest hint of strawberry lingering on the palate. I'd never heard of the wine before and I've never come across it since - something like *Clos de la Dame Blanche*, it's properly recorded in the notes back in the office, of course.' He was signalling that he was a professional who was thorough in his approach to the job.

They set off to view the grapes, stopping to examine the vines, looking for any sign of disease, both drawing on their experience of the task.

'So you need to know something about the 16th September Unit, Sam. And your people haven't heard of them?'

'We don't know enough about them. OK, we haven't heard anything of them for some years but Erik Blum's told us that British Security does know something about them. And I'm grateful that you've come.'

'I had a visit from one of my former colleagues to confirm that I could disclose to you what I knew - so long as I was satisfied it was necessary. Completely deniable, of course! No one would put it down on paper that I could disclose *anything* to anyone outside the Service. ... So you have a problem with these people?'

'Just so, they are involved in a drug smuggling operation generating a projected $10 M with the aim of buying something from what was once the USSR for use against Israel.'

'A large quantity of arms ... or a large explosive device. I'd hope that it was the former and act as if it were the latter.'

'As we are doing, Mark. But we need to get some lead on these people. There's a bank account in Basel through which the drug money is being laundered and there's a shadowy German operating that account. Down here in Cassis we've the drug smuggling part of the project, which is why I'm here, why the Golan has come to Cassis!' They laughed. Though from very different backgrounds they had warmed quickly to one another.

'Don't worry, I'm satisfied that you definitely need to know what I can tell you. First let me tell you of my background. So far as wine is concerned my family have been wine growers in Bordeaux since the late 1800's, wine's in my blood in more ways than one. But I served in the Army, the *British* Army, of course.' There was no likelihood whatsoever that Mark Gould would have served in anyone else's army. 'And they sent me to Northern Ireland in a security rôle, so I came into contact, sometimes direct, sometimes indirect, with all manner of Republican groups and splinter groups. We kept our ear to the ground, and a variety of informers and people with better imagination than evidence used to try to bend our ears, for a fee of course. Well it was ten years ago, in April 1991, that I came across the Unit that concerns you, the 16th September Unit. Not a very imaginative name but evidently indicating some grievance, some event in the past.'

'Our guess is that it has to do with the Israeli drive through the Lebanon in 1982 and the *Phalangist* massacres on 16th September in the Sabra and Shatila refugee camps in Beirut. The commission of enquiry concluded that Ariel Sharon, the then Defence Minister, should have known what to expect and prevented it. So the cabinet sacrificed him to public opinion, though he wasn't the only one criticised.'

'And now he's the PM! So revenge would be sweet.'

'Momentarily, yes. But if it were nuclear the result for Jew and Arab would be bitter indeed.'

'Bitter and long lasting. No, we don't want that to happen. So, to go back to the Emerald Isle, we heard in April 1991 that one of the Republican splinter groups was involved in an arms deal with the 16th September Unit. We were ready, of course, to seize the arms as they were landed or, if they were going to be delivered to the South - as was more likely - to alert the Gardai, the Southern Police. But nothing came of it, the Republicans lost some money on the deal and were hopping mad - for a while we British had a competitor in the 16th September Unit for Republican hatred, though of course we won in the end, 16th and 17th century wrongs are more important than ones suffered last year, aren't they? Mind you I'm not sure how *your* people regard us over the Mandate and the events leading up to 1948. You'll have to tell me some time, Sam.'

'I'll tell you when you visit us in the Golan. But what more do you know of the Unit?'

'Precious little else, I'm afraid. For more information you'd have to speak to the so called Chief of Staff of the Republican group - they call themselves the Continuity IRA now. And if you ask me there will always be something of that sort, a continuity group pursuing unfinished Republican business. When they've got all 32 counties I wonder what they'll want next, still that'll be the Eire government's problem. Unless they start legal actions in the British and European Courts for compensation for wrongs going back to the Tudors and Cromwell - and, by the way, Cromwell wasn't anything like as bad as they care to make out and we have that on a Southern Irish historian's say so, not that *he's* too popular with the good folks of Drogheda. After all you mustn't challenge the collective folk memory!' Sam noted that it wasn't just Irish Republicans who were stuck in a 17th century time warp.

'So the trail leads nowhere, it doesn't take us to the Unit.'

'No I can't get you there, not directly at any rate. But I can point you in the direction of the Continuity IRA. It may surprise you that there were lines of contact between our people and the Republicans but there were times when it was to the advantage of both sides to be able to speak to one another. I can give you an idea of how to establish contact. But I can't promise that there won't be any danger in it for you. They're pretty ruthless and if they thought you were in the pay of the British you would be in for a very unhappy time.'

'With the Unit's threat facing us I'll have to risk that, won't I?'

'Yes, I think so. I know I did and lived to tell the tale, but sometimes I wondered whether I'd pushed my luck too far, especially when informers were murdered by the IRA. A semi-naked body found in a ditch with bruising or signs of torture and gunshot wounds in the head - an Armalite rifle can make a very nasty mess. And I'd remember the last meeting I'd had with that unfortunate person, perhaps a week or ten days before. Once an informer was taken in by Republicans two days after I'd met him at a remote farm: a week later his booby trapped body was found by the roadside a quarter of a mile from the barn where we'd met. It brought me out in a cold sweat, I can tell you. I wondered whether it was meant as a personal warning. You drive around wondering whether there's a bomb in the next ditch with someone a couple of hundred yards away ready to set it off by radio or by a command wire. You open the door of a building wondering whether it's going to blow up around you. Not a relaxing way to live! Still I'm here in your pleasant and disease free vineyard, Sam, so my professional judgement mustn't have been too bad. At any rate I was successful in watching my back. What you need to know is how to contact the Chief. Well you need to send a message to him asking to meet. I've been told by my former masters what the current form of words is, don't bother to take it down I've got a note of it for you:

> "A visitor wishes to discuss the
> correspondence of Columbanus and
> Gregory the Great."

You send the message to O'Toole's Bar, which is out on the shore of the Atlantic, at Malin Bay in Co Donegal, you can use the 'phone, the number's on the note. I've been there, it feels as if you're on the very edge of the world, particularly when you're wondering whether you've made the last journey of your life and you're starting to pray pretty hard for survival. It's quite a journey, Sam. You'll need to fly to Londonderry and pick up a hire car, then it's over the Border, into the South, and perhaps 100 miles. Mind you they're Irish roads with twists and turns everywhere and if you hit foul weather, and I can tell you that there's no shortage of *weather* coming in off the Atlantic, if you hit foul weather you'll progress pretty slowly! On the other hand, if its fine you'll think you're in God's own country or perhaps *you* wouldn't want to think of it like that, Sam.'

'And whyever not? It's all the work of the same Creator. I'm ready to be overwhelmed by the Irish scenery. And in return for your assistance? What do your people want from us?'

'To hear that you've been successful with Operation Account, well that's what Erik Blum called it!'

'And nothing else?'

'To tell you the truth my former masters had ideas, but I told them, No! You'll be taking a big enough risk as it is,

Sam. I don't want you going there as a British stooge. If the Republicans were to suspect that you were there with any business to do but your own ... well I wouldn't give much for your chances of survival. So there you are, you've got your *entrée* to the inner circles of fanatical Irish Nationalism and I wish you well.'

'Thanks for that, Mark. You obviously had a lot of experience of these people.'

'Four years. Working in a number of places along the border, Fermanagh, Tyrone and South Armagh, they called that Bandit Country, where we had to helicopter the troops in and out of their fortified barracks!'

'A bit like the South of the Lebanon was for us! I recognise your fear of the roadside bomb set off by remote control. Dov and I were in a vehicle that was disabled by one. And we lay there with the dead and wounded waiting for the helicopter to lift us out, all the time wondering whether there was another bomb waiting to go off if *Hizballah* saw any sign of life by our armoured personnel carrier. Dov, who's my Number 2 here, served in the Lebanon with me.'

'You served *there*, Sam?'

'Yes, in the Golani Brigade. You'll meet Dov at lunch. we can reminisce together! It's strange, despite the constant danger, they were good times.'

'Then like me you know what fear is.'

'And like you I know how to handle it - you must have done to stand it for four years.'

'Not for four years non-stop. I did have breaks now and then and I wasn't on the front line all the time.'

'How often did you get away from it?'

'Two or three weeks every three months, though I was always subject to recall if something cropped up which only I could deal with.'

'Well, Mark, I admire your courage. I don't think I could have faced up to so much stress and for so long.'

'Well I was single - and for that matter I still am - I

wouldn't like to have taken a wife's worries into the field with me.'

'I'd be grateful if you avoided mentioning danger over lunch. Elizabeth my wife will worry about my going there, she isn't ignorant about the IRA and their factions, but try to play the risk thing down.'

'I'll do my best Sam. But if she asks me direct?'

'Tell her the truth. Not making the information available is one thing, deceit is another. If she asks, tell her there are risks but that they're necessary ones.'

'I'll do as you ask. ... We've seen the red varieties, let's see the whites. I think you said they were Marsanne and Clairette ... '

***

Sam had gone to fetch a case of wine for Mark and Elizabeth took the opportunity of asking the question that was troubling her, 'Mark, is it dangerous, what he's going to do? Will he be running a risk meeting these people?'

'The honest answer to that is, Yes, he will be running a risk. But your husband is a brave man and ... I'm not sure how to put this ... the Almighty has looked after him so far in the face of danger in the Lebanon and elsewhere and I hope ... I'm sure He will continue to do so. I survived there in Ireland for some time, Sam's only got to make one visit. I won't deny there's a risk, but it's a necessary risk when you look at the danger you're all trying to avert. Don't worry I'll be keeping in touch and making sure the information I gave him is up to date. But when he goes over that Border, if not before, he's on his own.'

'Thanks for being honest, Mark. I thought it was like that, I just wanted to be sure. He'll go with my blessing. Excuse me a minute, I'll be back.' Her voice had thickened and Mark knew that she was deeply concerned. He was glad that he had served in Ireland as a single man: it would have been impossible to have had a wife worrying about you, particularly if there were also children to think about.

***

As Sam saw Mark off he remarked about the sports car, 'A thoroughbred, Mark. I like the little British flags on the sides of the bonnet.'

'It's a Triumph TR3A but I wouldn't think about driving it where you're going! Those Union Flags would not be appreciated in Co. Donegal.'

'I expect not. And the "correspondence between St Columbanus and Pope Boniface"?'

'Something to do with putting down a Christian heresy. Your man is an amateur theologian and a poet, that's what he turns his mind to when he's not planning the violent re-unification of Ireland! Well I must get off now and head back up the Autoroute to Valence.' He picked up a gray cap from the passenger seat and put it on - evidently an essential part of a sports car driver's kit. 'Thanks for the hospitality. I'll keep you posted with any changes in the message or any development within the Continuity IRA that my old masters hear of. I'll be back here to learn how you got on but not to probe for information on the Republicans, that phase of my life is past.'

'Not completely, you've come here today!'

'Very true, but it was really just to try the wines of Cassis!'

'And your verdict?'

'The jury's still out Sam, until we've fixed a price for the 1999 and 2000 whites. See you soon.'

Mark was off, taking the car gently down the rutted drive. Sam saw him turn right onto the main road towards Cassis and heard the sound of his well tuned exhaust as he accelerated away. Well he was now ready to make contact with the Republicans. He hoped they would be willing to help. But would they? He hoped that Mark was right in thinking that they would be more than willing to do the 16th September Unit down in retaliation for the money they had lost on the abortive arms deal.

He was aware that Elizabeth had joined him when she took his arm. 'Sam, I know this visit to Ireland is dangerous. I don't want to discuss it, I just want to say that you have my blessing and prayers ... and my admiration, as always.' She wiped her eyes with the sleeve of her blouse. 'Come and help bath the children and then we'll go down to the harbour for dinner and a stroll and try to pretend that we are ordinary people on holiday. Wouldn't it be nice to be that, just ordinary people, for a change.'

Chapter 12

Saturday 23rd June 2001

Maria had been right, they would need to work through the weekend to have him ready for his first appointment with Dominique Garnier the following Tuesday. So 10 a.m. on Saturday morning saw Peter on his way to her house. The name of the street he had just entered struck him, *Petersgraben*, literally it meant Peter's grave! But in fact it marked the place where one of Basel's defensive moats had once been. It was only one of several city streets with *graben* in their name. He guessed there wasn't going to be any great risk in crossing the border into France for sessions with an analyst who might well belong to a terrorist cell. No, with the preparation Maria was giving him he should easily pass off as a genuine patient. And he wouldn't need to work hard to show the real hurt of losing Julia.

The hurt was still there but his involvement with Maria Bertorelli, a professional involvement of course, had brought a sense of excitement. In a carrier bag he had a copy of Maria's book, bought the previous day. It had been the next to last copy in the shop and the assistant had told him it was selling well. He would let Maria know the good news when he got her to sign his copy.

On reaching *Petersplatz* he glanced to his left and saw that the Saturday morning flea market under the trees in the square was up and running. Summer had come, it wasn't a day to be indoors, perhaps they could continue their sessions *al fresco*. He turned right into *Peterskirchplatz* and then left into *Petersgasse*, taking in two sides of the church in his perambulation. He liked this world of little streets with shops, hotels, restaurants and the university all mixed in together. He rang her bell, he was finding his visits interesting. When he remembered that he was being paid for this he congratulated himself for volunteering to be prepared in this way as a suitable case for Dr Garnier's treatment.

Maria was listening to an early Beethoven String Quartet. She was barefoot, wearing jeans and a cream silk blouse and she signalled to him to make coffee for both of them and bring it in. He sat and watched as she continued, immersed in the music, ignoring her coffee until the last movement was over. 'The *Quartetto Italiano*, Peter. An old recording but one I love. Perhaps it's the Italian in me that makes me think they're the best. They're so good in their interaction with one another. Thanks for getting the coffee, we'll have it and then get to work.'

'It struck me on my way here that we'd be better out of doors today. There's the flea market in the *Platz* for a start. We could wander about and talk, have coffee every now and then and break for lunch. How does that seem to you?'

'Provided you continue to be the model client co-operating, as you have done so far, and working hard it seems a good idea.'

'I'll try. By the way I've brought my copy of your book for signature. They told me in the shop it was selling very well and that they'd reordered a substantial number.'

She smiled at this but made an effort to restrain her pleasure, 'It's funny Peter, but I feel like a child, taking pleasure in what people say about it. It's partly that it's a tribute to Klaus but there's also the fact that it's nice to receive praise now and then.'

'Be childlike, enjoy the praise, Maria. You deserve praise, it's a super book!'

'Thanks, Peter. Leave it there and I'll sign it when we get back.'

She pulled on a lightweight navy blazer and a pair of flat shoes before they left the apartment and headed for *Petersplatz*.

Once in the square they began a slow tour of the stalls: clothes, books, radios, CDs, old vinyl records, cassettes and a multitude of other things. They made an unhurried examination of the wares on sale, spending most time on a stall with classical and jazz recordings and making a few purchases. At the back of the square a child of perhaps 10 years old was playing Bach on the cello. They stopped and listened, joining the applause when she had finished and adding their coins to her collection.

'What about a stroll round the Botanical Gardens, Maria?'

But she had found an up market second hand book stall, 'Once I've had a look through this lot, Peter.' There was a biography of Che Guevara, Dürenmatt's *Minotaurus*, Jean Anouilh's *Antigone* and Gogol's *Taras Bulba*. They spent five minutes going through the titles before she bought Gogol's tale of Bulba's martyrdom at the hands of his enemies and he acquired a spy thriller. She raised her eyebrows, 'Professional reading, Peter? Don't you think of anything but work?'

'Plenty else when someone can distract me, Maria. Now let's look at the Botanical Gardens.'

She held back for a moment, seemingly about to say something, but then changed her mind. They crossed the road into the gardens and Peter led them in the direction of the cactus house, opening the door and following her in. At the far end of the house she turned and said quietly, 'You know, I haven't been here since '91 when Klaus and I used to meet secretly. That was after we got back from Berlin ... ' Her voice failed and she turned away. He caught up with her and placed a hand on her shoulder. She turned to face him and he withdrew his hand. She forced a smile, 'When a relationship was as good as ours, good in spite of all the limits and restrictions, there's a strange pleasure in feeling the pain of the loss. After all you don't miss what's unimportant, do you?'

'Maria, I'm sorry I brought you here ... I seem adept in stirring up sad memories'

'No, Peter, don't apologise. It was necessary ... after

all the memories themselves aren't sad ones ... what is sad is that they can never be more than memories, a remote and distant country I can no longer visit.' She touched his arm, 'Come on, Peter, let's go and have a drink somewhere.' Their contact - hand on shoulder, hand on arm - had in each instance been momentary, as though to say, I'm not trying to make claims on you but I do want you to know that I'm sharing your pain and that I understand your sadness.

Despite Peter's good intentions they hadn't achieved much during their outing and after a light lunch they returned to Maria's apartment for a more structured session. With a Mozart Serenade playing very quietly in the background they got down to work over a succession of cups of coffee.

'Right, Peter, something I mentioned yesterday which you were going to think about last night: have you any memories, however faint or indistinct, of being abused, sexually or emotionally in childhood?'

'None whatsoever. There was never anything of that sort. I'm absolutely sure of it.'

'Good, we'll leave that alone. I don't want to attempt to create a fictitious past for you in that area. It sometimes happens that therapists suggest to a client that they *might* have been abused in childhood and the client latches onto the suggestion and it somehow becomes real to them - it's known as false memory syndrome. It can be a relief for a client to think they've put their finger on the source of all their problems, a cause for which they're not responsible can appear very welcome after a lot of distress. And the same lawyers who sued molesters on the strength of what the therapist unearthed now sue the therapist for unearthing what wasn't there in the first place. It seems that the only winners are the lawyers, but you already know enough about the glittering prizes awaiting legal success as I'm sure you'll be telling me shortly!

'Now let's focus once again on your relationship with your father, going back as far as you can, which seems to be that memory of getting lost as a young child.'

'Yes, I suppose the earliest memory is of our trip to Basel zoo. I was three then, or so I'm told ... and that's the problem because I'm not entirely sure that I can really remember the occasion ... it may be that it's become such an established part of family folklore that I've come to treat it as a genuine memory. No, I'm not doubting that it happened and that I got lost, or rather that *he* lost me, but I'm doubting whether the memory I have is authentic and first hand or one that the family have created for me.'

'That can be a problem. I don't want to interrupt the flow so remind me, once we've finished this afternoon, to tell you something about infantile memories. But tell me what you think you can remember and what you recollect of your emotions, how you felt, at the time and subsequently.'

'Truth to tell I don't remember any emotion on my part, so far as being lost was concerned. My father had met a lawyer colleague and while they were talking I slipped off back to the tigers. When he found me, fifteen minutes later, I was sitting there watching a tiger pace to and fro. My father was angry, very angry ... yes, I'm pretty sure that part of the memory is mine from first hand. He almost hit me but he restrained himself at the last moment.'

'And his anger wasn't something you had encountered before?'

'Or since ... it was a one-off event, specific to that situation. He must have been frightened out of his mind at losing me and anger was his response. It didn't last but it remained with me and I remember it still. At the time I was an only child - I've a sister who was born a couple of years afterwards and there was an older brother who was still-born. I don't think they expected to have another child after I was born, the pregnancy and birth weren't easy for my mother. So at the time I was the only one and might have remained the only one - I can understand my father's reaction.'

'And how did those events affect your relationship with your father?'

'I never wanted to see him like that again so I usually made sure I did whatever he wanted. He and my mother were a bit over protective at times. My father had his plans for me and *knew* that they were the best plans. So I was destined from birth to study law and be a lawyer like him.'

They broke for coffee.

'You said that you were destined to study law and be a lawyer but it hasn't worked out quite like that, has it? You studied law here in Basel but then you took off in another direction. How did your father respond to your decision to become a policeman, albeit a rather exalted one dealing with breaches of security.'

'You've pinpointed the next time of conflict Maria ... and this time there was tension within the family, with me out numbered two to one!'

'My father is a very successful commercial lawyer who specialises in international tax planning work for our leading corporations and their executives. He's done very well financially as a result of his labours and, of course, he wanted me to join him in the firm. But ... '

'But you had other ideas?'

'I did indeed! And he seemed to think that my plans weren't worth consideration - no I exaggerate there - he made clear that there were better things for me to aim at. But that wasn't the sort of way I wanted to spend my life. There should be more to life than making the biggest pile of money you can. I wanted to do something that was socially useful, not make the fat cats of business even fatter!'

'And did Julia share these ideals? Did she like you

being part of the security apparatus? Or would she have preferred a well heeled corporate lawyer?'

He didn't reply immediately. Then he spoke quietly, 'She didn't like my police work or my hours and she would have enjoyed being able to spend a good commercial income. It's odd that my choice of a job has strained relations within my family and has also helped to lose me Julia.'

'But it's a choice you stand by, Peter?'

'Most certainly I do. I just hope I get through my probationary period, its what I want to do, what I enjoy doing.'

'Why?'

'Because I feel the need to protect our country and I like the idea of being in the public service. And I couldn't face the routine of working in a law firm. Compare what I'm doing now, there's tremendous variety - meeting informers, keeping people under surveillance and even being psychoanalysed! If I'd followed my father into his law firm I'd have been helping to make the rich even richer and to dodge their proper obligations to our country and to other countries that can ill afford to lose out on the tax due to them.'

'So you see work as a kind of Crusade?'

'No, that would be too extreme a way of putting it, Maria. At the end of the day what I want to feel is that I've done something worthwhile and it helps that the pay isn't too bad - nothing like that of a top corporate lawyer but fully adequate for my needs. And there's probably something similar in your attitude to life and work, isn't there? If you gave up the academic part of your work and concentrated on the maladjusted among the top crust of Basel society you'd be doing very nicely indeed, wouldn't you?'

'The interrogator returns! I wondered how long you'd be happy just to keep answering my questions. I'll keep that discussion for another day, enough to say that I enjoy the discipline of the academic side and think it important to put something back into the system that's done a lot for me. But you'll have to take care with Dominique Garnier - don't start interrogating her too fiercely or she'll begin to suspect that you're not the maladjusted young man that you purport to be. And we'll have to invent an occupation for you, I somehow don't think you can tell her the truth on that issue.'

'I'll try to refrain from grilling her.'

'How about relations with your sister, is she a rebel against the paternal fiat like you?'

'In no way! She's the opposite, she toes the family line and is appreciated by my father accordingly.'

'And what does she think of your career?'

'Not much, she can't see why I'm willing not only to work for what she says is a pittance but also to disappoint our father by doing so.'

'Right, Peter, plenty of material there for us to work on. It will be far safer for you to build on a real situation and heighten the tensions and exaggerate the attitudes and feelings - just so long as you don't overdo it! We can heighten the family tensions and make your father more of an ogre crushing you with his dominance. Now that should keep Dr Garnier busy: early memories of a very possessive and sometimes angry father who later has very definite plans for your future, plans which you spurn; a sister who is a goody-goody, more than ready to go along with father's career plans for her and dismissive of your own career; your mother's death five years ago which we spoke about yesterday; and Julia's departure three months ago.

'Now let's talk about your mother and how you got on with her. Go back to your earliest memories of her ... '

'I've to remind you, Maria, that you've a seminar to hold on infantile memory or something of that sort. So I'm all ready, do I take notes or will there be a hand-out?'

She laughed, crunched up a sheet of paper into a ball and threw it at him, 'If you're not careful I'll be asking for a 10,000 word essay on the subject by this time next week! You were on target suggesting that your zoo experience might not have been your own memory at all but the memory of others which you had adopted in the past as your own. It's an area that interests me but I won't spend the rest of the evening propounding my theories. There's an interesting instance of Jean Piaget, who was an influential child psychologist. His memory was of an attempted kidnapping when he was two years old. He was in his pram in a Paris street with his nursemaid when she bravely fought off the kidnapper and was scratched in the struggle. He remembered the crowds of onlookers and the policeman vividly. And then when he was fifteen the nurse confessed that it had never happened. She had faked the scratches and invented the attempted kidnapping. Piaget's conclusion was that he had heard vivid descriptions of the event as a child and created his own "visual memory" of the nurse's fictitious report.

'And it's an open question just how far back into childhood your memory can go. Very few people remember much before the age of five and hardly anyone remembers anything before the age of three. So your zoo experience would be just on the border of memory, perhaps we could make you four and a half so as not to raise any problems in Dr Garnier's response to the story.

'You might like a closing quotation from our founding father, Sigmund Freud, whose presence seems to brood over my discipline,

> "It may indeed be questioned whether we have any memories at all *from* our childhood: memories *relating to* our childhood may be all that we possess."

And there we must leave it or I'll be late for the Faculty reception this evening. We won't work tomorrow morning but if you would like to be my guest for lunch we could spend the afternoon hammering out what you should bring out at your first meeting with Dr Garnier on Tuesday.'

'Could I borrow something on memory from you, Maria? It seems an interesting subject, though I'm more interested in adults - the sort of people I might need to rely on in court.'

She headed for a bookcase and extracted a volume. Then after a moment's hesitation she pulled out another from she same section. 'One's by an expert in the field and the other, a slender contribution, is from your favourite photographer of Swiss mountains.'

'I assume that's a certain Dr Maria Bertorelli?'

'Just so, Lieutenant Gruenweiler. Just so. And I'm afraid you'll find that most of us think we can remember events far better than in fact we can. Bear that in mind next time your case depends on someone's detailed recollections of what happened in a few fleeting moments.'

Chapter 13

Monday 25th June 2001

More likely than not Mustafa's women came from Marseille rather than from Cassis and probably most of their customers came from Marseille too, but as Dov would be using the prepaid mobile it didn't matter - no one would be able to trace the location from which his call was being made. He and Sam had carefully gone through what he was to say and he wondered why he was becoming stressed out about it, after all there was nothing to go wrong ... at this stage anyway. He dialled the number and waited. He had just decided that she must be out when he heard a woman's voice respond, *'Hello!'*

He began, 'Yvonne? ... Is that Yvonne Charpentier?' He hoped she spoke English.

'Yes, this is Yvonne. Perhaps you would wait while I put the baby down.' So there was a baby. But it wasn't likely to be Mustafa's - he hadn't been here long enough for one of his women to bear him a child. Still she spoke English and that certainly helped.

She returned to the telephone, 'My sister is visiting this afternoon and I was looking after her baby, you didn't think it was mine did you?' She laughed and he joined in.

'A friend gave me your name ... '

'And my telephone number ... '

'Yes and your telephone number. I'm in Marseille this evening on business on my own and wondered whether ... ' He stopped to find the phrase that momentarily had slipped his memory.

There was a moment's pause at her end before she answered, 'Whether I could hand back the baby and be available?'

'Something like that.'

'Wait a moment ... Mr?'

'Michael Williams.'

'Right Mr Williams, I'll find out when my sister is leaving.' He wondered whether there really was a baby-owning sister, still what did it matter? He was surprised that she sounded rather pleasant, not harsh as he had expected.

There was a rapid exchange in French in the background and then, after a minute or so, she spoke again, 'Yes you're in luck Michael. She's catching the 18.30 to Paris so I'd be free at, shall we say 19.30. Your friend didn't give you my address?'

'No but perhaps we could meet at one of the restaurants near *Le Vieux Port*, you won't have eaten? You could be free for the whole evening?'

'In one sense I am rarely free Mr Williams, but then if you mean that I am without any other appointments this evening ... then, yes, I am free in that sense!' Once again she laughed.

'Fine Yvonne, just name a restaurant and I'll be there at 19.30.'

'There was a moment's pause, 'You're here on an expense account? ... Good. Then we'll meet at *Le Filet Bleu*, in the *Rue des Tyrans,* you know it?'

'No, but I've a map.'

'Good, it's to the east of the Old Port. I'll see you at around 19.30 this evening.'

'And how will I recognise you, Yvonne?'

'I'll be wearing a red dress and ... you'll find me ... striking, I think that's the expression. I'll see you then.' She put the telephone down and he switched off his mobile. So the meeting was set up, she intrigued him, he liked her voice.

***

Dov parked his car in the *Rue Paradis*, arriving at *Le Filet Bleu* early, at a little after 19.15. He asked for a table in the corner, telling the waiter that he was meeting a family friend Mlle Yvonne Charpentier who would be arriving shortly. He ordered a bottle of Perrier water and waited. At 19.35 she arrived, the dress was red all right, a very bright red, both it and the wearer were ... well striking as she had said. The description really was apt . She stood nearly six foot tall in her high heels. Her hair was raven black and the dress, while it covered perfectly respectably between a high neckline and a point a little above the knee, set off a fine figure. Dov noticed how the eyes of the other diners, the women as well as the men, followed her to the table. She had both poise and presence. He rose to greet her while a waiter slid a chair from under the table, moving it back to let her sit.

'Un apéritif, Madame?'

"Pastis, s'il vous plaît.'

The aroma of a subtle perfume caught him. She didn't reek of the stuff, it had been judiciously applied. He was aware of a feeling of excitement deep down within his stomach. 'Well Yvonne, you said striking and that was understating things.' She was extremely well groomed; it was obvious that she had given attention to her make up, not that a clear complexion like hers would need much attention, and to her hair. He was surprised, she hadn't had much time since his telephone call for preparation, especially as she had been despatching her sister to Paris by train barely an hour earlier. Her deep blue eyes held his attention and he noticed that her gaze didn't waver. She was taking in his face and seeking to arrive at an assessment of the man across the table from her. He was being judged when he had expected to be doing the judging. The glass of *anisette* arrived accompanied by a carafe of water. She matched the spirit with an equal quantity of water.

'Thank, you Michael. I won't deny that I enjoy being appreciated.' She touched his hand, so lightly that he then wondered whether she had really done so. 'Thank you for the invitation to dinner. We'll talk about what I charge later, you never know, if the meal is good I might not charge you anything for the time we spend here in *Le Filet Bleu*. I hope you'll enjoy the meal, Michael, I wouldn't like to be responsible for disappointing you. Now would you like me to suggest what we might order?' There was something about all this that puzzled him she seemed to be trying to challenge him by her very directness and make him react. The worrying thought crossed his mind that she might be intending to report back to Mustafa Malik on the evening's events.

He remained on his guard and this wariness restrained him from being completely bowled over by her. If she were going to be direct he would respond in kind. So he threw in a casual comment, *'La Rue des Tyrans?* I was afraid it might be some sort of bondage establishment instead of a restaurant!'

She got the joke and laughed, 'Nothing of that sort, it's not my line, honestly, Michael. I'm a very straightforward girl as you'll find out. Now *les Moules Farcis* are particularly good here ... ' Straightforward? He wasn't at all sure about that.

'And who was it, Michael, please, who gave you my name and telephone number? I'd like to know whom to thank for letting me enjoy an excellent meal *and* your excellent company.'

He had been waiting for her to ask this. After all it was his reason for being with her. 'You wouldn't know him, a boating acquaintance who was given your details by a man who keeps his yacht at Cassis. He said that, from what his friend had told him, he was tempted to call you himself but he'd never been able to work up the courage to do so.' He was keeping it vague just as Sam had directed.

'And what did he have to say about me?'

'His friend had told him that you were ... a real cracker, great fun, good company and really lively ... '

'Really lively?'

He lowered his voice, 'Really lively ... you know, really lively.' He had intended to add "in bed" but the words suddenly seemed surprisingly out of place. 'His friend had been drinking, I think, and probably said more than he ought ... if I remember rightly he was someone from the Middle East.'

She took the bait, 'Yes that's where Mustafa probably comes from, though he never said as much. You've never met him? No, a strange man ... though a generous one. He too could be lively *in bed*, I can assure you of that Michael!' She had read his mind and articulated the words he had suppressed. 'But we fell out and it's ... let me see, it must be a couple of months since I saw him. In a way it's nice of him to put a good word in for me but it could bring the wrong type of man along. No, you're not the wrong type at all Michael, I'm not trying to warn you off. In fact I'm very glad you telephoned. Very glad. I was at a loose end this evening. Lets enjoy the meal and then the rest of the evening together, as I told you my sister and her baby have gone back to Paris so they won't be in the way. But no more talk of Mustafa, that's all in the past and I would rather forget him for the moment. But you Michael ... what do you do for a living?'

He was ready for the question, 'I'm a rep for a Swiss drug company. I'm on my second visit to the area. I worked for them back in the USA and then they moved me over to Europe a year ago.'

'And what do they manufacture?'

'Oh, the usual things, anti-spot creams, antibiotics, contraceptive pills ... all manner of cures.' He hoped she wasn't too conversant with the world of pharmaceuticals and moved the conversation to Marseille and Southern France. For the moment he wasn't going to learn anything about Mustafa.

***

'And your car?'

'Parked in the *Rue Paradis*, Yvonne.'

'So your car's in Paradise Street and where would you like to be, Michael, I wonder? On the way back to your hotel or with me in my apartment in the *Quartier du Panier*, in the *Rue des Cordelles*. ... I thought so! Well we can take your car round to the other side of *Le Vieux Port*, there's parking at the *Place Jules Verne*, then we can walk, its a warm evening.'

'Fine by me, Yvonne.'

They parked his car and made their way between a couple of stark modern apartment blocks into the *Quartier du Panier* and then ascended a narrow street of steps with ancient houses pressing in on them on either side. They passed along a succession of old, narrow streets. 'And this, Michael, is the *Rue du Refuge* where there was once a house of correction for loose women. The entrance was in the *Rue du Déshonneur* - It's now called the *Rue des Honneurs.* Quite a change! Something to make you think, isn't it? The exit was in the *Rue des Repenties.* And the regime? Harsh in the extreme. Whatever people say about the present there was no lack of hypocrisy in those days, was there?'

'You mean that the men responsible for the downfall of the women - if I can use that expression - were the ones organising their detention?'

'You have it Michael, you have it exactly.'

'Plus ça change, c'est toujours la même chose.'

'Such fluency, Michael! Very good indeed for an American!'

The apartment's doorway in the narrow street was unprepossessing, as was the stairway but the apartment itself was something different. Light and airy, furnished in Scandinavian style rather than with the usual heavy

French furniture.

'Let me take you on a tour of the place.' She took his hand and guided him to a door on the far side of the living room. 'Well here we are Michael, the whore's bedroom where all the work is done. How do you like it?'

'Very different from what I expected, Yvonne.' He paused suddenly embarrassed, 'I never called you that ... and I wouldn't think of doing so.'

She pressed on, 'Very different from Mustafa's place.'

'It certainly is!'

'But you like it?'

'Yes? But I don't like the expression whore's parlour.'

'Why ever not? After all that's what it is. You 'phoned for an appointment with a whore and that's what you've got, Michael.' He couldn't dispute that she had arrived at the only possible interpretation of his reason for calling her but when it was put that way, in such stark terms, it sounded all wrong. He was unhappy at the basis of their relationship. But then how else could he have engineered their meeting?

'But you're a nice girl, Yvonne. Not like ... '

'Not like you imagined a whore from Marseille to be?'

'Well ... well, yes.'

'Then count yourself fortunate, Michael. Coffee first? Good. Black or with milk? Sugar? You can look at the paper or at a book while I'm making it.' She disappeared into the kitchen and turned on a classical music station on the radio. He looked at the well filled book shelves. As he had suspected she was an educated woman ... and she was doing this for a living! No shortage of French classics or indeed of world classics. There was a row of Zola's novels. Yes, *Nana* was among them. Very appropriate. And yet was it? She puzzled and attracted him. It was over a year since he had slept with a woman. Still, he was doing this for his country!

Beside him was a waste paper basket and he idly picked up a blue printed slip and unscrewed it. A payslip for Lieutenant Yvonne Charpentier. And the heading read "Marseille Police Department". Either she was moonlighting, which seemed unlikely, or she was engaged in some sort of surveillance operation on Mustafa and anyone who came from that direction. Too early to challenge her on it though. He screwed it up again and dropped it back into the basket. It would have to be discussed with Sam but he couldn't do that from here. Meanwhile he would have to watch his back, they would probably want to tail his car when he left. It would have to be abandoned. He would give them the slip in the city, he ought to be able to manage that.

She returned with the coffees and sat opposite him in an armchair. 'Checking out my library?'

'It's pretty extensive, Yvonne? You appear to have read a lot.'

'Yes, we're not all uneducated, you know.'

'I wasn't suggesting ... '

'Of course not.' She smiled at his discomfort.

'You said we'd talk about your charges later on.'

"i've taken a liking to you Michael and I've decided to waive charges tonight. I want to go to bed with you so I wouldn't think of charging, especially after as good a meal as that.'

'But I wouldn't want to take advantage of you ... after all you've a living to make just like any other ... '

'Just like any other whore?'

'No, just like any other person. Somehow I don't see you as a whore!' He was sweating, wondering how long he could keep up the pretence. That payslip had changed the direction of the whole of the evening's enterprise.

'That's nice of you Michael, but wasn't it a whore you were looking for when you 'phoned me this afternoon?'

'Well ... yes, but having met you ... I just don't want to take advantage of your good nature.'

She threw back her head and laughed heartily, 'The whore with the heart of gold sort of thing? Really Michael

... or perhaps paying for sex adds to your excitement? Forget it, I'm not taking money off you. Particularly when you're a friend of a friend. Or at any rate a friend of a former friend.'

He tried to look puzzled, clearly she had spotted something. 'Whatever do you mean, Yvonne? Whom do we know in common?'

'Mustafa Malik evidently, and I assume he sent you along this evening. Either you are one of his people or the pair of you are bisexual.'

'What are you on about.' Dov was completely thrown by another abrupt change in the course of events.

'You were able to confirm that this place didn't look anything like Mustafa's bedroom. I wonder how you know that?'

He decided that attack was the best mode of defence, 'And I don't think that you're a whore, Yvonne. Your payslip in the basket ... ' He bent down and extracted the piece of paper once again.

'And so each of us has been rather careless with the result that each of us now knows who the other is! But before you get any ideas of rushing me to try to silence me and then departing, perhaps this will persuade you to remain sensibly docile for the benefit of both of us.' She produced a small handgun from beneath the chair. 'And I have a panic button connected direct to Police HQ. Perhaps you would like to tell me about yourself and your links with the friend we seem to have in common - Mustafa Malik.'

He was sweating. What should he to do? Should he come clean? Would evasion be of any use to him and, more importantly, to Sam and the others? 'Yvonne would you give me a moment or two to gather my thoughts, please. I can promise you I'll be rather more coherent if I can.' She knew where his car was and no doubt she had memorised the registration number. He wondered whether she had already 'phoned through the details to her HQ. If so they were probably taking the car off to a police pound somewhere on the edge of the city ... and the papers in it would lead them direct to the *Domaine du Cheval Rouge* outside Cassis! They could even be waiting now on the stairway for him. He wished he could ask Sam for his advice but that wasn't on. He made his decision and so he began, 'I'm well aware that you owe your loyalty to the French police, Yvonne. The story I'm going to tell you will stretch your credulity but, when you've heard it, you might conclude that as a human being you owe a larger loyalty to humankind.' He paused, the sermon over, and started to marshal the facts in his mind.

'I was stupid enough just now to indicate that I had seen Mustafa's bedroom. Let me first explain how it was that I came to be interested in him. I'm not an associate of Mustafa's, in fact I've never met him, though I've seen him on board his yacht, the *Viagra* - you know it?'

'Very well indeed, I've been on board as his guest. And I can assure you that he has no need for any drug to enhance his performance, certainly not so far as drive and energy are concerned.'

'I'm a serving soldier with the IDF, the Israel Defence Force.' He saw the surprise on her face. 'And I'm seconded to Mossad for an operation to counter what Mustafa and his people intend to do to my country. I assume that you're involved in keeping an eye on his drug smuggling? I can see from your expression that you are. OK, let's move on a stage: do you have any idea what the drug profits are to be used for by Mustafa and his people? No, not for them to lead the life of the rich, though Mustafa himself isn't doing too badly. The people behind it all are a terrorist group, the 16th September Unit. You won't have heard of them, they're a shadowy Arab outfit who have targeted Israel in the past and now they have a plan that has been described as the ultimate car bomb, only this time it won't be in a car and won't be a conventional bomb but a nuclear one. They need $10 million or $12 million to buy the weapon and that's why they're into drug smuggling. Mind you there's the added attraction for the Unit in that it's the decadent West that will suffer as a result of the Afghan heroin that they're selling to the dealers. Mustafa's job is to see that their containers of drugs move smoothly through the port of Marseille and at the same time he does a little smuggling on the side, on his own account that is, using the *Viagra* to meet boats from the North African coast.'

'And how, despite what you've just said, Michael, can I be *certain* that you aren't part of Mustafa's organisation and spinning me a yarn? And, even if I were sure that you were working for the Mossad, why shouldn't I report your activities to my bosses? Do the authorities in Paris know that Mossad are here doing just what they want on French soil - without any regard to French law? We want to nail Mustafa and stop this band of smugglers - think of the harm they're doing to our young people!'

'Yes I can understand what you're saying, Yvonne, understand it and appreciate it. But, consider for a moment, just what it is that the drug money is to be used for! Just think of the harm that a nuclear explosion would cause, not just to those in the target area, to Jew and Arab, but also to the world in general as the products of the explosion find their way into the atmosphere.'

'If only I could be *sure* of the truth of what you're telling me, Michael. Put yourself in my place for a moment. I've already broken the rules by not telling my boss that I'm seeing you this evening. If they find out that I've been in touch secretly with one of Mustafa's associates they'll think that I'm in their pay - a corrupt cop - and then I'll be without a job and most probably in jail, and I'm sure you know the sort of time that ex-cops have in jail!'

'But if I genuinely am who I say I am?'

'OK, that's not so bad - though I'd still be in trouble for not telling my bosses of Mossad activity concerning

Mustafa. What are you asking me to do?'

'I'm not quite sure of that, Yvonne. I'm not the boss of this operation - far from it I'm merely the gofer.'

'And your boss is?'

'Sam, that's as much as I ought to tell you for the moment. I'm certain that, if he could be sure he wasn't being lured into a trap, he'd meet you and tell you just what I've said but with rather more detail. If you blow our cover then we'll probably lose the scent we're following and the chances of the 16th September Unit succeeding will increase. You see they've already got most of the money they need.'

She had relaxed as the conversation proceeded, placing the hand gun on the arm of her chair. She moved her hand and the gun fell to the floor, bouncing in Dov's direction. She sprang to her feet but he didn't move. The gun lay at his feet, all he had to do was to reach down pick it up and turn the tables on her. He turned his gaze away from the gun to his captor. 'Yvonne, as a demonstration of my genuineness I'm going to get up and walk away from you towards the window. You'll be able to pick up the gun without any fear of attack. Then we can continue our conversation.' He did as he had said. She picked it up and returned to her chair. Then he went back to the sofa.

'Well you've made a point, one that I shall have to consider very seriously.' In her mind a host of conflicting thoughts jostled together: like many she regarded Israel with mixed feelings - she saw the Jewish people as both victim and aggressor and wasn't sure how to relate the one to the other - and there were the politics of work, that bastard of a Captain always taking the credit and treating her with the contempt in which he held all women, she certainly didn't owe him any loyalty, certainly not as an individual. And then there was another factor, a personal one. She had warmed to Michael. She had been lonely since she and Jean-Paul had split up six months ago.

She liked Michael as a man, so unlike that pig Mustafa to whom she had been assigned in an effort to penetrate the smuggling operation. Michael's refusal to take the chance offered by her dropping the gun had impressed her. 'Give me a few minutes, I'll make another coffee. Read a book while I'm away. There are some collections of photographs that you may like - they're on the bottom shelf.' She made for the kitchen, switched on the kettle and sat on a stool deep in thought.

Dov found a collection of Henri Cartier-Bresson's photographs and began to leaf through it, his attention being caught by one of a German unit marching through occupied Paris, a shot taken at some personal risk to the photographer. He was looking at it when she returned with a *cafetière* and cups on a tray. She looked down at the book, 'Yes we too suffered at Nazi hands, Michael. My grandfather remained in the fight against the Germans after our country surrendered. He served in the *Armée Secrète* and took part in the sabotage raid on the Oerlikon ball bearing factory in Annecy in November 1943. He survived the occupation, many of his friends didn't. ' She paused for a moment before continuing, 'And I guess we owe your people an apology for the way that some of the French treated their Jewish neighbours, some were very willing helpers of the Nazis ... OK, I'll keep my mouth shut and I'll keep you updated on what my people are going to do with the Malik Case. Cartier-Bresson spoke of *le moment décisif* - the decisive moment, well I've reached my decisive moment. But first I'd like to have a word with your colleague ... I think you said his name was Sam.'

'Yes, that's it, Yvonne. I'm relieved at your decision. I promise that you won't be compromised by us. I give you my word on that.'

'And perhaps you would like to tell me how you came to be in Mustafa's bedroom, Michael?' And so he told her of his recent visit with Sam and pointed out that he wasn't

Michael but Dov.

'You've finished your coffee, Dov? I think it's time to return to our tour of the apartment, though there's not a lot that you haven't seen already. You can tell me what you really think of the bedroom, now that you know that it's where a police officer sleeps.' She led the way into a small but elegantly furnished room, once more the furniture was Scandinavian. A light floral spread covered the bed and the curtains were of the same material. A plain oatmeal carpet covered the floor. The effect was of lightness and good taste. 'So you can see that its *décor* is very different from Mustafa's. You can stay the night? You haven't a wife or partner or even your Mossad handler waiting up anxiously for your return? No? Good! Don't let's waste any more time.' She turned to face him, her anticipation evident in her smile. Then she unzipped her dress, let it fall to her ankles and stepped out of it and lifted a black silk slip over her head. He feasted his eyes on her, it was clear that her lingerie bill must be pretty steep, her bra and panties were of very fine black lace. Her arms were around his neck and they kissed for the first time. He was breathless. Not long ago she had been threatening him with a hand gun but now ... His hands explored the fabric of her underwear, feeling her breasts and then her buttocks. They were firm to his touch. She felt his arousal, slipped off his jacket and then unzipped his trousers.

'Well Michael, do you want to give a demonstration of your wares. By that I mean, *of course*, the pharmaceuticals you told me you sold. Perhaps you'd like to demonstrate one of your contraceptives to me? But then as you're Dov and not Michael I assume you haven't any.' She laughed happily, she was happy and at ease with the decision she had made.

'They were supposed to be oral ones, I'm afraid ... but I have brought some *préservatifs* with me, not my company's, of course!'

She laughed at his allusion to his now discarded cover story. 'A wise precaution, Dov. You never know where I've been do you?'

'In Mustafa's bed by all accounts!' He immediately regretted saying it.

'Forget him, Dov, at any rate for the moment. In fact, though I saw his bedroom, I avoided his bed ... that wasn't for me - though I did find him some willing women. Tonight's for us to enjoy. Those memories aren't ones I'd want to cling onto. From the moment I set eyes on you I wanted to do this, not for money - I'm a cop not a whore - but because you attracted me. So, no Mustafa, no anyone else. OK? How to deal with Mustafa is for another day. By the way I'm on leave tomorrow ... we won't have to be up early in the morning'

'That's good news, Yvonne. And I'm a lucky man ... '

She led him to the bed and began to unbutton his shirt. Then she ran her hands over the front of his underpants, 'Promising, Dov, very promising indeed. It looks like we've a fulfilling night ahead of us.'

He had unhooked her bra and was beginning to slip her panties down. She stood there before him naked apart from her high heels. 'Now your turn, Dov.' She slipped off the unbuttoned shirt and removed his underpants and socks. 'Well we're both ready for action. Pass me a *préservatif* and I'll put it on for you.'

***

It was morning and he sat at the bedroom window while she showered in the bathroom down the corridor. He watched as people made their way to work along the narrow street below. This was turning out to be a very interesting assignment, better than guarding Mossad's HQ. Far better! He just hoped that Sam wouldn't be too put out by his disclosure of their activities. He felt pretty sure that he would approve, after all it could have complicated things if they had found the French police and customs watching them while they in turn watched Mustafa. Now with Yvonne on their side they would be warned of any police surveillance.

The door opened and Yvonne returned to the room wrapped in a deep blue bath towel. She stood beside him looking through the net curtains, 'Poor souls, off to another day's toil!' She dropped the towel to the floor, 'Perhaps, before we see your friend Sam, we could spend a while in *plaisir intime* ... ' Dov's grasp of French wasn't too thorough but he had a pretty good idea of what she meant.

Chapter 14

Tuesday 26th June 2001

'But, Sam, we *now* have a source of information within the Police Department. That could be very useful. If we'd continued unaware of their interest in Mustafa we could have run into trouble, bad trouble. You *must* admit that.'

'Provided always that we can trust her! *You* seem to have been swept off your feet by her, hardly the best way to come to a reasoned conclusion about her trustworthiness, is it? And doesn't it strike you as odd that *she's* as taken with you as you are with her. It's like a couple of teenagers after a high school prom. Life's not like that, is it?'

'And what would you have done in the circumstances, Sam?' Dov was angry and bitter. He had arrived back at *La Domaine du Cheval Rouge* floating on a cloud and this argument had brought him back down to earth with a vengeance. The Mums had taken the children out for the day to a local beach and left a light lunch for the others. Elizabeth, sensing the tension between the two men, was keeping out of the way. The argument had begun immediately they had sat down to eat on opposite sides of the big table in the kitchen. Esty's soup remained untouched and cold in the bowls before them. Dov had broken his chunk of *baguette* in half but otherwise the food was untouched. For men with healthy appetites it was indicative of the intensity of the debate going on between them.

Sam thought for a moment and then a smile crossed his face, 'Much the same as you, I expect. Sorry Dov, perhaps I'm getting a bit long in the tooth for work like this in the field. It's a fact of life that things rarely go as planned. Others influence what happens, often unconsciously, and the important thing is to limit any damage so far as possible or better still, and that's what you appear to have done, to turn it to our advantage. You're right it would have been very difficult if we'd been rounded up by French police or customs. We should have anticipated that they too might be interested in Mustafa and his activities. Being taken in by them would have hindered things and I'm sure that there would have been publicity which wouldn't have been missed by Mustafa's friends. So we now have the attractive Lieutenant Yvonne Charpontier as an honorary member of our team as well as beginning a relationship with Dov Levin. But be very wary, Dov, make sure that she's not taking us for a ride – a very enjoyable one at the moment, as far as you're concerned, I'll admit.'

'That's seems to be the way things are, Sam.' A note of quiet satisfaction had replaced the anger in his voice.

'There's just one thing, Dov, your relationship will bind her to us but also, if it begins to fall apart, she could go running to her masters to denounce us. You'll have to be careful and stick with her. You've got to do all in your power to keep her sweet, you realise that don't you, Dov?'

'I'll be very happy to have that as my agenda for the next few months, Sam, very happy indeed.'

'But you mustn't let the relationship cloud your judgement. You've got to keep an eagle eye open for any sign that she's not playing fair with us, any indication that she's decided that her first and only loyalty is to the Marseille Police Force or whatever they call themselves. So we'll have to ensure that's she's in it up to her pretty neck and has every reason to remain loyal to us. I'm not suggesting for one moment that we would want to do her any harm but she's got to have good reasons, reasons which have nothing to do with the emotions, for continuing to play fair by us. You understand that, Dov?'

'Understood, boss. After all I have no wish to spend time in a French jail or for you and the others to do so. I'll remain alert, I can assure you of that.'

Sam picked up a spoon and began his soup, 'Cold,

Dov! We've let it cool down. Here give me your bowl and I'll heat it in the microwave. Now tell me more about your new friend - our new colleague - and about the meal you enjoyed together. You can keep most of the *après dîner* matters to yourself though ... '

'So you'll see Yvonne, Sam?'

'Yes, that would be wise. I should be able to make a more dispassionate assessment of her than you could.'

'I don't dispute that but I think - I hope - that you'll find that what I've told you isn't too far off target. Where and when?'

'As soon as we can. You say she's got today off? Well what about later this afternoon? Let's make it on the promenade in front of *Notre Dame de la Garde*? They say the view from there's impressive. I'm sure you know her 'phone number by heart!'

'You might well be right about that, Sam. OK, I'll call her on her mobile in case she's out. You never know the police may bug their own people's landlines.'

'You've just given me an idea, Dov. No doubt the French have tapped Mustafa's 'phone line. First, they should have transcripts for the time before we came on the scene and, then, their tapping may well be more effective than our bugs and they may be picking up his mobile calls as well, so she might be able to let us have the old history as well as keeping us updated. That could be invaluable to us. I'm sorry I lost my temper, Dov, but the more I think about it the more I'm pleased at what you've achieved, though we've got to remain alert.' With which Dov completely agreed, the more he thought about things the more pleased he was at what he'd achieved the previous night.

'Yes, Sam, she'll see us in front of the Basilica at four p.m. I'll come to make the introductions ... '

'And see that the remainder of her day off isn't

wasted?'

'Jealous?'

'Not at all, I've got Elizabeth - if you hadn't noticed.' The tone was one of good hearted banter. 'And Elizabeth can go in advance and keep an eye on our backs, just in case ... '

***

They found a car park near the top of the hill with a flight of steps leading up to the promenade. A beggar had taken up residence on the steps, seeking alms from pilgrims or spare change from tourists - though the few coins on his plate evidenced no distinction as to their sources. Dov dropped a 1 Euro coin into his plate and received a muttered response, he didn't know whether he was receiving a blessing or being berated for lack of largesse.

'Generous today, Dov. You must still be floating on air.' Sam slapped Dov on the back good humourdly. They reached the top of the steps and turned onto the windswept promenade. Despite the brilliant sun the breeze made it cold. Elizabeth stood on the far side facing them and adjusting the controls on a video camera, a good excuse for her to linger there and be part of the scene. She had seen them and the absence of any signal from her indicated that she had noticed nothing suspicious. Yvonne was leaning on the parapet with her back to them gazing out to sea. She was wearing black jeans and a red sweater of a less striking shade than the previous night's dress. 'Right, Dov, let's find out whether your judgement's sound or whether we're walking into a police trap.' They made their way to the waiting off-duty police officer.

'Yvonne, it's good to see you again. This is Sam.' She turned and greeted them with a smile. He kissed her on the cheek and had the kiss returned. To Sam she offered her hand. He noticed her firm grasp. She was happy and at ease. Both men experienced a sense of relief. Sam put away thoughts of the link between kisses and betrayal.

'That's where the pair of you should be!' She pointed to a small fortified island near the shore and backed by a couple of long narrow islands, gleaming limestone rising out of an azure sea. 'The *Château d'If*! And under lock and key!'

'I thought that was for aristocrats.'

'Don't be too sure of that. But let's say you can have a stay of execution. But first I'd like a word with you, Sam. I have to be sure just what I'm letting myself in for if I play along with you and your colleagues. Dov can stay here and enjoy the view. You and I, Sam, will have a stroll round the Basilica and chat - I could even take the priest's place in the confessional box and listen to your guilty disclosures.'

'And by way of penance?'

'Not until you've come clean on your transgressions. Let's go!' She turned to Dov, 'If you find it too windy out here you can shelter in the shop.' She took Sam's arm, 'Let's head for the crypt. it's sure to interest you. You'll like the votive offerings - perhaps you'll place one there some day. If your friend's story is to be believed you'll have quite a deliverance to give thanks for. She pointed up to the gleaming gold Madonna and Child surmounting the tower above their heads, 'Your compatriots, I believe, Sam. We're in good company.'

The walls of the crypt were covered with plaques and paintings. Yvonne explained to Sam that they had been presented as thank offerings to Our Lady for deliverance from a variety of calamities. They moved slowly past, viewing the paintings, some of train crashes and some of near disasters involving early aircraft; works of art and of mechanical history. They were interesting from a variety of points of view, all placed there from a religious response to the close shaves that their donors had experienced. Thankfulness for deliverance expressed years ago and still in evidence. An unusual place to be, certainly unusual for a meeting of this kind.

Sam had the opportunity to begin his assessment of Yvonne. He sensed that beneath her calm surface she was on a "high" and hoped that it was her reaction to Dov and not excitement at being the bait in a police trap. He could well understand Dov's response to this woman, despite Elizabeth's presence outside the Basilica he felt himself being attracted to Yvonne. Towards a corner, where the wall was adorned with a fan shaped arrangement of ancient crutches, they came to a halt. 'Well Sam, to business. Dov told me in outline what had brought you here. I'd like to hear it from your own lips so that I can be sure about what I should or shouldn't do.'

And so he began at the beginning, keeping reference to the Swiss end of the operation obscure but giving as much detail of the Mossad operation as he felt safe. She listened intently, nodding now and then. He concluded, 'And so, Yvonne, I'm glad that Dov contacted you and found out the police and customs interest in Mustafa Malik. That's important information, something we ought to have realised was highly likely. It means we have to be careful if we are not to draw attention to ourselves.'

'But you could be working with the co-operation of French Security, wouldn't that be easier and simpler for all of us?'

'Yes and no. I can well understand you asking yourself why we shouldn't, if we're legitimate and above board ... '

'Kosher?'

'Yes, *kosher* will do as well as any other expression.' They laughed and he began to feel that she was with them, that they had got her on board.

'But, as I've told you we're already involved with another Security outfit who tipped us off about all this in the first place, the more people involved the more chance of a leak and that could mean that we would lose the scent ... it's a risk we can't afford.'

'But *I'm* a risk you can cope with?'

'The way things went between Dov and yourself last night, we haven't much choice, have we?.'

'True ... and that leads to what more you might want from me ... and what I might feel able to do for you, doesn't it?'

'That's about it Yvonne. What we already know is important ... the news that we're not the only ones interested in Mustafa's activities. But, as you've realised, there could well be more that interests us.' He checked to make sure that they not being overheard. 'You've got a tap on his 'phone?'

'You're probably right. OK, yes we have.'

'And you have access to the transcripts of his calls?'

'I've got copies in my desk, yes.'

'And it wouldn't be impossible for you to bring them home and for us to see them?'

'Not impossible but whether it would be wise ... if something went wrong and you were found with them ... '

'But if we only looked, noted down anything relevant and left them with you?'

'Better and safer. And you would want to see the latest transcriptions as they arrived ... or was your visit to the house to ... '

'To bug the place? Yes it was, I've got to come clean on that.'

'Well I reckon you need to nail Mustafa and his friends even more than we do, though Sam I don't know whether you've really seen the harm dope can do?'

'I was once a Rabbi with pastoral care of University students and I saw what drugs could do to a young life which otherwise had plenty of hope and potential. Make no mistake, Yvonne, I have no love for drug runners and pushers, none at all. But, so far as I can tell, the Unit's aim is to make the money they need to buy their bomb and then deliver it. Drugs are a means to that end, they moved into it to make a fast buck and in all probability they will soon be out of it again.'

'Yes, if they don't decide they want more cash for some other spectacular that they've thought up. Besides, Mustafa seems to have his own small scale operation - that's what we were on to at the beginning ... three months ago but then we realised he was overseeing something much bigger. But your interests and ours are the same, aren't they? We all want to put Mustafa and friends out of business ... no money, no bomb, isn't that what you're after?'

'Not quite, Yvonne. One thing we know is that they aren't far from their target of around $10M. If we wind up this end of things, if you haul Mustafa in, then they'll find some other route or some other operative, less colourful, less obvious than Mr Malik. Then we might have great difficulty in getting on their track again. Our interest is to keep this end of things running until we can get to the brains of the Unit or pounce on the bomb itself en route to our shores.'

'And all the time young people will be supplied with dope by these people, more and more will get hooked on the stuff!'

'If Mustafa's dope supplies run dry there's still plenty remaining from other sources, I'm afraid. OK, anything that puts a brake on the trade is good but in this case you must balance out the various sources of harm to people and go for the least bad option. And that's to let the trail remain in place so that there's a chance of preventing the nuclear explosion that's scheduled.'

'But Mr ... '

'Kagan, Sam Kagan.' He wondered at himself for giving her his real name and concluded it must be because he had decided he trusted her. And he asked himself what had brought him so quickly to that conclusion, the "halo factor" perhaps - he had felt her attraction immediately, had understood why Dov had responded to her in the way he had. A dangerous way of going about business in the world of international espionage and counter espionage. It was a technique that Mossad itself had often used with success, the pretty bait of the honey trap.

'But, Mr Kagan, how am I to know that you are what you claim to be? How am I to know that I can believe the story that you and Dov have told me? And, if you are from Mossad, how am I to know that you aren't behind the drug smuggling, that Mustafa isn't - knowingly or otherwise - one of your helpers. After all, some odd things have been done by security services and their offshoots. Just look at the Iran Contra business in Reagan's time.'

'You're wise to want to be satisfied, Yvonne. But how to do that is another matter entirely. You'll have to give me time to think about that.'

'OK, but don't take too long. I want to help and I'm already fond of Dov but, Mr Kagan, I'm not going to let myself become the wreckage left behind by some double cross! I have a job that I enjoy and I have no wish, no wish at all, to find myself as a guest of the French Prison Service. And, if I help you, it won't be for money but because I'm satisfied that it's the right and humanitarian thing that I ought to be doing.' Sam noticed how the "Mr Kagan" distanced her from him and withdrew the closeness that had begun to build up between them. He wondered how her "fondness" for Dov would fare.

'No, our interests coincide. I need to convince you as soon as possible of our bona fides. And Dov ... '

'I'll take the risk of spending the rest of the day with him and then he'll have to wait until you have convinced me.' An indication that at root she did want to trust them and was looking for reassurance. 'You probably won't see him until tomorrow morning, somewhat earlier than today as I'm on duty at 08.00 hours. Let's go and find him. And remember, next time we meet here you have to make a full confession if you wish to escape the penalties you face for breaking and entering the house of an innocent householder and installing illegal bugging devices.' She laughed as he winced. A thought occurred to her and she took up an idea she had alluded to earlier, 'Promise me that, if what you have told me is true and if you are successful in preventing a nuclear attack, you *will* place a votive offering - a thank-offering - here, officially or otherwise.' She looked at him and there was a twinkle in her eye, the idea amused her greatly.

'A picture of a mushroom cloud with an inscription something like, "The Government of the State of Israel and the agents of Mossad thank Our Lady for deliverance from the threat of a nuclear attack." ?'

'I should think that would do very nicely, that or something like it, Sam. I leave you to ponder the appropriate artwork ... and it might be as well to phrase it in Latin rather than Hebrew.' She was back onto first name terms, 'Let's find Dov. Then I can continue a pleasant friendship and you can begin to think about how to satisfy me.' She smiled again, 'Dov doesn't have to think too hard about how to achieve that.'

***

Sam remained on the promenade in front of the Basilica and watched Yvonne and Dov get into her Peugeot 304 and set off down the hill into the city. He'd collect Dov from the centre of Marseille the next day when he'd made contact on the mobile. For a few minutes he stood looking out to sea, taking in the islands and, in particular, the *Château d'If.* He could appreciate Yvonne's caution and her wish to stay out of anywhere like that.

Observed by Elizabeth, who was removing a disc from her video recorder, he went back to the Land Rover before setting off for Cassis. Elizabeth completed her filming and made for the Renault Espace, following Sam out of the car park. She would stay a few vehicles behind the Land Rover for the journey home making sure that there was no one on his tail. She wondered what sort of afternoon he had had and how Dov was getting on with his good-looking police woman friend.

Chapter 15

Tuesday 26th June 2001

Well, this was it! The house was a few yards back from the pavement, fronted by a small garden of tidy shrubs, a flight of five steps led up to the heavy brown wooden door whose small window was protected by a heavy iron grille. He had seen it all before, the day he followed Jakob Schmidt there from the airport. Now he was about to enter the house. Peter Gruenweiler rang the well polished brass bell push next to the equally polished plate, whose italic lettering declared this to be the abode of Dr Dominique Garnier, Therapist. The door opened and she greeted him, 'Monsieur Peter Gruenweiler? Come in. Let me take your coat, please.' She was a striking woman, though he would not have described her as beautiful, of medium height with short blonde hair.

'Thank you for being ready to see me so soon. I really appreciate it.'

She led him into the dark hallway, where she took his coat and hung it on a peg, and then onwards into a room to the rear of the house. Though they were in late June it was a dull day and the study too was dark. A tall window illuminated part of the large room with a weary light. A substantial sofa stood to the left of the window, angled so that it faced a large, heavy mahogany desk on the other side of the window. She indicated that he was to sit there and moved to her desk. It was illuminated by a green desk lamp that threw most of its light onto the surface and a little onto the face of Dr Garnier who had taken her seat and picked up a letter.

'Your GP, Dr Ax, says that he is referring you to me on account of severe anxiety. He adds that he heard me lecture at the University some time ago and that you have your own reasons for coming here rather than seeing a therapist in Basel. It would be useful for me to know those reasons, M. Gruenweiler.' Her gaze was steady and she had made immediate eye contact with him, though hers were the eyes of sympathy and not those of an aggressive interrogator. He took in her clothing, a dark green trouser suit with a small gold brooch on one lapel catching the light from the desk lamp. He decided that she had style and presence.

'I didn't wish to consult a psychiatrist in Basel for reasons of confidentiality and anonymity. I couldn't risk my employers hearing that I had been seen coming out of a psychiatrist's consulting rooms. And I wouldn't want my parents to know either. Psychiatrists aren't a breed that my father rates very highly, I'm afraid.' he smiled apologetically.

'During the course of our sessions we'll be exploring your parents' attitudes and their effect on your development but, perhaps, you could enlarge on why they should not know about your need of help in this way. After all, if you were suffering from high blood pressure you would tell them, would you not?'

'Well, yes.' He started playing with the signet ring on his finger, one of a number of routines that Maria had advised him to use. 'But psychiatric illness is something different, isn't it? It's not like a real illness, it means that you're not up to it, not up to living a real life. Unable to stand on your own two feet ... '

'So some people think, but they're mistaken. And your parents think that way?'

'My father does, certainly. I'm not sure my step-mother has an opinion on the matter ... My father has no time for people who are always looking for a prop, a support and just won't get on with it.'

'With it?'

'With life, their work and that sort of thing.'

'And you indicated that he has a particular view of the psychiatric profession ... '

'Contempt.' He started to fiddle with his wrist watch.

'That's why I wouldn't see one of your type in Basel. I couldn't have my father knowing.'

'And you M. Gruenweiler, what do you think of the psychiatric profession?'

'I don't really know, Dr Garnier. I'm wary but I'm here, so I suppose I'm hopeful to some extent. I need help, that's certain.'

'Well, that's a start anyway. How long have you thought that you needed help?'

'For the last couple of months. I kept planning to see Dr Ax but I kept putting it off. Every time I was about to make an appointment I became agitated and put it off.'

'But surely your agitation should have confirmed the need to get help?'

'I suppose it should, but I put it off.' His voice was rising - Maria had advised him to put some occasional aggression into it and then apologise. This seemed as good a time as any. 'There must be plenty people like me who aren't keen about coming to someone like *you*. Who feel they ought to be able to take care of themselves. Oh, sorry, I don't want you to think I don't want your help.'

'Good, I'm glad you used the word help: that's what I can give but *you* are the one who must get to grips with the problem and overcome it or at least mitigate it. So let's get going. Can you identify what triggered your anxiety, what brought it to its present intensity? Or perhaps we ought first try to identify when anxiety became a problem for you?' They were off and he was ready to feed her with the replies that he and Maria had prepared, untidy, partial replies that would be built on and added to as the sessions continued.

In the hall a clock chimed four. Dr Garnier looked up from the note she was making. She noticed that he was playing with the end of his tie. 'Perhaps this is a good time for a break. You would like a coffee or perhaps you would prefer tea?'

'Tea would be most welcome, thank you. Yes, most welcome.'

'Then I'll see to it. Not having a receptionist, I must see to these things myself.'

She left him to his own devices and wondering whether he was still under observation he continued fiddling with his tie. The room was very different from Maria's; hers was all lightness and simplicity. Here everything was heavy and dark. The furniture was heavy and the colours were somber. She had switched on a standard lamp as she left, lighting up the corner behind the desk. Behind him was a grand piano with its lid open and music on the stand. He got up to stretch his legs and inspected the music. 25 Préludes, Opus 31 by someone called Alkan, Charles-Valentin Alkan. He had never heard of him and he made a note to check him out on his return to Basel

Dr Garnier returned with a tray, which she placed on a small table. 'English Afternoon tea. I hope that's acceptable M. Gruenweiler? Good. Milk? And sugar? No. Well here's your tea. I must say you've worked hard so far, very well indeed for someone who was so doubtful about coming to see me! Perhaps your father could be persuaded to change, or at any rate modify his attitudes to my profession. It does help if I can see the family together.'

'Even at my age?'

'Yes even with adult patients. I find observing the family dynamics helpful. It can reinforce impressions formed earlier or open up new areas for examination.'

'No he wouldn't change his opinion. There's no chance whatsoever of me bringing my step-mother and father along. I'm very sorry but it's simply not possible. Still I'm glad we're making progress.'

'Right, let's recommence. You were looking at the music on the piano, when I came in with the tea. Are you musical? Do you play an instrument?'

It occurred to him that he was being given an opportunity which might be useful. 'I play the piano, or at any rate I did. There isn't space for one in my apartment. I miss it though.'

'Perhaps you would like to bring some music with you to your next session. Then when we've finished talking you can have a while playing before you leave. As you probably know music can be wonderfully therapeutic, especially when you're playing music yourself. Not before an audience, that can be very stressful if you're lacking in confidence, but by yourself and for your ears only. You have a favourite composer?'

'Schubert and Mendelssohn are both firm favourites, I wouldn't like to have to choose between them. By the way, who is Alkan? I've not heard of him before.'

'A Jewish composer who lived in Paris, just round the corner from where Chopin had once lived. He died in 1888 when a copy of the Talmud that he was taking from the top of his bookcase fell on him. Ironic, isn't it, a Jew being killed by the Talmud!' She sat down at the piano and, having turned over several pages of the score, began to play, slowly, rhythmically and solemnly. She was a pretty good pianist. The piece had a simple melody, tentative at first over a funereal base line. The tempo rose to a frenzy and then returned to its initial calm with the base almost alone at the end. She smiled at him and announced, 'Prelude No. 8 *"La chanson de la folle au bord de la mer"* (The song of the mad woman on the sea shore) by Charles-Valentin Alkan. My party piece, then I tell people that it's the state to which my work has reduced me!' He noticed she was now more relaxed than when the session had started, perhaps she too found the first meeting with a new patient stressful.

'Well done, I enjoyed that. Thanks for the introduction to Alkan, it's always good to widen one's musical frontiers, to find something new, and in this case accessible. Another Jewish composer to keep

Mendelssohn company.'

'In this case a Jewish-Jewish composer and not a Christian-Jewish one.' She left it at that, a somewhat enigmatic utterance and Peter wondered whether he should have mentioned the composer's racial origins, but then she was the one who had done so in the first place.

'Music's a rich tapestry like life.'

'Indeed it is. But you haven't come here for music lessons, have you. Drink up your tea and we'll get going once again. We've something over half an hour left and I'd like to complete an overall view of your life. Can we go back to your relationship with Julia. You met her five years ago, at a party wasn't it? And then she moved into your apartment a few weeks later. How did your father react to that?'

'Not with any great enthusiasm. Nothing too direct but you could *feel* his repugnance ... ' Off once again, feeding her the replies that he had prepared with Maria. A funny sort of game this but, then, his was a funny sort of job.

'That's as far as we can take it today, M. Gruenweiler. I think we've made good progress. I have booked you in for the afternoon, at the same time, a week tomorrow. If you care to bring your music then you can have the piano to yourself while I attend to one of my young patients. By the way that 's why I was a little surprised at Dr Ax referring you to me, the vast majority of my patients are children and, despite your problems, you are in no way child-like. Indeed you are, in many ways very mature, so I have high hopes of being able to help you - remember *help* is the important word - to help you to get through this difficult phase of your life. Until Wednesday, then.' She took his hand for the first time, held it for just a little longer than he had expected and then opened the door to him. He seemed to have succeeded, for the moment at any rate.

***

Back in his apartment he typed a report of the session for Maria on his PC. He used a floppy disc in order to keep it off the hard disc - you never knew what might become of the PC and he didn't want his personal details in unfriendly hands. It was as well that he was used to recording long and involved interviews. But before leaving Altkirch for Basel he had, nevertheless, sat in his car and made a list of the points that Dr Garnier had dealt with. Unfortunately Maria was out of town for the evening and he was due to see her the following afternoon. The next morning would see him in the office reporting to Erik Blum and doing some paperwork on another case that was due in court in a month's time, though he would not be required to testify.

Chapter 16

Wednesday 27th June 2001

The next morning Sam brought Dov back to the *Domaine* just before nine for a second breakfast over which they discussed how they could satisfy Yvonne that they were genuine. It had to be be clear, unambiguous and convincing. Sam was pretty sure of her goodwill towards them and understood her need to be satisfied.

'We could fly her to Israel and let our masters at HQ convince her, Sam.' A visit to the Paris embassy was another possibility that had come up during the debate.

Dov was deputed to find out whether either would be acceptable and despatched to meet her at *Le Filet Bleu* that evening.

Just after midnight Dov parked in front of the house, noticing that the lights were still on, and found Sam and Elizabeth waiting for him in the salon. 'Well she wants to go to the top.'

'The PM?'

'Not quite, not the present one at any rate, Peres is her choice. It seems he's the only one at the top she knows of and whom she'll trust.' Sam was reminded that he was here because Erik Blum had insisted on dealing with him and him alone. The only *kosher* one that Mossad possessed indeed!

'So Yvonne Charpontier wants an audience with Shimon Peres?'

'Or, the other way round, if we want her assistance - and there's no doubt that we do - Shimon will have to have an audience with Yvonne. It's not just that we want her to keep to herself what she already knows about us, it's our need for the information she already has and her continued co-operation, information on tapped 'phone calls and so on. We need her badly, Sam, there's no doubt about it.'

'Just as you do? Sorry, that's unfair, Dov. But I can understand the attraction.' Elizabeth gave him a quizzical look. 'OK, we let HQ know and see whether they'll be prepared to arrange it. If this went wrong it could be very embarrassing for Peres.'

'If we can't get her to help and the bomb goes off it would be even more embarrassing for all of us, Sam.'

'OK, we can but try! I'll take the TGV to Paris in the morning and communicate through our office there. So far as I'm concerned it will give me a good chance to have a long read. I've been meaning for a while to dip into a new anthology of war poems, this should be a good opportunity. There's the spraying of the vines to be finished, if you can, Dov. Otherwise you're free to eat in the Marseille Police Canteen, or wherever you go for meals with young Lieutenant Charpentier.' Dov pretended to box his ears and then they headed for bed, Sam setting the alarm for 6.00 a.m. less than five hours away - to give him plenty of time to catch the TGV.

***

Thursday 28th June 2001

As Sam looked out of the window of his return TGV, Marseille bound and insulated by skilful engineering from the sound and motion of travel, he watched the villages of France scurry past, villages hugging at their hearts their old memorials to war and death. Not on this line, only recently constructed for trains such as his, but on older routes shared now by stopping trains for less important passengers and by freight, were the stations to which soldiers had marched, ready to fight in the last century's conflicts. He reread Wilfred Owen's *The Send-Off*:

"Down the close darkening lanes they sang

their way
To the siding-shed,
And lined the train with faces grimly gay.

"A few, a few, too few for drums and yells,
May creep back, silent, to village wells,
Up half-known roads."

That delusive excitement of comradeship and of conflict anticipated. And all too quickly dispelled by the harsh reality of pain and mortality, when, despite everything, despite the fellowship of arms, you were alone, terribly alone with death waiting to recruit you into his wan host. Sam Kagan had never known anything like the carnage of the Somme or Verdun but he had experienced the steady attrition of warfare in Southern Lebanon, the toll taken by the roadside nail-bomb, by the sniper's bullet, by the *Katyusha* rocket. He had known the grief of nursing the dying in his arms, of hearing the last breaths of the mortally wounded and knowing that within a few hours he would have to bring such words of consolation as he could muster to a grieving father, mother or wife. But this would all pale into insignificance if the 16th September Unit succeeded. Mega-deaths was the word the strategists used, an obscenity, not a word for the man or woman in the street. Happy those instantly vaporised at the epicentre of an explosion: the fate of those on the edges, whether by quick and painful death or by gradual radiation sickness was another matter entirely.

He had to keep this in the realm of the possible and unthinkable rather than allow it to happen. The afternoon's negotiations with the Deputy Director had been hard work, clearly his masters doubted the reality of the threat. The guesswork of a gullible Swiss which he, Sam, was accused of having swallowed much too readily, even though the top brass had authorised the operation. For, when it came to it, the Deputy Director wasn't prepared to run the risk that Blum and Kagan were simply unhinged: if the threat did turn out to be real it would endanger his own skin in more ways than one. So he had agreed to contact the Foreign Ministry and they in turn had spoken to Sam and had reluctantly let him speak with Peres. And half an hour later Peres had called back agreeing to see Sam and Yvonne Charpentier in three days time.

Then followed the travel arrangements. They would call at the Paris embassy en route to the El Al flight to Tel Aviv. Yvonne would be issued with an Israeli passport to get her out of France and back again without leaving a trail for any of the French authorities. For a few days she would be Deborah Levi. Dov had checked with her late that afternoon. Yes, she could take a week's leave at short notice, she had to get it in by the end of the leave year in any case. This was all to the good, her absence would slow down any further work on Mustafa and in any case his was but one investigation of many for Yvonne's office and she had been able to shift its priority a little way down the scale.

***

Sunday 1st July 2001

Three days later Sam and Yvonne were back in an anteroom to Shimon Peres' office in the Foreign Ministry in Jerusalem. Their meeting with Peres was over and Sam had finished talking with one of Peres' aides. They had come off an El Al flight early that morning and been taken straight from the aircraft at Ben Gurion to a Mossad car. Yvonne had asked to see something of Jerusalem and Sam had promised a lightning tour of the city after the meeting with the Foreign Minister. They had breakfasted at the Foreign Ministry and had then cooled their heels for a couple of hours until the weekly Cabinet

Meeting was over and Peres returned to his desk.

'Well you've met one of our *Ashkenazi* aristocracy, Yvonne. I trust he's reassured you.'

'Yes I'm happy now I've heard it from his lips. It's not every day you meet a Nobel Peace Laureate. It was worth coming just to shake his hand.'

'And to encourage him. He's a strong dove but it does help when those at the top know that there are people world-wide who support moves for peace, however far that situation is from being achieved. Politicians like him don't meet too many outsiders without a personal or national agenda they want followed.' Sam refrained from mentioning Peres' rôle in obtaining the nuclear technology from France which had given Israel its bomb-making capability.

'Would you really think of going into politics as he suggested?'

'Only if I felt compelled by the situation in the country ... compelled and convinced that I could make a decent contribution. Israeli politics is such a mess with so many small parties and factions. It's the best case *against* proportional representation that can be made, certainly PR on the basis of our rules!'

'And what did he mean by calling you, "our incorruptible agent", Sam?'

'That's to do with a little difficulty I had with HQ over the Basel operation - that was when I met Elizabeth. What happened there stretched my loyalty too far. I won't go into detail but it caused me to leave Mossad. They had to talk me into coming back to head the team for this assignment, but I could hardly say no, could I?'

'And I can hardly say no, either. OK you've got me on your side but, as I've said before, I'm not in this for money ... nor for the love interest! I'm not receiving Dov's favours in return for services rendered ... that's not what's going on, is it?'

'In no way! I've suggested no such thing to him and I'm

certain no one else has. I've know Dov for some years, he's smitten by you, I can guarantee that.'

She looked relieved, 'It was just that it suddenly struck me that it's how the Mossad operates.'

'At times, yes. In the present case, *no*. A very definite *no*, Yvonne.' And she believed him: his "little difficulty" with Mossad HQ over the Basel operation – whatever that had been – reinforced her feeling that Sam was a man of integrity who could be trusted.

'So let me be completely clear, I'm helping you because I believe it's the right thing to do, not for any benefit in cash or in return for ... for the services of a lover. Because that's not how I think of my relationship with Dov.'

'The relationship of a week or so. My, you've both got it pretty bad! Though I'm pleased for the pair of you. But work at it, Yvonne, build a relationship that's based on more than the physical, that's multi-faceted and complete. I speak from the experience of some years of giving pastoral care to students. Good, sermon over. Now where do you want to go? You don't have any friends or acquaintances visiting Israel at the moment?'

'None that I know of. And with things as they are at present it's unlikely that they would want to come. How about the Wailing Wall? Then the Temple Mount.'

'The Western Wall - the *Kotel* - that we can do but with the present state of things the Temple Mount is out of bounds to non-Muslims. You'll just have to see it from a distance from the Mount of Olives or from the tower of the Lutheran Church in the Old City. You'll get a good view from either, though there's nothing like being there. I've been there, though according to the Chief Rabbinate I shouldn't have. You see there's the fear of walking on the spot which was once the Holiest Place, the part of the Temple where only the High priest could go and then only once a year on *Yom Kippur* - the Day of Atonement - but I'm pretty happy as to where that would have been and I kept away from that particular area. For a long time I'd wanted to enter the Dome of the Rock and see the rock itself. It was there that Abraham prepared to offer Isaac in sacrifice - we speak of it as *the binding* - it's a mysterious event - chilling and puzzling - where Abraham was told to do what, at first sight, is an act totally abhorrent to the Jewish religion, to offer his child in sacrifice ... to kill him. He didn't have to go through with it, of course, but the very invitation from the Almighty to do such a thing raises profound and difficult questions:

> *"So Abram rose and clave the wood, and went ... " '*

'A Jewish writer?'

'No a Gentile Englishman, or perhaps Welshman, Wilfred Owen a poet of the First World War. War poetry, it's one of my interests. It can speak with a powerful voice and as I've served in war zones it certainly speaks to me of the pain and sorrow. But to revert to the Dome, we can't go there today, which is a shame as it's one of the loveliest buildings I know. But the Wall, we will go there, though you'll have to go to the women's area. The other thing is that we must keep out of any area where there might be trouble - we don't want your picture on the front page of *Le Figaro* with the headline, "Frenchwoman survives Jerusalem bombing" '

'Better that, Sam, than, "Frenchwoman killed in Jerusalem bombing!" '

'Indeed. But you will come back here to see the place properly after Mustafa and the 16th September Unit have become ... well not history but, perhaps, a note in a file in Mossad HQ as a threat averted.'

'I'm sure that Dov will want to bring me Sam and I'm sure I'll want to come. But tell me, how are you getting on with the investigation? How near are you to those behind Mustafa Malik?'

'Not very near ... yet, I'm afraid. We've got a link between someone and a European bank but, unless he makes contact, preferably in person, we've nothing to go on. That's why we need your 'phone taps and details of the numbers he's called and who've called him. They're vital, so tomorrow we get working on them. OK?'

'OK, tomorrow. But now tell me about your time as a Rabbi, Sam, you seem to have done a variety of things in your life. Did I hear Dov say that you had a degree in electronics and computing?'

Chapter 17

Tuesday 17th July 2001

Peter drove his Opel Vectra off the car train at Goppenstein and headed down into the Rhône Valley. He'd chosen to go that way, through the Lötschberg tunnel on the back of a railway wagon, rather than take the longer road route via the eastern end of Lac Leman and up the Rhône Valley. Though they might return that way ... he would see how the day went. Maria had been subdued with little to say as they journeyed south from Basel. Her spirits had seemed to lift somewhat as they skirted the southern shore of the Thunersee. At Spiez they had stopped for a quick coffee before heading due south into the valleys that led up to the station at Kandersteg where they had driven onto the car transporter train for the journey through the Lötschberg Tunnel. Now conversation had dried up and each of them kept their own counsel.

Maria had warned him before they set off, 'I'm afraid I'm not going to be very good company today.' In response he had assured her that it was her day of remembering and that he was content to be there as her driver and companion. At Visp he asked her whether she wanted to change to the train there or at St Niklaus and was told St Niklaus - she didn't want to be with people on trains for too long. So they parked at St Niklaus station and took the train for the 12 miles into Zermatt. They sat looking out of the carriage, passing a mural of St Niklaus - Father Christmas - on one of the buildings. A few minutes later she broke the silence, 'Oh for the simple certainties of childhood when we believed in Father Christmas!'

'You ought to know better than to sentimentalise childhood too much, Maria. Even for the lucky ones it's not all so very easy and for some kids childhood can be a grim time of abuse or neglect.'

'That's all true but nevertheless ... there is something magical about children and Christmas. Of hopes realised, generosity, family warmth ... memories to be cherished. Alongside that the real world can seem so cold and unrewarding.'

'Growing up means taking blows, suffering disappointments, adapting to an adverse, perhaps antagonistic world. Maturity needs a positive response to all that sort of thing, you know that, Maria.'

'But to feel it ... that is rather different.' She sighed and then was silent for the remainder of the half hour journey.

They left the station and made their way through the town of Zermatt. 'I'm going to be even worse company for the next few hours, perhaps for the rest of the day. I'm sorry, Peter, but that's how it's going to be.'

'You needn't apologise Maria, I know something of loss at the moment.'

'She took his arm for a moment, 'Sorry, Peter, I'm being selfish - I know that the break up of a relationship can be like a bereavement. We'll talk more about that, say, tomorrow. OK? Good'

They approached the small cemetery and stood at the gate. On the far side a few people stood with their backs to them. She grasped his arm, 'It's Anna Bonner, Klaus' widow and the children. I don't know who the other woman is. We'll have to wait until they've gone. I should have realised that they'd come here today.'

So they waited and Peter was glad that it was a warm sunny day as it was nearly half an hour before the party turned and began to move towards the gate.

'Walk up the hill, Peter, so we don't meet them.'

Something in him counselled against complying, 'No, Maria, you were there at Klaus' funeral. You met her then, you should stay and meet her now.'

He saw a look of alarm in her face and then she said, 'OK, Peter, but only because you're here to defend me.'

They waited for two or three minutes. The unknown woman and the children passed them, then came Anna Bonner.

'Good afternoon, Frau Doktor Bonner ... ' Maria didn't know how to continue.

'Good afternoon, Doktor Bertorelli, I somehow expected you to come ... ' She too seemed to have run out of words. Peter saw Maria's face muscles tense up. But then she continued, 'Maria ... I *hoped* you would come. I'm so glad you have ... '

'Anna!'

The two women were in one another's arms and in tears. The others stood ten paces away. Anna Bonner said something to the other woman who indicated that she understood and left with the children. Peter, feeling very much out of place, looked enquiringly at Maria, 'I'll wait for you - don't hurry, take as much time as you need.' She nodded her acquiescence and set off in silence with Anna Bonner towards Klaus Bonner's grave. Peter took himself to the far corner of the cemetery where he could keep an eye on things from a decent distance. He sat on the edge of another climber's tomb whose memorial stone was adorned with carved ropes and climbing gear. He took from his pocket Bruno Bettelheim's, *The Uses of Enchantment*, he might as well be getting on with the reading that Maria had set him - did fairy tales really have meaning and importance? But, though he read, he kept a wary eye on the two women standing by the distant grave.

They turned and began to walk in his direction. He looked at his watch, they had been there for fifty five minutes. He got up to meet them and was aware that he had been sitting on cold stone for almost an hour. They met near the gate. Both women were red eyed but there was a tranquillity about them both.

'Peter, meet Anna Bonner. Anna, Peter Gruenweiler's a friend of mine from Basel - we share restaurant tables, no more.' There was an unexpected look of mischief in Maria's eye. They shook hands and Peter offered his condolences.

'I'm glad to meet you Herr Gruenweiler and to know that Maria won't have to go back to Basel on her own. Look after her, won't you. We've just had a wonderful hour talking about Klaus as we both knew him, sharing experiences ... sharing our joys and sorrows in a way I've been able to do with no one else since he died. Maria tells it was you who insisted that she remain at the gate when we left Klaus' grave. For that wise decision I thank you from my heart.' Despite her red eyes she managed a smile, 'Thank you so much, Peter.'

'Yes, Peter, we've had the most wonderful and amazing conversation. I wouldn't have thought it possible ... now, if you can bear with us a little longer, we're going to walk up past the youth hostel and look towards the Matterhorn itself. After that I need a little while at the grave on my own and then we can set off home. You have the rose we brought? Do you mind holding on here until I get back? Thanks.'

He watched the two women walk hand in hand through the gate and take the road to the end of the town and felt relief that his hunch that Maria should not avoid the meeting with Klaus Bonner's widow had worked out. He knew that things could have gone very differently with much anguish for Maria as well as for Anna and her family. He walked over to the grave with its simple granite tombstone. It recorded simply his dates and the inscription:

> *"Klaus Bonner, psychotherapist and mountaineer, who loved mountains and humanity and who died on 17th July 1997 climbing the Matterhorn, the mountain he particularly loved, leaving many to mourn him deeply. The world, a better place for his life, is diminished by his death."*

He swallowed. It was a good epitaph. He would like to have met the man. And he resolved to get Maria to talk about him, if not on the journey home then in the weeks to come. That was *if* he survived his encounters with his other therapist and so he returned to working his way through Bettelheim's book.

The women returned and Peter then walked Anna to her hotel while Maria went to be alone at the grave.

'You are ... friends Herr Gruenweiler?'

'Friends. We met through our work, though we aren't both in the same line of business. We eat together now and then, we're going to a concert next week ... '

'And you brought her here today.'

'She asked and I felt she needed to come, just as I suppose you needed to come. Grief isn't an easy thing to handle, is it?'

'And it's even harder when you have no public standing, no status in relation to the deceased. I was the widow but Maria as the mistress ... she got no recognition and that must have been hard, very hard. I once was angry with her, not now though. We've reconciled our differences, no that's not positive enough: we as women are reconciled to each other and for that I thank you, Peter. We stood at his grave together, then together we looked at the mountain with the evening light bringing out its relief and almost highlighting the point from which he fell.' She was silent, moved by memories, then she continued, 'Remember, look after Maria, she still has a lot of grieving to do.'

'Thank you Frau Doktor Bonner, I will do my very best. And I would like you to know that as I stood at your husband's grave, while you were on your way to view the mountain I really felt that I had missed something in not knowing him. I'm sure that there are many who still feel a deep sense of loss at his death.'

'Yes, but some of his projects are still running - the

good that he started isn't finished yet. That's one of the things that's helped me through it all.'

They reached the hotel and Peter declined an invitation to coffee; he needed to be there when Maria was ready to leave the cemetery. Anna's closing charge was, 'Remember she's going to be vulnerable for quite a while to come.'

***

From the time they got back into the car at St Niklaus, Maria hardly ceased to talk about Klaus. What had been held back for four years poured forth in a torrent, the dam-wall of restraint had at last collapsed and, with a strange cathartic joy, she spoke to Peter of her years with her dead lover. Peter proved a good listener, coming in now and then with a question and so confirming his interest and involvement in all she was telling him. They dined at a small brasserie in Aigle before joining the *autoroute* taking them along the side of Lac Leman and then round Bern and back to Basel.

Maria produced a CD from her handbag, 'Do you mind, Peter, it's the Duruflé Requiem. It's a work I love, I wish I were a believer but I'm not, not yet at any rate. But if I *did* believe, the final *In Paradisum* is what I'd hope for ... for Klaus and for all of us. The belief thing, its not like St Niklaus and children, it's much different, much more important. But that's for another time. Can we just listen to this and then be quiet?'

He put the CD into the player and it began:

Requiem aeternam dona eis Domine,
et lux perpetua luceat eis.
(Lord grant them eternal rest.
and let perpetual light shine upon them.)

A deep sense of tranquillity took possession of them and

when the disc had finished their silence remained unbroken until they reached the outskirts of Basel when Peter asked, 'Did you sing it with Klaus in your choir?' And the tear in her eye was the answer to his question.

'Peter, I just can't express my gratitude for having you with me today and especially for making me stay to meet Anna. I'm seeing her next week and, if we don't become friends, at any rate there's no longer any antagonism between her and myself ... and that's good for the pair of us. I wonder ... I wonder if you would like to stay at my place tonight. I'm not inviting you to bed with me, you can have the spare bedroom, but I would like to have someone round the place. Today has been quite cathartic and exhausting so I'd rather not be on my own ... and you've said that the emptiness of your apartment sometimes gets to you. We'll talk about Julia tomorrow, that's if you'd find it helpful. And by the way *you* have the makings of a pretty good therapist, I've certainly found you invaluable today - you really know how to listen and to encourage ... and how to share silence. Thanks, Peter, for being such a good friend.'

She squeezed his arm affectionately and he responded with the lightest of touches of his hand on her left knee.

'Yes, Maria, that sounds a good arrangement. I'll pick up some gear from my apartment first. There's some food in the fridge that we can have for lunch tomorrow. A lazy start with the papers, lunch and then a stroll by the Rhein. Therapy for the pair of us.'

Chapter 18

Friday 20th July 2001

Peter Gruenweiler sat at the piano in Dr Garnier's salon, playing a Schubert Impromptu. Their fourth session had gone well. Now he had her grubbing round in his early years, focusing on his relationship with his overpowering father. The spectre of childhood sexual abuse had been raised and he had succeeded in getting it dismissed from the scene. 'Don't be too forceful in dismissing the idea,' Maria had advised him, 'she will think she's onto something if you're too vehement in your denials!' He was finding the process tiring, keeping to a consistent story and reacting appropriately to any unexpected questions. Fortunately Maria had done her work well and there were not very many of Dr Garnier's questions that did not cover adequately prepared ground.

The opportunity of being alone in the salon had enabled him to bug both the telephone and the room itself. The downstairs lavatory had also been dealt with, though he wasn't sure who would be conversing there. Still, you never knew, someone with a mobile 'phone might make or take a 'phone call while responding to the calls of nature. He wondered whether he would have the opportunity to bug any other part of the house. Dr Garnier put her head round the door, 'I hope you don't mind being here on your own, M. Gruenweiler. I've got to take young George back to his parents. I'll be home in twenty minutes or so.'

'Fine by me. I'm enjoying playing. I miss having access to a piano. As you said it's very therapeutic.' He gave George, a lad of about twelve a smile and went to see them to the door, locking it behind them. He left the key in the lock, in that way she wouldn't surprise him while he distributed the remaining bugs and he could always say that he'd turned the key by mistake. He would give himself a quarter of an hour with five minutes as his safety margin. He set to and by the end of fifteen minutes had dealt with everywhere except the bathroom and a bedroom at the very top of the house. He returned to the entrance hall and removed the key from the door, no need now to block her way in.

When she returned he was attempting one of the Alkan Preludes. She sat and listened and when he had finished took over at the piano to make a point about some phrasing. 'You chose No. 13, so you're not superstitious. *"J'étais endormie, mais mon coeur veillait"* ... (I slept, but my heart was awake). It's from the Song of Songs. The waking heart ... I think that's what you may need more of - for your emotions, your feelings to be more awake. We'll have to see how we can work on that. But that's for our next session. I'll lend you Bruno Bettelheim's *The Informed Heart*, it's about living under extreme fear and terror - he was a psychoanalyst who was imprisoned in Dachau and Buchenwald in 1938/39.' She paused and he suppressed a desire to tell her that he had read Bettleheim on the significance of nursery stories - she might question who had put him onto Bettleheim. 'I wonder if you would like to be my guest this evening. I don't feel much like cooking and would like to eat out but not by myself. Don't feel obligated, you probably have something arranged.'

'As it happens I've a free evening, so I'd be delighted to accept but I'd like to pay my way ... ' He was soon to regret his ready acceptance of that invitation.

'No you'll be *my* guest. I'll book a table at *La Couronne* in Buschweiller. Do you know it? No? Really? You will enjoy it, they do fine duck - there's a Menu *"Tout-Canard"* which I enjoy.'

***

It had been a pleasant enough evening though there had been moments when it was clear that she wasn't entirely at ease. She had started to call him Peter and asked to be addressed as Dominique. The occasion for the meal had become clear early on when she had ordered Champagne, 'For a birthday celebration', though she had declined to say how old she was - he guessed that she was in her early forties. She had talked animatedly about her work with children traumatised by war and civil strife. She had spoken mainly of Kosovo and merely alluded to work in Jordan and the Lebanon. And once she had mentioned Gaza but then she seemed to shy away from any further mention of the place. Afterwards he had to wipe the car windows before they could drive away from the restaurant. An unseasonal fog was brewing up. It grew thicker as they neared Hésingue. It took twice as long as normal for them to reach Altkirch, so that it was gone midnight when they arrived at her house. He wondered whether she had known that fog was brewing up when she invited him to dine with her.

'I'm not going to let you go back to Basel in this fog, Peter. You'll stay here for the night and set off in the morning. You haven't got to be at your desk first thing have you?'

He did his best to reject the invitation, 'It really isn't that bad, it only means going back over the route we've just taken.'

'I won't hear of it. If you had an accident it would be on my conscience.' She took his hand, 'Come on in, I don't eat men and as you can appreciate it would be unprofessional to go beyond friendship with a client - although you seem one of the better adjusted of my clients, it's almost unfair to take fees from you.' She smiled as she unlocked the door and escorted him into the house. 'Coffee and a Cognac? Good, take a seat in the salon and I'll see to it.'

She had shown him to the bedroom in the top of the house, which, apart from the bathroom, was the sole remaining candidate for bugging, showing a disinclination to leave him there. Then she had suddenly announced that she was going for a bath and gone downstairs. He had almost installed the bug in the bedroom when he became aware of a rustling sound outside the door. There was just enough time to slip bug and tools into his jacket pocket before she knocked lightly on the door and came in. 'Not in bed yet, Peter? Is there anything I can do for you before you go to sleep?' She stood before him in a low-cut satin night-gown that left nothing to the imagination and made the thrust of her question crystal clear.

He had no doubt about what was on offer and he couldn't see any way out. It occurred to him that if he hadn't met Maria he might have responded to Dominique's overtures with some enthusiasm. 'Well, perhaps it's a little lonely up here on my own.' She was holding him tightly, her mouth on his - he tasted the Cognac on her breath - her body pressed urgently against him. She was desperate for intimacy and he wished that he'd had enough time to install the bug before she returned. This was all running far faster than he had imagined and he knew that in order to maintain access to her and her house he would have to co-operate. In one way his wasn't a bad job at all, if this was what it entailed - being entertained to an excellent gourmet meal before sex with your own personal shrink, and an attractive shrink at that. But in reality he resented being forced into such a situation. And especially so because of Maria - there was nothing physical between them ... well not yet. His thoughts of Maria discomforted him and, remembering Jakob Schmidt's visit to the house, he said, 'You haven't a lover, then ... '

'Not for some time ... not for far too long. Don't waste time on discussion, Peter, I've been waiting all evening for you. Get those underpants off and show me that I haven't been wasting my emotional energy.' She was a driven woman, anxious to dominate, lusting for his body. He had never encountered anything quite like this. She released him and watched him strip. 'Good, it certainly looks as if you're properly equipped for it, Peter.' He wondered whether she was checking that he passed muster as a Gentile. She opened a bedside drawer, 'There's a packet of condoms if you must, I prefer it without but you may want to use them, if that's what you would like ... ' He would certainly play safe and so he began to unwrap one, 'Here let me do it, I'm probably quicker than you.' She was certainly in a hurry.

'Do you like playing games, Peter?' There was playfulness in her voice.

He looked up at her, exhausted by the previous half hour's activity. A woman like this was a totally new experience and one that he could well do without: he was certain that there couldn't be very many women around with her sex drive. 'What kind of games, we've played enough for one night surely?'

She smiled, 'I once had a lover who owned a gun and

we made love with it under the pillow. We used to pretend that he was ... raping me, threatening me with the gun ... can we do that now?'

He was tired and a little confused, the wine and the Cognac as well as the exertion had affected him. 'OK, if you like that sort of thing.'

'Good, you'll like it, I know.' She fetched the pistol and ammunition from the wardrobe and placed them on the bedside cabinet. 'Now load it, Peter!'

He looked at her in disbelief, 'You want me to load it? That's highly dangerous!'

'The danger's part of the excitement, that's why I like it, it helps me to have a proper orgasm. It's far easier for most of you men. And don't pretend that you don't know how to load the thing, all you Swiss serve in the Army.'

He did as he was told and loaded the pistol, checking that the safety catch was on. He replaced it on the cabinet. To his consternation she leaned over him and took it, then kneeling over him, she moved the safety catch to off and pointed the pistol at him. He lay there in a cold sweat, so she had rumbled him, found out who he really was, she had hinted as much by telling him that he was better adjusted than any of her other clients. Wasn't there a spider whose females ate the males after intercourse? He wondered what use that memory was in his present situation. She had said that she didn't eat men – could he really believe her? He was preparing to plead for his life when she said, 'The other lover used to point it at me but I'm going to do the pointing tonight and rape you!' She put the gun under the pillow and descended on him with a vigour and urgency that shook him. What had he let himself in for? Was she mad, like the woman in her party piece, Alkan's Eighth Prelude? He was going to need all his wits about him if he was going to emerge alive from therapy. And if he didn't survive ... well he hoped Erik Blum would nominate him for a posthumous police medal or perhaps some of Erik's Jewish friends would have his name carved on Mossad's own memorial! He felt he too was going mad and was amazed at the speed with which these thoughts were running through his mind while this madwoman was giving all she'd got to these sexual gymnastics.

She lay beside him sound asleep. Now her breathing was slow and regular, not as it had been an hour earlier. Carefully he slipped his hand under the long bolster-pillow and withdrew the pistol. He applied the safety catch and then slid the pistol under the bed. That was one peril dealt with at any rate. He wondered what she would want when she woke in the morning. He wouldn't be staying to find out.

His mind went back to a session with Maria, when she had been asking him about the effect on him of Julia's departure. 'OK you miss her as a person, you miss the intellectual stimulus. What about the physical side of things? How important was that to you?'

'Very important but, surprisingly it's not so much the ecstatic moments of sex I miss as not having her there in bed beside me, not having her warm soft body close to mine.'

'But the sex thing?'

'I miss it, sometimes badly.'

'And you haven't found another partner, even for the odd night?'

'No, I haven't wanted that, even when I've been very stressed ... '

'You've no hang ups about masturbation?

'None. It's not that great but it's better than nothing.

No, I've no hang ups about masturbation.'

'And who do you think of when you do?'

'Julia ... or sometimes the girl before her, but that only lasted for a couple of months.'

Now if Maria went over the same ground he would have to admit, if not precisely rape at Dominique's hands, then something not very far removed from it. No, he wouldn't wait for her to broach the subject he would have to be open about it when he reported to her tomorrow - no it was already tomorrow, he would be telling her that afternoon. And it was his acquaintance with Maria herself that had made him less than eager for intimacy with Dominique. He would have to be completely honest with Maria about the night's events and tell her exactly what had happened. He was going to need advice on how to deal with the situation in Alsace. But he would not let on to Maria why, apart from being threatened with the gun, he had found Dominique's attentions particularly unwelcome.

He knew he mustn't sleep, he wouldn't be safe if he did. Downstairs the hall clock chimed three. He decided to try to recall everything he could remember from his police studies on the Swiss law of rape. It was an exercise that, combined with fears for his safety, would keep him awake for the next few hours until it was reasonable to get up and return over the border at Allshwil to the safety of Switzerland and guidance on how to keep Dominique in order. But his mind turned away to Bettleheim on fairy tales, trying to find one that reflected his recent experiences. Was there something of Oedipal conflicts in it all? He couldn't for the life of him see where *Jack the Giant Killer* fitted into all this! As his therapist, wasn't Dr Garnier a sort of mother figure? But then Maria was also his therapist and he didn't see her as having a mothering rôle. It seemed more likely to be in keeping with Bettelheim's other book, the one that Dr Garnier had given him, he couldn't quite remember the title - was it *The Instructed Heart?* - on living under extreme fear and terror.

At six he slipped out of bed, gathered up his clothes and made a silent exit from the bedroom. He dressed downstairs and let himself quietly out of the house. An hour later and after a shower he was sitting in his kitchen with a large cup of strong black coffee on the table before him. On his way home he had stopped at a *Bäkerei* and bought croissants and crispy rolls. He worked his way through these relieved that, despite the physical and emotional bruising of the experience, he had not lost his appetite for a good breakfast. As he ate it occurred to him that he had missed out on bugging both the bedroom and the bathroom. After all he could have installed the bugs before he left that morning. But then what if she had discovered him at it? She had almost done so when he'd been working on the bedroom before ... before all that had gone on in that bed. He was determined he would never again go beyond the ground floor of her house. She wouldn't be getting him up those stairs again! Another time if it were foggy he'd be ready to walk back to Basel rather than risk another amorous encounter with her. And once more he found himself breaking out into a sweat. Confessions lay ahead: Erik Blum in the morning and Maria in the afternoon. Neither session was going to be easy for him.

Chapter 19

Saturday 21 July 2001

'Do you really think you ought to persist with this, Peter? That woman ought to be reported to her Association for the most extreme and unprofessional conduct as well as being charged with criminal offences by the French Police – that's assuming she's sane! You've bugged the place, isn't that sufficient?'

'I bugged most of the rooms but not all of them, Maria. I won't pretend she didn't scare the life out of me last night and I can see the force of all you've said but, somehow, and I don't know why, I have the feeling that there could be value in remaining in touch with her. It's more a matter of intuition than of logical reasoning. It's not the way a policeman is supposed to proceed but it's one that sometimes pays off. I'm ready to risk it and see what happens. No it's not the sex angle, not that she's unattractive, not that she's bad company - dinner at *La Couronne* was a pleasant enough way to spend an evening - there's something disturbing her and I wonder whether she might not open up to someone prepared to lend a listening ear.'

'You were probably more on target when you said she was mad! What was the piece of music she played?'

'Alkan's *Prélude "La chanson de la folle au bord de la mer"*. I managed to find a CD of his *Préludes*, there's nothing odd about them. If you would like to listen to it you can borrow it. OK, we can pick it up from my apartment on our way to the restaurant. But do you honestly think she's mad? What do you as a professional mean by madness, insanity that sort of thing?'

'It's not a word I would use professionally, though for

our present purpose it's useful. We both have a good idea of what it means but it's not a helpful term in psychiatry. Her mind is clearly disordered at times though not for a great deal of the time. I know she's very bright, very able intellectually, a respected worker with traumatised children. And, no, before you ask, there's no truth in the assertion that genius and madness are closely associated.'

'But I think there's something disturbing her, Maria. Behind the efficient professional facade - and, until the question of music came up, I found her just that, very professional, without a great deal of warmth, but then that's the way you professionals usually need to play it isn't it, not becoming emotionally involved with your clients?' She wondered whether there was more in his comment than a general observation but she also noted the word "usually" and let his observation pass. He went on, 'There must be deep stresses, something has to be disturbing her, upsetting her badly, for her to behave as she did last night. With the telephone bugged as well as most of the house we should be picking up some idea of what goes on between her and the man who led us to her.'

'Jakob Schmidt?'

'Erik told you?'

'Yes, and to be completely honest, he's told me pretty well everything about the operation. He needed to do that to convince me that I must put away my quibbles about the sham client we're presenting to her - to Dominique Garnier - and help in making you appear authentic. And on that point, are you completely sure that she has no suspicions?'

'As sure as I can be, though when she pointed that loaded pistol at me with the safety catch off ... well, I really thought the game was up. Instead it turned out to be a variant of some sexual game she plays with her lover, the one who hasn't been available for too long - presumably that's Schmidt, we'll just have to wait and see.'

'I wonder if her distress is as much to do with the nature of what she's become involved in with Schmidt as with her relationship with him or with whoever else her lover might be. She's got a fine record for working with traumatised children, and that includes young girls who've been raped by soldiers, often by men who were their next door neighbours. She's worked in pretty rough places, pretty dangerous ones, Kosovo and before that in some pretty unsavoury refugee camps in the Lebanon and the, so called, Holy Land. She's a very committed woman. That's why Erik Blum had to tell me the whole story to obtain my co-operation.'

'Rape at gun-point ... could she be living out the experiences of her young clients?'

'I just can't tell you the answer to that. Sadomasochism isn't an area that I specialise in, fortunately or unfortunately, as the case may be! ... I suppose it's possible, but she ought to be experienced enough to be able to avoid that happening. Though I can perhaps imagine that with so much exposure to severely traumatised rape victims who've seen their friends and families brutally murdered before their eyes ... It makes me thankful that my work's so different and yet, at the same time, it makes me guilty for being too comfortable - the academic ivory tower, wealthy clients and so on.'

'Wealthy! Like me on a policeman's pay?' They laughed, glad to break the tension.

'For you, Peter, it's one of the perks of the job. Analysis and therapy, I mean. Still I hope you have enough money to pay for dinner, it's your turn this evening and I don't think the table you've booked is at McDonald's!'

He pulled a face, 'That's true, Maria, when I rang McDonalds they said we'd have to chance to our luck, though we'd probably find a table, if not we could always have a take-away to eat in the *Barfüsserplatz*!'

'In that case I'm not sure I want to dine with you tonight, Lieutenant Gruenweiler!'

'Then it's just as well that, after the disappointment with McDonald's, I managed to book a table in a little place up near the *Münster*, Dr Bertorelli!'

Their laughter was renewed. They needed to laugh. It had been a tense session: his experiences of the previous night had clearly scared him and it still showed - she suddenly felt a real emotional concern for his safety. And it occurred to Maria that *she* had invited him to spend the night at her apartment a few days earlier, after the visit, or rather pilgrimage, to Zermatt. But that had been a very chaste night with separate beds in separate rooms. There was no infringement of professional etiquette there, even if Peter had been a regular client. And she was aware of jealousy as well as anger in her feelings for Dominique Garnier.

'One thing before we end our session, Maria, and I must say I'm glad we keep the shrinking matters confined to this room, could it be that Dr Garnier's problem is caused by the tension between her genuine concern for the Palestinians and concern as a human being over what the 16th September Unit intends to do? You did hint at it earlier.'

Once again the reality of the situation asserted itself; they were not involved in games, this was for real and if they didn't get it right the consequences would be unspeakable. In that context personal hurts had to take second place to duty and the threat to millions posed by the Unit's plans.

'I suppose it turns on how much she knows of what the Unit intends to do. And I suppose you, if anyone, are the one to whom she might open up. I'd thought of telling Erik to pull you out. You know the risks you face, so, Peter, if you want to continue as her client I won't try to stop you, much as I ought to personally ... er, professionally.'

'I'll stay with it, Maria. It's too risky not to. But then *you*, Maria, might be the one she'd be more ready to confide in. Just think about it. Session over? Good. We'll collect the Alkan CD at my place and then see whether the table I've booked is an improvement on McDonald's!'

'You haven't really told me how Erik reacted to your report this morning, Peter.'

'First of all with stunned silence. Then with anxiety for my safety and, well you know Erik, "concern for my moral welfare" was the expression he used. He wondered whether I shouldn't be checked out by a police doctor and then, you'll never believe it, he enquired whether the condoms had been "intact after my experience of intimacy" - to which the answer was, yes.'

'At that I'm very much relieved, Peter. Though it would be as well to be checked out for your sake and the sake of any future partner.' She flushed slightly and deflected his attention with a laugh, 'I'd love to have seen you reporting to Erik this morning. No, Peter, don't get me wrong, I'm certainly not laughing at you but I can just imagine Erik and his response.' And he joined her amusement, after all there are some things where if you don't laugh you might almost end up in tears.

Chapter 20

Tuesday 31st July 2001

The information they had found in Mustafa's house during their break-in had been revised by a message picked up by a 'phone bug: there would be a gap in the arrival of containers into Marseille and then several in quick succession beginning with one arriving on 29th July.

Just after 8.00 a.m. on a slightly misty morning Sam and Dov, driving separate cars, followed Mustafa's Alfa Romeo up the hill out of Cassis. Initially he drove in the direction of Aubagne, going onto the A50 *Autoroute* beyond Carnoux-en-Provence. But then he surprised them by not heading for Marseille. Instead he took the A52 northwards until he joined the A8, the *Autoroute la Provençale*, and headed west. North of Marseille he switched to the A7, the *Autoroute du Soleil*. Passing Aix-en-Provence, he added a further 25 km before taking the exit for the Lançon-Provence service area.

Sam and Dov's hire cars, a Renault and a Mercedes, followed him off the *Autoroute*. For a moment they each thought they had lost him but then they saw him get out of his car in a corner of the parking area and stroll in the direction of the restaurant. Dov remained in his car while Sam followed Mustafa. He was in the cafeteria queue and Sam left him there while he bought a copy of *Le Figaro* and took the opportunity of visiting the gents before returning to the queue. That placed him six or seven customers behind his quarry. He watched as Mustafa purchased a substantial breakfast but, when his turn came, Sam limited himself to a *pain au chocolat* and an espresso. He found a table a little to the rear and to one side of Mustafa and kept him in view from behind his paper. Mustafa seemed to be in no hurry to finish breakfast and be on his way. He must be waiting for someone. Meanwhile Sam gave the impression of being immersed in his paper while he kept his undivided attention on Mustafa. If he hadn't he would have missed his quick nod towards a heavily built man on a nearby table, a nod that was returned before the man got up and left, followed a moment later by Mustafa. The man was standing by the exit while it was Mustafa's turn to visit the gents. As Mustafa came back into view the man left and headed for the truck park.

Mustafa got into his Alpha and remained there for five minutes before he moved off, followed by Dov and Sam. They rejoined the *Autoroute* and accelerated, not to the full 130 km/hour allowed but to 110 km/hour as it had begun to rain. Several vehicles ahead of Mustafa was a truck with a blue container on board. Mustafa and the truck were clearly staying within the speed limits to avoid attracting the attention of the *Gendarmerie.* It was the only container vehicle in sight and had to be the one Mustafa was shadowing. It would be easy to keep it in view from a comfortable distance to the rear. They headed north past Avignon and then Orange. At the next *Péage* point, although Sam and Dov had selected the longest queue to avoid getting ahead of their prey, they found that they were through first. That didn't matter, they could go gently and let the others overtake. But as they pulled away they saw that the truck and Mustafa's car were not following them but pulling over to the right and stopping.

Sam called Dov on the mobile, 'Go off at the next *Air de Repos.* We'll wait for them there. Just pray they don't take an earlier exit.' There was indeed an exit for Pélissanne and Salon-de-Provence around six km on and then a further ten km brought them to the rest area at Lamanon. They pulled off the *Autoroute* and parked near the far end of the area. The radio marker on Mustafa's Alpha would alert them to his approach and there would be no hurry to get back behind them, the important thing was to keep them in front.

'What do you think they're doing Sam?'

'Your guess is as good as mine. It could be that the truck has some problem with brakes or tyres - he might have decided that he needs some more air in them - if so lets hope it's nothing too time consuming. On the other hand it may be part of their technique to deal with anyone following them, though it wouldn't throw the *Gendarmerie* or the Police. We'll never know, I expect, but if you want the gents it's there. If I'm gone by the time you get back you can catch up with us, but no excessive speeds, please.' There was no need for the advice as it was nearly half an hour later that their instruments picked up Mustafa's car and they started their engines to continue the pursuit.

The weather had brightened and the sun was driving away the cloud. *Le Soleil* was asserting its authority over its *Autoroute*. The road surface had dried quickly and they headed north at the maximum 130 km/hour, wondering where their destination might be. They might need to take fuel and the longer the journey the more likely they were to be detected. They passed Montélimar, Valence and Vienne, rolling north at a steady pace in moderate traffic, Dov taking the lead and Sam keeping well back. At Givors they took the A46 *Autoroute* to the east of Lyon and then the A43 into the city. Sam heaved a sigh of relief, Lyon appeared to be their destination. They weren't, after all, heading for Paris or beyond. Once they appeared to be approaching their final destination he would overtake Dov and attempt to locate the yard or depot. Assuming that Mustafa stayed with the truck his radio beacon would locate them both even if Sam lost sight of the car.

They came off the motorway, turned north and passed the small aerodrome of Lyon-Bron before heading into a *Zone Commercial*. Handy for the Unit to have a depôt from which light aircraft could make quick deliveries within France and possibly beyond. The truck indicated a left turn and so did Mustafa. They made their way into a small yard with a warehouse at the back. Sam noted the name of the place, *Lyonstor*, drove on to the end of the road, and took down its name, *rue Anatole France*. He turned the car and watched Dov drive up the road and park facing him. He got out and joined Dov, 'We'll stay here for, say, half an hour and then see whether the container's been taken into the warehouse, then, Dov, its somewhere decent for lunch. We've been on the road for four hours plus and deserve a decent meal.' Half an hour later they drove past the yard to see the truck minus its container preparing to leave. There was no sign of Mustafa, though his car was parked near the gate. They felt satisfied that they had identified the distribution centre for the Unit's supplies of heroin. They had also established the nature of one of Mustafa's tasks as the Unit's man in Provence. Only time would tell whether this information would prove to be of any use to them or to Lieutenant Yvonne Charpentier of the Marseille Police. Sam was wondering how they could use it to their advantage.

***

South of Lyon they turned off the *Autoroute*. Sam soon

spotted a *Routier* restaurant with a number of trucks parked outside and he led the way into the car park. He joined Dov as he was locking his car, 'They say that if you see a good number of trucks outside a *Routier* you'll get a good meal. Well, Dov, let's see whether they're right in this case.' It was 2.15 but the restaurant was still open with a couple of dozen customers scattered round the dining room. From the number of lorries parked outside it seemed that some of the drivers were back in their cabs enjoying a post-lunch siesta before returning to the *Autoroute*. Lunch was 10 Euros - and that included the wine! They found a table out of earshot in the corner. Promptly a carafe of red wine together with two glasses was delivered to them by a young woman who took their order for the main course and directed them to the buffet of hors d'oeuvres in the middle of the room.

'Looks like a good choice, Sam. We're not going to starve here!'

'No chance of that! They've obviously kept replenishing the supplies through lunch time. With the fish they've got here it's not difficult to avoid ham and the like. And, by the way, go easy on the wine - it may be free but we don't want any trouble with the *Gendarmerie* on our way home.'

Dov nodded, he too would avoid ham - today - to keep Sam company. Though he himself wasn't strictly observant he had no wish to give offence to others, especially to someone like Sam whom he respected. No, respected was too weak a word, worshipped was more like it - worshipped as the one who had saved his life in the Lebanon and who now had got him away from the Mossad gatehouse, into this demanding assignment and into the arms of Lieutenant Yvonne Charpontier of the Marseille Police. Not the strong arm of the law but rather the tender arms of a loving young woman. These days Dov was over the moon, his feet hardly touching the ground.

Dov poured the wine and tasted it, 'I don't need your warning to go easy with this, Sam, it's not like our wine from the *Cheval Rouge*!'

'Having your own vineyard is spoiling you, Dov. You won't be wanting to go back to Tel Aviv when the operation's concluded.'

'Now that you mention it, Sam, I must admit that the thought had occurred to me that it wouldn't be a bad idea to stay on, particularly if Yvonne ... '

'Became a fixture in your life? Your "significant other", an "item" with you or whatever the current phraseology might be.'

'I know it's early, Sam, but we do seem to get on well and to be suited to one another. And I haven't felt like this over a woman for many a long year.'

'Well I hope it all works out, for both of you. I wouldn't like Yvonne to think that she'd been "used" by us and then dropped but that doesn't mean that you're being offered as a sacrifice to keep her happy - in any case that wouldn't work out for either of you, would it?'

'Have no fear of that! We're both very fond of one another - location "Cloud Nine" or somewhere like that!'

'Well good health and long life to the pair of you, Dov. *L'Haim*.' Sam raised his glass took a sip and pulled a face, 'You're right Dov, nothing at all like our home brew is it?'

'Or like your products on the Golan?'

'That's certainly true, our Cabernet Sauvignon with the *Yarden* label is quite something and we've another five reds including a Yarden Merlot and some blends. All that seems a long time ago and yet this operation has only been running for a couple of months. Erik Blum came to us in June. About time for a review of progress. I know we did one for HQ recently but that doesn't really get to one's inner feeling about the way it's going. It might seem too subjective but I often find that my gut feeling about something is more on target than a dry factual analysis.'

'And your current gut feeling?'

'Well fed and likely to be overfed if these plates heading in this direction are ours.'

Their empty starter plates were taken away and replaced with plates of well done steaks and *frites*. Dov refilled their glasses, drank half of his and declared it considerably better with food. Sam shifted the carafe onto a neighbouring table to remove the temptation to imbibe more. They tucked into their steaks. Not bad, not at all bad. France was a civilised country, when truck drivers ate this well and for five days a week or however long their working week might be! The empty plates joined the carafe on the other table when they had chosen desserts from the buffet, Sam checking that the cream on the *pâtisserie* was synthetic. Over coffee they returned to pondering progress.

'OK, let's have your gut assessment of the situation so far, Sam.'

'First of all the sobering thought that we're over half way there - half way to 16th September - and as yet we haven't made a great deal of progress. That worries me. Well, there are three established points of contact with the 16th September Unit: us here in Cassis, the bank in Basel and, as an offshoot from that, the French shrink, who is possibly also Jakob Schmidt's lover. Blum will be told when Schmidt contacts the bank again and one of his people has signed up with the shrink as her patient and has bugged her place.

'At our end we've bugged Mustafa's house, enrolled Yvonne to give us the benefit of the police's official bugging of his place and 'phone calls, including a mobile they managed to get a look at and find its number. We know that Mustafa does a bit of private drug smuggling on the side and this morning we've seen him in action escorting the Unit's drug container, watching the tail of the truck. So we can probably be sure that the industrial unit on the edge of Lyon is the place where the packages of heroin are broken down into smaller quantities and sent on to the wholesalers and dealers. Vile Afghan dope ruining decadent Western youth as they see it. But the detail of the drug side of the operation isn't much help to us. If we let the information get through to Yvonne's bosses they'll be only too pleased to move in and stop it. And what would the Unit do then? Find another route, after all they have almost the price of the bomb already and it won't take much effort to rake in the remainder. More coffee?' Sam went off to refill their cups.

'Thanks Sam. If only we could locate Schmidt, he seems to be the biggest player, the one who holds the purse-strings.'

'And that might be done through the Basel side of the operation or by us here if there are any calls that can be traced back to Frankfurt or wherever Schmidt lurks. And then there's the Irish link with the Unit, the Continuity IRA deal that fell through. We've had feelers out for three weeks now but there's been no response at all. It may be that the Irish outfit doesn't exist any longer. As you know we're due at Mark Gould's place in Valence on our way back down the *Autoroute* this afternoon, perhaps he'll have something useful on the Irish connection that will get that moving.'

'I was wondering, Sam, if there was an emergency in

Cassis, so that Mustafa had to contact his bosses urgently ... well that might give us something to go on, he might have to be less careful in his communications than he has been so far and with our bugs and the police surveillance ... '

'We might get a fix on Schmidt? Yes, it's worth a shot. We'll have to think up a suitable emergency. When's the next container due in Marseille? A week's time? Yes, that might give us something to use. Well let's get off to the Englishman's place and see what his lifestyle's like. You've got a copy of the route in your pocket? Good. It's down to the south of Valence and just across the Rhône in what's called the Ardèche. I've been wanting to see his home since we first met him.'

***

An hour and a quarter later they drew up in front of Mark Gould's house, pleasantly located on rising ground to the west of the Rhône. A short flight of steps led up to the deep blue front door with a spotless brass door knocker and letterbox. The threshold too was brass clad and gleamed fiercely. As Sam remembered it, that was how the Brits ran their army with plenty of spit and polish to keep the other ranks in line and morale high. The Israel Defence Force operated rather differently. Sam rang the door bell and, as they waited, they turned away to enjoy the view of the river in the distance. On the other side of the driveway were some token vines, not enough to constitute a vineyard but enough to tell the visitor that the owner was serious about wine. They were reminiscent of the few rows of vines next to the visitors' car park at the Golan Winery at Kazrin.

Sam had expected a servant to answer the door but it

was Mark himself, apologetic that his "man", Antoine, had gone home early and wouldn't be there to attend to them. He had discarded his jacket but not his tie. Sam wondered if he ever appeared without one. 'Sorry about that chaps, but Antoine did get a bite ready for us before he left. But first a glass of wine, there's a rather nice *Saint-Péray* in the fridge, it's a sparkling wine, the grapes are Marsanne and Rousanne. Would you like to try it? If not there's an extraordinary *Hermitage Blanc* in there as well.'

'We had a couple of glasses of very ordinary *Vin Ordinaire* with lunch, so we mustn't ... '

'Come now, Sam, this *Hermitage Blanc* is rather special, no that's underselling it. It's 1942 in fact, a gorgeous vintage. Funny stuff these *Hermitage* whites they can outlive the reds ... some of them can be pretty grim for the first few years but after 10, 20 years or even longer - why, this one's been round for all of 60 years, made when France was in the hands of the Hun - they can be absolutely wondrous! Yes, it will have to be the *Hermitage* and you aren't in a hurry to go are you? After a decent meal you'll be fit for the road and if not we've got plenty of bedrooms here and you can be on your way after breakfast, that's if the Scotch Malt in the porridge doesn't push up the breathalyser reading too far.' He was an extrovert and an enthusiast - you couldn't help liking him and he was the most hospitable and generous of men.

'I think we would be disappointing you Mark if we didn't join you in a glass or two of your ancient *Hermitage*. Go ahead and open it we'll see whether our palates can begin to do it justice.'

'Come through into the salon and make yourselves comfortable, you've been on the road for quite a while today I imagine.' He led them into a generously proportioned room with an assortment of armchairs and sofas. 'Make yourselves comfortable while I get the wine. If you need the bathroom it's in the hallway, the second door on the right.'

Dov flopped into an armchair while Sam walked to the French windows and took in the view of the garden and the river in the distance. Mark seemed to be doing well from dealing in wine. Oh to be an English *négociant* in this corner of France! Yet he knew that amid all this comfort and an occupation that he obviously relished Mark lived with the recurring demons of his tour of duty in Ireland. No, Sam didn't begrudge him this small *château*. He wondered whether there had ever been a Mrs Gould to share it with him, certainly there was no sign of a female presence round the place.

Mark returned with the bottle and produced a waiter's corkscrew from a sideboard drawer. He drew the cork and lifted it to his nose to check that, despite its considerable age it was in good order. Then he took three glasses from the same sideboard, pouring a little into one glass which without any show of theatricality he tasted before half filling the other glasses and handing them to Dov and Sam. Finally he half filled his own glass.

'Treat it with reverence gentlemen. There's not too much of it around. I was given it by a lady of my acquaintance who found it in the depths of the basement of her *château* along with hundreds of other bottles of great vintage wines. That find certainly solved her financial problems!'

Dov waited for Sam to comment but it was to him that Gould addressed his question, 'Well Dov what do you make of it?'

Dov guessed at an appropriate response, 'Rich,

intense and ... splendidly fruity. It's amazing to think that it's been sitting for all of 60 years waiting to be uncorked and poured out.' From Mark's face he was relieved to deduce that he hadn't said anything too stupid.

'And you Sam?'

'Apples and pears ... there's a hint of nuts,' he took another sip and after a pause added, ' and there's something herbal, it's only very slight but it's there I think.'

'Pretty good Sam, your palate has been trained I can tell, no offence to you Dov but Sam's the one who's got the background. He hasn't been wasting his time at the Golan Winery and for that matter neither have his colleagues at Kazrin, they're certainly raising the standing of Israeli wine in the trade – I've recently done a little research on the subject. Well, how has today's pursuit of Mr Malik gone?' He looked in Dov's direction, drawing him into the conversation.

'A success I think, we followed through to a depot on the edge of Lyon and Mustafa followed the truck into the yard.'

Sam broke in, 'Which wasn't very clever. If I'd been watching the truck's tail I'd have stopped short of the entrance to the depot and watched for anyone showing up in the next few minutes after arrival. As it was if the police had been keeping the place under surveillance they would have pounced and nabbed truck, container, dope and Mustafa all together.'

'So where does that get the two of you?'

'I don't think that the mechanics of the heroin smuggling and distribution are very relevant to our investigation. We could shop them to the Police and Customs but that would only send them off to take another route for the dope and they haven't got far to go to find the price of the goods they're after from the

Ukraine. We want to keep Mustafa there in Cassis. We'll have to consider how we can create some sort of emergency for Mustafa Malik at our end and see whether that makes him contact his bosses in a way that locates them for us.'

Gould nodded, 'That makes good sense though it's a shame not to be able to put dope smugglers behind bars, still first things first. My good news, besides the 1942 *Hermitage Blanc*, is that we've got another contact point for the Continuity IRA. I know you haven't had any response from the one we gave you last month and I just hope this one's up to date and effective.' He took an envelope from the sideboard and gave it to Sam. 'The question's the same but the telephone number's different. And again I caution you to make no mention of who gave the particulars to you - I'm very comfortable and happy here and I don't want some wild Irishman out of my past leaping up from behind my vines and shooting me dead on my front door step!'

Sam had visions of Mark slumped down on the brass threshold, bloodstains there would never do! He kept the thought to himself. 'I can and I do give you my solemn word on that Mark. We're more than grateful to you and your masters.'

'Former masters, Sam. All that's behind me, I'm a simple British expat earning a crust as a *négociant*.'

'I somehow don't think that word *simple* applies to you in any of its senses, Mark. But I take your point.'

Gould smiled in acknowledgement of Sam's compliment. 'Well how about a light *repas* and then a look at my *Saint-Joseph* vineyards along the road.'

'Sounds a great idea!' Despite their late lunch Dov was always ready for a decent meal. He suspected that what Mark had awaiting them would be considerably superior to the average snack and he wasn't disappointed. The side table in the dining room was replete with a variety of dishes and it was clear that Mark had gone to some expense and trouble to provide this *repas* for them - though the effort had no doubt been expended by Antoine, his "man" - it was no mere snack that was on offer.

'Help yourselves and don't be afraid to go back and take more, I'm here on my own at the moment and I don't want to be eating it for the rest of the week. I've majored on fish, fresh salmon and smoked trout, so it shouldn't clash with your dietary rules though it probably won't be *Glatt Kosher*.'

'It will do admirably, Mark. Thanks for your consideration, you're a fine host.'

'It's a real pleasure to have you here Sam and you Dov, you'll have to bring the ladies and the youngsters here some time when my fiancée Karine is around, at the moment she's scouting out new supplies in Chile.

'Now fill your plates and take your seats at table. I'll get the remainder of the *Hermitage Blanc* from the salon and we'll ration our drinking to that one bottle. Over our meal we can talk about the Continuity IRA and the other Republican outfits you might encounter. I'm hoping that the bait of giving one in the eye to the 16th September Unit will be sufficient encouragement for them to help you - and let you get back out of Ireland in safety! I hope you don't mind the music, I like to have something in the background.' It was very much background but Sam soon detected what could only be Jewish themes played by a small group including a clarinet - another indication of Mark Gould's hospitality and welcome – it was clearly *Klezmer* music.

***

Just after 10.00 p.m. Dov and Sam arrived back at the *Domaine du Cheval Rouge*. Mark Gould's *repas* and an enthusiastic tour of his vineyards had kept them for longer than they had planned but they had enjoyed him sharing with them his expertise in viniculture and vinification and they had also spent a while swapping military stories. They were more than ready for bed - tomorrow they would give thought to prompting Mustafa to breach telephone security. They had seen him following the truck straight into the depôt - if he could be careless in that way he might, in an emergency, be careless with his communications.

Chapter 21

Wednesday 1st August 2001

After breakfast the next day Sam and Dov sat at the kitchen table at the *Domaine* working through the transcripts of the latest 'phone taps. Generally they seemed to be of little consequence, Mustafa was not involving himself in much more than the trivia of an idle life - calls to order magazines and CDs, calls to women he knew or whose acquaintance he wished to make. Here and there they found possible small nuggets, information that might be useful - long distance and international calls. The French police had done their work for them, identifying the other parties to the calls. Yet after a couple of hours they had found nothing that appeared to lead anywhere useful apart from confirmation that the next consignment was due into Marseille on the 7th of the month.

'So how do we get him to contact his boss in a hurry, Sam?'

'Yes, as we were saying yesterday we need to provide the impetus by giving him an emergency to report - no good leaving it to chance!'

'But nothing so dangerous that he might pull out or be pulled out by his masters - we don't want him making a run for it do we?'

'No, that's certainly true. Let's try to analyse what he does when the containers with their drugs come in through Marseille. First of all he keeps a weather eye open for any Customs interest in the container, I suspect that there will be some genuine imports in them with the dope hidden towards the back. Then he follows it for its journey to Lyon to ensure that no one else is taking a special interest in it. So far the French authorities haven't troubled him, largely, it seems, because he also has a legitimate line of business with containers that are completely in the clear - North African basket work and that sort of thing. That's all the French police and Customs have been able to connect him with. We must have been lucky, the list we found in his desk on our visit doesn't tally with anything the Marseille Police have for his shipments. And it was well worth keeping an eye on him with yesterday's run to Lyon.'

'I just hope he didn't realise we were following him, Sam. I hope his eyes were so much on the tail of the truck that he didn't see us back down the road.'

'I don't think so. The hire cars couldn't be traced back to us and we managed to keep a good way down-wind of him. Once we'd worked out what was happening it wasn't too difficult to keep out of the way.'

'And, so far as we know, that yard on the edge of Lyon was the container's final destination.'

'Yes, unless it was taken on further with another truck and another watcher. But the fact that it was taken off the trailer and into the warehouse suggests otherwise. My guess is that Lyon's a big enough market for them - probably any excess goes on to Paris and, then, that little aerodrome is close to hand. But distribution's not our problem or concern. The main thing, Dov, is that we've managed to sort out Mustafa's personal rôle in part of the enterprise.'

'So if he were unable to be there for his escort duties ... '

'They might have to find someone else to take his place and that might need a 'phone call from our friend to his boss?'

'It might *but* perhaps they already have alternative arrangements in place, someone for Mustafa to 'phone as a stand-in.'

'Yes, there must be a fall-back plan.'

'In which case we'd have to deal with the stand-in as well as Mustafa, Dov, but making it look purely coincidental!'

'However else, Sam? But we'd need to be able to locate him or her. It could be that they would simply turn up at the Lançon-Provence service area make contact with the truck driver and head north as Mustafa did yesterday.'

'Except that Mustafa has *first* to keep an eye on things at the Marseille Container Port. If there is a stand-in and he's not local then he'll have to come here to deal with the first part of the surveillance operation. That being so Mustafa might want a word with him to give him a briefing. Considering Mustafa's sense of self importance I suspect that he'd insist on doing that anyway. It wouldn't do for him to have some outsider simply stepping into his shoes without Mustafa giving him his orders, keeping control of things.'

'I think you've got something there, Sam. Incapacitate Mustafa and then keep an ear open for his 'phone calls and an eye open for visitors. Followed by a little further incapacitation and an even sharper ear open to Mustafa's 'phone calls!'

'And the next container's due in ... '

'In six days time. Enough time to discuss with Paris Station what to use on Mustafa and his stand-in and enlist any help we need. For some reason the Marseille Station people want to keep out of this.'

***

Saturday 4th August 2001

Three days later they were back around the table together with Tanya and Michael from the Paris Station of Mossad. If direct contact were to be made with Mustafa those involved had to be strangers who would then disappear from the scene as quickly as they had come. A couple of photographs of Mustafa lay before them on the table. Tanya was to be the bait, a busty blonde of a little over medium height, it was unlikely that Mustafa would fail to notice her.

'And how should I dress to attract him, I've brought a selection from my wardrobe.' Tanya indicated a suitcase and suit bag next to the kitchen door.

'As short as possible, I should think. The shortest of your mini-skirts and a tight tee shirt will do fine.'

'So I'm to be one of Mustafa's *Jupettes*?'

'That's right - make it a skirt that's short enough to catch his eye, Tanya.'

'And how do I find him, or rather how does he find me?'

'There should be no problem there, he's usually to be found around six in the evening in a bar down by the harbour, the *Bar du Port*. He sits there with a glass of wine talent spotting. A *jupette* and those legs ought to do the trick! Don't overdo it though, he likes to feel he's making the running, seducing rather than being seduced!'

'From your description of the man, Sam, I'm pretty certain I don't want to be seduced by him and I assume that once I've doctored his drink I'm free to leave.'

'Yes, promise him another meeting - the day after tomorrow, if you like, and by that time the last thing that'll be interesting him is short skirts and long legs.'

'And Michaerl, remember we don't want him written off completely, only written out for a few days.'

***

Sunday 5th August 2001

Tanya got to the *Bar du Port* a little before 5.30 p.m. and ordered an ice cream and a Pernod. She sat to one side, under the shade of the awning, and quickly disposed of the ice cream, indicating to the waiter that the dish could be removed: eating ice cream was hardly a sophisticated activity likely to appeal to Mustafa. She diluted the Pernod and sipped it, deciding that Arak from Ashkelon was a superior member of the family of aniseed drinks found round the shores of the Mediterranean. The thought brought a momentary longing for home, to be back in Israel, that is, not Russia where she had been born. But with the longing came the realisation that her work in Europe was to enable Israelis to live in peace - or as near as they could get to it with the present Palestinian unrest.

A strange job this, she was the bait in the honey trap for the unwary. She had done it often and with considerable success, Arabs, Europeans, sometimes Germans and Austrians. She didn't mind the work even if she had to become intimate with her victims, after all Mossad had recruited her from a Tel Aviv massage parlour. She wondered which of her clients there had been Mossad's talent spotter. She smiled to herself at the attitude of the young man who had interviewed her for Mossad, it had been very much an arm's length interview - as if he were afraid of catching something from her. Fortunately there had been nothing to catch and she very much hoped it would stay that way. She had told him in no uncertain terms that if he wanted to recruit her he had better show more respect to a former Moscow University language teacher forced by lack of other work into her present employment and, to her surprise, he had done so and been most apologetic at the end of the interview.

She glanced at her watch, 5.50 p.m., she touched up her lipstick and arranged her legs to best advantage, making sure that her skirt was no lower than she felt decency demanded. She was wearing a white mini-skirt and a tight fitting dark blue blouse. The blouse wasn't low cut but to someone sitting in the empty chair on her left it gave, through the gap that the buttons couldn't quite close, occasional tantalising glimpses of her white bra. Her glass was empty and she ordered another Pernod. One of her attributes was that she could down a substantial quantity of alcohol without it having much effect on her, which was useful when she needed to drink someone under the table. She noticed that the waiter couldn't resist a lingering look at her legs. She smiled at him and decided she quite liked him. There was a gentle, melancholy reticence about him and she wondered whether she could rid him of it if she tried.

6.00 p.m. had passed and she was beginning to wonder whether Mustafa was going to appear when she saw him on his way along the harbour-side. She wondered whether to concentrate on him or on her drink and decided to give him a quick glance and then look away, it was more likely to give him the feeling of being the hunter rather than the hunted. It worked and a moment later he was there standing beside her table, addressing her in French, 'If you're alone Mademoiselle and not expecting company, perhaps you would be willing to allow me to join you at your table?'

She looked up and smiled, 'So long as you don't intend to take advantage of an innocent young woman.'

Her attire and her come-hither smile belied her assertion of innocence and lured him on. He was already imagining a night together in his splendid circular bed back at the *Villa des Pins*. He sat down on the chair on her left, 'Well Mademoiselle, your innocence is very attractive and must, of course, be respected. To be honest I'm a little tired of being on my own and I'm in need of company to brighten up the evening. You look as though you could cheer me up and add a little interest to my evening drink. By the way, you're occupying the table I take most evenings at this time, so I felt justified in asking for the pleasure of sharing it with you. What's that you're drinking? It looks to me like Pernod.'

'And you're quite right, it is Pernod. What do you usually drink at this table?'

'One of the dry white wines from Cassis but as this is a special evening, special, that is, on account of your company, it will be Champagne.' He looked around,

'Waiter a half - no make it a whole bottle - of Lançon Black Label, and two glasses.' The young waiter nodded and Tanya was conscious that he was still having difficulty keeping his eyes from continuing his inspection of her legs. She caught his envious glance in Mustafa's direction. Yes, she liked the look of the young man, there was something about him that attracted her, a strangely compelling mixture of innocence and longing. She resolved to pay a second visit to the *Bar du Port*. She needed a break from following the commands of her Mossad masters in these matters. She wanted to be in charge of her own sexuality for a change. Yes, she might find it satisfying to give the waiter what Mustafa, despite all his hopes, would not be getting, not from her anyway!

'By the way, I'm Mustafa - Mustafa Malik.'

'And I'm Tanya.' She was happy with her real name and saw no reason to change it for her encounters. 'You're not French or are you?'

'No I'm Lebanese, though when bedlam broke out there I had to move out. First it was Cyprus, then here. This is a good place if you like food, wine and sailing.'

'And women?' She had noticed his eye on her blouse and couldn't refrain from making the comment.

'Yes, *and* women. Though you're something special, if I may say so.'

'Thank you, Mustafa. So you enjoy the idle life here?'

'Idle? No not all the time anyway. I'm in business, import/export and that sort of thing. I've got to find some way of paying for my lifestyle, you know. Work hard, play hard! That's my motto. And having good friends to share it with. How about you, Tanya? What do you do?'

'I do some fashion modelling, not that I *need* to work - a couple of years ago an aunt left me enough to keep me going - but it's sometimes good to work for a change. One shouldn't be *too* idle - just idle enough for pleasure but not boringly so, don't you think so?'

'Perhaps you'd let me photograph you some time,

Tanya. My yacht would make a nice setting.'

'You have a yacht? Is it in the harbour?'

'No. I keep the *Viagra* in *Port Miou*, just round the corner from here. You know the place?'

'The *Viagra*!' She was laughing loudly, 'Is that what you call your yacht?' Her foot touched his leg momentarily, 'You don't look as though you need *Viagra* to get you going.'

'To be frank, I don't - but it seemed a good name for the boat. It gets people talking all right! And it made you laugh so it must be good!'

'I'd like to see your boat sometime, Mustafa. Yes, a photo session on the *Viagra* sounds a fun sort of thing. I'll do it when I'm free.'

'You're not free at the moment?'

'No, I'm very expensive.' She watched his face. He clearly wasn't sure what she was telling him. 'I mean it's nice to be spoiled by an attractive man.'

'Then you must let me spoil you, Tanya. When will you be free?'

'This evening I'm off to Lyon for a photo session there tomorrow afternoon and I'll be back in two days time. I could see you then, if you would like that.'

'Of course. First a drink here, I'll make sure that the waiter keeps this table for us and for no one else, then dinner at my favourite restaurant. After that we play it by ear.'

She wasn't too sure where the ear came into his bedroom activities. She pressed her foot in assent against his. 'Yes, I'd like that, Mustafa. I'd like that *very* much. It's a shame I've got to go off to Lyon this evening, I think we could have had quite a time together, but it won't spoil with waiting, will it?' She touched his hand and smiled. She knew she had him where she wanted, she could do whatever she liked with him. In a way, she was beginning to think that, if she hadn't known what he was involved in, she wouldn't have minded spending the night with him. Really he wasn't as repulsive as she had expected, in fact he wasn't repulsive at all but on the surface rather pleasant. But then wasn't that typical of life, some of the most dangerous people were, despite their evil purposes, rather attractive and even quite likeable. And knowing what she did of his drug smuggling and that somehow he was a danger to her people - though she hadn't been told exactly how, she was guessing that the money bought guns and explosives for some terrorist outfit - she knew she would be prepared to kill him with her bare hands if ordered to do so.

They had each had a couple of glasses of Champagne and it had contributed to their shared sense of well being. She just hoped the Champagne would last long enough for her purposes. Then she saw Michael approach and take a table next to theirs. The waiter appeared and Michael ordered a mineral water and a coffee. She remembered that he was a strict tea-totaller and she wondered what he thought about working with a state paid whore.

'Tell me about your business, Mustafa.' The request seemed an appropriate one from a girl who enjoyed being spoiled by attractive businessmen.

'We bring in baskets and rugs from Morocco and other parts of North Africa. Then we send electrical goods back in the containers. It keeps me in the lifestyle to which I've become rather easily accustomed - a couple of decent cars, the *Viagra*, the *Villa des Pins* and, *of course*, a couple of servants to look after the house and the garden.'

Her foot was touching his leg again and she noticed him flush slightly. With a warm smile she said quietly, 'I really am sure, Mustafa, that you don't need any *Viagra* to make you function adequately.'

Her comment was received with a look of satisfaction on his part. 'Unfortunately you will have to wait to find that out, Tanya. Unless, of course, you feel able to postpone tomorrow's photo shoot.'

Michael came over, nodded formally to Tanya and addressed Mustafa, 'Aren't you the owner of a 10 metre yacht berthed at *Port Miou*? The *Viagra*, isn't it? I'm Mick Ryan, by the way.'

Mustafa rose and shook hands, 'Mustafa Malik, good to meet you. Yes, the *Viagra's* mine. You like it? You're a yachtsman too?'

'Fine yacht, I'd say. Yes, I sail back in the USA. My boat's berthed in Maine. It's quite a coastline there.' As they conversed Tanya's hand moved over Mustafa's glass and dropped the contents of a small glass phial into his Champagne. It would incapacitate him but do nothing worse.

Their yachting conversation over, Michael went in search of the waiter to pay his bill and Mustafa returned to his seat. 'Sorry about the interruption, Tanya. I always enjoy a chat about boats, especially when mine's the 10 metre ocean-going craft that's the envy of the whole *calanque*. Wait till you see her, wait till you see the *Viagra*! More Champagne?' He filled their glasses and quickly drained his. Her errand for Mossad was now accomplished and, in all probability, she would never see Mustafa again, that was the nature of her work. They continued to talk about boats and the sea until she looked at her watch and announced that she had to be on her way to catch the train to Lyon. No, she had her car and didn't need a lift. Yes, of course, she'd see him here in a couple of days at the same time and at the same table, she couldn't think of anything nicer.

***

Monday 6th August 2001

The next evening Tanya was again at the *Bar de Port* for an ice cream and a Pernod. She wore the same white mini-skirt but had opted for a white tee shirt to accompany it. Good, it was the same young waiter and again his eyes were on her legs. She had noted his name from the slip on which her order had been recorded the previous day, that would help to establish rapport with him, to make him realise that she had noticed him. Fortunately she was the only one on that side of the bar and she hoped they could talk without him being too awkward.

'Bon soir, Mademoiselle, une glace et un Pernod, ce soir aussi?'

'Well done, Pierre, it's good to be remembered.'

He flushed and responded, 'It's my job to remember what my customers like.'

'Excellent, Pierre. My name's Tanya, by the way. And what time do you finish work here tonight.'

He looked surprised, 'Late, past midnight, I fear. Though tomorrow's my day off.'

'That's fine, I just wondered if you would like to give me a guided tour of the area, show me the cliff paths and the places to see. How about that for tomorrow? We could eat out and give you the chance to be waited on for a change. How does that sound?'

'Incroyable, Mademoiselle!' His eyes were on her legs again, she hoped he was interested in more than just her legs. He paused a moment. 'That I would like greatly. I will give you my address and telephone number when you leave. And you will wear walking shoes and wear jeans as the going may be rough in places and that,' his eyes indicated her skirt, 'would not be very suitable.'

'Fine I'll dress properly for our walk, Pierre. *A demain!*'

She enjoyed the ice and the drink but didn't stop for a second Pernod as the bar was filling up. She caught Pierre's attention with a smile, *'Et maintenant, Pierre, l'addition et l'adresse, s'il vous plâit!'*

***

Tuesday 7th August 2001

Pierre had been right, stout walking shoes and jeans were necessary. The weather was glorious with a clear blue sky, marked only by vapour trails. He had shown considerable reserve when Tanya had called for him earlier that morning and, at first, she had found it hard work to keep the conversation going. But, before long, they had become at ease with one another. As the walk had progressed he had lost himself and his inhibitions as he explained to her what she was seeing in the way of geology, bird life and vegetation. Pierre knew the area well and was pleased to enthuse about it to Tanya. They had walked beyond Cap Canaille and then retreated from the path to a quiet spot among the trees and scrub. Their picnic lunch over, they lay back on the grass, relaxing and enjoying the warmth of the sun and the sound of bees busily gathering nectar from the clover and other flowers. Below them the sound of the sea was mingled with the cries of the gulls. Snatches of more musical birdsong reached them on a gentle breeze. Now they were quiet together, quiet and yet comfortable.

'Now use your ears and listen, Tanya, see how many different sounds you can hear.' They were quiet for some minutes, perhaps five or ten, when he asked, 'Well what did you hear?'

She catalogued the sea and its gulls, the bird song and the drone of bees adding, 'Walkers with a dog or perhaps two dogs but fortunately they kept out of our way.'

'But for me, Tanya, the best sound was your quiet breathing ... so close, so very close to me.' His hand grasped hers and he raised himself on his elbow and looked down at her with that gentle smile that somehow spoke of intense longing.

She smiled back and authorised him to proceed with the words, 'Please, Pierre, please.' He responded tentatively at first, not believing his good fortune, then satisfied that she really wanted it, he let his kiss linger. His hand was on her breast. She sat up and unhooked her bra, 'That should help, Pierre.'

'You mean it?'

'Of course, I do, Pierre.' As he slipped his hand under her tee shirt she reached down to his jeans, unbuckling his belt and undoing the zip. She let her hand explore. 'I like what's in here!'

He coloured but succeeded in moving her bra out of the way, beginning his own voyage of discovery. 'Tanya, it's like a dream. Tell me it's real ... You know, I see so many pretty women in the bar and they're all inaccessible, pleased to show off their bodies and to tantalise. It's like they're saying, "You're only a waiter, you can look for a moment but my body's for men with money, not paupers like you." And I thought that you were just like all the others.' He was crying quietly, tears of happiness.

'You've not done this for a long time?'

'No, Tanya, not for a very long time. Tell me you're real that you're not a dream.'

'I think that your hands and your penis are assuring you of that, Pierre. But this isn't the best place for intimacy. But let me give you a treat ... you've got a handkerchief? Good you'll need it in a moment, we don't want your jeans stained. I suspect you'd like me to bring you to a climax before we leave?'

'I'd be stupid to say no wouldn't I but what about you, don't you want to come?'

'Perhaps you'd like to come back to my apartment? We'll see how we get on together there.'

'Please, Tanya. I can't think of any better idea.'

'Neither can I, Pierre. But first your afternoon treat.'

She rubbed gently so as not to hurry things but it was only a minute or two before his orgasm came and their lips met for another lingering kiss.

'That was good, Pierre? Well I think we can do better still without our clothes in the way, don't you? Let's tidy up and be on our way. Thank you for bringing me here, it's been a wonderful afternoon. When do you have to be back at work? 11.00 a.m. tomorrow? That gives us, let me see, 21 hours together, I hope you have enough stamina, Pierre!'

They began the walk back to Cassis and he slipped his arm around her waist – a lot had happened in the last half hour and he still could hardly believe his good fortune.

***

The apartment had been empty when they arrived. Michael, who had been warned to clear his things out and make himself scarce, had retreated to the *Domaine* to discuss the situation with Sam and Dov. She took Pierre by the hand, 'We're a bit warm and sweaty after our exertions. I think a shower is called for and in the interests of water economy it might be a good idea to shower together. You approve, I can see that, so lets strip off and freshen up.'

They stood in the bathroom relishing their view of one another's bodies, then she took his hand and led him to the shower.

'Erect again, Pierre! I wonder what you're expecting next.'

He smiled his gentle smile, 'And I wonder what *you* are expecting, Tanya. I somehow think it's the same thing for both of us, at least I hope so.'

'We'll just have to see, won't we?'

The powerful shower engulfed them with a torrent of warm water and their hands, unrestrained by clothing, explored one another while their lips made and remade contact. She turned the water off and stepped back, finding soft white towels. 'Lets dry off and see what we can do next. I've got some condoms in the bathroom cabinet. You can choose what you fancy ... different types for different purposes. Now, if you would like a drink first, slip on a bath robe and come into the kitchen.

***

The doors from the bedroom onto the balcony were open and, in the last of the evening light, Cap Canaille was just visible in the distance. Moonlight would soon be reflected on the calm sea. They lay contentedly together .

'You've been making up for lost time, Pierre?'

'Not lost time. Time waiting for this, time waiting for you, Tanya.'

Her hand moved to his penis and she asked the question she had wanted to ask as soon as she had seen him naked before her, 'Pierre, are you Jewish?'

'Yes, but don't hold it against me, Tanya.'

'No, I don't think I'd do that ... you see, I'm Jewish as well!' His answer was all that she had hoped for. What had started out as a routine assignment had turned, for her into something very special, something very different. She just hoped her Mossad colleagues would understand because she was going to be much less useful to them from now on, indeed she would be saying farewell to her employment with them. Still she could offer to recruit a successor, one or two of the other girls at the massage parlour might be pleased to have a change of employer. Having your work place burnt down by the ultra-orthodox, or whichever group it was that had resorted to arson to clean up Tel Aviv, was quite an incentive to look for a safer job - that and the risks inherent even at the best of times in such an occupation.

***

As they had expected, two days after his meeting with Tanya, Mustafa made a telephone call to a Marseille number. He had been unwell for a couple of days and needed Saeb to attend to a job for him. Saeb should call that evening at the *Villa des Pins* for a briefing. Yvonne had quickly identified the recipient and his address for them. So they had located Mustafa's stand-in, now to put *him* out of the way. and see whether Mustafa would then call his boss.

Their problem of how to remove Saeb was solved within minutes by Yvonne herself. She called to tell them she had the answer and, when she appeared an hour later, it was to announce that Saeb had a criminal record of dealing in stolen cars. In the past five years he had done time, not once but twice, for the offence. She would have him taken in for questioning on a similar matter - with the number of cars stolen daily there would be no problem in finding several thefts about which to quiz him. The attention of the Marseille police had shifted away from Mustafa for the moment, there was always too much work on hand and most investigations didn't get the time they merited. This was good news for Sam and his team - it would keep Yvonne's colleagues out of their hair, or rather out of Mustafa's, for the time at any rate.

They discussed the way in which the prospect of Saeb's arrest could be engineered and decided at last that it would have to be on the basis of Mustafa's telephone call. Sooner or later someone at police HQ would review the transcripts of the 'phone taps and it would be noted that Yvonne had had access to them. If she were to initiate Saeb's arrest without reference to Mustafa's 'phone call someone might well put two and two together and start asking why she had kept quiet about the connection. Fortunately there was nothing in the transcript to indicate the nature of the job that Saeb was to oversee or the date and time. That information remained exclusively in the hands of Sam and his team.

'It'll please my boss, he likes to have something happening on these cases even if it really amounts to precious little.' The Marseille Police functioned like many other such organisations with a good deal simmering quietly on the back burner, going nowhere.

Sam advised caution, 'Don't grill him too hard and don't make too much of his connections with Mustafa - indeed you can let him know that you're aware of his visit to Cassis but pretend ignorance of his destination here. And give him plenty of opportunity to consult with his lawyer in private. In that way we can be sure that word will get back to Mustafa of his deputy's inability to escort the next consignment in two days time.'

She returned to Marseille to put Saeb's arrest in hand and to dine in the city with Dov later that evening. Over dinner she was able to report that Saeb was already sweating it out in a cell at Marseille Police HQ and that she would be questioning him at around 10.00 p.m..

It worked according to plan. Later that evening Saeb's advocate called on him at the Police Station and, at a little after midnight, Mustafa received his call from the advocate. Saeb had been arrested in connection with a stolen car enquiry, the Police knew that he had been in Cassis, but evidently they had temporarily lost him there as they had no idea whom he had been visiting. Mustafa's response was a terse, 'Thank you,' and instructions to the advocate to put the frighteners on Saeb to make him keep his mouth shut. Evidently he did this effectively, as Yvonne was able to report the next afternoon that at her second session with Saeb, which had followed a further visit from the advocate, Saeb had been a very frightened man indeed.

Sam was later pleased to relay this information to Tanya, who had defended Mustafa as "not all bad" at the debriefing session. 'That's your Lebanese gentleman friend, Mr Mustafa Malik, for you Tanya. If he and his henchmen know how to make a tough like Saeb wince you can be sure he'd not be too gentle with the likes of you if you got in his way!'

'I don't intend to get involved with Mustafa, though I'm not sure how I'll avoid bumping into him when I'm seeing Pierre.'

'Well just take care, Tanya, and don't undo the help you've been to us, that's all.'

They sat back and waited and, sure enough, Mustafa made the expected International call. He made it from a pre-pay mobile. And it was a Mossad bug in the office at the *Villa des Pins* together with a spot of luck that got them what they were after. Evidently the call was to another mobile which was not functioning well. It was frustrating, they could hear Mustafa but not the other party to the call. Evidently Mustafa was being told to call another number which was working. They couldn't hear the number given to Mustafa and were despairing of achieving anything when they heard him saying the number to himself as he redialled the call. He counted in Arabic but Sam was able to translate and then check that he had got it right afterwards from the tape they'd made of the interception. From Mustafa's side of the conversation it appeared that another member of the 16th September Unit would be sent and would be with Mustafa within 12 hours. Almost certainly it would be a mere functionary but, nevertheless, they would try to follow him back to his base. More important was the German landline number that Mustafa had unwittingly given them. There, in all likelihood, was to be found the man directing the operation, the one who held all the strings and was co-ordinating the task.

They had made progress ... well perhaps. Only time would tell. The call had been made to a Herr Johann Tannenbaum. But to their disappointment the number of the landline turned out to be a pay-phone in a restaurant in Frankfurt-am-Main. They were not a lot nearer to identifying the brains behind the operation or the location of the nerve-centre of the Unit. They would have to consider sending in a Mossad agent to the restaurant with a photo of Jakob Schmidt on the off chance that it was Schmidt who had taken the call and that he was a regular there with an address known to the proprietor of the restaurant. The agent would pass himself off as being from German Security and do his best to scare the restaurateur into saying nothing to Schmidt about the enquiry.

***

Thursday 9th August 2001

And in Paris a defiant Tanya had told the Station Chief that from now on she intended to lead a chaste life, both privately and professionally - she was planning to join a nice Jewish boy with the hope of ending up under the bridal canopy! His disappointment was personal: he had fancied some time with her himself. And why did it have to be now of all times that she had suddenly decided on a life of wedded bliss? Next week his wife was off to their apartment in Menton for a whole month and he had planned to secure some satisfaction for himself during her holiday. Well, like last year, it would have to be one or two of the young Scandinavian women who found their way to Paris at this season to extend their cultural experience. And that young fellow at Mossad HQ would have to start interviewing women from the cat houses of Tel Aviv once again, or perhaps he did so regularly to keep supplies going for their world-wide operations. There were plenty of funny jobs involved in setting up Special Missions! So he gave Tanya his blessing and told her that he would always be delighted to see her or to take a call from her.

You never knew, she might find a chaste life with her young waiter lacking in excitement and once more combine the activities of those two of the oldest professions that had once met up in a Jericho inn some millennia ago.

Chapter 22

Thursday 16th August 2001

'Look, Dov, I sometimes have my doubts about how much Yvonne should be told of what we're doing. Yes, I know that she can't be kept completely in the dark ... she won't co-operate if she feels we're using her and not trusting her ... but just think what will happen if her bosses discover that she's been working with us and passing police information in our direction. She's not Mossad after all, she's got no reason to keep her mouth shut if things get nasty. If she knows she's for the chop she'll sing! Remember the prospect of having old customers for jail companions isn't a pleasant prospect for a police officer and the screws themselves are hardly likely to be very obliging. Just what is it that's causing her to co-operate with us, Dov?' Sam's mood of caution and introspection was due to the current lack of any real progress.

'Partly our relationship, Yvonne and myself. But, its more than that, she's with us, sees the need to help in order to avert a catastrophe. We can rely on her, I give you my word for it. She has access to the police taps and transcripts, that's what's made her so indispensable, Sam.'

'Don't think I'm not grateful to you Dov for recruiting her to our enterprise ... '

'I don't think I recruited her, you know. If I remember rightly you sent me along to her on the assumption that she was one of Mustafa's women of easy virtue. And we fell for one another.'

'And it's possible to fall out of love, Dov! Just, for the purpose of argument, suppose that the two of you did fall out and that she, in a fit of remorse and conscience - after all she's got a good career ahead of her - and perhaps out to get her revenge - decided to come clean with her bosses ... well where would that place us?'

'I see your point, Sam, but that's not going to happen!'

'What you mean, Dov, is that you *hope* it won't happen. In personal relationships you never can be so sure, sure with absolute certainty.'

'And where does that leave me?'

'It leaves you and all of us all having to proceed with care. We think we're onto the leader of the Unit, only time will tell on that, but we still need to have the latest transcripts of the police 'phone taps on Mustafa. There may be more for us to learn from our friend at the *Villa des Pins*.'

'So it's keep the love life going! It's my official instructions, my leader's orders. And who am I to disobey or even think of disobeying for that matter.'

'That's about it Dov, just keep the lady sweet - for the moment anyway. You'll have to think of what you're wanting from your relationship with her when Basel Account is over.'

'What I want is, I think what you would want in the circumstances, Sam. After all I didn't set out to use her, the ... emotional part of the relationship's genuine on both sides ... '

'And lasting, Dov?'

'I hope so, I very much hope so.'

'So when it's all wound up and we say farewell to Cassis and the *Domaine*, what of yourself and Yvonne?'

'Well I like this life, Sam.' He indicated, with a wave of his arm, the house and the vineyards, 'I've no wish to go back to gate duties at Mossad HQ. As you know I'd be more than happy to stay here at Cassis. Then Yvonne could continue for as long as she wanted in the Marseille Police, until she wanted a family, of course.'

'Of course! You've discussed it with her?'

'Not yet, Sam. Perhaps it's a little premature ... '

'Perhaps, but take care that you keep things on a steady keel, we don't want complications.'

'And what can she be told, Sam? I've told her quite a

lot and, after all, she's had a meeting with Peres.'

'Wholly deniable, of course, and she made the trip on false papers which we collected back once we were through Customs at Charles de Gaulle. Just keep quiet about my trip to Ireland, the Brits know but I don't want half of Europe to hear of it.'

'OK, Sam. And I assume that *your* marriage to an SVR agent didn't create any problems?'

'None that couldn't be overcome and she was *ex*-SVR by then.'

'Well at any rate France is a friendly power so far as we're concerned!'

'Friendly? Yes, at times!'

'And at present?'

'Hard to say, Dov. Self interested and commercially driven is perhaps the best summary of the French, after all they first sold nuclear technology to us and then later on to Iraq. Perhaps there's a touch of remorse over Vichy and the unstinting co-operation some of them gave to the Nazis. So we continue to proceed with care and in extreme circumstances evacuate rapidly! And if we have to quit we *all* go and go immediately. Understood?'

'Understood, boss.'

***

'I'm in need of a break, Sam, and I *would* like to find a Russian Church some time.'

'A trip to Paris then, the Russian Orthodox Church there has a good choir. But you know to keep quiet about what we're doing. Take care what you say to other Russians - let them think you're on holiday from Israel, which will be partly true. Not a word about Cassis and the *Domaine*!'

'I can promise that Sam.. I'm so grateful to be out of Moscow with its snoopers making life unpleasant. And grateful to you for both your children, my grandchildren.'

She gave Sam one of her great Russian bear-hugs to emphasise her gratitude. The reference to *his children* was not entirely accurate as only the younger, Ya'akov, was Sam's: Olga, the elder child born in Basel's Women's Hospital, was of different paternity but that in no way affected Sam's love and care for the child of whom he was the adoptive father. So far as he was concerned both were his without distinction.

'But Mum, you don't want to go to Paris alone. I'll come with you.'

'Not with the children, Elizabeth. Esty can come with me if she thinks she would enjoy the trip. How about it Esty?'

'Well I'm not sure ... though the idea of a few days in Paris does sound attractive.'

'It's no trouble at all. You take the TGV from Marseille straight through to Paris and I can get someone from the Paris Station - our Mossad Station that is, not the SNCF's Gare de Lyon - to meet you from the train and take you to your hotel and keep an eye on you while you're there.'

'Keep an eye on us indeed, Sam! Whatever next! We may be mature women but we're certainly not geriatrics needing to be looked after. Of course we'll go and, yes, someone can take us to the hotel. Then we're on our own out on the town - a Russian and an Israeli in Paris. Go ahead and book the train and the hotel for next week for Esty and myself, that's if Esty agrees.'

'Yes, I'll go but ... what about feeding the rest of you. There'll be three hungry mouths, four if you count my son's lady friend, not to mention two children!'

'Don't worry we'll get by, we can cook, after all Dov and I were in the IDF and we survived.'

'You need proper feeding not just "getting by", Sam, survival just isn't good enough! I'll prepare meals for you and freeze them, I'm not having you starving in my absence. After all that's why I'm here at the *Domaine* in the first place. I'll get started on it this afternoon. Oh, I'm quite excited. A trip to Paris!' Esty Levin had a sense of duty and she needed to be needed - she wasn't going to let them down. But a trip to Paris! Now that really would be something to tell her friends in Netanya about!

***

Monday 20th August 2001

Four nights later Mrs Feldman had taken charge of her grandchildren and shooed Sam and Elizabeth out the door to have a quiet meal on their own. 'Not as nourishing as you'd get here, I'm sure, but it'll do the two of you good to have some time on your own - why should Dov and Yvonne get all the romance? So they made for Cassis to have dinner at the *Restaurant Aristide Bruant*. It was new establishment to them, a visit they had been promising themselves for a while.

They ordered a bottle of white wine and asked the waiter to leave them with the menu until they were ready to order. Armed with an English *A to Z Gastronomique* to aid their understanding of the complexities of French cuisine, they worked through the menu. If possible Sam would aim for food that didn't contravene the rules. He had learned in his line of business not to draw attention to his origins. Nothing here would be truly *kosher* but he would avoid the obvious things, like pork and shellfish which were out of bounds. The problem was that French cooking seemed to go out of its way to create problems with its abundant use of butter and cream in meat dishes and the use of shellfish.

A *Civet de Lièvre Diane de Châteaumorand* was rejected: it was likely to include bacon and its sauce, "thickened with the blood of the animal," wouldn't do. Though all this was academic as the meat in the dish was that of the hare, a creature which, though chewing the cud doesn't part the hoof and is therefore declared, like the pig, to be unclean. Sam was reminded of a newspaper report he had once seen of a hog - was it in Indonesia that it had been found? he couldn't quite remember the detail - which chewed the cud and split the hoof. The report had said that "the Jerusalem rabbis" were devoting their attention to this culinary problem, but like so many matters appearing in newspapers they never followed up the report with an announcement of the definitive status of this unusual creature. He would have to rely on his own judgement as a Jerusalem rabbi if one ever chanced to end up on his plate.

And a seemingly straightforward fish dish was also problematic, you could order what you liked and it was more than likely that the tantalisingly tasty sauce would contain shellfish, the produce of the sea but "without fins and scales" and therefore forbidden. And in France there was little chance of finding refuge in the choice of a vegetarian dish: to include such in a menu seemed to the majority of *restaurateurs* to be evidence of gastronomic apostasy.

In their vineyard at the *Domaine* there were indeed several grape varieties but he wasn't going to undo that! The injunction was that they should not sow two varieties in the same vineyard; a Gentile had done that years ago and he and Dov were merely keeping it going.

After ten minutes study and constant reference to their book they settled for *Provençal* tomato and red pepper soup followed by wing of ray grilled with butter and, despite the waiter's efforts at persuading them, without the rich seafood sauce that he assured them would make it "a truly enjoyable experience".

'How do you regard all this Sam, it can make life rather difficult, can't it? Remind me again of your line.'

'Yes, it can make things difficult but in extreme circumstances life comes first - these are secondary rules but rules they are to be applied as best one can in normal circumstances. The rules are there to be obeyed and I try to do so. But it's also a question of identity, a matter of belonging to a people, of remaining in a tradition stretching back several millennia and not giving offence to other Jews ... a counter to the extremes of modern individualism and the behaviour of iconoclastic solipsists.'

'You sound as though you're delivering an address to your students, Sam. Solipsists indeed! You don't have to impress me with your vocabulary, you know.' She laughed and took his hand, 'You impressed me the first time I knowingly saw you, knowing who you really were, back there in the Basel court. Oh, Sylvia had told me about you but seeing you was rather different. A bit like that line from one of your war poems. How does it go? Let me see:

"I was your enemy my friend"

or something like that.'

'The line is:

"I am the enemy you killed my friend."

Not altogether apt but I take your point. The irony is that the one who died, poor Vladimir, was on *your* side. In our individual roles in that business we were enemies but now ... friends, spouses, lovers.'

'And parents,' she said softly. A shadow had passed over her face at the mention of Vladimir and his demise but it was the thought of love and parenthood that had brought a tear to her eye. Happiness and fulfilment were precious indeed.

'And talking of parents, Elizabeth, I'm going to have to be up early to take your mother and Esty to the station in Marseille to get the TGV to Paris. Still that will be no bad thing, it will get me started on my own trip by air. Are you sure you'll be OK on your own? Dov won't be back at the *Domaine* from Paris for two days, I'm not too happy at leaving you there by yourself. It's a nuisance that he's had to go to Paris as well.'

'And why not on my own, Sam? I've been accustomed to looking after myself for long enough, the odd night by myself doesn't distress me at all.'

The soup bowls were removed and the elderly waiter brought the grilled ray, enquiring, yet again, whether they didn't, after all, wish to have the excellent sauce that should accompany the dish. Reluctantly he moved away, marvelling to himself at the austere taste of these Americans and wondering whether they wouldn't soon be asking for tomato ketchup to accompany the fish.

Their conversation turned to the children and, after a sorbet and a coffee, they called for *l'addition* and prepared to leave. The waiter was somewhat mollified by the generosity of their tip and decided that, on balance, he could put up with the eating habits of Americans provided they were generous. As they left Sam caught sight of Mustafa sitting alone at the table next to theirs. That was something he could have done without. The tables were in adjoining alcoves and separated by a screen so that they hadn't seen him arrive in the restaurant and he'd been unusually quiet. As they left Mustafa's eyes followed them or rather they were on Elizabeth, he drank in what he saw and relished it. She was quite a woman, an attractive American with a court record too, whatever that had all been about. He had seen her around the place and out of curiosity had followed her back to the *Domaine* one day, or, rather, to the turning off the main road that led to the *Domaine*.

Elizabeth satisfied herself that the children were sleeping quietly, showered and found Sam waiting for her. He took her in his arms, 'Friend, wife, lover and mother of my children I'm a fortunate man indeed.'

'And I'm a fortunate woman. How long, I wonder before Operation Basel Account is over and we're back home in the Golan with the shadow of doom removed?' It was not often that she articulated her fears about the plans of the Unit.

'Not until they're ready I fear. It's essential for them to

be caught red-handed so that the world is made aware of the dangers posed by stray nuclear devices. So at a guess a under a month. We're working on the basis that their title gives us the date they want to set the thing off.'

'16th September? That's ... let me see ... less than four weeks away.'

'27 days to be precise. I'm counting down and I'm sure they are. They're almost there so far as funds are concerned! Only another half million dollars to go, so the Swiss tell me. We've done well to identify Mustafa's boss and my visit to Ireland may shed some more light on the Unit. Then we watch and wait, our people in Germany are watching for Tannenbaum or Schmidt like hawks, they must have doubled that restaurant's turnover with the number of meals they're taking there looking out for him. Once they're on to him they won't let him slip out of sight. But now my wife and lover let's end the day on a perfect note.' His hands explored her body and he delighted in its smooth undulations and as she responded with vigour and delight, the shadows of the nuclear threat dispelled temporarily for them both.

Their exertions over he murmured, 'Let us sleep now ... ' He was quoting Owen out of context but nevertheless it gave him pleasure to repeat the line. Yet his mind was too active for the sleep of which he spoke. In his mind he was going through their conversation earlier that evening in the restaurant, anxious to reassure himself that he had given nothing away to Mustafa. He hadn't been there when they entered the restaurant and there was no knowing when he had arrived, they must have been too engrossed in their conversation to notice. It was bad luck his being there and at the very next table, still their run of good luck couldn't go on for ever. And he immediately dismissed the idea of "luck", it demeaned both the Deity and man. You did your level best and, at the same time, relied on the Master of the Universe: Sam knew no other method and those principles had stood him in good stead so far.

And alongside him Elizabeth feigned sleep as her mind too was active. She was troubled by her memories of the night four years earlier in Basel when, in self defence, in her bedroom in the Hotel International, she had shot dead Vladimir, her SVR colleague. True the court had, thanks to the evidence from Sam's bugging of the room, returned a verdict of manslaughter and the demonstrators from Women Against Rape had given her a rapturous reception as she left the court, but self forgiveness was harder. Throughout she had been her sternest judge, after all Vladimir had been more than a colleague: before he had become arrogant, coarse and self centred he had been her lover.

At last Elizabeth fell into a disturbed sleep. Sam found that sleep's embrace continued to elude him. In any case he often got by with four hours a night, finding his way downstairs to read in the early hours. He made himself a coffee in the kitchen and took it to the lounge. He had brought his new book of war poems - the Oxford Book of War Poetry - from the case that lay in the bedroom, packed and awaiting his departure for Ireland the next day, no, it would be later that morning. The clock in the hallway chimed two to remind him.

He turned to the back of the book, interested to see what modern poets were writing on war and conflict, modern wars were smaller but no more pleasant than those which in the twentieth century had filled the world stage. A little way into his reading he came across Sheamus Heaney's poem, *The Strand at Lough Beg, In Memory of Colum McCartney.* The footnote told him that McCartney, a relative of Heaney's, had been killed in a random sectarian shooting in the late summer of 1975. Sam's impending departure for Ireland to contact, he hoped, the Continuity IRA, focused his mind:

"What blazed ahead of you? A faked road block?"

The line caught his eye – he trusted that he would meet no such thing on Irish roasds. He finished the poem, read it a second time and put the book down. His coffee was cold and he felt within him the chill of concern. No longer was he a single man, unfettered by responsibilities and free to hazard his life without the burden of care for others. Upstairs slept Elizabeth and the children. He hoped this Ireland trip would prove uneventful apart, of course, from yielding valuable information on the Unit. Once Operation Basel Account was over, *that* would be it - so far as active, front-line duties for Mossad were concerned. *If* he got what he wanted, a senior position at HQ, fine. If not, he told himself, he wouldn't lose much sleep over it - though he'd regret not having the opportunity to shape the Institute's future - he'd return to the vineyards of the Golan with real pleasure and contentment. He went to make another cup of coffee and then took a stroll round the vineyard in the moonlight, strangely out of place in his dressing gown and slippers. The tranquillity was almost tangible. Deep within himself calm now prevailed. So far as he was aware Mustafa would have gained no information of any significance apart, perhaps, from their Jewish identity, but then there must be plenty of other American Jews wandering about the Riviera and Provence and even settling down to live for a while in France. There was nothing to alert Mustafa in that.

***

Mustafa had paid the little blonde and sent her on her way back to Marseille. She hadn't been bad entertainment, nothing wonderful but not too bad a performer. He had wondered whether she was under age but she drove a car, so she must have been old enough. He stood on the balcony, with a glass of Cognac in his hand, thinking of the American woman, Elizabeth whom he had seen earlier in the evening. A woman who was going to be by herself in that large house outside Cassis. He'd be leaving here in a couple of weeks, temporarily at any rate, so this might be his last chance of becoming acquainted with her. He'd think about it. Indeed he had a few thoughts about her as he waited for sleep to envelop him. His official work here was nearly over. Once it was complete and he'd reported to his leader he'd come back here and resume his own personal business of smuggling drugs which he'd been running in parallel with the Unit's efforts. The easy life, with easy women and plenty to spend on his pleasures was irresistible. The American woman might not be in the easy category but he wanted her badly ... and he would see to it that he had her. It would make up for that leggy little blonde, Tanya, who hadn't turned up again at the *Bar du Port*. Damn that stomach upset that had put him out of commission a couple of weeks ago just when he should have been meeting her.

***

Meanwhile Tanya had a problem. She needed to be frank with Pierre, if she hadn't cared, and cared deeply for him it wouldn't have mattered. But not late at night. Tomorrow was his day off, she would speak to him after breakfast.

***

Tuesday 21st August 2001

Pierre found her at the breakfast table reading a book. 'Up early, Tanya?'

'I wasn't sleeping well so I came through here,' she smiled at him aware of the tension inside her.

She poured him a second coffee, filling the large bowl to near the top.

'There's something you need to know, Pierre.'

'It's not to do with Mustafa, is it?'

'It's not that ... but you might want to leave me after what I have to tell you. No, it's not him. But you need to know that I once sold sex for money.'

A look of horror crossed his face, 'Tu est *pros* ... *prostituée*?' He struggled to get the word out.

'*Non, j'étais prostituée*. Not now. It was two years ago. Let me tell you about it, I must explain how it happened.' She tried to read his expression but without much success. 'I lectured at a University in Moscow but succeeded in getting out of Russia to Israel,' she wondered whether she should have mentioned that country but she had to be as open as possible. 'I was having difficulty in finding work when a friend who was also out of work suggested that we join some other Russian girls in running our own *bordel*, our own brothel, as a cooperative. We ended up with six of us girls plus a couple of men we trusted to keep us safe. We had no nonsence from our clients and we were working for ourselves. It wasn't as bad as you might think but it wasn't the best of ways of earning a living either. I was the book keeper ... and so spent less time with our clients, which was something.' She had known it would be difficult to tell him but it was proving harder than she had expected. 'After eighteen months I was recruited to another job and that was what brought me here.'

'Weren't you trying to pick up Mustafa when we first met at the café?'

'Yes and no, Pierre. I had no intention of going to bed with him but what I was up to is something I can't say ... for the moment at least.'

'Under cover work of some kind, you're not working for a gang?'

'No nothing unlawful.' Though she wondered how

lawful Mossad's activities were. 'It's your day off, Pierre. I would like you to go away for as long as you need and then come back and let me know your response to what I've told you. I'm not asking for a decision now, take time, get it right. I'll be here waiting for you. And, by the way, let me assure you, I'm clean. You're in no danger of catching anything unpleasant from me.'

'Yes, Tanya, it's been a shock. I do need to be by myself ... to have time to think ... see you later.' He took his jacket from the coat peg and made for the door, turned back to kiss her on the cheek. And he was gone. She remained sitting at the table and began to cry. Her life of new-found happiness was beginning to unravel, hadn't she been really stupid to tell him about her past?

***

He returned at just after four o'clock to find her still sitting at the table. She saw from his face that he was relaxed, he'd clearly come to a decision.

'Still at the table,Tanya.'

'I didn't feel like doing anything much until I knew your response, Pierre.'

'When you told me this morning, my first reaction was shock and I thought you must be telling me this to get rid of me. I went back to my apartment over the café and sat and thought for some time and then I remembered your face as you told me all this. I knew you were hurting, that it wasn't easy telling me and that that you were doing so out of respect for me ... out of *love*. And as I *know* that I love you I've come back to say thank you for being open, honest and loving.' He took her hands raised her from the chair and kissed her gently. 'Now sit down and we'll talk. Once I'd made up my mind I went to see my uncle who owns the café and told him that I was in love and had moved in with a wonderful girl. He's sent round a bottle of Champagne for us to celebrate,' he indicated a duffel bag he'd brought, 'It's wrapped up up to stay cold, we'll open it shortly once I've told you the rest of my news. My uncle has a restaurant a little way eastwards along the coast. He's always wanted me to manage it but I've never had the confidence. Well I've just told him that we'll manage it together – after all you have book keeping experience, though I didn't tell my uncle where - that's if you're willing, Tanya. We can go and see it tomorrow as my uncle wisely doesn't want us on the road tonight with a half bottle of Champagne inside each of us! Will you come and have a look at the place tomorrow morning? - there's a substantial apartment going with the job.'

She mopped her eyes with a tissue, 'Of course I will, Pierre. I'm so very grateful to you, so very grateful.'

'And I'm grateful to you for being so honest, open and loving to me, Tanya.'

'Well don't delay, you've plenty of experience popping Champagne corks.'

'Tanya, I promise never to say this again, and you have plenty experience of love making.'

'I don't, you know ... plenty of experience of *sex*, yes. But *love making*? That experience has been entirely with you, Pierre.' She found a pair of Champagne flutes in the cupboard and placed them on the table.

He removed the foil and the cage, worked the cork and poured two glasses. 'To our loving future together.'

They chinked glasses and drank.

He began diffidently, 'I wonder, Tanya ... I wonder if you can suggest how we might make love and at the same time ... '

' ... drink Champagne? I've never done so but it should be possible. Move your chair around to the side of the table, no don't turn it, keep it facing the same way, facing me. Now if we place our glasses and bottle on the end of the table ... yes, I think you've got the idea ... '

Chapter 23

Tuesday 21st August 2001

The strong wind gusting in from off the sea caught the car door as Sam opened it and nearly wrenched it from his grasp. In front of him was his destination, O'Toole's Bar, a building that had seen better days. Its decor of dark green walls and reddish brown woodwork was just distinguishable in the prematurely fading light of the wild August evening. Here it felt as though summer had never come. Fifty yards away a solitary street light provided a minute addition to the illumination. Besides his hire car there were six others parked in front of the pub; automatically he noted their numbers and memorised them, you never knew when such information might be useful, even vital. He turned and took in the scene: beyond the parking space was the road he had taken from Londonderry, and past that the narrow beach festooned with seaweed that the receding tide had deposited there. A couple of small boats were drawn up on the beach next to their lobster pots. The cables on a small sailing dinghy rattled insistently against its mast. To the right he could just make out the rise of the land to a high cliff top. The spray from the sea caught his face. No doubt this was a place of beauty on a fine day but not now: tonight it was fully exposed to the elements and those elements were powerful, as another gust told him. He wondered whether this wasn't going to be a waste of time, still he would soon know and time was running short. There was little to be gained from standing here outside O'Toole's. As he locked the car the first drops of rain mingled with the sea spray and he made for the door of the bar.

The outer door was set in the side of a small porch, evidently to limit the effects of the prevailing westerlies off the Atlantic, and there was an inner door into the pub itself. The two doors and the thick walls shut out the wildness of the weather and he found himself in a warm smoky atmosphere with the bar immediately in front of him. He glanced around and noted eight or nine men in a couple of groups, they were returning to their conversations after a momentary pause to see who the newcomer was. A small dark haired man left one of the groups and took up his place behind the bar:

'A fierce night out there, Sir, but you're more than welcome here. It's a drink you'll be needing.'

'A pint of Guinness is probably what the visitor has.'

'And not just the visitors, Sir, if you look around you you'll see that quite a few of our regulars are partial to it too. So it's a Guinness?'

'Please.'

Their conversation continued as the stout was run into the glass and the head allowed to settle.

'On holiday?'

'Yes, a friend recommended Co. Donegal as a place where you can get away from it all and he sure was right.'

'From America, if I'm not mistaken?'

'New York. We stand out a bit, I suppose.'

'Yes, but there's no real shortage of your folk in these parts. All looking for their roots, y'know.'

'Not mine, I'm afraid. My people came from Poland.'

'That's fine, Sir, like us you Poles are a good Catholic people. If you're staying over the weekend Mass is at six o'clock on Saturday evening and at noon on Sunday. Father Ryan's usually with us here on a Tuesday night but not today, he's been called out to a farmer who's dying.' He crossed himself.

'Sadly I've got to be on the move. Londonderry tomorrow ... '

'It's better round here to call it Derry, Sir. I hope you don't mind being corrected but it's wiser to use that name and it saves a little breath for other things.' He laughed and slapped his hand on the counter. The chatter in the bar had continued with the occasional burst of laughter. The barman's admonition reminded Sam of when he had been corrected by a waitress in the south of Cyprus for referring to Turkish Coffee, she too had hinted that one's personal safety could be compromised by such careless talk. Some words, unbeknown to the speaker, could carry a dangerous emotional resonance.

'Thanks ... I don't know your name, mine's Sam Charles, by the way - call me Sam, the barman back home does.'

'Good to meet you Sam,' he pushed forward his hand and they shook in greeting, 'I'm Dominic O'Toole, this is my place, I couldn't afford to employ myself, if you know what I mean.' He laughed again and his amusement was genuine, a man living contentedly in his own small world. Sam wondered whether he had ever been out of Co. Donegal. 'Well your Guinness is ready for you, Sam.'

'You'll have one too?'

'Only if you press me. Yes thanks, I need to dilute the blood flowing in my veins!' He set to and drew a pint for himself.

'No music yet? I was told you had music here on Tuesday evenings.'

'Oh, give them a little time, Sam. A couple of them are here but the others have yet to come. Over there to your left - the tall bald headed man, Tom, he's the main fiddle player and he's good at it too, as you'll soon hear. The fellow next to him with the blue jacket and short dark hair, he's not here so often as the others, he plays the *bodhrán* - you probably haven't heard of it but it's a sort of one sided goatskin drum played with a short two ended stick. They'll probably get going around half nine but you're in no hurry yourself?'

'None, Dominic, none at all.' He raised his glass, 'Your health, Dominic.'

'*Slonche*! That's what we say here, it comes to the same thing but it's an assertion of our identity. A nation once again and we don't like to forget it! We bought it with God knows how much blood over the centuries.'

'Slonche! then, Dominic. The goatskin drum sounds like those big things they play in the North, they use goatskins on them too don't they?

'It's the Lambeg drums you'd be thinking of, great warlike things - sure they use goatskins too - from Protestant goats up there, here we use Catholic ones for our *bodhráns.*' The pair of them laughed heartily. It was a friendly place to be, particularly when there was so much weather outside coming straight off the Atlantic. Sam relaxed.

'Thanks for the lesson on Irish drums, Dominic. I'll take my glass over there to one side of the fire and make myself comfortable. You would never know that it's a world of wind and spray and rain outside.'

'Enjoy the turf fire, Sam. Enjoy the warmth and the smell of the burning peat. When I come back from visiting my sister in Boston and get the fragrance of the peat in my nostrils I know I'm home and, I'll admit it to you, it brings tears to my eyes. We all need to come home don't we? And what about some food to set you up for the rest of the evening - I'd recommend the steak pie, it's done with Guinness, and some chips and cabbage to go with it. I've got to recommend it of course, my wife's the cook.' he pulled a wry face. 'You look like a man with a decent appetite.'

'You've persuaded me, Dominic! You make it sound as though the evening's going to call for some measure of stamina. When does the musical party finish?'

'Two or three in the morning generally.'

'We can drink until then?'

'Yes ... not officially of course, but the Gardai leave us alone, we don't give them any trouble and they don't give us any, besides my brother's a Garda sergeant at the local station!' He laughed. 'We lock the front door at eleven, of course, to keep out the curious but we're still in business for those already here and then if anyone with a genuine thirst turns up after hours we can usually accommodate him. Take a seat and the food will be with you in about ten minutes.'

Sam sat to one side of the large fireplace watching the glowing pile of peat and taking in the scene. The outer walls were thick and the windows small, so that the tumult of the storm was shut out and there was a sense of calm within the pub. The bar had one public room, its walls dark with the combination of the original woodstain and years of tobacco smoke. Smoke from the fire, as well as from cigarettes and pipes, had rendered the ceiling a mellow buff colour. The effect was surprisingly pleasant, there was a richness and sense of comfort about the room. The clientele obviously felt very much at home there. Possibly some spent more time here than in their own homes.

Another couple of musicians, apparently an accordionist and a banjo player, came in dripping with water; there was now even more weather outside O'Toole's bar. The barman returned from the kitchen and took their orders, engaging them in animated conversation in what had to be Gaelic as Sam was unable to comprehend the odd word that came his way. He drank his Guinness, it wasn't as bad as he'd feared, in fact it was rather good, quite like Porter in that other Catholic country where he'd been a few years ago and where some of his roots were - Poland. But *his* people had attended *schul* on Friday evenings and Saturday mornings, not Mass on Saturday evenings and Sundays. It was just as well that the Guinness was drinkable as his instructions were to have a glass of it and the note he'd received in front of him on the table. He took the folded note out of his pocket and placed it beside the glass. He didn't need to read it again, the message was short and to the point:

"Tuesday evening 21st August, O'Toole's Bar, Malin, Co. Donegal. Get there in time to eat, place this note on the table and just keep drinking pints of Guinness. That will slake your thirst and keep the Irish economy going! You'll be contacted while the musicians are playing. Then do as you are told and you will in all probability meet the man you wish to contact."

That was it, typed on a tired sheet of paper by an old typewriter, and it was unsigned. From his pocket he took a guide to Co. Donegal and began to read about the area. If the weather lifted he might have a quick look around the district the next day before heading for ... Derry - good, he'd got the name of the place right.

Dominic arrived with a very substantial helping of the beef pie and bowls of chips and cabbage. 'My wife's compliments, Sam. She says you will have her to contend with if I don't take a clean plate back to the kitchen. And I wouldn't recommend your taking her on!' He left him to the food, drink and his thoughts. And Sam's preoccupation was with the thought that, after sitting in O'Toole's Bar for six hours or so, he might reach three o'clock in the morning without anyone having appeared to speak to the man with the Guinness and the note. He knew he would have to go carefully with the drink if he were to be in a fit state to speak to anyone and, just as important, take care of his own safety. It was not a situation he relished, he was accustomed to taking the initiative not to being dangled on the end of a piece of string to amuse others. And he wondered whether his contact was already here in the bar or yet to arrive. Which of his fellow customers or the barman might it be? He looked around and tried to guess but no one was obviously a Republican paramilitary. Certainly none of them looked like his idea of a Volunteer, the young, totally dedicated and ruthless foot-soldiers of the Organisation and its ever more militant offshoots and splinter groups like the Continuity IRA. But there might be a member of the high command among those relaxing with him in the bar. Time would tell. At any rate he hoped so. He turned a page of his guide book and began to read about the town of Donegal and its history.

At a little after 9.30 the musicians began to show more interest in their instruments than in their glasses and cigarettes. The man pointed out by Dominic as the fiddler took his instrument out of its case and began to attend to his bow, treating it with rosin. The banjo man played a few notes and the accordionist joined him. Their beginning was tentative as though they were feeling their way. The fiddler called out something about a Scotch reel and they really got going. Sam continued with his reading, his plate pushed to one side and his glass nearly empty. Dominic interrupted his thoughts;

'Y'should feel honoured, Sam, they usually converse only in Gaelic but, as you just heard, Malachi announced what they were to play in English. They're glad to have an American guest with us.'

Sam wasn't sure that he wished to be noticed in this way. He assumed that Dominic had told them where he hailed from, but that was only to be expected, after all he was an obvious outsider sitting on his own, wearing a smart sports jacket and engrossed in a book. 'Well get them a drink from me, Dominic.'

'Tis a good idea, Sir. I'll do that, but first you need a pudding to keep the pie company. Bernadette's got a fine bread and butter pudding, rich with currants and sultanas it is. I can bring you one?'

'Y'can,' Sam replied, slipping into an imitation of the barman. Not a *kosher* meal exactly but that was the least of his problems at the moment. 'My compliments to Mrs O'Toole on the splendid pie - and she certainly knows how to make chips.'

'That she does, decent Irish potatoes, the right oil and a little care. The Irish potato! A reminder of the famine, you'll know all about that I expect? It'll be in your book, no doubt.' Sam nodded and Dominic continued, 'No credit to the Brits, no credit at all but, then, there's precious little credit due to them for the way they've treated us over all the centuries and for the way they go about things in the North even now, if you understand me.' The landlord was nailing his political colours to the mast.

'I understand well enough, Dominic. As an American, a latecomer to those shores mind you, I'm glad we fought for our independence from the Brits. But sadly you Irish were too near to them, just across a strip of water after all, too near to win your freedom quickly. You've got most of it now ... '

'81% of it, 26 out of our 32 counties - but that's not freedom! You'll excuse me, of course, but so long as our country is partitioned in this way there will be brave boys and women ready to die for the Cause. But that's not tonight's agenda, Sam. It's music you're here for isn't it?' He paused just long enough to inject doubt into the statement and then continued, 'So sit back enjoy the welcome, the warmth of the peat hearth, the food, the Guinness and the music itself - you won't find a better bunch of players in many a long mile.' Two more musicians arrived, another accordionist and another fiddler, they stood just inside the door, the rain dripping from their raincoats and their instrument cases. 'Right I'll order your pudding and you'll have another Guinness? Good, but first I'll attend to Mairtin and Pat, looking at their state it'll be an act of mercy to serve them a drink.' Sam listened to the music aware that there could be little doubt of the political complexion of O'Toole's Bar, its proprietor and his customers. If he was going to make contact with the Continuity IRA that evening then he was certainly in the right sort of place.

The newcomers hung up their coats, left their instruments with the other musicians and came towards Sam. Nodding to him and murmuring a greeting they took their places facing the fire and began to dry their rain-soaked trousers. Dominic brought them a couple of glasses of a hot dark liquid. He replied to Sam's unasked question, 'Hot toddy, Bushmills with a drop o' hot water and sugar. Wonderful mixture, does more good than anything the medical people can give you!'

'Charge it to me Dominic.' And as he said it Sam wondered whether he wasn't being foolish, making himself look the bounteous American. Dominic said something to the two men who smiled in Sam's direction and raised their glasses to him. He returned their greeting and raised his in return. Dominic returned with an immense helping of bread and butter pudding and a glass of toddy, 'Just to let you try it!' By the time Sam had finished his pudding the two newcomers had dried out - or rather their trousers had done so - and joined their colleagues, who were taking a break for sandwiches which Dominic had brought out on a couple of heaped plates. Sam returned to reading his book and wondering how long it would before contact was made.

At eleven Dominic came over to replace his empty glass with another of the interminable pints of Guinness. 'Peter's got to go early tonight so they'll be playing the Soldiers' Song in a moment, our National Anthem here in the Republic, you'll see everyone get up and of course you'll do so as well.' Clearly Dominic didn't want any awkwardness in his bar.

'Of course I'll be upstanding with the rest of you, Dominic.'

'But there's no need to stand hand on heart like you Americans do at home.'

'Thanks, you're a good host.'

Dominic returned to the bar and Sam sat back

enjoying the music. He could tell that the musicians were playing as much for their own pleasure and enjoyment as for the entertainment of their fellow drinkers. He watched them: Malachi their leader engrossed in his fiddle playing; one of the accordionists, eyes down studying his fingers as they moved over the keys; the other gazing heavenwards with partly closed eyes; the player of the one sided drum - Sam recollected that Dominic had called it a *bodhrán* - using a device like a screwdriver to adjust the tautness of the skin before he recommenced his drumming. There was a gaiety about some of the music but much of it was wistful, possibly the melodies of patriotic ballads though there had been little singing. Then they struck up what he knew must be the Soldiers' Song as Dominic had nodded in his direction and the others were on their feet. Sam joined them immediately and watched their faces, outdoor men with complexions wrought by wind, rain and sun - probably more of the first two than the latter. Faces that told him little more than that they were men at peace with themselves and the world in which they lived. There was no one whose features remotely suggested involvement in an illegal terrorist organisation.

The *bodhrán* player must be Peter, he was the one who was leaving early. He packed the instrument into its case, made his farewells and headed for the door. He had a slight limp, dragging his right leg as he walked. At the door he paused and nodded towards Sam who returned his valedictory greeting. Their eyes met and Sam noticed the intensity of the man's gaze. He held Sam's eye with an unwavering look. Then he opened the door and disappeared out into the wind and the rain. Sam looked at his watch, 11.15, and they might be at it for another four hours! Sitting waiting and wondering was something for which he was temperamentally well fitted, yet he was beginning to feel tense once again. Still O'Toole's Bar was a warm refuge from the storm outside, the beer and the food had been good and he was enjoying the music. He looked at his glass, he had consumed two and a half pints plus the hot toddy. His bladder confirmed this and he went in search of the gents. With a nod of the head Dominic indicated a door to the right of the bar and Sam headed there.

He was washing his hands prior to returning to the bar when one of the other guests entered. 'You're looking to meet someone, perhaps?'

The man was holding the note that had been lying next to his glass of Guinness on the table. 'I see you have my invitation in your hand, my friend. You want a word with me?'

'No, I'm only the go-between, Sir. I'll be taking you to the man himself.' Sam was relieved as the speaker's manner and appearance didn't indicate anyone of standing and authority in the Continuity IRA. 'You're finished here?'

'When I can find a hand drier.'

'You won't find one of those electrical things here, neither will you find one of those godless condom dispenser things, as you know this is a pious Catholic country.'

Sam saw a roller towel on the door but opted for a paper towel and slowly dried his hands. He was aware that his pulse had quickened, waiting was over at last. 'OK I'm ready.'

'Right we'll be on our way, we've only to go upstairs. You go in front and do exactly as I say.' The man's right hand was in a deep jacket pocket and Sam had little doubt about what he held. They crossed the passage and went through a door into the private quarters of the pub. The kitchen door was open but there was no one there; Bernadette O'Toole was not around to witness him climb the stairway towards the back of the building and pause at the top while the man followed. 'Right along the landing now and it's the first door on the left.' Sam followed his instructions and found himself in a small bedroom with a single bed along the wall it shared with the landing. In the opposite wall was a small fireplace with a peat fire burning. The curtains were drawn closed and a small table stood in front of the window and on it a whiskey bottle and two glasses. 'Take a seat, Mister.'

Sam turned to the fireside chair with wooden arms to the right of the fireplace. 'Not that one, Mister, that's for the man himself. You take the other chair and place it in front of the table ... No, facing the table. Now sit down. I'm sorry about this but he insists, he does, that you have your eyes blindfolded and your back to him.'

'Don't I get the benefit of a priest before you shoot me?' Sam put as much humour as he could into the words, hoping to hide the mounting unease he felt.

'Now 'tis not an execution you're at but a wee chat with a friend of mine. We just like to look after our security. Now relax and join me in a nip of this while we wait. We've got five minutes to kill before he's due. That's the only killing that's to be done ... tonight at any rate!' The man laughed at his attempted humour and poured out two substantial amounts of whiskey, 'Tis an atrocious night out there and we must needs fortify ourselves.' He put a glass in Sam's hand and raised his own, 'To Ireland free and undivided!'

Sam opted for the politically neutral, *'Slonche!'* But it was the phrase *L'Haim - To life* - that possessed his mind, never had life seemed so desirable to him. What if they were to think that the Brits had sent him ... hadn't it been madness to come here and put himself in this danger? Possibly it had, but it was a calculated risk and once the calculations had been made - and that had been done some time ago in the company of colleagues whose judgement he trusted - you got on with the job. He just hoped they hadn't decided he was a British agent. He shivered at the thought of the feel in the back of his neck of "the cold-nosed gun" of Heaney's poem. And now his thoughts were on Elizabeth and the children. He knew he was there for them and for many others who would be in the gravest danger if his nerve or his powers of persuasion failed. He was glad that he had just made a visit to the gents, to be sitting here in these circumstances with an over-full bladder would be agony.

'Time to bind your eyes, Sir.' Sam put down his glass and noticed to his surprise that he had emptied it. His custodian wrapped a cloth round his head, checked that it wasn't uncomfortable and that it completely blocked Sam's vision. 'But we don't tie you to the chair, though I warn you that if you attempt to turn or get up you will be shot. My gun's got a silencer and with the music down in the bar and the weather outside no one would hear a thing. And my friend that you'll be speaking to has just such a gun as well.' There was a call from the bottom of the stairway. 'You understand what I've just said? Really understand, after all we don't want any tragedies tonight, not with the weather as it is.'

'I understand completely, though I must protest.'

The man went to the door, 'Our American friend is ready to meet you, Sir, though he's protesting somewhat.'

Sam sat waiting as he heard slow footsteps on the stair, then a few words murmured in the doorway between the newcomer and his custodian, who was evidently being dismissed - for the time at any rate. The newcomer stood in the doorway, or so Sam judged, and spoke. Sam was surprised at the quiet, almost accentless voice - perhaps that of a teacher, 'You're very welcome to Ireland Mr Charles. I trust you have enjoyed your evening here at O'Toole's.' He sat down in the armchair and continued, 'I'm told by one of those in the bar that you have been a model guest, standing immediately for the Soldiers Song and listening attentively to the music. For them that's fine but for me what I'm interested in is what you want with the only Organisation with the nerve, the will and the total dedication to make sure the Brits clear out for good, licking their wounds and never wanting to defile our Irish soil again. But first let me introduce myself to you, I won't give you my name, it's enough for you to know that I'm a member of the Council of the Continuity IRA and speak for the Chief of Staff. Now it's for you to tell me about your own standing and your business here in Co. Donegal on such a wet night. One thing though, my colleague has told you the rules of this meeting but just for your safety I'll repeat them: if you turn or attempt to get up from your chair you will get a bullet in the head. I'm sorry it sounds, perhaps, a little unfriendly, and we are above all a hospitable folk, but we live in serious times.'

Sam knew that the next few minutes would be the most difficult and probably the most significant of his life. His script, which he had rehearsed time and time again, was etched on his mind, but in the real world and particularly a world such as this, on what now felt like the edge of the world and the very edge of life itself, you had to play it by ear, identifying every nuance in the other's voice. And his task was made no easier by the blindfold he had been forced to wear, it, together with the whiskey, was having a disorientating effect on him.

'I'm glad you've agreed to meet me, though I would be lying if I said I was enjoying the manner of our conversation. But perhaps you have a name I can use when addressing you - that would humanise things to some extent.'

'Joe will do - it's not my real name, of course, but then I don't suppose that Sam Charles is yours either - and I take your point. Still, with your background, you must appreciate that in a war situation we have to play games - serious games - like this.'

'Yes, I understand what you're saying, Joe. But must it go on for ever, this running battle against the authorities with all the civilian casualties and destruction? And there's the loss of your own people, your Volunteers.'

'You're no stranger to long running warfare are you,

Sam Charles? Since 1948 and indeed since long before that you Jews have been in conflict with the Arabs in Palestine. Your problem, as Jews, is that you aren't agreed on what you're after. For just how much of the place will you settle as your Promised Land? Your settlers and the religious lot want the whole place. I'm surprised that they stop short at the Jordan River, didn't some of your tribes live on the eastern side of it? Or so they taught me in seminary.'

'I'm here, as you know, to ask for some help, some information.'

'Indeed I know that but I'm enjoying our wee chat, Sam. It's interesting to know how others feel. What are your own ideas of the proper borders of Israel?'

It wasn't a subject they had expected to be discussed when he had spent long hours on briefing sessions for the mission. He had no idea what sort of response was expected or what would turn things sour and send him away at best empty handed or possibly with a bullet in the back of his head. He would be *moderate* in what he said, and that would be no problem for that word had increasingly come to characterise his thinking on the subject. And he would use the opportunity to build up some rapport with his interrogator. 'Like you, Joe, I'm basically a military man and the question a military man has to ask is, "What can we satisfactorily hold and defend?". The more realistic of our politicians see it that way. Samaria the PLO can have, though I have reservations over the Jordan Valley. You've been there, yourself?'

'Years ago when we seminarians visited the Holy Land, as some foolishly call it. Back in the days when you had to go through the Mandelbaum Gate to reach East Jerusalem and the Temple Mount.'

'You've not wanted to go back again.'

'Perhaps and, then, perhaps not. The struggle here takes all my time, my energy and emotions. But perhaps when at last it's all over and we've got the whole of Ireland to ourselves ... ' He stopped speaking and Sam heard what he took to be a light drumming of the man's finger tips on the arm of the chair. They were silent for a while until the man spoke again, ' "The fools, the fools, they think that they have pacified Ireland. But they have left us our Fenian dead. And while Ireland holds these graves, Ireland unfree shall *never* be at peace." *Never* is a long time Mr Charles but there will always be fine, bold lads and girls willing to continue the armed struggle until we are ... in our entirety ... a Nation once again. We will settle for *nothing* less.'

'You're quoting from one of your politicians?'

'From one of our *martyrs*, Padraig Pearse. Possibly a madman - he had strange mystical ideas on the significance of blood shedding, but then this is a Catholic country of a peculiar, un-practical kind, a land that gets excited by bleeding crucifixes, statues and the like. Pearse was more use to us dead, as a potent symbol, than as a Soldier of the Republic. I can tell *you* this, though it's not for quotation to anyone else, that if I'd been around at Easter 1916 I wouldn't have followed him into the Dublin GPO. But, of course, it was the Brits who were stupid enough to put him and his colleagues in front of the firing squad after the rising and make them into martyrs and so inspire generations to come. The days of the executions of Pearse and the other fourteen went by and our people felt that they were "watching a stream of blood coming beneath a closed door." Pearse was surely right when he said of the Brits, "The fools, the fools ... ". With those executions the Brits turned a dubious, botched event into a triumph for the rebels. It was no coincidence that it took place at Easter: for the Cause it was *resurrection* indeed. There's many a Volunteer's grave with the words:

> *"A fuair bas ar saoirse na hEireann." "He died in the cause of Irish freedom."*

Their many deaths over long years were not futile, the Island for which they fought and died *will* be ours again, not just part but the *whole* of it, *all* the 32 counties of Ireland!'

His voice, at first quiet and intense, had risen both in pitch and volume as he progressed. The peroration over, there was a pause and Sam once more heard the fingertips tapping on the arm of the chair.

Sam broke the silence, 'And *my* people have six million dead as an eternal reminder. For us all "Never again" is the watchword. That's why I'm here seeking your help, Joe.'

'Are ye now? Well I'll be listening to your request. But first I'll trouble you with something more from Padraig Pearse:

> *"Life springs from death: and from the*
> *graves of patriot men and women spring*
> *living nations."*

Your nation is evidence of just such a resurrection, Mr Charles. There's much there that I admire and much I don't. And you'll be pleased ... and relieved ... to hear that the admiration just about outweighs the other.'

'You're not entirely strangers to the soldiers of the Palestinian cause are you Joe?'

'And why might you be thinking so, Mr Charles?'

'In the intelligence world there are stories going around of an arms deal between certain Palestinians and the Continuity IRA that came unstuck and that you were swindled by them in some way. *If* there is any truth in that it seems possible to me that you might be disposed to have your revenge. It really isn't very pleasant to be taken advantage of, is it?'

There was silence in the room. The wind outside had dropped and rain was no longer beating on the window. Sam wondered whether these words had antagonised the man. Below in the pub a door was opened and momentarily the sound of music could be heard. The sound sent the man's finger tips into action again and it was a couple of minutes before he replied.

"What is it then that you would be wanting to know, Mr Charles?'

'People, places, names, addresses, telephone and fax numbers, internet addresses, anything of that sort - for the Palestinians and anyone else working with them. I'm not anxious to know about your organisation, indeed I'm anxious *not* to know anything about it.'

'Which is just as well for your personal health and safety, Mr Charles. And can I take it that you won't be talking to the Brits, carrying wee bits of information to them?'

'That I can promise, Joe. After all the Brits were in charge in Palestine and didn't do my people too many favours when refuge in that land offered them a chance of surviving murder by the Nazis.'

'Yes and your Irgun assassinated Lord Moyne, an Anglo-Irishman with anti-Jewish views who opposed your return to Palestine. Did you know he was from the Guinness family? Yes, the brewers of that fine dark, velvet liquid you've been drinking downstairs this very night. "The curse of the Guinnesses", so the superstitious say - and we've no shortage of such people. But to my mind simply the result of cause and effect, sowing and reaping if you're of a religious disposition, with nothing mysterious about it whatsoever.'

'Is that so? Are you a priest, then?'

'A priest? God forbid! No, I left that path before it was too late. It's less stigma here in Ireland to leave the seminary than to leave the priesthood, that's for sure.'

'Well you can take it I'll keep my mouth shut. I'll report back to my masters with whatever information you can give on the 16th September Unit but as for O'Toole's Bar and its customers I will be entirely silent. After all I might want to come back for a few days fishing some time.'

'I would like to think, Mr Charles, that it would be to an

Ireland both free and undivided, but that may take longer than my lifetime or even yours. But don't worry the struggle goes on, it has gone on over the centuries and it *will* continue until we win. Yes I have the information you seek and I will let you have it. Indeed I anticipated that this would be your request and I have it here with me. I will leave the note of it on the bed and you can have it when I'm gone. It has been interesting speaking with you Mr Charles. I wish you and your people well in what they seek, though I would counsel a greater degree of ruthlessness. Too much reliance on politicians can be futile. If I may quote from one of your Hebrew Psalms which we used to chant in the seminary:

> *"It is better to take refuge in the Lord than to put confidence in princes." '*

The man paused, 'You may remember, Mr Charles that it continues like this:

> *"All nations surrounded me; in the name of the Lord I cut them off!"*

I would advise you and your people to avoid being surrounded by hostile nations if you wish to survive. Do come back to fish, this is a fine country, fine enough to die for, though we also need people to live for it.'

'I'm grateful to you, Joe, your information may save many lives, many innocent lives.'

'Then I'm glad to have been here, to have helped you and to have had your company, Mr Charles. Our Organisation isn't one of mindless, unfeeling killers, I can assure you of that. As you can hear the winds and rain are back. I'd counsel you to spend the night here at O'Toole's and be on your way in the daylight after one of Bernadette O'Toole's Irish breakfasts, but tell her to leave out the bacon and black pudding! A good bowl of porridge with a wee drop of Irish Mist will set you up pretty well for the day. And her soda bread is an experience in itself. So, good night and don't get up, I don't want to have to put a bullet in your head! That would spoil the evening and be regrettable both for you and your organisation. Now you'll just sit quietly on that chair and wait for my friend to remove the blindfold. The note of what you want to know is on the bed.'

'Good night and thanks.'

'Safe home, Mr Charles.'

'Safe home, Joe.'

Sam heard his feet going down the stairway, it was definitely the walk of a man who limped. He had no doubt about it. He had been speaking with Peter the *bodhrán* player, the gentle tapping of his fingers on the arm of his chair was also strong evidence in support of this theory. Sam was aware of his custodian returning to the room, 'Time to remove the bandages, Sir. I'm glad to find you alive and well and not a martyr to some cause or other. Your visit to O'Toole's has been worthwhile, I trust.'

'Indeed it has, I very much enjoyed the beer and the music, not forgetting Mrs O'Toole's fine food!' He went to the bed and picked up the sheet of paper which had been left there. Carefully he folded it and placed it in an inside pocket. Tomorrow he would transmit it to Mossad HQ.

' 'Tis a fine sense of humour you have, Mr Charles. Would you be joining me in a wee night-cap, there's an awful lot of that John Powers whiskey still in the bottle.'

'Not for me, I've had enough for one night but please help yourself and drink to your own health and mine as well if you like.'

'That I will down below. But we think it would be better if you spent the night here in this room. No, we're not holding you prisoner or anything like that but it wouldn't be a good idea for you to go back into the bar, people might wonder where you've been all this time. I'll bring you a hot drink if you fancy a less powerful night-cap, if you understand me. OK I'll do that and then you can sleep. Would you be wanting a call in the morning? When? OK I'll tell Dominic to call you at 7 o'clock. The bathroom's next door.'

He went off to tell Dominic and to get the drink while Sam studied the sheet of paper, committing the details to memory in case he was parted from it. He would have liked a mobile 'phone but his hosts had forbidden him to bring one and he couldn't have been sure of the line being secure, no doubt the Brits' GCHQ was still picking up everything it could in the border areas. It would be interesting to see the view from the pub in the daylight and he was looking forward to Bernadette O'Toole's breakfast. A good night's rest and then off to Marseille via Londonderry - or rather *Derry* - and Heathrow. *Safe home*, he hoped. It was a nice friendly expression. And some words from earlier in the evening came to mind, *"We all need to come home don't we?"* How true that was, but the task of safeguarding his home had so often taken him far away from hearth and family. He wouldn't be sorry to see this operation through and quit Provence for the Golan.

Chapter 24

Wednesday 22nd August 2011

'So, apart from running up a shrink's bill - no, two shrinks' bills - and having bugged the home of one of them, we haven't much to show for a couple of months' work, Peter.'

'It's as you say, Erik. And the bugs haven't told us anything. I wish I'd been able to bug the bathroom,and the top bedroom', he grimaced at his memories of that place, 'but I've never had the opportunity to be there on my own again. It's almost as though they know we've planted the things and are making sure that there's nothing for us to hear.'

'Either that or they're accustomed to proceeding with extreme care, professionals who are always alert to security risks. She may use a mobile outside the house or she may make or take calls when working at the hospital, so it wouldn't be easy to break into those conversations if she does either of those things. Or, again, it may be that we're wasting our time, that we're proceeding on a false premise: it could be that Schmidt's visit to your Dr Garnier was a one off and that there's no relationship at all between the two of them, either professional or personal. I suppose the test of that will be when Schmidt makes his next visit to the bank - and that should be soon from what our friend Balthasar tells me. Schmidt gave him some cock and bull story about his sudden departure from *Die Drei Könige* at their last meeting – something about being afraid of being kidnapped. You'll just have to keep up your appointments with your two lady shrinks for the time being, Peter.'

Erik Blum's visits to Peter's office these days generally ended up with them standing at the office window gazing down on the trams in *Binningerstrasse* below and pondering where their investigation was heading. It certainly wasn't proceeding with the inevitability of a tram taking the accustomed route to its terminus. Perhaps the Zoo, just beyond *Viaduktstrasse* which crossed over *Binningerstrasse*, was where they ought to be: it was where he had got lost as a young child - his mind teemed with the facts and supposed facts that he'd been feeding to Dr Garnier. There were plenty of animals there which appeared warm and cuddly but which, given a chance, would be more than happy to take a bite out of your leg or any other part of you that came their way. Peter often asked himself whether Dominique Garnier was other than the concerned, professional therapist he encountered on his regular visits to Altkirch, whether in a corner she would be ready to use that gun on him.

'And what have your Israeli friends discovered at the Marseille end of things?'

'As you know they've established how the drug smuggling is done - drugs in containers through Marseille which they then take to Lyon and distribute onwards. A Lebanese who looks after those consignments, the "official" ones, as well as doing some smuggling with his yacht as a private sideline. They've been very successful with their 'phone tapping. Though they haven't yet managed to pinpoint Jakob Schmidt they did trace a call from their drug man to Schmidt at a Frankfurt restaurant. The place is run by Middle-Easterners and they've been wary of asking for Schmidt's address in case word gets through to him about their interest. So they're going there in relays, eating meals - it must be good business for the place - and keeping an eye open for Schmidt. Of course when he emerges from cover to call here at the bank we'll make sure we don't lose him again and the Israelis will have to watch him like hawks once he gets back to Frankfurt.'

'And once they've run him to earth in Frankfurt, Erik?'

'Who knows? Persuade him to tell all after they've watched him for a bit longer I suppose - they seem set on letting him lead them to other members of the Unit rather than wringing the truth out of him immediately. Knowing what Schmidt's planning I shouldn't think the Israelis will be too gentle if he declines to co-operate. After all we're only weeks away from their supposed target date and progress so far hasn't been brilliant.'

'The Israelis would be ruthless, you mean?'

'Just put yourself in their shoes, Peter. If someone planned to blow up your splendid city of Basel with a nuclear device, how would you go about getting the truth out of him about the weapon's location?'

'With some measure of subtlety, Erik. I'd be wary of killing him in the process and the knowledge dying with him. But, yes, come the end, if he still held out, I don't think the interrogation would bear much resemblance to the procedures outlined in our training manuals!'

'And let's hope that Jakob Schmidt really is the brains of the operation and that he does know exactly what's planned. Now, how's it going with Dr Garnier, no more hair-raising nights, I hope?' He spoke of it lightly now, but he had been desperately worried at the risks being taken by his young assistant when Peter had reported some weeks ago on his night *chez* Dominique.

'Calm, gentle and showing no signs of wanting to repeat the experience, though she did apologise. There are times, though, when she seems to lose the thread of what we're talking about, to be preoccupied, perhaps, by something else. It could be the stress of what she's into with Schmidt ... that might be an indication that we ought to persist with this thing for longer.'

'Perhaps, but it might be something else on her mind or even the approach of early senility. And how are you getting on with our own in-house shrink from the University? Or should I ask?' He nodded towards the photograph on Peter's desk.

'Oh, that's just to remind me of my twice weekly appointments.'

'Of course, Peter ... and might she have a similar photo to remind her that she has to put up with you twice a week?'

'That's quite possible, Erik.'

'Take care emotionally, won't you.'

'Yes, we're both taking care, we're both emotionally bruised from the past. But I'm grateful that you sent me to her, Erik. I've found the whole area of psychology and therapy fascinating.'

'Not more fascinating than working in the Security Service, I hope! You're a good Police Officer, Peter, I don't want you deciding to take up some half baked therapy as a career.'

'Don't fret, Erik I'm very happy with my official duties and with having you as my boss.'

***

In Tel Aviv the Deputy Director closed the file with a sigh. Not much real progress yet at *any* point. Sam Kagan was growing a fine crop of grapes, a Swiss Security Officer was in therapy and Mossad's German unit, supplemented by a few irregulars for variety, was tied down in Frankfurt keeping a Middle-Eastern restaurant in business - at any rate their *hallal* meat would probably be *kosher* though he couldn't think of many of his men to whom that would matter. And they still didn't know where Jakob Schmidt was to be found. He might indeed be in Frankfurt or he might be ... anywhere. That was the problem. And if they couldn't find Schmidt they would have to keep their eyes open at all their ports and frontiers, which they always did anyway. And if the thing were already in Israel, lurking malignantly out of sight? Heaven help all of those living in Israel or the Territories, a nuclear device would be no respecter of Semites, Jew or Arab. When he reported that evening he would tell Sharon that progress was as good as could be expected. He just hoped that he wouldn't be called upon to elaborate on that bald statement.

Chapter 25

Wednesday 22nd August 2001

Elizabeth sat at the table in the kitchen of the *Cheval Rouge*. She had eaten an early lunch and was enjoying the coolness that the thick old walls and the stone floor gave. Outside the heat was almost beyond endurance; it was certainly not a time for physical exertion, though the evening would bring relief. Both the children were asleep and she was glad to have some time to herself. Her concern for Sam's safety resurfaced, being busy hadn't allowed her to brood on the subject but now that she had time to think she also had time to worry. The telephone rang and she was relieved to hear his voice. He'd had his "wee chat" and all his business had been completed satisfactorily - he would be flying out of Derry City Airport in half an hour. He'd be back at Marseille Marignane in the late evening and perhaps she could bring the children and meet him? She assured him that there was no problem, she couldn't wait to get there and see him back safe and sound once again. They assured one another of their love and then Sam rang off, saying he was going to have a coffee before boarding his flight to London.

Elizabeth returned to the table and her thoughts. Her glass was empty and she went to the fridge to refill it from a carton of orange juice. The house had a dignified calm about it. She liked it here, and in a way she'd enjoyed the two days on her own with just the children for company. But she really longed to be back in Katzrin in the Golan, in their own little house. It was quite modest, small indeed compared with this, but it was their home. Sam's trip to Ireland had been the only really scary bit of events so far. And now he was safely on his way out of there. The operation itself seemed to be going smoothly but with an absence of hard facts, she was anxious though that it should succeed - not just for the sake of those who would be the victims of a bomb but also for Sam's sake. She wanted him to have another success to his credit. And she knew that, despite all his efforts to hide the fact, civilian life hadn't suited him and he had missed the excitement and comradeship of Mossad. She hoped that after this was over he would get the post for which he had made a bid when agreeing to return to field duties, even though that was likely to mean a move from the Golan to Tel Aviv.

Yes, the operation was going smoothly, quietly rather, too quietly with not enough to show for their time and effort. Perhaps Sam's "wee chat" with the Irish Republicans would have provided a fruitful lead.

How far all this was from the life of her childhood and from her university studies in Moscow in English and computing! After that had come the excitement of recruitment to the KGB's First Main Directorate with work abroad in the USA and Canada for several years, involving industrial and commercial espionage, followed by the spell in London, where she had begun to feel more and more alienated from her chosen profession. And that had led to the Swiss visit and the events in Basel four years before. It had led to jail, a murder charge and the trial. And to Sam coming into her life. She recalled the first time she had seen him knowing who he really was – not the American journalist he had pretended to be at their earlier meetings - from her seat in the court, just in front of the public area. She had been excited at what Sylvia, her advocate, had told her of him, excited and bewildered. And the bewilderment had increased when he had failed to appear as a witness, a witness whose testimony, Sylvia had assured her, was going to change the whole outcome of the trial. But in the end he *had* arrived. Late, dishevelled and dirty from the road where he had lain comforting a badly injured woman trapped under a tram. His testimony to the events on the night of Vladimir's death had set her free ... and ensured his arrest for a variety of contraventions of Swiss law.

Memories swirled around in her mind and thoughts of those months in London occupied her. She had fallen in love with her employer, Peter Lewis. And, although his love for her had been genuine, the old emotional ties to his wife Ruth and the effect that their looming split was having on their son Michael had prevented him from breaking free of his marriage. And by the time that this had become clear Elizabeth was carrying his child, Olga, who had been born during her time of residency in the Basel remand prison before the trial. She thought of Peter, a kind but indecisive man, whose hesitancy had got them into the emotional mess from which he had ultimately emerged only slowly after a breakdown. For her the way of recovery had been through the concerns of pregnancy, concern for the girls who shared the prison wing with her and the sudden appearance of Sam Kagan. She thought of Peter, he usually visited them in the Golan three or four times a year to see their daughter, having adopted the status of uncle - through coming to Israel he had found some new customers for his scientific glassware business. She had arranged to see him and Ruth his wife in Paris later in the month.

And she thought of Vladimir. His death still grieved her. It was true that during their years together as agents of the KGB, later the SVR - same thing, new name - he had become coarse and self centred. But he had been the first man she had really loved and in the early years he had returned her love and shown care and consideration. It was those memories of their good times in the USA and in Canada that made her feel so guilty over his death. He had drugged her and attempted to rape her in that Basel hotel room. She had acted in self defence and shot him, she didn't know whether she had really intended to kill him, she had acted as the drug - *Rohypnol* - had begun to take effect and her consciousness was ebbing fast. She had acted instinctively to defend herself and her unborn child. *That* she knew but still she couldn't shake off the sense of guilt and regret for the death of one who had once been dear to her - another Vladimir to be sure, the unspoiled colleague and lover of the early days, but not completely unrelated to the man who had tried to rape her.

She let her thoughts go their own way and they took her further back to her gentle, caring father who had died during her childhood and to her drunken step-father, her mother's second husband. What a relief it had been to go to university and then to have the excitement of being recruited into the KGB. How special that had made her feel!

They were a succession of men who had, in their different ways, shaped her life, Sam most of all. He had brought happiness and stability to her life and she was profoundly grateful. She got up from the table and climbed the stairs to the children's bedroom. They were both sleeping peacefully. She knelt down and kissed each on the forehead. How she loved them both, one of Peter's and one of Sam's - though Sam treated both equally as his and gave each his unstinting love. She hoped and prayed that their lives would be rather less dramatic than hers had been, that they would be kept from danger, from evil doers and from wrong. She was dragged from her reverie by the insistent ringing of the door bell.

Immediately she opened the front door she recognised Mustafa, though she didn't allow the recognition to show. 'Can I help you?'

'I saw the sign and I'd like to make the purchase of some of your wine, please.'

She noticed that he spoke good French and she wished they hadn't left the old sign advertising wine sales there by the roadside near the end of the drive. She could smell drink on his breath. This was a visitor she could do without and whom she would send on his way as soon as possible. There was no tasting room, the whole thing had been very casual with customers doing their tasting in the kitchen. While she was debating within herself whether to tell him they weren't open for business she found that he had somehow manoeuvred himself into the hallway. OK, she would sell him something and get rid of him quickly.

'Come into the kitchen, we've nothing formal like a tasting room but you'll find it comfortable enough.' Because the occasional visitor had to be entertained in this way they always ensured that there was no incriminating paperwork in view in the kitchen, even though this was the room where discussions and planning took place. She had no worries on that account. She led the way and turned to ask him, 'Are you interested in red or white?'

'Both I think, *if* they're palatable.'

'We have one red and a couple of whites - they're all V*ins de Pays*, ... Monsieur? I didn't catch your name ... '

'Jean Renard. And yours?'

'Elizabeth.'

'You're not French, though you speak it pretty well.'

'American.' She refrained from passing a similar comment on Mustafa's accent, better not to let him think he was an object of interest.

'I'll try the red first, the grapes are?'

'*Grenache* and *Mourvèdre*, traditional red grapes of the area. They blend rather well I think you'll find.' She poured him just under half a glass.

He went through the usual motions, swilling the wine round the glass, viewing it against the light of the window, inhaling the bouquet and then sipping it. 'Not bad, not bad at all, Elizabeth. In fact it's very good rather like yourself, young and fragrant, if I may put it that way without offence.'

'You're here to buy wine and not make comments about the vendor.'

'Then I'd better explore the wine further,' he took the bottle and filled his glass to near the brim. Then he drained it quickly. 'And the whites you mentioned?'

'The first is the *Blanc de Blanc*, a blend of four varieties: *Marsanne, Clairette, Ugni Blanc* and *Sauvignon*.'

'I've never come across the middle two ... *Clairette* and *Ugni Blanc*. Is the stuff any good?'

'That's for you to say, after all the palate's an individual thing. But I suspect you've been drinking *Ugni Blanc* for years.'

'I doubt it, I don't drink rubbish.' An aggressiveness was surfacing.

'But you enjoy *Cognac*?'

'Of course.'

'Well, they make it by distilling the wine of two or three grape varieties and *Ugni Blanc* is one of them. It doesn't make a brilliant wine on its own but blended with other varieties, it's worth trying. They use it a lot that way in Gascony.'

'I'll give it a try, you seem to know what you're on about. You're part of the American take-over of the French vineyards, I assume?' He reached for the bottle she had produced from the refrigerator and, without rinsing his glass, half filled it.

'No take-over, I can assure you. My husband and I run this vineyard and another towards the headland. We enjoy it here, that's all.'

'And what does your literature say on this?'

She picked up a leaflet and quoted, *' "Nez*: grapefruit and lemon. *Bouche*: peach and pear leaving a delicate flavour of fennel." But what one finds, *really* finds, is always an individual matter and it's affected by what you've just been drinking or eating.'

He had drunk most of the glass and was about to empty it with a second mouthful. *'Pas mal ... pas mal du tout.'* His French was becoming slurred. She must get him out and gone. She wished they had a dog on the *Domaine*, a decent guard dog would have made this fellow think before doing anything stupid. Although he'd not really misbehaved she could see trouble on the way. At the back of the table drawer behind her was a small handgun, that was her security. Sam had told her to keep it near her bed when he was away but she had left it in the kitchen. The drawer was locked so that it wouldn't be found by a child.

'You might like a copy of our tasting notes.' It was her opportunity to unlock the drawer and pretend to be looking for a copy. 'Sorry I'm not sure where we've put our supply, have this one instead.' She would give him the copy from which she'd already quoted. She had only partly closed the drawer.

She picked up the leaflet and handed it to him. As she moved back he grabbed her and held her against himself, 'Let's find out what sort of *bouche* this one has. You're obviously a fine vintage Elizabeth. The *nez* is distinctive, a very pretty perfume.'

She tried to push him away but he was too strong for her. The perfume was Calvin Klein's *Escape* - Sam had sent her a bottle of it when she was in the remand jail in Basel and Sylvia her advocate had got into trouble for letting her put some on in the interview room. The perfume held such happy memories for her. At the moment what she needed was escape with a small "e", if only she could get out of his grasp she knew she stood a good chance of beating him out of the room and the house. But then that wasn't an option, the children were upstairs and she would never leave them alone with a drunken stranger in the house.

'And now it's time to sample you Elizabeth.'

He was pressing her against the table. Despite it all she stayed calm, drastic action was called for. She rammed her fingers into his nostrils and split his nose. Mustafa staggered back, blood pouring from his torn nose and rage contorting his face. As she grasped the gun at the back of the drawer he reached for a French cook's knife held in a wall block by the cooker. Elizabeth retreated to the other side of the table and faced him across it. The table provided only limited protection, should he decide to throw the knife ... well she wouldn't give him the opportunity.

She raised the gun, 'Drop the knife Monsieur Malik.'

Hearing his name brought him to a stop momentarily. He stood there with the blood dripping down the front of his shirt, 'And how do you know my name, woman? Who *are* you anyway?'

She didn't answer but repeated her instruction, 'Drop it on the floor.' Once more a look of hate crossed his face and he drew back his arm ready to throw. The gun's safety catch was off and all she needed to do was to pull the trigger. To her horror she found she couldn't. She froze and time seemed to freeze with her. Afterwards when she thought about it she couldn't be sure why she had held back. Perhaps it been the memory of killing Vladimir, a memory that she had called to mind minutes before? But if that was the reason she couldn't find any linkage between the two men. There was no similarity at all, this beast was nothing like Vladimir, she had never shared ties of love and affection with Mustafa Malik. The knife just missed her head, hit a wall and clattered back across the floor, upstairs a child whimpered and, her momentary blockage overcome, she shot Malik in the shoulder at the same time as a shout came from the front door of the house. She didn't care who was there, it couldn't be a worse visitor than the one who lay writhing and screaming on the red tiled floor of the kitchen. Mustafa Malik could look after himself for the moment. She rushed into the hall to find Mark Gould standing in the doorway, the very model of the well groomed Englishman. Dov was with him.

'Thank God you're here, Mark. Mustafa's lying screaming on the kitchen floor and he may have a knife, so take care.' She gave her gun to Gould who was already on his way across the hall.

'Good afternoon, Malik, my friend tells me that you've been just a little bit too troublesome. You do know that you're making quite a mess on this clean kitchen floor, don't you?' Mark kicked the knife well beyond Mustafa's reach and instructed Dov to return to the front of the house and keep a lookout.

Malik stopped his blabbering to look up from the floor, 'Get me to hospital I'm losing blood and the pain's excruciating!' Indeed he was an exceedingly bloody and repulsive sight.

Mark turned to Elizabeth, 'First of all wash yourself well if you have any of his blood on you - you never know what it might have in it!' Mustafa continued to whimper, 'Stop it man, just bite your lip for the moment. Soldiers don't cry. We'll attend to you when we're ready and not before.' He turned his attention to Elizabeth, 'Are you all right. Tell me quickly just what happened.'

'He came here smelling of drink and wanting to buy some wine. He sampled some - too much in fact - and then tried to take advantage of me, he was going to rape me.' She sounded calm but she felt as though she were standing outside herself, listening to others conversing. It was all so unreal and Sam wouldn't be back for hours.

'Scrub your hands well, Elizabeth.' A child's cry could be heard upstairs, 'That's your first priority Elizabeth, see that the children are all right and then come down here and give me a hand ... bring a couple of pillows. By the way, as well as thanking God for my timely arrival, you can thank Dov for alerting me to Mustafa's visit to the *Domaine*. Now we've got to think what to do with him. Right, Elizabeth, if you're satisfied that your hands are completely clean and free from infection run off and see to the children. Dov's outside keeping an eye on things. I can call him in if you want them amused later on. Now I'll devote my attention to your visitor.'

Elizabeth washed her hands and scrubbed her nails

and then set off for the nursery. Mark turned his attention to Mustafa who was now lying quietly on the floor. The blood around his nose was beginning to congeal and the flow was easing. The pain in his shoulder had been partially anaesthetised by the impact of the bullet but not to the extent that he wanted to risk moving.

Mustafa gave Mark a sad and bewildered look. 'Get me to hospital, please!'

'All in good time my friend. But first I need to know a few things about you and what you're doing here in Cassis. I'd like the skipper of the *Viagra* to co-operate and tell me something about himself, you've plenty of time and if you lack the inclination then I'll have to provide a little encouragement. So, Mr Mustafa Malik, what brought you all the way from Beirut to Cassis?'

Mustafa lay there sullenly. He wasn't going to talk. He was still bewildered at the turn of events. He had come here looking for a little fun and it had turned out so very differently.

'Come on Malik I really would like to know.' He aimed a kick at the wounded shoulder, nothing too violent of course but it was enough to persuade Mustafa that the co-operation sought by his inquisitor was mandatory and not an option. He winced and began to cry. 'Come on be a man, Malik. Why did the 16th September Unit send you here?'

As Mark lifted his right foot, as though to deliver another kick, Mustafa began his response, 'You seem to know a lot. Who are you?'

'Now Mr Malik, you really don't seem to understand the rules of this game: *I* ask the questions, *you* give me the answers. If you would only grasp that we could get this unpleasant business over very quickly.' He pointed the gun in Mustafa's direction. 'We don't want to waste any more bullets, do we?'

Mustafa glowered and remained silent. Mark kept the gun trained on him and started to search the pockets of his jacket, removing wallet, diary and mobile 'phone. He placed them on the table and turned to Mustafa, 'Let's see what this lot have to tell us about Mustafa Malik and his friends and acquaintances.' He scrolled through the names and numbers on the mobile, recording them on a sheet of paper. It was fortunate that Mustafa hadn't had the opportunity to destroy the 'phone's micro-SIM card. He had read of a Frenchman who on arrest had eaten his to keep it out of police hands. There were several numbers outside France and among these were two in Germany. Now for a few more questions ...

He took the pillows from her and sent her back to the children. Mustafa groaned and Mark walked over to where he lay, 'I've brought you a couple of pillows, raise your head and I'll slip one under.' Mustafa complied and lay back with his eyes closed. Mark immediately placed the other over his face, pressed the barrel of the gun against it and pulled the trigger. Mustafa rose and fell back with a final gasp.

Mark got up and stood above the latest martyr of the *Jihad*. He looked down and murmured, 'I trust the wine and your allocation of 72 maidens are to your liking old chap. And I wonder if they supply tasting notes with each goblet.' The pillows would have to be burned and Mustafa's remains disposed of. They would have to get this mess out of the kitchen, it wouldn't do to have any more visitors calling to buy wine from the *Domaine* today. He went out to instruct Dov to get rid of the notice on the main road and then he returned to the kitchen. He was satisfied that he had got everything out of Mustafa that was worth having. They now had some more German telephone numbers. Malik hadn't come up with Jakob Schmidt's address, though he had identified Schmidt as the boss to whom he reported. Well, he wouldn't be sending any more reports. He didn't expect Sam to be too pleased at his actions, that didn't matter - he wanted to show them that he was still useful and capable of acting decisively, not a redundant British spy well beyond his sell by date. In any case Malik would have had to be despatched, they couldn't have run the risk of sending him to hospital where he might have blabbed, either consciously or under anaesthetic.

Elizabeth appeared, 'The children are happy for the moment, can I help?' She looked down at Mustafa, 'He's quiet, has he passed out?'

'He's asleep.'

'Where are we going to take him when he wakes, he's got a bad shoulder wound that needs hospital attention.'

'He's not going to wake and he won't need a hospital.'

'You mean he's dead? Surely the wound wasn't that serious, has he bled to death then?'

'You're right on target, Elizabeth, Mustafa's dead. As an act of kindness I shot him. Of course I didn't do it until he'd coughed up the information I was after. So the chap won't be troubling us any further apart, that is, from our having to remove his mortal remains. Make sure the children are kept out of here and don't let any stranger through the front door if anyone gets past Dov. In fact it would be a good idea to move Mustafa to the safekeeping of one of your outhouses. I'll make use of these kitchen gloves, please, if you don't mind. And have you any rolls of thick polythene anywhere? You have? Good, what width? Don't worry, I'll have a look outside.'

Mark set off through the back door of the kitchen leaving Elizabeth looking down on Mustafa's body, the head still covered by a pillow. How long ago was it that he had rung the doorbell and asked to buy wine? Perhaps three quarters of an hour, but to her it seemed more like a lifetime ago. And how long had Mark Gould been here, perhaps for half an hour and in that time he had interrogated Mustafa and then killed him. Killed him and shown no signs of concern. He was a cool and efficient operator, indeed a cold and ruthless one. And all the time he was so very polite and precise. He seemed so very English. It was just as well that they were on the same side.

***

'A nice cup of tea please, Elizabeth. I reckon I've earned it.'

He was certainly tidy and well organised. When she had returned to the kitchen it had been to find the floor washed and disinfected and all trace of Mustafa removed. The body must be in one of the outhouses wrapped in polythene. She wondered what his plans were for its disposal. No doubt he had worked that out, perhaps even before he killed him.

'Darjeeling, with a trace of milk and without sugar, if I remember rightly.'

'Precisely so, Elizabeth. I'm glad to have made an impression.'

'You've done that and no mistake, Mark Gould! First of all, thanks for turning up just when you were needed. I don't know what I'd have done without your help.'

'You'd already winged him, Elizabeth, and at the worst you could always have finished him off.'

'Wounding to save your life is one thing but killing's another thing entirely. You see there was a previous occasion when I was in Basel working for the SVR ... '

'When you shot one of your SVR colleagues who was attempting to rape you?'

"You know? How?'

'My old masters let me have some notes of the trial. Useful background information on Sam and yourself. From my reading you both impressed me and I'm glad to have met you and to be working with you.'

'Thanks. But it is a little disquieting to have a stranger knowing about those events.'

'Why, Elizabeth? After all they were very public,

weren't they? And in any case I'd read the reports of the trial in the French press.'

That afternoon, when she had hesitated, those memories had almost cost her her life. In that short moment, when the memory of shooting Vladimir had held her back from firing, she might have been hit by the knife. She was beginning to show signs of agitation and Mark noticed her hand shaking.

'Sit down Elizabeth, your need of a drink is greater than mine. What do you want?'

'Tea, any sort with a couple spoons of sugar. It might counter the shock. By the way how long is it until Sam lands at Marseille Marignane?'

He turned round from filling the kettle, 'There's a few hours to go. As you know I promised to meet him back here after his return which was the reason why I was in the area this afternoon. Dov called me with news of Mustafa's visit and I broke a few speed limits to get here. By the way I spoke to Sam before he left Londonderry, he's had a useful visit. Probably with the information he's got from the Continuity IRA and with what I've been able to extract from Mustafa's 'phone we'll be on our way to locating the leadership of the 16th September Unit.'

'And eliminating them? Like you've eliminated Mustafa?'

'Why not? It's war isn't it? We eliminate a few of them or suffer untold casualties and a world scale catastrophe.'

'It's just that it seems so cold, so ruthless ... '

'But so necessary, Elizabeth, so very necessary. It's no game we're playing, no game at all. They're very determined and we can't give them any leeway whatsoever - they wouldn't give us any, not an inch, you can be completely certain of that!'

Tea was ready and he poured her a mug adding a plentiful quantity of sugar and a little *Cognac*.

'It's just that I'm not born to kill and I don't want to learn the trade.' She drank and was quiet. Her thoughts were back with Vladimir, she had come to live with what had happened that night in Basel but there remained an indelible sorrow over his death at her hands. Still, the manslaughter verdict of the court had helped and she felt that by serving some time in the Remand Prison in Basel she had, to a degree, begun to expiate her guilt. Mark Gould poured himself a cup, leaving it to cool and Elizabeth to her thoughts while he went off to liaise with Dov. First of all they had to dispose of Mustafa's car quickly - after that, once Sam was back, would come the disposal of his mortal remains.

Chapter 26

Wednesday 22nd August 2001 (evening)

Sam had drowsed through most of the Air France flight, wondering to himself how the operation would end. So far things had gone slowly with information being obtained, collated and evaluated and the jigsaw assembled laboriously. Smoothly but all too slowly - there were so many pieces of the jigsaw still missing. He wondered whether their luck would hold out or whether they would find themselves in a cul-de-sac, led there by chance or worse still by their opponents, aware all along of Mossad's interest and merely setting them up. Once again he rejected the idea of luck as unworthy of both man and his Maker.

The pilot's instruction to fasten the seat belts brought him back to the present: Elizabeth would be waiting for him at Marseille Marignane Airport, he would soon be home with her and the children. At their temporary home, near Cassis, at any rate. It had been hard to tear themselves away from their real home in the Golan for this assignment. But then it was only a temporary absence. Within a few weeks, they would be back there again - of course, that would be if all went well.

He reopened his book at Heaney's poem. He was grateful that his journey back from Donegal to the airport at Londonderry had been uneventful. No faked road blocks or indeed any official military ones. No cars tailing him - there had been precious few vehicles on the roads he had travelled. That corner of Ireland would be a place to visit again one day when, if the rain chose to clear, he might have a chance of viewing the countryside he had traversed, seeing little but the short stretch of the road that had been visible, through mist and rain, in front of his car. He finished the narration of the disposal of the remains of a terrorist victim:

*"With rushes that shoot green again, I plait
Green scapulars to wear over your shroud."*

What did that word - *scapular* - mean. He had looked it up before he left for Ireland. Yes, that was it "a short monk's cloak". Clearly a very Irish touch.

The aircraft had circled around Marseille and was now approaching from the south. Sam looked down wondering if he would recognise anything. Then he was pleased to see the *Basilica de Notre Dame de la Garde*, on its hill some 500 feet above the city, illuminated and standing out unmistakably. He recalled his first meeting there with Dov's Yvonne and his promise to instal a votive offering in the crypt if the operation were successful. The gilded Madonna and Child surmounting the spire gleamed brightly. The Marian cult put him off but that didn't prevent a wry smile and a muttered, 'Well despite what they've made of her she was a nice Jewish girl!' Mrs Feldman would be pleased that he was taking the Christian view of the Madonna's pregnancy. The passenger next to him began to say something and then thought better of it. Next Sam picked out *Le Vieux Port*, crammed full of yachts, and the *Pannier* Area to the north. He wondered whether Mustafa was there with one of his women, young blondes all of them. The *Nouveau Port* with its miles of berths for the world's shipping was now below them. Soon there would be another consignment of the 16th September Unit's drugs on its way through the port, perhaps it would be the last. It still partly mystified him why Mustafa was involved here, perhaps it was to bribe the Customs or shipping officials to avoid the risk of a container being opened. But so few were checked that his presence seemed both a waste of manpower and a source of risk for the Unit. It was a conundrum he would like answered, a loose end that annoyed him. Perhaps the simple answer was that it allowed Mustafa to have fun with the local women and do his own private drug smuggling to feather his own nest.

The aircraft made a gentle landing and taxied to the terminal. He was seated at the front and had only hand baggage; he would be with Elizabeth in a couple of minutes. The thought buoyed him up as he strode through Immigration and then emerged from a deserted Customs area. He looked around but there was no sign of Elizabeth. He was disappointed, he had been longing to see her and the kids. Then he saw the Englishman, Mark Gould, and his heart sank. Something must be wrong. Gould took him by the arm and directed him away from the crowd. 'It's all right Sam, nothing too serious, your wife and the children are all right. Good, we're out of the throng so I can explain.'

'No one said that there was anything wrong when I 'phoned in earlier.'

'There was a good reason for that, nothing had happened at that stage, Sam. But let me repeat Elizabeth and the children are all right, they've come to no harm. But you must let me explain. Would you like a drink?'

'No, Mark, but I would like to see Elizabeth and the kids without delay.'

'Fine, let's go to the car, it's in the short stay place, P1, the nearest to the terminal. We'll be there in a couple of minutes during which time I can outline what went on earlier this evening.'

'And where's Elizabeth?'

'In an apartment my people have in Cassis, just at the back of the town. The view from it is quite splendid, especially of Cap Canaille in the setting sun.'

'Come on, Mark, you're not a realtor trying to sell me the place. Facts and quickly please!'

'Sorry, Sam. Right, the facts. At about 3.15 this afternoon your friend Mustafa decided to pay a call to your *Domaine*. I was in the apartment at the time enjoying the view of Cap Canaille, it really was quite splendid ... '

He paused and brought himself back to the facts, those that Sam wanted. 'Your chap, Dov, called me as the other members of your team weren't around. He was quite alarmed, said that Mustafa had just driven up in a car, an Alpha Romeo, and that he was heading for the house. He'd tried to 'phone Elizabeth to warn her but had got no reply though he knew for sure that she was in. I was there in under seven minutes and Dov reported that Mustafa was inside the house.'

'With Elizabeth and the children?'

'Yes. But to go on, Dov and I approached carefully, made our way in only to find that Elizabeth had dealt with him.'

'Sold him some wine and sent him on his way?'

'Shot him in self defence and glad to have help arrive.'

Shot him? Elizabeth? Oh, no! Not that!'

'She's fine ... your Elizabeth is a tough young woman.'

'But after what happened in Basel! You're sure she's OK?'

'Completely. Have no fear on that account. And the children were out of the way upstairs and heard and saw nothing. Nevertheless I thought it wise to move her out to my apartment for a few hours while we dispose of Malik's body.'

They had stopped walking. Sam looked around to make sure no one was within earshot, 'She killed him then?'

'No, Sam, she winged him, put a bullet through his shoulder. I got what information he had out of him and put him out of his misery.'

'You killed him, Mark? You killed him in cold blood?'

'In cold blood? I suppose it was. I didn't get worked up or excited about it. It certainly wasn't in anger, it was a cerebral thing, Malik had to be got rid of. Just imagine the problems that a visit to the local hospital might have thrown up for us! We could have ended up on the wrong side of the French Police and their Security people - and you know how leaky French Security is. After all, that's why they don't know you're here, isn't it?'

'Your logic is impeccable, Mark, but I don't like what's happened.'

'Nothing untoward would have happened if Malik hadn't come knocking on your door and then tried to molest your wife. You were right about Malik coming to the house to buy wine. He enquired about the prices of your wines, and then sampled them becoming more and more intoxicated in the process.'

'And less and less in control of himself, Mark?'

'As you say. The wine was just a pretext to get into the house. His real interests were, I'm afraid, sexual.' So it wasn't only blondes that attracted Mustafa's attention! 'But, of course, your wife knows how to defend herself, the KGB obviously did a good job with her unarmed combat training. She tore Malik's nostrils open with her fingers.' Sam wondered how Mark knew about her background but didn't waste time asking. He would tax him with it some other time. Mark continued, 'But then Mustafa drew a knife on her and that was his undoing. Your wife went for a small handgun in the top drawer of the table, I must say I admire her dexterity. But, when she tried to fire, it malfunctioned, you really ought to make sure that your weapons are serviceable, old chap. Dov and I were on the doorstep when she got it to fire and winged the fellow in the left shoulder and that put an end to his antics. Elizabeth's fine and the children were safely out of the way upstairs, so you've nothing to worry about.'

Nothing to worry about indeed! Sam knew that the effect on Elizabeth of attempted rape and of gunfire would be devastating. 'And where are they - where did you say you'd taken Elizabeth and the kids?'

'My woman, Lisa, came over and took them to her apartment, the next one to mine, you know.' It was the first Sam had heard of Mark having an apartment in Cassis. 'We needed them out of the way. You see I asked

Mustafa a few questions and encouraged him to reply truthfully. Which he did, after a little encouragement. And we've got his mobile with its SIM card. I'll put you completely in the picture later, of course. You'll want to see your family first before the detail but it was useful, very useful.'

'And Mustafa, how do we dispose of his body? I assume you have some ideas on the subject.'

'That's not too much of a problem, Sam. He's wrapped up in polythene under a pile of poles in one of your sheds - awaiting disposal, you might say! He's well beyond needing first aid. As I've already said, it was necessary to ensure that he kept his mouth shut. What's a little tragedy for him compared with what he was planning for your people?'

At one and the same time Sam admired Mark's calm resolution and was revolted at his cold efficiency. 'So I have a body to dispose of? Your ideas, please!'

'As a matter of fact I have given it thought. That yard of yours could do with a new surface. Order some hard core tomorrow for delivery as soon as possible and then some ready mixed concrete. We can give poor old Mustafa a substantial waistcoat. We'll just have to make sure that we bury him away from any point where someone might want to put a drain or anything of that kind at a later date! We wouldn't want his rest to be disturbed, would we? Your digger's in working order, I checked it before coming here. So much easier than manual grave digging.'

'And we would live with a body under the yard for the rest of our stay in Cassis? Elizabeth couldn't put up with that.'

'I can't think of a better idea. I'd offer my apartment but digging up the floor there might draw attention to ourselves, don't you think. Or perhaps you would like to drive the body over to Marseille and dump it somewhere in the hope that the police will think it's a gangland killing.

No, using him as the basis for a resurfaced yard seems the best option. But, as I had a hand in his demise, I would like to have a say in his final disposal.'

'And I'm the one who provides the resting place ... '

'It was your place he drove up to and your wife he pulled the knife on, Sam.'

'And his car?'

'Driven away by Dov wearing gloves to be parked in Cannabis Row - what's the place's real name, *La Canebière*, isn't it? - in the middle of Marseille. Then they'll tow it away to some police pound soon enough. Don't worry, it's well away from the *Domaine*.'

'A *very* efficient operation, Mark!' Sam couldn't disguise the chill in his voice.

'Just so, an efficient operation. You won't believe it, but I did feel a little regret at having to put him down.'

'Put him down indeed! Like having a sick animal disposed of! I'd be prepared to believe anything about you Brits, especially when you assure me it's true, you know that!'

'And your visit to our friends in Irish Occupied Ireland? Did you enjoy their hospitality?'

'Indeed I did and I look forward to going back to Co. Donegal some time, if only to have a look at what the weather didn't allow me to see this time.. The music was good and so was the food and the Guinness. But I suspect that if you'd been the one who'd called in at O'Toole's Bar you might have found yourself in a similar situation to Mustafa.'

They recommenced their walk to the car.

'I don't think so, Sam. After all I spent four years on and off in undercover operations in South Armagh - Bandit Country we called it in those days when our troops had to be helicoptered in and out of fortresses near the border. Long years of it! So I think I can claim to know a little about the sort of people you were consorting with at O'Toole's Bar last night. And also about the ways and means of surviving their malicious intentions.'

Last night! Was it only last night? For Sam the narration of this evening's events at the *Domaine* had put all else out of his mind. All he wanted was to see Elizabeth and hold her close. He knew that neither of them would sleep that night, the news of the afternoon's events had shaken him and he knew that for Elizabeth old traumas would have been unleashed once more.

They had reached the car and from then on their conversation was of generalities and trivialities - you never knew, the car might be bugged by someone or other, possibly by their own people. And, after all, you didn't want your boss to know everything you thought ...

***

'No, Mark, I'm not having Mustafa's remains under the floor of my barn or under the yard. What we'll do is take the body out into the Med and give it a well weighted burial at sea. We've a motor launch in the marina at Cassis. We'll take Mustafa's remains there just before midnight and put them on board - Dov will put to sea with them. Then you and I will take the *Viagra* to sea from its mooring in Port Miou and rendezvous with Dov. We'll drop Mustafa's weighted remains over the side and then make it look as though Mustafa's taken the *Viagra* out and fallen overboard. After that we'll come back into Cassis in the motor launch with Dov ... and hope that we've seen the last of Mustafa.'

'It would be easier to cover him with a load of concrete, Sam.'

'Which is just what we're not going to do.'

'And Dov's policewoman - Yvonne - is she going to be told?'

'I've been thinking about that Mark. I don't think we can tell her.' His conversation with Dov before his visit to Ireland had convinced him that they had no alternative but to trust her, but to burden her with the knowledge that one of their number had killed – indeed murdered - Mustafa Malik wouldn't be fair. 'Let's just hope that she'll be convinced by our efforts and believe that he fell overboard. It's as well that she's away visiting her mother in Arles at the moment.'

***

They lifted the heavy, sacking-wrapped bundle from the foot of the launch, the remains of Mustafa Malik weighed down with a load of stones, and lowered it carefully over the side. It disappeared from sight immediately and then a few bubbles broke the surface of the sea. To Sam it seemed a sad lack of proprieties to be committing Mustafa to the deep without any ceremony whatsoever. His canvas shroud would lie on the sea bed and the green *scapulars* of Heaney's poem would be provided not by plaited reeds but by the swaying seaweed. But then, for Mustafa Malik, a monastic cloak was wholly inappropriate: he had been more satyr than monk, his earthly predilections erotic rather than ascetic.

Sam returned to the *Viagra*, started the diesel motor and turned the yacht out to sea on a southerly course. In the cabin an almost empty vodka bottle rolled around the table with a glass to keep it company. Sam had swilled a little vodka round the glass, handling it with a clean handkerchief so as to leave no fingerprints. He stood for a moment at the helm and then made his way to the stern and climbed down into the launch's inflatable that Mark was commanding. From the launch they watched the *Viagra*, the pride and joy of the late Mustafa Malik, disappear into the dark. For a while the sound of the yacht's motor remained audible and then it was gone. Someone would find the deserted vessel in the next day or so and, they hoped, conclude that an inebriated sailor had fallen overboard. It was time for Sam to get back to

Elizabeth and the children. He hadn't wanted to leave her but the immediate disposal of Mustafa's body had been imperative. Sam knew that it would be a while before the afternoon's events were wiped from Elizabeth's memory or even before their intensity began to lessen.

In the back of the launch Mark Gould sat on the cushioned seat with a beatific smile on his face quietly singing to himself, *"What shall we do with the drunken sailor?"* Sam looked in his direction, so calm and so relaxed. So very English and so very cold. The previous evening Joe had reminded him of the Jewish experience of the Brits during the Palestine Mandate. Now he felt a moment's sympathy for Joe and his Irish cause. But his sympathy was only momentary: the murder of civilians was always an evil thing. In the circumstances Gould had done the right thing, that couldn't be denied: it was his absence of any regrets that stuck in Sam's throat.

PART 3

Days of Fear

No passion so effectually robs the mind of all its powers of acting and reasoning as fear.

Edmund Burke, On the Sublime and Beautiful

Chapter 27

Friday 24th August 2001 (23 days to go)

André and Michael from the Paris Station had reached them about an hour before Mark Gould's expected arrival and were sitting around the kitchen table with Sam, Elizabeth and Dov. Mark Gould would be making a visit to a wine grower at Châteauneuf-du-Pape while on his way south. Mrs Feldman and Esty Levin were with the children in the front lounge. Mugs had been filled with strong coffee and plates of biscuits passed around the table.

Sam was summing up their discussion, ' ... and so to summarise, we're now certain that the 16th September Unit is directed from Frankfurt am Main:

First, there's the experience of the Continuity IRA, that's where they made contact and they had a couple of 'phone numbers there, one's now discontinued unfortunately but the other is live. And there's the address of a restaurant where they met Schmidt.

Second, that's where the late Mustafa Malik 'phoned when he needed a replacement for his number two to watch the tail of the latest container load of drugs on its way to Lyon. Unfortunately it turned out to be a restaurant payphone but it's the same one that the Irish mentioned. So Schmidt still eats there on occasion or they're in touch with him. So that's better than a mobile, though you can get some idea of where the call from a mobile is picked up from.

Thirdly, there are two Frankfurt am Main numbers on the deceased's mobile, one of which is the same as the IRA's live number. We need to follow up those numbers urgently. Keep the restaurant surveillance going and intensify our cover there.'

'You're really sure this is a genuine threat, Sam. I don't want to go troubling the Germans if there's nothing there.'

'Put that response down on paper and put the file

away if you like - then wait for the enquiry after the explosion, André. If you do nothing I'll find my own way of getting the help we need ... that's if you don't want to play ball.'

André was needled, 'I never suggested we wouldn't give you all the assistance you needed.' He dropped his voice, 'We even sent you our hottest property, young Tanya, and now she's found true romance with a waiter from Cassis and the Boss is impossible to live with - he had his eye on her, we could all see that - and his wife's about to go away with the kids to the *Côte d'Azure* ... all his well laid plans have come apart! You could see him walking with a spring in his step when he got the results of her last medical check up. Of course he played the responsible employer, concerned for her well being but his pleasure at her being free of any STDs was rather more personal than that. OK you want the numbers traced, the 'phone tapped and a watch put on the subscriber and that on the restaurant stepped up?'

'That will do quite well for a start. Oh yes, and on anyone connected with the subscriber, André. I don't want to find that the father's the subscriber, while his son's the head of the Unit and we're wasting our time watching the old man.'

'Trying to teach your grandmother to suck eggs, are you Sam? We'll do all that we can for you. As for the 'phone tap we may be able to manage an unofficial one, I've a contact in Frankfurt in DeutscheTelecom who might be able to fix it for us without our having to go to the top and give them explanations.'

'Fine André, the more low key and in-house the better. When is it likely to start?'

'Tomorrow if you don't detain us here for too long!'

As though on cue Mark Gould rang the doorbell and was let in to join them. Elizabeth made fresh coffee as introductions were made. Then they returned to the table, Mark taking a seat next to Sam.

'Mr Gould,' André began and Mark knew that a lecture was about to begin, 'I'm grateful to you for your rescue of Elizabeth from Mustafa Malik but must express concern that you took Malik's fate into your hands without any consultation. That action might have cost us vital information.'

'Thanks for your gratitude and no thanks for the rest! When I put a bullet through Malik's brain I was fully satisfied that I'd got from him all that there was to get. In an organisation like the 16th September Unit the members are only told what they need to know. Malik's rôle was to keep the way clear for the containers of drugs being imported through Marseille and to watch the tail of the lorry as far as the distribution depot in Lyon. On the side he had a lot of fun, funded by his own smaller scale drug smuggling activities. I was completely satisfied that there was no more information to come and I didn't want him pulled apart by your people before he went to his grave. As an act of human kindness I despatched him. After what had happened to him Malik couldn't have been left alive, he would have been far too dangerous in every way. Now you can take it that our discussion on this subject is closed.'

There was silence, a silence which Sam for one relished. Initially he had responded like André, who had now met his match and he conceded as much. 'I've made my complaint and you have responded, Mr Gould. So we can move on. Now, with our serious business over - Sam will fill you in Mark - Michael and I would like some of your wine to take back to Paris. At any rate Michael will take it back to Paris in the car while I head for Frankfurt. I'm assuming, of course that there are trade discounts for the members of the Institute. While that's being sorted out I'll 'phone to book my flight to Frankfurt.'

'Just make sure that they book you to Frankfurt am Main and not to Frankfurt an der Oder.'

Mark couldn't miss having a dig at André who came

back quickly with, 'An unlikely mistake as my grandmother was born there and my grandfather had a textile business in the city. They were both Brandenburgers. The next time I'm there I'll think of your advice.' He took his mobile from his pocket and wandered off to the other end of the kitchen for some quiet to make the booking.

Sam, Dov and Michael set about loading the car with wine while Mark and Elizabeth exchanged knowing glances.

André returned, his booking arranged, 'Is that your count down chart Sam, over there by the kettle? The one that's showing 23 today?'

'Yes, it's the countdown to the big bang,' he said quietly, 'the number of days to 16th September. I'm pretty certain that that's the date when they plan to set off their nuclear device. The chart's there to give us a sense of urgency about the task. And your flight? 14.15 hours, fine, Michael had better be taking you to the airport now. Enjoy Frankfurt, André!'

Hands were shaken, farewells said and the men from the Paris station seen off.

'While we're out here, Sam, perhaps you would like to give me a hand with unloading some wine for *your* consumption here at the *Domaine*.' Mark had come in a Jaguar with a substantial boot which he opened to reveal his cargo of wine. 'This is a gift for you, a dozen each of Côte Rotie, Hermitage and Châteauneuf-du-Pape. I did have some for that pair from Paris but I changed my mind for some reason!'

'Really, I wonder why?' And they both laughed. 'And to drink with our lunch, Mark?'

'A couple bottles of the Côte Rotie even though they've spent the morning bumping around in my boot - sorry, trunk to you - and then a quiet afternoon to sleep it off in one of your armchairs. There's nothing we can do for the moment as far as the Unit's concerned until the activities in Frankfurt throw up something.' The mention of Frankfurt provoked more laughter on Mark's part until Sam said quietly, 'I asked him afterwards about his grandparents and he told me they'd lived in Paris. He was just getting his own back on you, Mark. But he really did know there were two Frankfurts in Germany.'

***

André acted quickly and called up some of Mossad's German personnel to reinforce the surveillance operation before he took off from Marseille Marignane. On his arrival in Frankfurt am Main he reminded the Head of Station that it was a counter-terrorist operation, that the device concerned might be nuclear and that they were not to be too surprised if it was all the product of someone's fevered imagination. In that way André covered both options and didn't have to commit himself too firmly. He met with his DeutscheTelecom contact and the unofficial 'phone tap was put in hand using a junction box a street away from the suspect's apartment which had now been located from the number on Malik's mobile which tallied with the Continuity IRA's information. The subscriber was indeed Jakob Schmidt and accordingly the operation was given the name *Operation Leiter* (Operation Ladder). In Mossad HQ the *Operation Leiter* surveillance record would eventually form a sub-file of Operation Account. André wrote the name in his diary and added the figure 23 to the page, he didn't like being over dramatic, it was as well to keep an eye on the possible time-scale, but he wouldn't have let on to Sam that he was following his lead.

***

Schmidt evidently had a dislike of telephones and of contact with his fellow human beings. For in the first couple of days he didn't lift the handset or venture outside the apartment, in a fairly unremarkable low-rise block in an unremarkable suburb of Frankfurt. On day three he made a call, ordering the delivery of a pizza with extra anchovies and chilli and no, definitely, no ham. They decided he was either Jewish (unlikely), a Muslim (possible) or someone who just didn't like ham (again possible). The next day he emerged from the apartment block after a 'phone call for a taxi to take him to a local clinic. He returned three hours later and walked slowly to the entrance of the block. Then once again telephonic silence. Perhaps he was using a mobile. They were picking up nothing on any of the mobile numbers they had obtained from Mustafa Malik's mobile.

***

Wednesday 29th August 2001 (18 days to go) Frankfurt

Day five, early morning and it was Daniel's turn to sleep in the bunk of the surveillance van. They had changed the vehicle the previous night, feeling that the first had been there long enough and that it might be attracting attention. You never knew, there could well be insomniacs in the apartments round about, standing at a window with a milk drink or something stronger in hand wondering what was going on when the never-moving van regularly disgorged young men. Silvan was on the point of nodding off when a taxi drew up. He shook himself and woke Daniel. They needed to be ready to follow if Schmidt were to be the passenger. It was good to get out of the van onto the pavement, to stretch your legs and fill the lungs with fresh morning air. They got into the car, ready to follow. Three minutes later, at 05.33 as Daniel recorded in his log, Schmidt emerged, walked slowly from the door and climbed into the taxi. Then they were off. Daniel's guess was that their destination would be the airport.

They crossed the city and joined the A5 *Autobahn*, heading north. Silvan drove and Daniel called in on his mobile to say that the destination was going to be different from his earlier guess. At the second service area the taxi pulled off the *Autobahn* and drew up near the restaurant. The driver helped Schmidt out and walked with him to the restaurant. There they found a corner table and the driver went to the counter to get their breakfast. Daniel followed him while Silvan bought a couple of newspapers and found a table from which he could observe Schmidt without himself being noticed. Two or three minutes later Daniel joined him with coffee and a selection of rolls and jams, 'The driver's a Turk, I'd guess.' Silvan nodded. Schmidt's driver was unloading a similar assortment onto Schmidt's table. Both parties commenced breakfast, neither showing any sign of hurry.

Twenty minutes later a man with a dark complexion, suggesting Middle Eastern origins, joined Schmidt and his driver. Daniel headed past them on his way to the gents. In his small back pack, which he carried under his arm, was a video camera recording the occupants of the table. He got some more shots from the other side on his way back, changing his angle of approach to make sure he had the likenesses of all three men. Then Silvan was despatched to the gents, they might have a long journey before them.

At 06.53 the others show signs of being ready to move, heading for the gents themselves. Daniel and Silvan stayed put, they could see the entrance to the gents and from their inspection of the place they were satisfied that there was no other way out. Five minutes later the three emerged and Schmidt and his driver returned to their table while the other man left them. Had they passed something to him? Ought they to try to apprehend him? While they were chewing over these questions the other returned with a wheel chair for Schmidt who was helped into it by the two men. He shook hands with the Turk who set off, presumably for his taxi. The newcomer wheeled Schmidt across the restaurant to a lift whose doors responded immediately to the button and they disappeared from sight. 'Where?' was the word on the lips of the two men. Beside the lift was a staircase and the took it, taking care to let their quarries out of the lift and on their way before they reached the top. They were on a footbridge spanning the *Autobahn* and at once they knew what was intended. Schmidt was about to transfer to a vehicle on the other side of the *Autobahn*!

They could do little but follow and watch the transfer of Schmidt into a People Carrier, whose registration they noted, which then set off slowly to join the southbound A5. They might have commandeered a vehicle, but they were dubious about the wisdom of a hijacking, and there wasn't enough time to steal a locked one. They watched Schmidt leave and reported back by 'phone. 'You should have anticipated that,' they were told, 'you should have nicked a car in advance.' They raised their eyes heavenwards at this and went back across the A5 to drive north to the next exit and then follow Schmidt's track southwards, wondering all the time where he might have gone. A car despatched from Frankfurt entering the *Autobahn* two junctions south failed to encounter Schmidt's transport. He had succeeded in shaking them off his tail.

***

'You saw the pair who followed us over the footbridge, Bashir?'

'Ja, Herr Schmidt.'

'I may be mistaken but I think it shows the value of the precautions we take. Not a very subtle ploy but it has worked ... though I suppose they've learnt a little wisdom from the experience.' He laughed heartily until he was seized by a spasm of pain and had to fight to catch his breath. 'Somehow, Bashir, I don't think I'm going to be around too long to play these games. Still, this is the big one and I do expect to be around for the finale, that's good enough for me.'

'Nonsense, Herr Schmidt, you've got plenty of time ahead of you.'

'If only it were so Bashir, if only it were so! Thanks for your loyalty, you'll be able to go back to your family in Beirut when this is all over. You've booked them into a hotel in Malta for the whole month of September? Good, make sure you're there with them as well. That's an order, an order from the top. We'll need you there. Understood? Good. Now to the airport, I always think of it as a flying railway station with those great train-shed roofs of glass. A wonderful place. The Zurich flight is in a couple of hours, we're in good time.' He didn't tell Bashir that Zurich wasn't his final destination or how he was going to get there. He didn't need to know and it was safer that he shouldn't, the men at the service area had probably got the registration number of Bashir's car. But a fat lot of good that would do them! Bashir would change back to the genuine plates later that morning. His pain had lessened and he dozed off with a smile on his face. How he loved the chase, keeping at least a couple of steps ahead of his pursuers. To travel purposefully was indeed better than to arrive! That was his version of it anyway. But the arrival this time would be quite something, something historic! And this was Day 18 of the countdown. There were less than three weeks to go and the oncologist had given him two months at the outside. It might be a closer thing than he'd first thought or than he'd just hinted to Bashir. Yes, there were good men backing him up but he was the one who had planned it and put it all together, he *must* see it through! He *would* see it through! For nineteen years he'd lived just for this and

Sharon's coming to power had only added to his determination.

At Frankfurt Airport he put a call through to the bank in Basel, confirming the dinner appointment at *Die Drei Könige* for eight the following evening. Then he made a call to Dominique, who was at the hospital, he'd be with her in the early evening. Next he took a taxi into the city to the *Hauptbahnhof* and purchased a railway ticket to Freiburg im Breisgau with cash. From there he would take a taxi over the border from Germany into Alsace to Neuf-Brisach where he would take another taxi for the remainder of the 90 km taxi journey to Altkirch and Dominique. So he would avoid crossing into Switzerland and the possibility of passport examination. His pursuers would be expecting him to arrive in Basel by air and even if they kept a lookout on the railway they would expect him to be on an international express arriving in Basel SBB Station. Not finding him today wouldn't worry them overmuch as he was booked to see his Swiss banker at *Die Drei Könige* tomorrow evening, though they would have missed out on tonight's destination. Well, they could enjoy the ambiance of *Die Drei Könige* for as long as they liked – only he wouldn't be there. All the necessary cash for the bomb had already been transferred and after he had gone Dominique could use the balance at the bank for whatever would best benefit the Palestinian people, he would give her control of the account before he breathed his last.

At the station buffet he bought sandwiches and coffee. He was tempted to have a *Schnapps* but decided against, it would interfere with his drugs. Another quarter of an hour to his train. He sat and drowsed again and thought of Dominique, her warm soft body and her devotion to the cause. He was a lucky man he told himself and he believed it, even though he was involved in a race between two count downs. He had made up his mind to stay with her until it was all over.

From thoughts of Dominique his mind moved to the last few days: from his observation of the vans parked outside his apartment and the two pursuers this morning it had been very clear to him that they were on his trail. They, he didn't know whether it was German Security or the Israelis – probably the latter - could have pounced when he went to the clinic or when he set off this morning, but they hadn't and had they done so Bashir's brother would have gunned them down from his position across the road. And they hadn't stormed his apartment, an eventuality for which he had made plans which they would not have enjoyed, so they must be wanting to know where he would be going next in order to roll up the organisation with as many of its personnel as possible. Well, they had made a big mistake, one which they would regret to their dying days.

The *Inter City Express* was announced, it was dead on time – they ran things well in Germany. He climbed on with his one small suitcase crammed with his medication, found his seat and settled back to enjoy his last journey by rail. He opened his paperback copy of Wittgenstein's *Tractatus Logico-Philosophicus*, told himself that he'd really like to understand a little more of it before he died and wondered why. His eye skimmed the page and was held by the words:

> *"6..374 Even if all that we wish for were to happen, still this would only be a favour granted by fate, so to speak: for there is no logical connexion between the will and the world, which would guarantee it, and the supposed physical connection itself is surely not something that we could will."*

'Really?' he said to himself. The phrase "The Triumph of the Will" came to mind. *That* man's will had left Berlin a smoking ruin in 1945: which had not been the *Führer's* intention. Jakob Schmidt's will would soon leave Tel Aviv a smoking and radio-active ruin: which, most definitely, was his intention. And there was one simple favour he wanted from God, fate or whoever or whatever it was. Or rather it was two favours, that the 16th September 2001 would be an unforgettable day for the cause, a killer blow to Zionism, and that he would still be in this world to know that his work, his long laid plans, had been a triumphant success and that he had been the agent of vengeance. His eyes wanted to close, he was tired but he was also quietly jubilant, it was like an intoxication. The last of the money had been transferred to Basel two days before but it was not needed for the purchase of the bomb, it was surplus to requirements. They were all set to roll. Finance? Ticked off. Procurement? Taking place. Delivery? All in good time - 18 days hence. He looked out of the window as the ICE sped on, saw the German landscape rushing by, and smiled to himself at the thought of the frustration of his pursuers. And then Herr Schmidt returned to pleasant thoughts of Dr Dominique Garnier and her warm body before he took several pills, washing them down with a swig from a small bottle of spa water.

Chapter 28

Tuesday 11th September 2001

She had been leafing casually through the local paper while enjoying a mid-morning coffee when a headline and a short report took her eye. Tanya had just finished work on the accounts for the previous week, she preferred to do the bookkeeping in the spacious apartment over their restaurant in La Ciotat. They were doing reasonably well, it was yet early days and Pierre had some good ideas on improvements that they could make. She turned her attention back to the paper:

Yacht Found Drifting Without a Crew – Owner Missing

On September 2nd a 10 metre yacht, the Viagra, was found drifting, seemingly abandoned by its crew, 160 kilometres south west of Marseille. The yacht was normally berthed at Port-Miou, Cassis. The owner of the vessel, Mustafa Malik, is reported missing from his home in Cassis and the possibility is being investigated that he had fallen overboard. Marseille Police have yet to release a statement but it is believed that an empty bottle of vodka was found on a table in the cabin and that it is possible that M. Malik could have fallen overboard after drinking to excess. This is only rumour: M. Malik had the reputation of being a lively and popular host who loved to party and it is not known whether there were any others aboard the Viagra with him when he left port."

There had been rumours of Mustafa's disappearance

circulating for a few days and she wondered whether he had indeed fallen overboard in an inebriated state or whether some rival drug gang had disposed of him. On the other hand it wasn't entirely impossible that some of her former colleagues ...

She went down to the restaurant to tell Pierre but would be keeping her suspicions to herself.

***

Sam changed the count-down chart to read 5. There was now so little time to go and there was total inaction on all fronts. Nothing had been heard of Jakob Schmidt for nearly two weeks and Mark Gould's despatch of Mustafa had ensured that there was nothing to follow up on the drug front. To their surprise there had been a successor at Mustafa's house but he hadn't taken over the *Viagra* - perhaps the salvage bill for the yacht had outweighed the anticipated pleasure or profitability of its use. This reinforced Sam's conclusion that the *Viagra's* smuggling operations had been Mustafa's personal and private operation and nothing to do with the 16th September Unit. Meanwhile they had picked up nothing of value from 'phone taps, either from their own or from those of the Marseille Police. Mossad HQ had insisted that Sam remain at Cassis on the off-chance that something would turn up but nothing had. The situation was both frustrating and frightening.

Elizabeth and the Mums had gone into Marseille for the day and Dov was with Yvonne. So Sam had decided, on the spur of the moment, to go sightseeing. All was in order with the vines and in his restless state he couldn't stand the idea of doing nothing for the whole morning. If anyone wanted him he could be reached on his mobile. He pulled up at the main gate, west of Aubagne, of the depot of the *Premier Régiment de la Légion étrangère*. Its identity was announced in gleaming gold letters on either side of the entrance. Through the gate he could see the parade ground and in the distance a substantial memorial. An NCO in khaki fatigues came over to his car. On his chest he was wearing his medals, proper medals and not just campaign ribbons. Sam asked for *la musée* and was told to head back towards Aubagne and take the first road on the left. Two or three minutes later he climbed out of the car, having entered by a much less impressive gateway.

He spent around an hour upstairs looking at the exhibits including a Russian machine gun captured from the Iraqis in the Gulf War. A glass case had a model reconstructing the battle in 1942, against Rommel's *Panzerarmee Afrika,* at Bir-Hakeim in north Africa: now he knew why there was a Metro station with that name beside the Seine in Paris. He remembered Elizabeth's pleasure at coming across Stalingrad station when they had honeymooned in Paris. 'Stalin was a swine but it's good to see the city and its battle remembered, Volgograd doesn't have any of the resonance of Stalingrad does it?'

Back on the ground floor he went into the Great Hall with its paintings of past leaders of the *Légion*. He looked at his Michelin Guide, "The crypt contains a touching list of the dead." There was the crypt down a few steps from the Great Hall but roped off to keep visitors out. A notice by the steps explained that on the walls were the names of 903 officers of the Legion who had died in the service of France. *Officiers*, not the NCOs and the *légionnaires*, he noted. It took something away from the description of the Legion in the booklet he had bought on arrival, *" ... une famille pour les hommes venus des quatres coins du monde"*. His thoughts went back to the memorial crypt at the Golani Brigade Museum in Israel. How often he had been there, sometimes by design and on other occasions when he had found himself in the vicinity of Golani Junction. There each of the fallen had a file with his photograph and an account of his decease. Death made no distinction between soldier and officer and neither should a memorial. There he had remembered fallen Golani Brigade friends and acquaintances with whom he had once served and had looked at the files of some of the more recent dead. 'From the four corners of the earth', yes the Golanis were just that and they *truly* were a family.

He stood gazing out of the door that led from the museum to the parade ground. The regimental memorial was a hundred yards or so in front of him, a flat sided stone block surmounted by a great bronze globe, with bronze, life sized *légionnaires* at its four corners. It carried the inscription *HONNEUR ET FIDÉLITÉ* in gold letters. An appropriate military motto, he thought. A coach party arrived and was taken into the Great Hall by an under-officer who began to tell them about the annual commemoration of the events of 30 April 1863 when Captain Danjou's 64 men resisted 2,000 Mexicans for over 9 hours at Camarón. So long ago but clearly a formative event in the history of the *Légion*. The Captain's wooden hand was a sacred relic of the Légion, paraded annually on Camarón Day.

Honour and loyalty. Not a bad combination at all; sometimes loyalty to a cause could take you too far and honour, better still an understanding of what it meant to be truly human, was there to draw a line, a boundary, which you crossed at your peril. And yet a sense of affronted honour could either boil or fester and lead to an unrestrained response against which loyalty, to be an effective corrective, needed to be wide and generous, loyalty to humane and generous principles, loyalty as wide as one's shared humanity itself.

There were circumstances where there was no alternative but to fight for one's very survival, he and his people knew enough of that, but there had been many, many wars driven by the pride and arrogance of nations and their leaders. Wilfred Owen's *"Parable of the Old Man and the Young"* came to mind. It was so powerful because it took the "binding of Isaac" as its subject and then moved on to have the Angel say:

> *"Offer the Ram of Pride instead."*

And then came the concluding lines:

> *"But the old man would not so, but slew his son,*
> *And half the seed of Europe, one by one."*

Not a mistake the French made with the *Légion*, this supposed "family for men from all four corners of the earth": when military ventures turned to calamity the only French casualties would be from its limited number of officers and from the few Frenchmen in the ranks. Honour, loyalty - and a good press!

Sam had had enough of the military world for the morning but he was glad he'd come, it had made him think. He would read Owen's poem when he got home. He would have the *Domaine* to himself for a while, the peace and space would be welcome ... for a while, at any rate, until the others returned in the early afternoon. Then he would spend time reading to the children while the women saw to the evening meal. Parenthood had brought to him a greater sense of fulfilment than anything else in his life had done.

He was restless and stressed. What would they do if 16th September dawned and they *still* knew nothing of the Unit's detailed plans? The *Légion's* marching song came to mind, Edith Piaf's *"Non, je ne regrette rien"*: If Sam's mission were a failure would he be regretting mistakes made along the way? He hoped not and that even at this late hour there would be a breakthrough.

***

3.15 p.m. (French Time), Tuesday 11th September 2001.

They sat silent in front of the television in the lounge at the *Domaine*. Sam had been reading to the children when Mossad's Paris Station had called him with the news. He had hurried downstairs, switched on the TV and called the others to join him.

Smoke rose from the twin towers of the World Trade Center and the sequence was being shown and re-shown of the second aircraft, which they were later to learn was a Boeing 767 on United Airlines Flight 175 from Boston to Los Angeles - or so most of the 56 passengers and all the 9 crew had supposed when they boarded the flight that clear September morning - striking the south tower. The vast cloud of fire and smoke which then burst from that tower both gripped and shocked them. As a New Yorker from Crown Heights, Brooklyn Sam was particularly shaken by what he saw. Working in those towers were sure to be some of those who had been at school with him. Men and women who had done well for themselves in banking and broking firms, moving on from Crown Heights to better addresses in Brooklyn and New Jersey. Some with weekend places in the Catskills or on the Connecticut coast. And they would have families - families and young kids!

Black smoke billowed upwards but otherwise the towers stood strong and impassive, veiling the tumult and terror they must contain within. Surely those on the floors above the fires were helplessly trapped, it was impossible to imagine any safe path through the twin infernos. And those below? It was a fearfully long way down to the ground. Fire escape routes there must be, but would they be capable of evacuating so many swiftly enough?

The TV pictures began to alternate between Manhattan and scenes of Washington where smoke rose from the Pentagon. There were suggestions of other missing aircraft which were presumed to have been hijacked. There was talk of 50,000 people working in the twin towers.

4.02 p.m. The south tower began to collapse and debris, smoke and dust billowed over lower Manhattan. There were cries of 'No!' from those in the lounge. The scene appalled them and it was Mrs Feldman who spoke again, 'Poor souls!' She hugged the children to herself as though to protect them from the evil and violence of the scene. The others remained silent. Elizabeth was in tears. She could stand it no longer and went to make a pot of tea. In her KGB and SVR days when she had been engaged in industrial espionage she had worked in the sort of commercial enterprise that was located in those towers. Despite her covert activities she had liked her colleagues, finding the vast majority warm hearted, decent, friendly folk. Her imagination was painting a vivid picture of what it must be like in there. It was unspeakable.

As she waited for the kettle to boil she felt Sam's hand on her shoulder. His voice was thick with emotion, 'And such evil was most probably done in the name of religion. How perverse can you get?'

The 'phone rang. It was the Paris Station. The message was terse: Could it be that their quarry had fooled them and that they were now watching the operation he was funding? Michael would be with them that evening to review the position. Sam arranged to collect him from the airport.

'Paris, Elizabeth. They're wondering if we've got it wrong. They think that Jakob Schmidt's target might be New York and Washington, not Israel. They're suggesting that we might have been set up as a ruse!'

'What do you think Sam?' In a way it was a relief to have your attention diverted legitimately from the horrors of the TV screen.

'My mind tells me that it's possible. My intuition says that the threat we're trying to counter is real and that Israel *is* the target. Whether it's the same bunch of fanatics I don't know, I can't guess, but we can't just shut up shop. September 2001 may have yet more horrors in store.'

'Intuition Sam, that's supposed to be a female quality!'

'Not exclusively female, after all it would be an insult to your sex to suggest that rational thought was exclusively a male preserve. Women may have stronger instincts but men aren't entirely lacking in that respect! Often things are finely balanced and the ultimate decision turns on a hunch rather than on pure logic. Reason there must be to throw out the impossible and balance alternatives against one another, but in the end it's often the solution that *feels* right that's followed.

'Well I have a gut feeling that the threat from the Unit is real and that we're on target - if only we could find Schmidt. We should never have let him go to earth. It was bad enough for our people to lose him between his apartment and the airport at Frankfurt. But what have the Swiss achieved with all their efforts with the shrinks? They've had Schmidt's French shrink's place under observation but they've seen nothing at all of him. His banker's heard nothing more since Schmidt's non-appearance for dinner at that Basel hotel, though there's around $1¼ million left in the account that's still waiting to be shifted. Perhaps they don't need it and they got the bomb for a bargain price in the Ukrainian bazaar. Elizabeth, I'm at my wits end, today's Tuesday 11th and our guess, a not unreasonable one, is that there's a bomb to go off in or over Israel on Sunday 16th. That gives us no more than four days to act and we still have no idea where Schmidt is! ... Last seen leaving an Autobahn service area near Frankfurt and then ... nothing ... vanished into thin air!'

She pulled him close, there were no words for a

situation like this.

4.27 p.m. The north tower began its catastrophic collapse. For those fighting their way down fire escape routes to the ground the race for life was ending abruptly and violently. Sam and the others watched the scenes of people fleeing along streets, pursued by more vast clouds of dust and smoke. It added to the cloud of fog enveloping Lower Manhattan created by the south tower's collapse 25 minutes earlier.

'Who organised all that?' Dov had been sitting in stunned silence until now. 'The people we're after or others?'

Sam looked up, 'I can't even begin to guess. All I can say is that they're wholly evil whoever they are.'

Elizabeth wiped away a tear, 'It's all so unreal, like "Towering Inferno" and "Airport" all rolled into one. Everyone's going to be saying that. But *this* was real people not actors. Real death, not the screen version.'

***

At 11.00 that evening Sam, Dov and Elizabeth sat in the lounge with Michael. On their first meeting Sam had instinctively disliked Michael and concluded that he was one of the ruthless sort, without much subtlety, who was intent on his career to the exclusion of most other things. However he had worked with people like him and he couldn't fault his assessment of the situation.

'As I see it there's a considerable likelihood that yours has been a trail designed to lead us and our friends away from what the terrorists intended. The media are talking of the New York operation as the worst terrorist action ever.'

Sam broke in, 'And if there is a nuclear attack on Sunday?'

'Then the New York record won't have stood for very long! OK, we accept that there really is the possibility that your threat - by that I mean of course the one you're seeking to counter - that your threat is genuine. And, of course, we can't risk it happening. So it's been decided to send a team into that French therapist's house to tear the place apart and if necessary to wring out of her the information on where Schmidt's hiding. If it's necessary we'll tear her apart as well. If only we'd snatched him from the pavement in Frankfurt instead of thinking that he'd lead us to other members of the Unit. Perhaps you'd like to let your Swiss fellow know our intentions as a matter of courtesy. We wouldn't want to interrupt his underling's therapy session, would we?'

'I can't argue against that Michael. We've got to do something. I'll ring Erik Blum from the kitchen. Elizabeth can make some more coffee at the same time. You can watch CNN while we're away.' He switched on the set and headed for the kitchen.

'So that's it Erik, they plan to send in a team to search the place and interrogate Dr Garnier tomorrow afternoon. ... What's that you say, you've already arranged to send in your Swiss shrink to reason with Dr Garnier ... when? ... at 14.30 hours tomorrow afternoon. ... OK. I'll come back to you on that. ... Yes, we're feeling the strain too. Like you we've been propelled forwards by today's events.'

'That's the situation, Michael, Erik Blum has his own plans for tomorrow afternoon. As you know they have one of their men enrolled as a patient of Dr Garnier. Well his Swiss shrink, the woman who primes him with what he's got to tell Dr Garnier, is going there tomorrow to reason with her.'

'To reason with her! What sort of a game do the Swiss think they're playing? What we used to call parlour games? Our team won't be asking the woman anything, they'll be telling her what they want to know and getting it!'

'Michael, there are more ways than one of getting information out of people ... '

'And how many days have we got left until 16th September?'

'Four days before 00.01 hours on 16th. I know time's tight but we ought to see whether Erik's plan works.'

'What have Blum and his people discovered apart from the banking transactions that started this whole business off?

'We had Schmidt in our power in Frankfurt but then lost him on a German *Autobahn*, if I remember rightly, Michael. I'm asking that Erik be given a chance.'

'So when's this Swiss shrink going there?'

'Two thirty, 14.30 hours, tomorrow afternoon, it's the earliest Dr Garnier can see her. And it's the same time here, of course.'

Michael paused for a moment's thought, 'OK, Sam, she can have one hour for her mission. We go in the moment she leaves or at the end of an hour, whichever comes first. Yes, it's probably not a bad plan. At the cost of one hour's delay we will have two bites at the cherry. Dov can drive me to Mulhouse and on to Altkirch, there won't be much going on at this end whatever happens. I'd like a look at the TV first though.' The mention of Mulhouse brought back memories for Sam, it had been there in the Railway Museum at Mulhouse that his own liberty had been negotiated with Erik Blum.

They returned to the lounge to see the now familiar images of the doomed towers and hear talk of thousands of dead. Sam wondered whether, in a few days time, they would be hearing of megadeaths, that obscene expression of the nuclear planners, in Israel. If so the images beamed world-wide wouldn't be of the gradual destruction of buildings, but of something brighter than a thousand suns ... followed later on by satellite views of a vast radioactive crater.

Chapter 29

Wednesday 12th September 2001, 2.30 p.m. Altkirch

Dr Maria Bertorelli took her seat in the salon and faced the older woman who opened the conversation, 'As I understand it, Dr Bertorelli, you wish to speak to me about one of my patients, Peter Gruenweiler. That is so?'

'Yes, Dr Garnier, Peter is a friend of mine and from some of the things he has told me recently I have felt concern.'

'As you know, without his permission I am unable to discuss his case, though if you know him well, you should be aware of the extent of his psychosis.' Maria patted herself on the back for the effectiveness of her coaching of Peter for his rôle as Dominique Garnier's patient. 'He is your lover?'

'No, well perhaps ... a friend whose company I both enjoy and find helpful. No, we're not established lovers, just finding our way together.'

'Though if you have brought his written permission for me to discuss his case, that is a different matter and we can talk about him.' Maria produced Peter's signed authority from her handbag and passed it to the other woman.

'I trust you wouldn't be offended if I speak to him to satisfy myself that this is what he really wants. I won't keep you a moment.' She went into another room to make the 'phone call and Maria waited tensely for her to return. She was praying that Peter had his mobile switched on as Erik had instructed. If he hadn't it would sink the whole enterprise. She studied her finger nails and almost got up to walk around the room but forced herself to remain seated. Through the French window she could see the rain falling heavily and she could make out roses in the weak light. She almost jumped when she heard Dr Garnier's voice from over her shoulder, 'Yes, he says I'm to discuss his case with you. Though I would counsel you against mixing up friendship and your professional activities.'

It was a cue that Maria took, though with a certain diffidence, 'That's wise advice but Peter has told me that you have not always heeded it.'

There was silence and Maria was telling herself that she had blown her chances of success when the other woman replied, 'If he's told you that I won't deny it. I suppose you intend to report me for gross misconduct with a patient?'

'No Dominique, I wish to do no such thing. I'm concerned for Peter and for you. Peter's concerned for you as well. Over the weeks he's seen you going downhill, losing the thread of conversations and clearly under great stress. I've come here as much as a woman as a professional.'

Her abandonment of Dr Garnier for Dominique had its effect; the other woman's face relaxed a little.

'I appreciate that Dr Bertorelli - did you say that it was Maria? Good, Maria then. I appreciate that you are genuine in your concern. I'm very much alone, without anyone to whom I can open up. I don't suppose you've ever had a dying lover? Never known what it is to see the one man who has really meant something to you ... meant everything in fact ... to see him dying little by little ... bit by bit ... dying in pain ... to see him reducing more and more to a skeleton day by day? To see what cancer can do.' The room was silent, the rain pattered on the window.

'No Dominique that hasn't been my experience, though I do know enough about bereavement, the loss of one deeply loved, the loss of the one man who meant everything to me. My lover died four years ago, he fell to his death while climbing the Matterhorn. The wound has yet to heal fully, the process has begun, thanks partly to Peter - as I have told you Peter and I aren't long time lovers but he has shown wisdom and understanding. Through him I have become reconciled with Klaus' widow.'

'Your lover was Klaus Bonner, the psychotherapist? I once worked with him. You are both a very fortunate woman and an unfortunate one, Maria'

'Yes, a fine man. My colleague at the faculty and for six years my lover.' Despite herself tears were forming in her eyes. 'But Dominique tell me about your situation.'

'First my confession about my night here with your friend, Peter Gruenweiler. It came soon after Jakob came here and told me that his cancer was inoperable and terminal. He'd lived with it for some years but it was now rampant. They gave him three months and no more. And he had a project that had to be ready for this month, for this September. It had become his life's work the one thing he must achieve before he died. I was in such a state that I took the opportunity that the fog provided - I hadn't planned for Peter to stay here the night but when the chance offered itself ... Well I took it. It was a sort of test, could I find someone to replace Jakob in my affections. We had been lovers for twelve years, no thirteen. Your friend was a good lover, if that interests you.' She managed a smile, 'But he was no Jakob and I knew that I would never find someone to replace him. I knew that soon I would be *une veuve* - a widow - in all but the formal title.' She paused and once again the pattering of the rain on the window was the only sound until the clock in the hall chimed three quarters and Maria was reminded that she had to keep their conversation on course.

'Dominique, what's Jakob's project that has to be completed this month?'

'It's secret, I can't tell you. In a way I'd like to because it frightens me!'

She followed her intuition, 'Isn't it the delivery and detonation of a nuclear device on the coast of Israel?'

The other woman looked at her with incredulity, 'Maria how do you, how could you know? And the place is Palestine not Israel!'

'It was picked up by Swiss Security and the Israelis know as well. Peter is from Swiss Security, I'm not going to hold anything back from you. I'm here to ask you to help. If you don't the Israelis are waiting to storm the house and they won't be *asking* you to help. No, they'll be applying various interrogation techniques that both of us have treated patients for. They say "once tortured always tortured". I hold no brief for the Israelis, except to say that, faced with the threat of a nuclear explosion here or in Basel, I wouldn't be following the rules and ethics of our profession in trying to find out the details before it was too late.'

'I can't tell you, Maria. It's Jakob's life's work. He's put everything into this.'

Maria had forgotten the number of the clock's chimes, she had lost track of time and didn't dare to look at her watch, 'Dominique, there are many legacies that you can leave but surely the effects of a nuclear explosion isn't one of them. You and Jakob may hate Jews ...'

'But we don't, it's Zionist Israelis we hate. We're not anti-Semitic. Maria, have *you* ever seen the inside of a refugee camp. Can you envisage what it's like to live day in day out in squalor, without hope of any betterment of your situation, to see your children and their children suffer?'

'Dominique, there's not much time left. Just listen a moment.' Maria was beginning to shake, the tension had got through to her and was showing itself, 'You worked with Klaus, remember the work you did together?'

'Yes with traumatised kids, he was brilliant.'

'And you've seen the effects of cancer at first hand?'

'You don't have to remind me of that - I've got to give Jakob another shot of morphine in half an hour.'

'I had no idea he was here, Dominique!'

'Yes, he's been here for the last two weeks.' The weeks when there'd been no 'phone calls to monitor. 'He's in the bedroom at the top of the house.' She smiled a wistful smile, 'It's not the most convenient place for him to be but that's where we used to make love.'

'Listen Dominique, if that bomb goes off there will be thousands of men, women and children who will get all manner of cancers including leukemia. You've worked with kids, you've loved them, you've worked in places like Gaza and Beirut which have been grim. Do you want your legacy - yours and Jakob's - to be that, a modern plague afflicting Palestinian and Jew alike. Dominique ... you've done so much good in your life, so much as a therapist! Don't let this happen, please don't. As a woman I'm pleading with you, as Klaus Bonner's grieving lover ... .' She broke down, she was drained, totally and utterly drained, she had no more arguments, nothing else to use in persuading her. She knew she'd failed in her mission.

Again the sound of the rain on the window, harder than before. There was a long pause then, 'Maria ... you have persuaded me, though it's with a heavy heart that I do this but Jakob will never last out to 16th September. He's probably got ... no more than 48 hours left.' She was crying and she wiped the tears away with her sleeve. 'If I give you the information the Israelis will keep away?'

'Yes, they won't come if they can find the thing in time. There will be no need.'

'No interrogation ... no assassination squad?'

'None.'

Dr Dominique Garnier got up from her seat and went to the desk in the corner. She switched on her PC, waited and then began to type. She printed out not one but three items, giving only one of them to Maria. 'Here's the information you need: the ship, the date and the port - you probably realise that it's set to go off on 16th September, the anniversary of the massacres at the Sabra and Shatila camps by the Israelis' Phalangist friends. And I swear to you that this is the truth, I'm not fooling you. Now I must attend to Jakob. No, don't go just yet it won't be long. It you want music the hi-fi's in the corner. If you don't mind Bach's organ music - there's a CD in the machine - you just need to press Play. I'm glad it was you and not the Israelis who called. Thank you for the conversation and ... I'm glad that you have Peter Gruenweiler as a friend, despite all his neuroses which I now suppose may be more apparent than real!' There was warmth and gratitude in her smile. 'Just wait a little longer, I won't keep you long.' She took a couple of steps into the hallway and turned, 'There's one more thing you ought to know: Jakob was engaged to a nurse who was murdered there in Shatila on 16th September 1982. You, Maria, will understand the effect that the loss has had on him. *That* is what lies behind all this. If you had come here on Monday I would have told you nothing but, after yesterday's events in America, violence and revenge have lost their attraction.' Dominique Garnier turned and headed for the stairs.

Maria tried to reply but the words wouldn't come. She went back into the room and looked at her watch, three fourteen, she had just over fifteen minutes left before Mossad's squad were due to call, she had made it - if the paper she held told the truth. Once again she began to shake. She went to the hi-fi and switched it on. the Bach Fantasia in G Major began. She walked to the window and looked out at the dismal afternoon. Peter and the others would be getting pretty wet out there.

***

'Jakob, I've been dealing with one of my patients who arrived unexpectedly. How are you?'

His skull-like face looked up from the pillow, 'I suppose I've slept for most of the time. Have you the morphine ready to dull the pain?'

She nodded and produced the syringe. While she injected him he lay back on the pillow, 'Thanks Dominique for all your love and care over the years. Thanks for all we've done as comrades in arms ... I'm beginning to be afraid that I won't reach 16th September. Still we'll see. The night is coming ... '

'Yes, Jakob, we'll see. And thank you for all your love over the years ... thirteen years, almost ... There's something from the bank that needs your signature, I'm the witness. Let me help you.' With difficulty he signed, the time for reading documents was long since gone. She added her signature. She was struggling hard with her emotions. She went to the wardrobe and took out the pistol. 'Remember the silly games we used to play here, pretending to rape one another?'

If a skull can smile then Jakob managed to do so. Certainly the pain had eased and his face was almost tranquil, 'Dominique my love ... ' He closed his eyes.

The pistol was almost touching the side of his head when she pulled the trigger, he rose from the bed and fell back. 'Farewell Jakob,' she whispered, 'Night has come for us both.' And she remembered the day that Spring when she had told him that, if necessary, she would be ready to die for him.

Maria heard the shot as she stood at the window and she subsequently reckoned that it must have been six or seven seconds later, when she had reached the third step of the stairway that the second shot rang out, causing her to stop momentarily before continuing her wild rush upwards. Dominique had said he was at the top of the house so she knew where to go.

The bedroom was a scene of horror. The two bodies, with horribly damaged heads, lay on the bed which was already saturated with blood. Blood was also spattered over the walls. There was nothing she could do for either of them, that was very clear and her next instinct was to get out of the room, out of the house and to get the information to Peter and Erik. If the Israelis had come they couldn't have created more of a mess. Somehow she reached the front door and struggled with the lock before it yielded. She opened the door, saw Peter down the road under the trees and passed out on the doorstep.

Peter Gruenweiler was almost hit by a passing car as he rushed across the road followed by Erik Blum. They scooped Maria off the step and carried her back into the hallway, closing the door and hoping that they hadn't attracted the attention of any other passer by and that the car driver would have a short memory. Maria didn't appear to have any injuries and came to quickly, muttering disjointedly about guns and a butcher's shop. Gradually she became coherent and gave her account of what had happened.'

'Your piece of paper with the information?'

'In my handbag in the salon. But please get me out of here.'

'As soon as we can Maria.' Peter got her a cup of water and then pocketed the cup to ensure that no fingerprints were left for the French police.

Erik had found the note in her handbag and was talking to a Mossad agent on his mobile. 'The ship's the *Königsberg*, the port Haifa, she docked earlier today 12th September, and its in a container. Now read that back. Good, you've got it. Good hunting then! Make sure you let Sam know.'

On the end of the bed were two sheets of paper, the other items that Dominique had typed. One asked the parish priest for one requiem and one grave for herself and Herr Jakob Schmidt. The other was an authority for the Basel bank account to be operated by Dr Maria Bertorelli and Herr Peter Gruenweiler, for the benefit of work among traumatised children. There was a spot of blood on the bottom left hand corner. It was as though it had been sealed with blood, but there was nothing to tell them whose blood it was. Blum wiped the blood off on the duvet and pocketed the document. He left the other note for the parish priest of Altkirch to deal with.

Peter Gruenweiler was the worse affected of the two men. It had probably to do with his relationship with Dominique Garnier as his therapist as well as his experience with her and the gun in the bed that was now the scene of such bloody and violent death. He went straight to the bathroom and was sick down the lavatory before being ordered by Erik Blum to clear all the bugging devices out of the house. In Blum's words, 'The French police are going to have enough to keep them busy here without evidence of further odd goings on.'

Thirty minutes later they were ready to leave. Erik called up their car with muddied French plates and pushed Peter and Maria out the door in front of him, the rain was still falling in torrents and with luck nobody would have been around long enough to see anything untoward.

***

Later Erik Blum called the police chief in Mulhouse, whom he'd met occasionally, and explained that a young colleague who'd been consulting Dr Garnier in Altkirch had spoken to her earlier that day and found her very agitated and hinting at suicide. When he'd called back later as arranged she hadn't replied (that call had recently been made to add verisimilitude to Blum's account). Of course the young officer was probably a little up-tight but, in general, Blum trusted his judgement and it would be worth checking that all was well. No, he wouldn't give his colleague's name, he wasn't too keen to have it known that he was consulting a shrink. Blum put the 'phone down relieved that they would be likely to check on the place. He didn't like the idea of their bodies lying there for weeks and he felt responsible for preventing colleagues from the French force from having to deal with decomposing remains. Corpses, particularly, those with gunshot wounds were bad enough without decomposition to contend with as well. He was glad his stomach was stronger than Peter's but if it had been his therapist ... there was no telling.

***

3.20 p.m. Cassis

The Mums were looking after the children in the morning room while Sam, Elizabeth and Dov sat around the table in the kitchen watching the mobile that lay in front of Sam. They had said little since 2.30 pm. when Maria had been due at Dr Garnier's house. Though Sam had been praying silently but fervently for her success. They were beginning to think that she had failed in her mission when the 'phone rang:

'Michael here in Altkirch. Mission successful, the Swiss shrink has got the info! She's come up trumps. Erik Blum's over the moon and sends his greetings. We want you back at HQ or somewhere near it. More information later. Must go now.'

'Thanks, Michael.'

Sam switched off the 'phone and began to sob. He had never reacted to anything else in this way but the enormity of the threat and the nearness to 16th September had created within him a tension such as he had never experienced before. Elizabeth too was in tears and Dov went to make a pot of tea and to tell the Mums that they had good news at last.

***

7.30 p.m. Basel

Peter and Maria sat looking at one another across her kitchen table. Both had been very subdued since their return home. 'If I'd known what would happen ... '

'You didn't know! How could you? And even if you had I think you would still have gone there.'

'Well the threat's out of the way, a mushroom cloud removed from over people's heads.'

'Yes and no. They may have to defuse it or something of the sort. The Israelis are working on that now.'

'And it's 12th September, the day after those horrific events in the USA! Yesterday it was public horror and today something on a smaller scale but far more personal!'

'Yes and we'll know in three days whether Dr Maria Bertorelli has saved the planet.'

'Don't joke, Peter! I thought it was all buttoned up and over. I need sleep though, see you in the morning - sleep in the other room tonight and, if you can't sleep ... '

'Yes?'

'Pray for whoever's defusing the thing.'

***

Meanwhile Erik Blum had left them to themselves and was back in the office. Before leaving Maria's apartment he had visited the bathroom and noted two different makes of toothpaste and two toothbrushes. And there were two bathrobes on the back of the door. Either Maria liked to ring the changes or else Peter had moved in, perhaps as an occasional visitor or perhaps on a more regular basis. He wished them every happiness - they'd certainly earned it.

Chapter 30

Wednesday 12 September 2001, 21.05 hours

Their car pulled up at a side entrance to Marseille's Marignane Airport. Dov leant across from the driving seat and shook Sam by the hand. 'All the best my friend. Good luck. No, that won't do. May God go with you. It's a dangerous task you've got before you.'

'Look after the two Mums as well as Elizabeth and the kids, Dov. Knowing they're all in your hands will let me give my undivided attention to the task in hand. It's nearly over. We can all go on holiday when I get back.'

'Where, Sam?

'I fancy Switzerland. Erik Blum's promised to take us on tour - if we survive. Be seeing you.' He headed for the gate and was met by an official who, satisfied with his credentials, led him to a car which headed at once for the end of the runway.

In the dark they could see the aircraft's landing lights coming quickly onwards them and then slowing. The official listened to the message on his radio, 'Oui, Monsieur, c'est votre avion. Your 'plane ... I regret you have missed the duty free shop. You must climb into the hoist and we'll get you up onto the flight deck.'

The El Al freighter, a Boeing Jumbo 747-200, came to a halt fifty yards away and the hoist was moved into place. Sam shook hands with his companion, climbed into the hoist and bade what he hoped would be only a temporary farewell to French soil. As he came level with the cockpit he saw the captain in the doorway and stepped onto the flight deck. The hoist backed away. The door was closed and after a few words with the control tower the Jumbo started to taxi away. They took fuel and in twenty minutes they were airborne again with the lights of Marseille below them. Sam got a glimpse of the gilt statue of the Madonna and Child on the top of the

Basilica and then they were out over the Mediterranean, at the eastern end of which lay their destination. He remembered the promise he'd made to Dov's young policewoman that he'd place some record of their deliverance from the menace of the 16th September Unit in the crypt. He prayed that he'd be returning here to do just that. It would be interesting finding a way of doing it with words of studied ambiguity, which didn't attract too much attention.

'You must be very important cargo, Mr Kagan, for us to be diverted here to collect you. We were just getting ready at Schiphol when we got the message. We took enough fuel to reach Marseille and a little more besides, I wouldn't have liked to land here with nearly full tanks. Who's paying the bill for your trip?'

He wondered whether to be forthcoming and decided to confuse things a little, 'The Institute, I expect.'

'On a lecture tour or something of the sort?'

'Yes, something of the sort', he agreed. 'Do you mind if I try to get some sleep, I've a heavy day ahead.'

'Make yourself as comfortable as you can in one of the spare crew seats. I'll wake you when we're half an hour out of Ben Gurion. By the way my brother, Eli is on the Mossad payroll too. Sweet dreams, that's if you folk ever manage such a thing.' And Sam was reminded that his recent nights had often been disturbed by nightmarish dreams. He put on his *kippah* and prayed quietly:

> *'Wherever I go - only Thou! Wherever I stand - only Thou! Just Thou; again Thou! always Thou! Thou, Thou, Thou! When things are good, Thou! when things are bad Thou! Thou, Thou, Thou!'*

It was an old *Chassidic* song he had heard the *Lubavitchers* sing in Crown Heights. It brought him back to his childhood. And it somehow fortified him for what he now faced. He fell asleep murmuring, 'Thou! Thou! Thou!' The aircrew went about their tasks, checking on their position and heading, looking forward to being back in Tel Aviv early the next morning.

***

Thursday 13th September 2001, early morning

Sam shook hands with the crew and disappeared down the steps to the tarmac at Ben Gurion's El Al freight terminal. A Mossad car was waiting and Sam recognised the driver and was in turn recognised by him, 'Sam, I heard rumour that you were back with us and then you disappeared again and I thought I'd got it wrong. Been in Holland, then?'

'No, Dan, the South of France. They used the Jumbo as a taxi and dropped into Marseille to collect me.'

'Wow, you must be important or what you're doing must be!'

'A little of each I expect, Dan. And now straight up the coast to the docks at Haifa and don't worry about speed limits but do make sure you keep the car on the road! Now the last time I saw you your son was hoping to get a signing with the Maccabees. Did he make the team? ... ' And they began that inconsequential chat which typifies the meeting of old friends and acquaintances. Sam hoped it would keep his mind engaged. Time enough, on arrival in Haifa, to ponder the practicalities of the search for the bomb.

But that was easier said than done. There was little time left. By Sunday they would know whether this was a hoax or dire reality. And Tuesday evening was Rosh Hashanah, the New Year. What sort of New Year for Israel, for the world for that matter? The events of Tuesday 11th September had changed things in an alarmingly incalculable way. And the strife between Jew and Palestinian showed no signs of abating. A world of terror. A world at war? Possibly, and if the threat to Israel proved genuine and they were unable to avert it? He found himself asking Dan to repeat something that he had just told him.

They passed through Petah Tikva - the Gate of Hope. So many hopes had been fulfilled in this land. Yet so many hopes had been dashed, were now being dashed. The hopes of ordinary Jews and of Palestinian Arabs. Bethlehem, spruced up and refurbished for the Millennium, was now deserted by tourists and marked by the signs of battle. Jews went to discos or family celebrations fearful of being part of the carnage wrought by the next suicide bomber. Both were Semitic peoples yet they were at war. They passed Netanya with its high rise hotels and apartment blocks, scene of some of the recent suicide bombings, and continued northwards up the Mediterranean coast. It began to rain as they neared Haifa and Sam sensed, rather than saw, the mass of Mt. Carmel to their right. Here Elijah had called down fire from heaven upon his sacrifice after the abject failure of the Baalite priests to achieve such a demonstration of divine power. The task between now and Sunday was to ensure that the fire bound up in the elements did not break forth on all and sundry, Jew and Arab.

A phrase from the Christian Scriptures came into his mind - "the elements shall melt with fervent heat". Well they wouldn't if he had anything to do with it! Not for the time being at any rate. They now had less than three days. He looked at his watch: there were just 68 hours left to be precise. He knew he was only about 120 km away from their house at Kazrin in the Golan, but he felt an immense distance away from home and its comforts. He longed to be with Elizabeth and the kids. He longed for the warmth and comfort of having them in his arms. Home could be defined in many ways but for Sam Kagan it was above all people and relationships.

Sam was suddenly aware that the car had stopped. 'Well here we are Sam, it was the Haifa docks you wanted and that's where I've brought you. Fifty minutes and most of it with all four wheels on the road! All the best Sam. *Mosel tov!'* Sam got out and waved as Dan drove the car away to the parking lot. The dock security boss was coming toward him. The task now was to get the search under way with all necessary urgency and thoroughness but without panic and alarm.

Chapter 31

Thursday 13 September 2001, early morning

The Haifa Customs chief shook his head, 'We can't do it, we haven't the manpower and the importers would never stand for it. Opening *all* the containers from the ship? Never! And in any case who'd pay the overtime *if* we had enough staff? What did you say you were looking for?'

Sam gave him the benefit of the doubt, it was 4.45 in the morning, the poor man had been summoned from his bed and was still half asleep. Sam guessed he had been to a rather liquid dinner the previous evening and was not at his best, 'A nuclear bomb, Roni. Nothing more, nothing less. You see we'd rather like to have the opportunity to defuse it before it blows a great hole in the coast of Israel. Your help would be valued but if not we'll see to it ourselves. But whether you help or not you can keep your mouth shut about what you've just heard.'

At that point Shlomo Ya'acoby the dock manager arrived, another unfortunate dragged unwillingly from his bed. His security chief introduced him to Sam and then retreated to the comfort of his car. The dark shape of the *Königsberg* towered above them and Sam seemed to sense an emanation of malice from the ship. Behind them was some heavy machinery on a low loader, the yellow flashing lights on the tractor providing an eerie effect as it waited for its police escort before moving off out of the docks. It had begun to rain and the location was not the best place for their discussion.

'Right Mr Kagan, let's move off the dockside to my office and try to sort things out. As I understand it you want to turn out everything from the containers. That's a vast operation, we've never done anything like it before. Did you say the Prime Minister's Office has ordered the action?' They followed him to the car and were driven half a mile to the offices.

Sam got ready for his explanation and the dock security man set to brewing tea. 'What I'm now going to tell you mustn't get beyond these doors. If it does we're going to have the most frightful panic you can imagine, people fleeing the Israeli coast in their hundreds of thousands. Understood? Good. Well, we have information that there's a nuclear bomb in one of the containers on the *Königsberg* and you can take it that it's not a museum item but intended to be used in earnest very soon.' He avoided naming 16th September, it wasn't relevant to the search which would start immediately, with or without the assistance of the dock company, and if it became public knowledge the nearness of the date would only add to the terror of the population. 'Every one of those containers has to be emptied and searched thoroughly and as soon as possible. The question is how we organise it Shlomo - the job's got to be done immediately, if possible under cover if not then out in the open. We've got no shortage of manpower, as many of the IDF as we need and we can use IDF bases for emptying the containers. And they've got wagons to carry the things. So how many containers are there and how long will it take to get them off the *Königsberg*?'

'There are 119, you're lucky she's a small ship and not fully loaded. But this isn't good for the importers, they're not going to be happy at having their consignments torn apart by the military.'

'A little happier than being torn apart themselves by a nuclear blast! Perhaps you'd like a word with the PM's office?'

'It's not that I disbelieve you but if ... '

'If I were nothing more than a crazy nut? OK, here's the number, get in touch but don't waste any time over it. And when you've spoken to them call your staff into work - we've got to get those cranes working at once.'

Shlomo Ya'acoby left the table to use the 'phone on his desk. Sam finished his tea and indicated that he wanted a refill. Roni Fattal the Customs chief sat without a word gazing at his mug of tea, which was untouched, he seemed numbed at the threat. Outside the low loader with its heavy load made its way past towards the dock gates, illuminating the scene with its yellow flashing lights. Somehow it added to the disorientation Sam and the others felt. Sam looked forward to getting the opening under way, better to be doing something than waiting. But he knew that for him personally it would be a matter of waiting until the thing was found, then it would be action for him and the disposal team, working against the clock to defuse it. He wouldn't be happy until the bomb was found, and even then not until it had been made safe.

Sam wondered whether he was seeing the last days of Haifa and to his surprise some words in the Christian Scriptures came to mind, "they were eating and drinking, marrying and giving in marriage, until the day when Noah entered the ark, and they did not know until the flood came and swept them all away, so will be the coming of the Son of Man." It was Christian apocalyptic, last days Messianism. He had remembered it from a study he'd once made of Christian Messianic expectation while he was in the *yeshiva*. Would it be better for these people in Haifa to be blotted out without warning or to know what threatened them and to be able to mend their ways, or more likely to be swept away by pure terror. It mustn't come to that.

He thought of the report he'd had of the debate earlier that night over what they might do in the face of the menace. The action favoured by most of the top brass had been to make the *Königsberg* put to sea again and take it's terror cargo elsewhere. But some had argued strongly for dealing with it at Haifa. Where would the explosion be and what would be the effect of radioactive fallout drifting back eastwards from wherever the ship might be in the Med when the thing went off? And there was always the risk that it would then prove to be the ultimate Arab propaganda coup with claims that Israel was undertaking a nuclear test or something of that kind. To the outside world that might appear more likely than a story about a free gift from some unknown terror group, the 16th September Unit, being turned away by its intended recipients. It would be a wonderful excuse for another Arab invasion. Was the present morale of the IDF adequate for a threat of that order? Finally his argument, presented for him by Mossad's Deputy Director, that they knew where it was and had time to immobilise it, had won the day or rather the night. He had been told that it had been an exhausting debate and he prayed that the final decision was the right one. Once the search was under way he would speak to Elizabeth and the kids on the 'phone and then get some sleep. He would need to have all his wits about him once they had located the thing and were attempting to render it harmless, he'd promised Moshe from the Weizmann Institute that he'd be there with him.

***

Friday 14th September 2001

Nothing found and mutterings of scaremongering among the military and others.

***

Saturday 15th September 2001

The Sabbath before the New Year. Sam woke and called control: 98 containers had been checked and no bomb found, though some very odd items had turned up which were not listed on the manifest or import documents. 21 containers remained and they should be cleared within the next couple of hours. They would call him as soon as anything was found or the job was complete. He told them to make sure that the very last container was checked even if the bomb were found earlier: it wouldn't do for there to be two bombs or a bomb and a dummy. He picked up his book of war poems, surprised at his inner calm in the tense situation. Then he thought of Elizabeth and the kids, if things went wrong they would never see one another again, and he began to sweat. He took a photograph of the family from his wallet and looked at it. Then he opened the book and slipped the photograph in for use as a bookmark. The last poem took his eye and as he read on it gripped his mind and imagination, it was an imagined broadcast prior to a nuclear attack telling parents to give their children the appropriate pills "one and two" and proceed to their nuclear shelters. Well shelters weren't likely to be of any avail to Sam and his colleagues if they couldn't find and defuse the thing.

***

11.00 hours, Haifa

The telephone rang. A voice from the Control Office, 'Sam we've got egg on our faces, the last container has just been cleared and there's nothing there, not the slightest sign of a bomb. We've been taken in. My next call's to the PM's Office and I'm not looking forward to Arik's response.'

Sam was shaken. Emotionally washed out, he didn't know whether to be relieved or weep. His plans for a management rôle at Mossad HQ had just gone down the pan but that was the least of his worries. Despite his emotions his mind was clear and focused. 'Don't do anything yet. There's the chance that the weapon could be biological.'

'OK Sam, I'll see what I can manage on that score but

I'm not too hopeful. The politicians will probably want all this out of the way as soon as possible, they'll announce it as a Customs swoop aided by the military. Sorry, Sam, I feel for you. Do you think your Swiss friends set you up?' Eli rang off and Sam sat immobile for perhaps five minutes. Eli wasn't sorry, he was twisting the knife. Sam hadn't expected this. The kids could hand back "pills one and two" and their parents could put them back in the green containers! No need for shelters, except that he needed one to hide himself from the fall out of Mossad's wrath. Again his mind asserted itself. All his instincts continued to tell him that Erik Blum was trustworthy, totally trustworthy. If anyone had set Sam up then they had set up Erik as well. And, as Sam thought of the way the Swiss had discovered the secret of the *Königsberg*'s cargo, he remained convinced that the threat was real. He must have a word with Bern.

Erik wasn't available and Sam was put through to Peter Gruenweiler who was with Maria Bertorelli when he took the call. 'Sam Kagan here. We've turned out all the containers, ALL of them, and there's nothing nuclear! I've instructed them to look for anything biological but that's not what our intelligence told us. The Customs are tearing the *Königsberg* apart, crawling round the bilges and tearing cabin walls down. Any ideas? You didn't pick up anything from Dominique Garnier apart from her typed notes, did you?'

'Maria's here I'll hand the 'phone to her.'

Sam put the question to her, 'No there was nothing else. All I know, all I was told was on paper. Sorry, Sam, I'm worried for you. My guess is that there's a real threat. I don't think she misled me intentionally. Though, perhaps she might have been fooled by Jakob Schmidt or maybe she didn't understand him. I'll put you back to Peter.'

'Hello, Sam. That's about it I fear. We know the money's genuine and we know it's gone. What else can you want that sort of amount for?'

'What else indeed. There really was nothing there? Erik told me you searched the place.'

'We did in the short time we had. And we took the PC's hard disc as well as a box of floppies. We've been through all the files ... nothing there, nothing at all. The only things we took, apart from the two notes she typed for Maria, was a book by some philosopher.'

'Which philosopher, Peter?'

'Wittgenstein.'

'*Tractatus Logico-Philosophicus?*'

'Just that. You know it.'

'Had to study it once. There weren't any notes, underlinings, pieces of paper, that sort of thing. I wish you'd sent it on to us.'

'Only a photo he was using as a bookmark, some old railway locomotive, a steam one. Erik's got the book somewhere.'

'Nothing there then. Thanks, can you get Erik to call me when he gets in? Thanks again. See you some time when this is all over, whatever *this* might be.'

***

13.50 hours, Haifa

Shlomo Ya'acoby had just returned from lunch. He looked across the desk at Sam, 'I've enjoyed your company, Mr Kagan, but it will be good to have my office back now that all this has come to nothing. You must be bitterly disappointed or mightily relieved.' Here was another person quietly amused at their failure and ready to put in a bill for the upset caused to his business.

'Puzzled, Mr Ya'acoby, rather than disappointed. Very puzzled. Everything indicated that our information was genuine. Yet we've looked in every one of the 119 containers and dug around in the bowels of the ship and there's nothing, nothing whatsoever that I'm interested in, though the Customs have seen plenty to keep them amused. You're sure we've seen everything? There weren't any containers that were unloaded before I came on the scene, were there?'

'No, you've seen them all. Look here's the ship's manifest. There are the container numbers, the ones we've used for your control list. Apart from the locomotive there was nothing else on the ship, barring its crew and a few rats.'

Sam sat quietly. Thoughts of another ship on it's way came into his mind and then a thought struck him, 'The locomotive? What locomotive, Shlomo?'

'The one that left here on Thursday morning. It was there when we were introduced to one another. It went off on the low loader while we had our meeting here.'

'It went where, Shlomo?'

'Hold on, I'll check?'

He pressed a button on his 'phone, 'Michael, that old locomotive that we off-loaded a couple of days ago. Where was it headed for?

'Tel Aviv. Where in Tel Aviv? The train station. OK, thanks.' he turned to Sam, 'You heard that. You don't think that ... '

Sam was already on his mobile, 'Eli. No I don't want to hear what Sharon thinks. *You* listen to me. The disposal team, they're still on standby. Good. Get them to the train station at Tel Aviv. Get them there by chopper and I'll see them there. Yes I'm coming down by chopper. I think the bomb might be in a locomotive that came off the *Königsberg* and it's sitting there right in the middle of Tel Aviv.' He laughed, 'If it does go off those countries with embassies in Tel Aviv will wish they'd located them in Jerusalem. Oh, yes, and find someone who knows something about steam railway locomotives and get him down there immediately.'

Then he called up his chopper, instructing Shlomo to make sure there was clear space for it to land safely on the dockside. It would be with him in three minutes. Next he rang Erik Blum who had just got back to his office and hadn't had time to pick up his 'phone and call Sam. 'Erik, I'm sorry there isn't time for civilities. ...... Yes, its Sam Kagan here. That book of Wittgenstein's that you carried off from the house in Altkirch. ...... Yes, that's it. Have you got it there? ...... Good man. Right there's a photo as a book mark. A locomotive. OK, what kind? ...... Steam. Colour? ...... Black. Number? ...... 13657. Anything on the back of the print? ...... Nothing. ...... Ah yes, the maker of the paper? ...... Something in Russian. That's probably all I need. But stay by the phone for the next hour or two. My hunch is that the bomb's in that locomotive, which has been sitting in the middle of Tel Aviv, ticking away while we've been tearing containers and the ship itself apart! I'll call you for a chat sometime - if we survive this, Erik. In the mean time many thanks.' He finished the conversation as he left the entrance to Shlomo's office. He could hear the chopper coming in to land. Sam Kagan prepared for the crouched run to its open door. In a few minutes he would be in Tel Aviv and then he would know, or at any rate he hoped so.

***

14.20 hours, Tel Aviv.

The bomb disposal team had been there for ten minutes when Sam arrived. The locomotive stood on the back of the low loader on public display. It was indeed number 13657, just as the photograph in Schmidt's copy of Wittgenstein's *Tractus* had indicated. A meaningful bookmark for the German, just as Sam had so recently placed a family photograph in his book of war poems. There was no doubt now, none at all. Sam gathered the team together and briefed them quickly, 'You all know what your jobs are. We thought the thing was in a container but I'm certain it's here inside this locomotive. We've got to locate it and make it safe. Who's our railway expert? Not here yet?' Another chopper came into sight and landed an elderly man who hurried over, seemingly more interested in the locomotive than in Sam and his colleagues. He held out his hand to Sam, 'Nahum Ben-Shefi. That's a fine piece of machinery you've got there.'

'That's as may be, Nahum, but your task is to tell us where you would hide a bomb in it. I'm Sam Kagan, by the way.'

'I wouldn't dream of doing any such thing. Put a bomb in a locomotive. I don't go round playing at being Lawrence on the Hejaz Railway.'

'We're not asking you to put a bomb in it. We think someone else has and want your advice on where to look. Is there anything funny that suggests it's been nobbled?'

'Oh, I see. Well I'd go for the firebox, the boiler or the water tank in the tender. Let's have a look.'

'Right, Nahum. Perek, you go with him in case there are any anti-personnel devices.'

They started with the tender, checking the water tank and finding nothing. Then it was onto the footplate and with some difficulty they opened the firebox doors but found nothing in there, the space was empty and cold. Suddenly Nahum realised, 'They've fixed a plate over the boiler fire-tubes, you can't see through them! There must be something inside the boiler itself. Let's look at the other end, the smokebox.' He climbed down and hurried to the front of the locomotive climbing up and struggling with the fastenings on the door of the smokebox. A member of the disposal team joined him and together they managed to open the door. Here too there was a plate covering the fire-tubes. 'There's no doubt, the thing's been nobbled. There's something in the boiler that shouldn't be there. I've never seen a steam locomotive's boiler looking like that before.' He stood there fascinated.

'Can I take a look at the thing, please. I've brought my camera, I'd like a photo.'

'Hold on Nahum, I'd like to set our friends in action to get the foreign body out of the thing.' Sam got the team organised. Shimon, a sergeant-major from the bomb disposal team, climbed into the firebox and examined the plate over the fire-tubes. He shouted that it appeared to be fitted with an anti-personnel device and he was joined by another soldier with a bag of tools. The others moved back while they did their work. They reappeared on the footplate gave a thumbs-up sign and moved to the front to make the smokebox safe.

Sam looked at his watch, it was 15.22 hours on 15th September. He wondered at what time the nuclear device was programmed to explode. They had taken 42 minutes on the anti-personnel device on the firebox, another 42 at the front would take them to 16.04 hours. That would make it 7 hours 57 minutes to 00.01 hours on 16th September. That was the amount of time they could, *perhaps*, count on to make it safe. That always assumed the timer was accurate and not running fast.

They had decided not to evacuate the area and so draw attention to the threat they faced. The public looked on from a distance behind barriers that had been set up by the military, having been told that the locomotive was being prepared for steaming. Meanwhile the group were drinking tea though there was little conversation. Moshe the scientist from the Weizmann Institute had been quieter than the others throughout. Sam remembered his confident performance, explaining the workings of an atom bomb at their meeting in Mossad HQ back in June. Moshe was the expert who had seen one of these Russian weapons or at any rate something like it and who would be responsible for making it safe. The bomb disposal team would be giving assistance but they had never seen anything of this kind: the technical assessment and decisions would be entirely his. Sam noticed that he was shaking slightly and he manoeuvred him clear of the others, 'Moshe, I can see that it's getting to you. I'd be the last to pretend it wasn't a risk and a huge one at that.'

Moshe looked at him before replying, 'It's not so much fear for my skin as fear of failure. I feel so lonely, so utterly alone. If I botch this we all go up with it, you, me, men women and children. Vaporised in a moment or rather less than a moment. And we'd be the lucky ones!'

'Don't worry Moshe, I'll be in there with you and the IDF engineers while you do it.'

'But you're not a technical expert!'

'No but I'll be either in there with you or standing out here. I'm not going until this thing's safe, so if it goes off I might as well be in there with you as standing next to it.'

Moshe grasped his hand, 'Thanks Sam I appreciate that.'

There was a shout from the front of the engine, Shimon and his squad had made the blanking plate safe. They climbed down for a cup of tea. While one team of engineers moved in to unbolt the plate in the smokebox another dealt with the plate in the firebox. The smaller plate at the front proved more troublesome and it was another 45 minutes before both were removed and they could look into the gutted boiler. It had been stuffed with wood chippings and the engineers moved in to clear them.

17.05 hours

They had cleared the debris and located what they had spent days looking for. They were face to face with Russian military surplus goods in the form of a thermonuclear bomb. The sight produced a sense of hushed awe. The locomotive standing there outside the railway station in Tel Aviv was a latter-day Trojan Horse, its belly pregnant with war and destruction. That something so small could pack such a destructive punch seemed incredible. Moshe confirmed its identity. He had no doubt about what lay in the boiler of the locomotive. They all believed him and were fearful. The next few hours would prove crucial, it hardly needed saying. But the engineers had spotted two more anti-personnel devices which had to be removed before Moshe could confront the bomb itself. By 18.15 hours it was ready for him.

'Well Sam here we go, death or glory.'

'They're not necessarily alternatives, Moshe. It can be death and glory. But that's a subject for discussion when we have fewer immediate demands on our attention. I just hope that your version is the correct one.'

They climbed into the firebox accompanied by Shimon and another of the bomb disposal engineers. Moshe had a set of diagrams in a binder. The floor of the firebox had been lined by the engineers with plastic board covered with a layer of the wood chippings to make a cushion which they had then covered with thick polythene sheeting. The cavity of the boiler was illuminated by electric lamps set up by the engineers. Moshe began a slow and careful examination of the device. The engineers appreciated the need for care, rashness wasn't part of the make up of a bomb disposal man. Bravery and a cool nerve, yes. Impetuosity? Certainly not! Instinctively they knew they could work with this man. Not only did he give it time, he also clearly knew what he was looking for. He consulted one of his charts and muttered to himself. Then he turned to the others, 'An update on the Russian bomb I've seen, that's the one on this chart, but it should be OK. I could do with a cup of tea though.'

Tea was sent down in a flask and they all drank while Moshe continued to study his charts. Sam looked around him, it seemed ludicrous that the four of them should be enjoying a tea break cheek by jowl with the bomb.

Moshe looked up from his charts and produced a calm and relaxed smile, 'Perhaps it's time for Rabbi Kagan to say a prayer before we set to and try to draw this thing's teeth!'

'If it's the wish of everyone.' There was no dissenting voice and so he prayed:

> *' Deliver us from our enemies, O our God,*
> *protect us from those who rise up against us,*
> *deliver us from those who work evil,*
> *and save us from bloodthirsty men.*
>
> *'O our Strength, we will sing praises to thee,*
> *for thou, O God art our fortress,*
> the God who shows us steadfast love. Amen.'

'Right Moshe, we're in your hands now ... and the hands of God.'

The break and tea had done Moshe good and now he went to work carefully and thoroughly, calling for a variety of tools as he unscrewed sections of casing and disconnected wires. Sam looked at his watch and was amazed to read 20.33. Time might be short, very short. But he wasn't going to ask how long. In no way would he try to hurry the work or break Moshe's concentration. He lay on the floor of the firebox watching intently while he prayed, as he had done since climbing into the firebox over two hours before. And he thought of Elizabeth and the kids back at the *Domaine*. He took the family photograph from his book and studied it. Elizabeth would be worried out of her mind. No, she would be very anxious but she would be in control of herself. The kids would have no idea what was going on outside the railway station in Tel Aviv, and he was grateful for that. His attention came back to matters in hand when Moshe dropped a pair of pliers. He picked them up again and carefully removed a small piece of metal from the bomb.

'And that gentlemen is it. I've made doubly sure that the thing won't explode. It's completely safe now.'

Shimon took his hand vigorously, 'Superb my friend. You'll have to join my team. You were like an old hand at it.' He removed one of his sergeant major's armbands and slipped it over Moshe's sleeve. 'If ever you're out of work at the Weizmann, you know where to come!' Then remembering that word should be passed on to the others he climbed out through the firebox door onto the footplate and shouted down to those on the ground, 'All clear, he's done it. HE'S DONE IT!.' There were a dozen of them and they always counted themselves privileged to have been the first to hear. They let out a cheer, repeated as Moshe and the others appeared and climbed down.

'Sam pulled his mobile from his pocked and pushed a key, 'Elizabeth. It's good news, the thing's defused. I'll be back to you in a moment or two when I've spoken to Sharon.'

He pressed another key, 'PM please. Sam Kagan calling ... Good news Mr Sharon, the very best. The thing's been made safe by Moshe Kahn of the Weizmann and by Sergeant Major Shimon Eifermen and his bomb disposal team. You'll be down here with the Chief of Staff as soon as your chopper can get you here? Great. The boys will be delighted to see you.' He looked around and found that most of the men were down on the ground in tears. They had borne up through the work but now the enormity of the threat averted had got to them. Sam was conscious of tears in his eyes, tears of relief, thankfulness and gratitude. It was dark, the Sabbath was over. Sam Kagan prayed a belated prayer:

> *'Sovereign of the universe, we have heard in the new week tidings of joy and gladness ... you have blessed and prospered the work of our hands.'*

He could hear a chopper coming towards them, the PM must have been considerably nearer than in Jerusalem. He was ready to ask that Moshe and Shimon, with his team, should be considered for bravery decorations - but that proved unnecessary, the PM and the Chief of Staff had a bag of the things with them!

Sharon had taken Sam aside, 'We're glad, very glad that you stuck to your conviction that there was a real threat. If that thing had gone off it would have been a disaster and a history changing event. Though, of course, you'll never have the publicity you deserve.'

'Publicity isn't something I've ever wanted, Sir, and it's not something the Institute seeks. To have saved life on a huge scale and served my country is quite enough.'

'However anyone could have wanted to do such a thing is unimaginable – whatever could have induced Schmidt to such a barbaric act?'

Sam took a deep breath, 'You know the reason for the name of Schmidt's group, *"The 16th September Unit"?* - Yes, the massacres at Sabra and Shatila but you wouldn't have been aware that Schmidt's German fiancée, a nurse, was among those murdered there. If *that* hadn't been *allowed* to happen we wouldn't have been confronted by *this*.'

There was a moment of silence, 'You have a reputation of blunt speaking Mr Kagan, I'm aware of the circumstances of your departure from the Institute after the Basel operation.' Sam thought he had said farewell to his job at HQ, but Sharon continued. 'And that's a quality we need. We politicians don't need officials who tell us what they think we want to hear – or rather what we might want them to tell us - they're not what we need, we need honesty even when it hurts. You've done yourself no harm, Sam, by your blunt speaking. The *Memuneh* will be wanting a word with you very shortly and what he'll propose will not disappoint you. Well done and very many thanks from myself and the Cabinet.'

Sharon shook Sam's hand and set off for his chopper pondering the press release to be issued to down-play the nature of the threat they had just faced. And that locomotive must be sent on its way to the Dimona nuclear plant before it became a subject of public curiosity.

Sam pondered the title of the Mossad boss - *"the one in charge"* or *"the appointed one"* - plain, unvarnished and to the point. He wondered whether *he* would ever be the one in charge. Did his ambitions go that far? Elizabeth was certain to have a realistic view of the matter.

And in three days it would be Rosh Hashana, a new year with the nuclear threat removed, a High Holy Day indeed.

PART 4

Last Things

Such is the patriot's boast, where'er we roam,
His first, best country ever is at home.

Oliver Goldsmith, *The Traveller*

Chapter 32

Tuesday 18th September 2001, Rosh Hashana (Jewish New Year)

Dov had collected Sam from the airport and he dropped him at the door of the *Domaine* with apologies for having to rush off: he and Yvonne were taking Mum Levin and Mum Feldman to dinner that evening near the Old Port in Marseille and the ladies were already in Marseille shopping. Sam knew, however, that it was really a scheme to let Elizabeth and himself have an evening alone together with the children.

Elizabeth met him on the threshold, 'Sam ... ' Words stuck in her throat and tears began to flow.

'Elizabeth my love, my joy, my everything ... ' He too was overwhelmed by the emotion of the occasion but choking back his tears he murmured, 'Safe home, safe home once more.'

The sound of scampering feet told them that Olga and Ya'akov had torn themselves away from their toys to greet their father. They swarmed around their parents before clinging to Sam's legs, attempting to drag him into the house. He released Elizabeth and scooped one up in each arm. 'My word the pair of you must be growing fast, you're much heavier than when I went away last week!'

Olga looked at him with her serious face, 'That's because I eat my vegetables, like Mummy tells me.'

'That's a good girl, Mummy's right, they're good for a growing girl ... and for a growing boy.

Ya'akov pulled a face, 'I don't like vegetables, but it's all right, I don't need them 'cause you say I've grown in days.'

'If you eat your vegetables, Ya'akov, then you'll grow even more. Now, if your Mum will get me a refreshing cup of tea, I'll be able to recover from my journey and hear all that you've been up to in my absence.'

Elizabeth led the way across the hall and into the kitchen where Sam lowered his young charges to the floor and pulled a chair to the table. 'Ah, cookies, well done Elizabeth.'

'Don't thank me, thank my Mum. She cooked them this morning. It's her kindness and sense of mischief together: you see they're Easter biscuits, a bit late for Easter 2001 and too early for 2002, but she said that having you back again, after the risks you took with that,' she lowered her voice so that the children wouldn't hear, 'that b-o-m-b, its going to be like resurrection having you back!'

'Mummy, what's a b-o-m-b? Is it a bomb like you hear about on the TV?'

Elizabeth looked at Sam before replying, 'Well yes, Olga, it was just a little one but your father was very brave and we're very,' she choked back tears of happiness, 'very proud of him, he's a very brave man and many people owe a lot to his bravery. And he's been given a med ... ' she looked at Sam who shook his head, 'No Sam,' she whispered, 'let them see it, we're proud of you.'

He went back into the hall for his bag and produced the medal for their inspection. 'What's it for Dad? Little Ya'akov's face was a picture of puzzlement.

'Well, it was for working in a team to keep people safe.'

Olga's response was immediate, 'It's like an Olympic medal, isn't it Dad? Did you have to stand there while the band played music?'

'Sorry, children, they couldn't afford a band but it was the Prime Minister who gave them to us but by then we were too tired to get excited and sing.'

'You've got to wear it Dad, like they do in the Olympics. You need a ribbon, I've got some for my hair I'll get it!' She was off running across the hallway and up the stairs to her bedroom.

'I'll show you my new soldiers that Uncle Dov and Aunty Yvonne gave me,' and Ya'akov too was on his way across the hall.

Elizabeth laughed, 'No peace for the tired, I'm afraid but the tea's brewed and you can catch your breath for the next 20 seconds before our energetic pair are back again. Have a biscuit, my Mum will expect them to have gone by the time she gets back.'

He sipped his tea, 'Safe home, Elizabeth. It's an Irish expression that they put on the back of their roadside signs with the names of their towns. I've never been so glad to be home ... ever.' He rose and took her in his arms. From upstairs came the sound of a dispute between the children. 'Yes, it really sounds like home doesn't it!'

That evening, the children bathed, read to and asleep; and dinner, prepared earlier in the day by Mum Levin, out of the way they sat in tranquillity as the late evening sun streamed through the window of the sitting room; together at peace, the dark cloud of nuclear menace dispelled.

Neither wished to break the silence which had, somehow, become more meaningful than a thousand words but, at last, Elizabeth spoke, 'So it's goodbye to this, to our own vineyard at the *Domaine du Cheval Rouge*. It's been a good time, despite the threat.' Her face changed, 'And despite what happened with Mustafa.'

'I'm sorry you had that experience - they should give you a medal too, do you want me to ... ?'

'Thanks but no thanks, Sam. I don't want reminding of it. It seems that each time you're involved in an operation I leave a dead body for disposal.'

'You didn't kill Mustafa, remember that, you merely winged him as Mark put it. *Mark* was the one who did the killing, not you, Elizabeth.'

'Thanks, Sam, you can remind me of that whenever I get morose about it.'

'But, taking up what you said, yes, we'll be on our way soon. It does look as though the Institute is going to offer a headquarters post ... '

'So you won't be out in the field any more?'

'No, I'd probably be based in Tel Aviv but with liaison visits elsewhere.'

'And where would we live? Must we leave the Golan, Sam? I love it there. Remember when all this began, the weather, the summer flowers, the eagles at Gamla? Must we give up all that and live in Tel Aviv?'

'Perhaps we can manage both, keep the house in Katzrin and spend the week in an apartment near Tel Aviv. Like you I love the Golan and the Upper Galilee, that's where I lived when we first came to Israel from Crown Heights, Brooklyn. And that's where my parents are buried. I've only recently realised just how strong the ties are which bind me to the land, it's almost mystical. But therein lies danger, when you yield too readily to the mystical then reason tends to go out the window! There are Palestinians who feel as strongly. They see the land they once owned being settled by our people, they see olive orchards that their families have tended for generations being torn down by our tanks in reprisal. It must be heart-breaking.'

'You always see both sides of a case Sam. Is that a benefit or a hindrance?'

'Some of each, Elizabeth. I always have had a reputation for having an independent mind and I'm determined to stay like that. But the idea of home is a rich and varied one: people, place, ideas, culture - though firstly and principally it's people. For me home is, Elizabeth, Olga and Ya'akov.'

It delighted her that he so readily accepted Olga, Peter Lewis' child, as part of the family, 'And any others that God sends us ... '

'Elizabeth, you have something to tell me?'

'Well Sam, I think it's quite likely that our two will have a brother or sister to adapt to next year ... '

He pulled her close. Together they wept tears of pure joy and gratitude. There would be big changes for them in the New Year.

Chapter 33

Thursday 20th September 2001

A young military attaché from the Israeli Embassy had delivered the letters to her apartment by hand, informing Maria that they weren't being asked for an instant reply and leaving immediately. Peter was sleeping in, still shaken by the carnage at Dominique Garnier's house.

Maria sat looking at her letter and then she put it on one side and picked up the letter that Eric Blum had given them the previous day. It simply told them that Balthasar Feuerbach had accepted the validity of the transfer of the account to Peter and herself and would be happy to advise on the investment of the money pending its use to help traumatised children. Also attached was a bank statement showing a balance, at 12th September 2001, of a little in excess of US $ 1.4 million. She wondered what the intended use of money had been. Tainted money, the profit of drug dealing, but she knew it was better in the hands of Peter and herself than swelling the bank's coffers or helping the Swiss Government along, perhaps paying for a few metres of the *Lötschbergbahn's* new railway tunnel or a new office block for someone.

Peter appeared, seemingly weary despite the late hour of his rising. 'Did I hear visitors?'

'Yes, someone from the Israeli Embassy with a couple of letters. Here's yours.'

He used a knife from the table to open the envelope and began to read:

Embassy of the State of Israel
Bern, Switzerland

20th September 2001

Dear Herr Gruenweiler

My Government has instructed me to write conveying the heartfelt gratitude of the President of Israel and of the Prime Minister and Cabinet for your selfless work during Operation Account. What you achieved and the discretion shown will not be forgotten by any of us. In the event of your visiting Israel you will be a most welcome and esteemed guest of the State.

In recognition of your achievement it has been decided on the unanimous recommendation of the Cabinet to bestow on you the State of Israel's highest Police decoration for gallantry, the Medal of Valour, and to recommend that you are declared one of the Righteous Among the Nations. Unfortunately the sensitivity of the matter precludes public recognition of this but that is, sadly, inevitable in the circumstances.

My Government would like the presentation to be made in Jerusalem but, in the event that you are unable to come, there could be a presentation in the Bern Embassy.

It is my hope to meet you personally very soon and to convey my personal thanks and admiration for your achievement

Ambassador of the State of Israel"

'I take it yours is the same? You should have

something better. You were the one who got the information out of her.'

'But you were the one who was raped at gunpoint in the interests of the State of Israel!'

He winced, 'You don't have to remind me of that! I was dreaming about it last night. I really am going to need a shrink if this goes on!' He took her hand, 'But you'll see me through, fellow Righteous Gentile!'

'You've still got your sense of humour and that's a good indicator of mental health, Peter. Will you accept it?'

'Whyever not, Maria?'

She squeezed his hand and he was about to release hers, 'No don't take your hand away Peter. I didn't sleep last night. No it wasn't the horror of Altkirch, though that will be with me as well for some time to come. It was this.' She indicated the bank statement that Erik had provided the previous day, 'I was thinking about how to spend it properly ... and I was thinking about us. Peter I have two questions to ask. First, will you marry me? And, before you answer that, the second one, which is will you come with me to Palestine to work with kids?'

'Pour me a coffee, a strong one please, while I recover, Maria.'

She found a mug and poured him some, 'Hot enough? Good.'

'What a night! What a morning! Well, Maria, in what order do you want me to give the replies?'

'Any order you like.'

'The answers are Yes and Yes, though such is my confusion, I don't really know in what order I've answered them!'

'You're sure, Peter? Really sure?'

'Totally, I like my apartment but I would be lonely there on my own if you were in Gaza City or wherever it is that you have in mind for our activities. I *had* noticed you prowling around the Internet yesterday, you know!' They were in one another's arms dancing around the kitchen.

'More coffee, Peter? The last lot seems to have livened you up.'

'Not the coffee, more your offers which were impossible to refuse.'

The doorbell rang, Erik Blum's voice came over the intercom and Maria pushed the button to open the main door for him. A couple of minutes later he was at the apartment door and Maria let him in. 'Peter's just gone for a quick shower, he was late up this morning. Give him five minutes and he'll be presentable ready to report to *Major* Blum.' Erik smiled, he had heard of his promotion the previous day. They conversed inconsequentially until Peter appeared, showered and dressed but unshaven.

'Good morning Peter, taking life more easily?'

'Well I am on leave Erik.'

'Of course, you've earned the break. There's just two matters.'

'Not again!'

'What do you mean, Peter?'

'I'll tell you in a moment. First of all let me hear what you've got to say.'

'Have Dr Bertorelli and Captain Gruenweiler receive letters form the Israeli Embassy? Letters like this one which I received this morning?'

'Yes they came by hand, Peter read his just before you came so we haven't discussed it ... there were other matters ... '

'Erik did you say, *'Captain* Gruenweiler?'

'I did indeed, that's the other thing I've got to congratulate you on!'

Maria kissed him, 'Bravery in the face of two shrinks, that sort of thing?'

'Something of the sort. You two look like cats with a bowl of cream, so you're obviously pleased with recognition by the Israelis. The Foreign Ministry and our heads of Security were keen for us to accept, help to cement relations between our countries, heal old wounds, keep commerce flowing, that sort of thing.'

'There's a slight complication, Erik. We're going to work in Gaza City. I'm not sure that Israeli medals round our necks are going to make us specially welcome. Look, sit down while I make some more coffee and let Maria explain.'

'Well Erik, we've been planning our future this morning. Peter has just asked me to marry him and, of course, I've accepted with alacrity and enthusiasm.' Peter smiled with pleasure and at her modified account of the proposal, he took her hand. 'Then I've asked him to come to Gaza City with me - there's a psychiatric unit being set up there for traumatised kids. It's going to be run by a charity whose boss is an old colleague of mine and, as you know, we have the money that Dr Garnier transferred to us, over US $ 1.4 million of it. And I'm not going to see that wasted. I'm determined to be there and see that Dominique gets value for every last cent of it. It's probably a three year project. I feel I owe it to Dominique and to those kids. I've been in my ivory tower here at the Faculty for too long! Its time to get out into the world and earn my keep and Peter's going to give a hand - he's got the makings of a good therapist Erik.'

'And he's got more than the makings of a good policeman, Maria. That's why he's been promoted. But you say three years? Perhaps we can get him leave of absence, even an attachment to some aid agency in the Palestine Authority's Area.'

'You mean in *Palestine*?'

'OK call it Palestine then. But the medals?'

Peter responded, 'I'd not be too happy about visiting Jerusalem, at any rate not before settling down in Gaza City. Perhaps we might receive them at the Embassy here and then entrust them to Major Erik Blum to keep them locked up in the safe in his office.'

'That would keep everyone happy, I think.'

'What do you think Maria?'

'Yes that ought to be OK. It will be thanks enough to know that Tel Aviv is still there and that there aren't thousands of extra cancer sufferers as a result of a crazy enterprise. It's strange, but ever since it happened, there's a question that's kept running through my mind and to which there's no answer ... its this, "What would have happened if Jakob Schmidt hadn't been dying of cancer upstairs in that house?" I know there were the events of the previous day in the States and a number of factors that made her provide the information we needed so desperately, but my intuition tells me that it was my argument that it would cause many, many cancer cases of young and old that hit home. She wasn't a bad woman, misguided and a bit crazy' - she looked at Peter who nodded, 'but not bad.'

'And Jakob Schmidt?' It was Peter's question.

She shrugged her shoulders, 'Like you I never met him alive, so I don't know what set him on that track. Probably the best of sentiments, sympathy for the Palestinians, anger at what had become of them, but mixed with a festering desire for revenge at the loss of his fiancée 19 years ago. So he decided to lash out at one of the factors in the equation, the State of Israel, ignoring the damage he would do to Arab as well as to Jew ... and ignoring the other players in the political game, the other Arab states and the regime in the Authority Area. We'll never know about him. I'm going to the Funeral Requiem, it's probably next week, and I doubt whether the priest will know anything more of Jakob than his name, probably not even his date of birth. And I wonder whether he really was Jakob or whether that was an assumed name and identity. I don't expect we'll ever know. Or know whether he was the originator of the whole enterprise, though I suppose he was. But Dominique's a different matter. The money's going into a trust which will perpetuate her name and Peter and I will be the trustees. Your friend Balthasar

Feuerbach is going to help us with free advice and banking and he's getting his lawyers to draw up a trust deed free of charge.'

'You've been busy since I last saw the two of you! Congratulations on your engagement and every success in your work in Gaza. I'll sort things out on the medals and take soundings about some indefinite leave of absence for Peter - I've no wish to lose him to the service and, you never know, the time spent in the Middle East might be useful to the service, particularly if you both come back fluent in Arabic! I'll leave you to your celebrations and arrangements. Once again congratulations!'

They showed him to the lift and returned to the kitchen. Maria opened the fridge and produced a bottle of Champagne, 'When I couldn't sleep I came in here and put it into the fridge, just in case we had something to celebrate today!'

'Bollinger Grand Année 1990! Not cheap bubbly. When did you buy it? I hadn't noticed it in the winerack.'

'A couple of days after the trip to Zermatt. I knew you'd set me on the path to recovery, though I also knew it would take time. I hid it in the back of the filing cabinet and ... and I looked at it from time to time and wondered and hoped ... Peter!' She clung to him, 'Peter, thank you for saying Yes and Yes!'

They lay together in bed, their nervous energy spent; relaxed, happy, tranquil and almost asleep. He stirred, raised himself on his elbow and murmured, 'You don't look very much like a shrink, Maria.'

She began defensively, 'And what should a shrink, a female one, look like? What sort of caricature ... I think this is where we came in!'

'Déjà vu, all over again, as an American once told me.'

'Don't poke fun at Americans or I'll report to Major Blum that you have an inferiority complex, Peter.'

'Maria, I'm so happy, ridiculously happy. I'm almost tempted to think I'm imagining it all, that the bangs at the Garnier house were nuclear explosions and that we're drifting in some celestial paradise ... '

'And drinking decent *Bollinger*? I believe that in the Muslim paradise the men drink wine and have a bevy of lovely maidens to keep them happy. But understand this, Peter Gruenweiler, Maria Bertorelli is not prepared to share you with a bevy of others - or indeed with any other woman! She sat up in bed and refilled their glasses. 'And also, Peter, it seems that you're something of a fantasist. I'm going to have to work hard on your therapy.'

'Which is?'

'Long sessions in the psychiatrist's bed and not on her couch! And, to change tack entirely, we're going to have to learn something about Islam and the Palestinian culture if we're going to be much use out there. We're going to be busy, so I hope you won't be short of energy for your nightly therapy.'

He drained his glass and pulled her down on top of himself, 'There's little danger of that, Maria, very little ... '

Chapter 34

Friday 28th September 2001

The afternoon was sunny but fresh and its brilliance added to the poignancy of the proceedings. The Requiem over, the *cortège* had driven from the church in Altkirch to the *Cimetière Communal* on the edge of the town. From near the gate of the cemetery a French TV crew was filming the procession, led by the parish priest and the two coffins, making its way along the gravel paths for the interment. Maria Bertorelli walked by herself toward the end of the procession, past large family tombs in the form of classical edifices, some of them with rusting metal doors. Erik Blum had refused to let Peter attend lest he be recognised as a regular visitor to the dead therapist and questioned. On balance, Peter had been relieved to be ordered to stay away. The television interviewer approached, 'I believe that you're Dr Maria Bertorelli from the University of Basel.'

'I am, can I help?'

'Perhaps you could tell us something about the late Dr Dominique Garnier and Herr Jakob Schmidt?'

'See me once the interment is over and I will try to help - but it will only be about Dominique. I have no idea who Herr Schmidt was, none at all.'

Maria had come prepared for this and she faced the camera with the cemetery wall and the cupressus trees in the background. Most of the mourners had left and the gravediggers were shovelling earth into the grave. She wore a black coat reaching to just below the knee with a mere hint of a burgundy coloured scarf at the neck. As always her hair was immaculately set.

She began quietly, 'We can only guess at what happened at Dr Garnier's house in this town two weeks ago but her death has robbed psychiatry of a woman who was greatly respected for her academic and practical contributions to the discipline. When she spoke at the Faculty of Psychiatry in the University of Basel she was invariably challenging and stimulating. She drew on her wealth of experience working with traumatised children, including young girls - and boys - who had been raped during the, so called, ethnic cleansing in the Balkans. Besides this she had worked, on and off, for some years in Palestinian Refugee Camps in Palestine itself as well as in the Lebanon and in Jordan.'

She paused while a train rattled past on the nearby railway line and then resumed, 'For that reason I am delighted to be associated with a trust which has just been established in Basel, thanks to a very generous gift from a donor who wishes to remain anonymous, to perpetuate Dr Garnier's work. And I am grateful for this opportunity of making known the existence of the Dominique Garnier Memorial Trust. It will work principally among Palestinian children traumatised by recent events but not exclusively so. If Jewish children can also be helped, then help will be given to any traumatised child irrespective of race or creed. That, I believe, is what Dominique would have wished.

'We mourn her passing and its manner. We salute her work. We *will* perpetuate her memory.'

'You saw Dr Garnier often?

'From time to time.'

'And your memories of the last time you met her?'

'It was a while ago,' vague but she couldn't be other than a little misleading, 'I spoke with a passionate, caring woman. A therapist of high standards and commitment. Her loss is a sad one. Thank you.'

The interviewer indicated to the cameraman that the interview was over and accompanied Maria down the road towards her car. 'Isn't that the second loss in recent years to your Basel Faculty of a specialist in traumatised children? Wasn't there a mountaineer who was killed a couple of years ago?'

It was like a kick in the stomach but she controlled her emotions, 'Yes, you're right. Klaus Bonner died four years ago, his career cut short by a climbing fall on the Matterhorn. He too is commemorated by a memorial trust, so, like Dominique, his good work continues. Thank you for filming today's events, it is important that Dominique should be remembered. Now, perhaps I might have a little time on my own to mourn her passing.' She turned back towards the new grave, pausing a few yards from where the diggers had almost finished their work. It was in a grassy patch next to a few recent arrivals with marble headstones. She would ensure that there was a suitable inscription to remind visitors of the woman buried there. But how to commemorate Jakob Schmidt? Perhaps the word *benefactor* would do: he had been so in death if not in life. The thought came to her of using words from that much thumbed edition of Wittgenstein's *Tractus* that Erik Blum had carried off with him from the house of death two weeks before:

> *"Death is not an event in life: we do not live to experience death." or*

> *"Our life has no end in just the same way in which our visual field has no limits."*

Maybe she'd have the last sentence inscribed on the stone or perhaps:

> *"The solution to the riddle of life in space and time lies outside space and time."*

Yes, perhaps *that* would be appropriate - the words had an enigmatic quality, an acknowledgement of the mystery that surrounded all life - and death itself. Certainly the deaths of Dominique and Jakob were shrouded in mystery.

Her tears flowed, some for Dominique Garnier and some for memories of Klaus Bonner. But they did not continue for long. Her sorrow was real but now it was manageable. And she would be back with Peter in less than an hour. Yes, she knew she was moving on. Now she was beginning to let go of a past whose memories had once been such a burden.

At the cemetery gate Erik Blum was waiting by the car. He had not wanted Maria to be alone and had also been wary of anyone recognising her from that afternoon visit to *Maison* Garnier. As they drove away he remarked, 'Did you see that yellow post box in the cemetery wall next to the gate? Who do you think would post their letters there ... I have a professional interest, of course, we security people are used to hunting for dead letter boxes!' It was as near as he got to humour.

They didn't return direct to Basel but headed into Altkirch, driving up the *rue de Ferrette* and past number 17A. Someone had left a wreath outside the door and the flower troughs were evidently being looked after by a neighbour. They wondered if the bedroom had been cleaned and the bloodstains removed. Would the house sell readily after its recent visitation by violent death? At the top of the road, where they turned the car and prepared to head out of Altkirch, they passed the Gendarmerie. Blum whistled, 'I didn't know *that* was there. It's just as well they weren't watching us the other afternoon! And now a gentle run back to Basel. With the big threat over, the urgency seems to have gone out of life, doesn't it?'

'Unless you're in love, Major Blum.'

'Ah, yes, love, Dr Bertorelli. I suppose that was what prompted the carnage we both witnessed here just two weeks ago.'

Sam Kagan was the last to leave the cemetery. As he watched from a distance everyone had gone and the the gravediggers had completed their work, packed up their spades and departed. Finally, when a good-looking young woman in a black coat had left the grave and walked towards the gate, he moved to the graveside. He stood for some minutes before the fresh mound of earth covering the coffins of Dominique Garnier and Jakob Schmidt and asked himself the question, *'Why?* Why had Schmidt gone to such extremes?' And within himself, conscious of his love for Elizabeth, he had found something of the answer. He could appreciate what his feelings would have been on losing his fiancée or wife in the circumstances of the slaughter at Sabra and Shatila. But it would have required the warping of his moral sensibilities to lead him into such a project. Years before, his father's death from a terrorist rocket attack on the *kibbutz* in the Northern Galilee had left him stunned and bitter. That had lasted for a while but the bleak feelings had lifted and he had remained faithful to his father's commitment to the acceptance of the "stranger within the gates". Indeed the presence of many of his father's grieving Druse and Palestinian friends at the funeral had been a powerful incentive to move on emotionally. For Schmidt this hadn't been possible, the wound had festered, and the outcome had almost been one of horrendous devastation and a lasting plague of radioactivity.

Sam had wanted to be here this afternoon, to see the end of things for these two misguided people. Despite it all he hoped they were at peace. He took one more look at the grave, turned and headed for the gate. He knew that he would never be here again. He had already seen the house where they died and noticed the wreath outside the front door: there must be patients who mourned the loss of their therapist. Now he would drive into Basel and renew his acquaintance with the city he had last seen four years earlier. Tomorrow he would be seeing Erik Blum. But Sam Kagan hadn't realised that earlier that afternoon Blum, always alert and watchful, had spotted him in the distance and left him to his own devices. Of course Blum would enjoy pulling Sam's leg about it when they met.

Chapter 35

Sunday 30th September 2001

'Well, Sam, you asked for a permanent return to the Institute in a senior rôle after the Basel Account assignment was over ... and we did have one all ready for you - heading up the Special Operations Division, *Metsada*.'

Sam nodded, he would have relished the challenge of taking charge of Mossad's clandestine combatant branch which definitely needed sorting out. He wondered to himself just what they were about to foist on him instead.

The Deputy Director continued, 'The post we're offering you is as Director, Operational Planning and Co-ordination. But in the aftermath of 9/11, the anthrax attacks and intelligence reports on continuing Iraqi activities, we've no choice but to strengthen our research in identifying and countering advances in nuclear, germ and chemical warfare and any attempts to attack us with such weapons. So we're taking immediate steps to increase our personnel in that area and add it to your portfolio. So, Sam, you won't be hidden away down some long line of command, you'll report to me direct and when I'm away you'll act as my Deputy. And your salary will reflect your status, so you'll be offered something between what they're paying me and what the Operations and Services Directors get. I would have been happy, of course, for you to get the same as I do but the finance people wouldn't agree to *two* Deputy Directors.'

'Yes, we're in a very different world since the 11th September. And I wonder what sort of world it would have been if Jakob Schmidt's device had exploded on 16th ... that's always assuming the thing was in working order ... it was USSR surplus goods after all and probably rather shop-soiled.'

'You needn't have any doubts, Sam, none of you got

medals on false pretences. The people from Dimona have had a good look at the thing and their assessment is that there was a 99.9% chance of it working. We take our hats off to you, we really do.'

'But, Dan, we were no braver than any other bomb disposal engineers. If you're going to be killed in an explosion it makes little difference whether it's likely to be a big one or a small one.'

'Point taken, Sam, but when you know that so much depends on drawing the thing's sting it must make the hair on the back of your neck stand on end and concentrate the mind.'

'And make you pray as never before!'

'Thanks Rabbi Kagan. I haven't forgotten that praying is just one of your varied rôles! But will you take the job? ... the PM and the *Memunah* are both anxious that you should start at once.'

'As so often there's no choice is there? If you really believe that I'm the one for the job and our political masters think the same way I can't very well say, "No thanks", and head off back to the Katzrin Winery in the Golan, much as Elizabeth and I would like to do just that. Indeed it's what we really long to do but with the new threats ... well there's no choice. Of course I'll take the job.'

'You're sure you don't want time to think it over, to have a word with Elizabeth. I know it's urgent but a couple of days is neither here nor there.'

'It's OK, Dan, Elizabeth's still in France but she and I discussed things on the 'phone yesterday evening – of course there were no details which would have breached security – we spoke in general terms but we were going over ground well covered in the past. She insists that in the present situation I should, I must, take on whatever task you have for me. Our future, everyone's future depends on accurate intelligence and swift counter action. Where's my desk?'

'Next door, in the room that communicates direct with this one, we're going to be working closely from now on. Thanks for agreeing to take the job and congratulations.' He rose and shook Sam's hand warmly. 'The *Memunah* will be in to see you shortly.'

'Thanks, Dan. I know we've had our differences in the past but somehow I think we'll be able to work well together.' While their discussion had progressed each of them had been thinking of their past relationship and its occasional stormy patches, particularly Operation Basel Formula which had precipitated Sam's resignation from the Institute.

'You'll have plenty of liaising to do with academic scientists, *Shin Bet*, the military and *Lekem*. OK I know that *Lekem* was officially disbanded in 1986 after the Jonathan Pollard affair but the work of *Leshkat Kesher Madao* - the Scientific Affairs Liaison Bureau - goes on within the Foreign Affairs Ministry. They've continued gathering information on developments in the world of science and armaments from open and covert sources. No doubt now they will suddenly find they've more money at their disposal to expand their activities but there's a limit to how fast you can do that. Your first task is to ensure that the information we already hold is reviewed at once and properly re-assessed. At the same time you'll work with *Lekem* on expanding the trawl for information. For instance we'll need to establish to whom chemical suppliers world-wide have been selling certain chemicals that might be used to make nerve gas.'

'You know, Dan, that my expertise is in operational matters and computing ... '

'And rabbinic studies ... '

'Indeed those also. Well I would appreciate it if I could choose a scientific adviser to help me with assessing technical matters.'

'Fine, we've got some of those.'

'I was thinking of young Moshe Kahn from the

Weizmann Institute. He did an incredible job as a bomb disposal engineer here in Tel Aviv the other day. He impressed me as a good team member who doesn't mind getting his hands dirty.'

'Or risking his life to protect others. If he's willing to come on a more permanent basis you can add him to your staff, certainly.'

'Just one thing, Dan, it occurred to me when you sent that Jumbo from Amsterdam to collect me ... you will remember the El Al Jumbo that crashed near Schiphol in 1992 and its cargo of chemicals? *We* aren't planning to wage chemical war are we? If so I want no part in it, none at all!'

'Purely for research Sam. We've got to find out how to counter the stuff and minimise the damage. You can be assured that you'll never have to be involved in any decision on the use of the stuff. I can promise you that.' No, Sam knew that they would never involve *him* in such matters. He just hoped they would refrain from using the weapons they dreaded in the hands of their foes. His hope was that they would go no further than holding them as a deterrent, like their much denied nuclear weapons whose manufacture Shimon Peres - Nobel Peace Laureate and now one of their doves - had instigated by obtaining French technical assistance for the construction of a nuclear reactor at Dimona - a *quid pro quo* for Israel's part in the 1956 Suez *débacle*. He smiled to himself remembering that the government had once claimed that the Dimona installation was only a textile plant. Fabrication indeed!

'You'll want to get settled in I expect, let's have a look at your room.' The Deputy Head was leading the way towards the communicating door when the telephone rang. He turned to his desk to take the call, placed his hand over the mouthpiece, muttering, 'It's Langley, Sam. Just go through and make yourself comfortable, I'll join you in a moment when I've found out what Uncle Sam wants.'

***

And so Sam Kagan was back on the permanent staff of *HaMossad leModi'in uleTafkidim Meyuhadim* - the Institute for Intelligence and Special Operations - Mossad for short. An organisation with a long string of glittering successes over the years but also with some recent dismal failures. He would do all in his power to restore its reputation and defend his country - especially now that the world's danger rating had just moved up several notches.

"Sword, famine and pestilence", these had been three national disasters feared and suffered by Israel of old. Now Sam Kagan was personally charged with the defence of the nation against the super plagues of the modern world. Sitting behind his desk he felt far less adequate than when he arrived in the Deputy Director's room less than an hour before. From his briefcase he took a framed photograph of Elizabeth and the children and placed it on the desk. And then he began his new duties with a short and fervent prayer before picking up the telephone and calling Elizabeth. He gave her the news of his new job but no details. Particulars would follow when she arrived at Ben-Gurion Airport in a couple days time. And once again he smiled to himself as things clicked into place in his memory - it had been David Ben-Gurion who had sent Peres off to negotiate with the French for the nuclear reactor. Sometimes a dove could pack quite a punch! And beyond any doubt the nuclear threat had deterred rogue nations - so far at any rate.

***

Elizabeth experienced very mixed emotions as she took in what Sam had just told her on the telephone. He had merely said that he had got the job and that it was more demanding than anything he had expected. So they wouldn't be back living in the Golan with snow-capped Mount Hermon a little way to the north. It would be the urban sprawl of Tel Aviv for the family. And gone would be the low key, relaxed work of the vineyards and the winery at Katzrin that had been such an enjoyable change for Sam. She had at one and the same time wanted Sam to get the Mossad job and hoped that they wouldn't give it to him. She wondered what it would entail for him - and for the family. He had sounded happy with the decision and so she was willing to accept the situation. Though that acceptance was tinged with regret, she was proud on his behalf. His ability and courage had been recognised and she knew that he would relish the demands of his new job, whatever it might entail. She longed to know more but that would have to wait until she got back to Israel, perhaps in just a couple of days.

All along she had known in herself that Mossad would give Sam a management job, certainly she had been sure of it since his return from Tel Aviv at the end of the mission. Perhaps they would be able to keep the house in Katzrin and use it at weekends and for holidays. However she wondered about security, would they be keeping Sam and the family cocooned in case of kidnap attempts. She knew the risk to security that a kidnap would present. Still, they would learn to live with whatever restrictions and limitations were necessary. To be together as a family would be enough.

She went in search of Dov and the others to tell them. The Mums were in the kitchen chatting over the preparation of lunch and they accepted the news with resignation.

Mrs Feldman was philosophical about the move, 'Well our French holiday had to end some time. I think I'll enjoy being back in Jerusalem with my Russian friends. Being here does have some drawbacks. Mind you it'll be a shame to miss the grape harvest after seeing all the work Dov and Sam have put in and the bunches swelling on the vines.'

'Perhaps you'd like to stay for just a little longer, Mum, and keep Esty company while Dov sees to the harvest and the wine making?'

'Yes, we'll think about that, though I'd miss the children. You'd have to let them speak to me on the telephone. Where will you be, the Golan or somewhere else?'

'Tel Aviv, Mum. That will be nearer to you in Jerusalem so we'll be able to call on you more often.'

'And I'll be able to call on you more frequently, Elizabeth and make sure your looking after my son-in-law and grandchildren properly. What do you think about all this, Esty?'

'I think my son probably has his own plans and that he's not going to need me as housekeeper for very much longer. So the time for a move back to Tel Aviv is just about right.'

Dov appeared at the back door of the kitchen in search of a cup of coffee. 'Hi Dov, Sam's got the job at HQ and we're going to be heading home soon.'

His face betrayed his lack of enthusiasm for the move, 'That's what I've been afraid of for some time. Out there are hectares of grapes that we've worked hard on, through rain and shine, to bring to peak condition. Now we're just going to hand it all over to someone else, pack our bags and go! And besides there's Yvonne ... we're due to visit a jeweller in Marseille tomorrow.'

Esty caught the news at once, 'Congratulations my boy, I like the girl and it's about time you gave me more grandchildren, Dov!' She enfolded him in a mighty hug and the others took their turn in congratulating him.

Elizabeth switched on the kettle, 'You came in from your beloved vines for coffee Dov so I won't delay making it. By the way it's not that bad, Sam left a message for you when he 'phoned: if you wish to stay on and continue to run the *Domaine* you're free to do so, the IDF are agreeable to you retiring on a pension. It strikes me that it would fit in very well with marriage to Yvonne: then she wouldn't have to give up her job in the Marseille police.'

She watched the smile of contentment on his face, Sam had been bang on target in guessing what Dov longed for. Getting the Mossad job he wanted had not made Sam forget his friend Dov. A good leader did his best look after his loyal troops. And she was glad for another reason: despite memories of her encounter with Mustafa Malik, she liked the *Domaine* and they would be able to come here and visit Dov and Yvonne from time to time. And she asked herself what kind of a situation she and the family would be returning to in Israel, despite efforts at securing a truce, violence between Jew and Palestinian continued to escalate.

Later that day when the travel arrangements had been made for herself, Mrs Feldman and the children to fly out to Israel on the following Wednesday - Esty Levin was staying until the wedding in November after which she would be on her way back to Tel Aviv - Elizabeth sat by herself in the lounge thinking. The Jewish New Year and the High Holy Days were now past, they were into another year, 5762 in the Jewish calendar. And what it held she couldn't begin to guess. The different calendars emphasised the different worlds of Jew and Gentile, yet they were worlds that met and in large areas merged. It was a complex relationship with its tensions and delights: common roots and old antagonisms.

She thought of her own background and the relationships and events that had formed her. A secular Communist upbringing within the old Soviet system. A devout Russian Orthodox mother who had imparted some of her Christian values. A father who had died when she was young and a drunken stepfather who had tried to abuse her. Her sense of escape and adventure on being recruited by the KGB. Working in Canada and the USA for the KGB and its successor the SVR - same thing, new name! - with Vladimir as her work partner and, for a time, as her lover.

She sat eyes closed immersed in her memories. Her first meeting with Sam came to mind, a shared table over dinner at the Hotel International in Basel, when he had passed himself off as a journalist. Then the next day, the Sunday before the carnival, when together they had enjoyed glorious weather in the Alps. She remembered with a shudder that evening in a Basel hotel room when she had shot Vladimir who had drugged her drink and attempted to rape her. She had been carrying Peter Lewis' child and had fought to defend it and herself from Vladimir's attack. Images passed through her mind of the Basel remand prison, her trial for murder, Sam's intervention as witness and her conviction on the reduced charge of manslaughter. And then marriage to Sam after he had resigned from Mossad on a point of principle. Marriage and a second child, although Sam always treated both without distinction as his. Happy years in the Golan and then this year, or at any rate several months of it, in Cassis. And next? Only time would tell. She would be with Sam and the children - that was enough for her happiness and peace of heart and mind. And within her their next child was slowly growing and developing.

Tomorrow Peter Lewis and his wife Ruth would be calling so that Peter could see Olga - he was a good father who continued to show responsibly for their child. Elizabeth had invited Mark Gould to lunch to meet Ruth. Both were Brits and both were in the wine trade so it would be good for them to make the acquaintance of one another. Once the children had been put to bed for the night she with her mother and Esty would begin tidying up the house. She needed it to be in rather better order for tomorrow, she didn't want Ruth thinking that she lived in a tip! Besides she didn't want to leave Esty and Dov with too much work before the wedding. And tomorrow she would book flights with El Al back to France in a couple of months time, she and Sam were not going to miss Dov and Yvonne's celebrations. She prayed that no crisis would keep Sam at his Mossad desk in November and prevent his attendance at the wedding.

Chapter 36

Thursday 18 October 2001

The *Operation Account* file lay on Sam's desk, where Ehud had placed it, for him to see the latest addition. It was the letter page of the Jerusalem Post of 11th October 2001. Ringed was a letter from Rabbi Mendel Gur of Leeds, England:

> **Ashkelon Railway Project**
> Sir, - My pleasure in hearing of this project, full of tourist potential, was dashed when I read that the steam locomotive concerned was being brought from the Ukraine. Don't the organisers of this project realise that the railways of Israel are of 4 ft 8½ in (1,435 mm) gauge and not the 5 ft (1,524 mm) of the Russian railways? Tsar Nicholas the First had been persuaded to adopt this wider gauge by an American adviser. Perhaps those behind the project intend to lay tracks of the Russian gauge at their site outside Ashkelon but this means that the locomotive will be confined to those tracks.
> I had hoped for the day when it would be possible for those of us who love the smell of steam, hot oil and half burned coal to travel on a steam hauled special from Tel Aviv to Jerusalem. The sight of a steam locomotive in Jerusalem station, which strangely has the appearance of an English rural terminus, will have to be delayed until someone gets it right and imports a suitable locomotive. Indeed <u>any</u> train reaching Jerusalem would be welcome. Next year in Jerusalem? Perhaps it will be a little longer than that - we

can but hope!

Rabbi Mendel Gur
Leeds, UK
President, Israel and Middle East Railway Association

'And what can we do with the locomotive now, Sam? It's been sitting in an army base since the people at Dimona removed the bomb from its innards and they want rid of it. The thing's a nuisance. People know that there was a bomb but they don't realise it was nuclear.' A lorry had removed the locomotive with the defused nuclear weapon from Tel Aviv to an IDF camp near the Israeli bomb factory at Dimona on the edge of the Negev by a circuitous route, passing through a couple of military bases en route to ensure it wasn't followed.

'If the thing hadn't been made safe it would have had rather more nuisance value, Ehud, until then it was "full of *terrorist* potential". Put the locomotive on display in one of the southern towns with a large Russian population, it'll remind them of home when they go out to buy their pork! But if you'd rather have it in kosher hands then the Rabbi in Leeds is probably your man, despite the gauge problem.

'However I think there are other things to exercise us this morning, the CIA people are due at 9.15 - that's 25 minutes time - the meeting will take up most of the day. Have you got the Sarin file ready? And our chemical warfare expert is here? The technical expert, that is. Good. We'll have to hope that our informant is mistaken but act as though he's spot on target!'

At that moment Zvi from Admin appeared brandishing a sheet of paper. Despite Sam's efforts to get rid of him he wasn't going to leave without receiving an explanation. 'Is this a joke of some sort or is it an effort to add to someone's expenses?' He slapped the sheet down in front of Sam, 'Just look at this!'

It was an invoice from a firm in Marseille:

> *"To the cutting, inscription (per the attached sheet) and fixing of a brass commemorative plaque in the Basilica de Notre Dame de la Garde, after having obtained the approval of the Church authorities, Euros 500 (including TVA)."*

Sam looked up, 'I was keeping a promise I'd made to one of our helpers in the operation. It's peanuts after all.'

'We've got the Audit Section coming in next week, what will they make of it, particularly the inscription?'

Sam turned the invoice over and scrutinised the attachment:

Ave Maria. With heartfelt thanks to Our Lady

whose intercession averted certain catastrophe.

Jacob and Family, 16th September 2001

'It looks correct and in order to me, that's what we asked for.'

Zvi looked puzzled, 'Are you all right Sam, it's an unusual request from an Orthodox Rabbi!'

'It's OK, as I said just now I promised one of our helpers I'd do it. You see the late Dr Dominique Garnier responded to our lady's intercession, our lady was a Swiss shrink called Maria Bertorelli. The capitalisation may not be wholly appropriate but the words themselves do tell the truth. Using the name Jacob seemed preferable as it was Israel's original name, one which wouldn't give too much away to the curious. It's ironic that the perpetrator of the intended outrage was also Jakob. Tell audit to come to see me if they want to know more.

When I go to Marseille for Dov and Yvonne's wedding next month I'll get you a photo of the plaque. By the way, it was to Yvonne that I promised the plaque. Now take it all away and let me get on with my preparation for this morning's meeting in 20 minutes time.'

Chapter 37

Monday 5th November 2001

'I wonder, Sam, if we could drive up the coastal plain and stop off at Megiddo?'

'Of course, Mark, it's on our route back to the Galilee and the Golan.'

Erik Blum sat in the back of the car lost in thought.

Three hours later they had completed their tour of the excavations and Sam and Mark stood on the top of the mound of Megiddo gazing out along the Vale of Jezreel. All was tranquil and at last the sun had broken through.

'Peaceful isn't it, old chap?'

'Indeed it is. The place of battles!'

'Yes, I refreshed my memory on the flight to Tel Aviv from Liddell Hart's book on the Great War. I've always wanted to see the place where Allenby annihilated the Turkish armies with such small loss of life. Just listen to what Liddell Hart says of it:

> *"When full deduction is made for the advantageous conditions of September, 1918, the conclusion remains that the triumph immortalized by the already immortal name of Megiddo is one of history's masterpieces by reason of the breadth of vision and treatment. If the subject was not a difficult one, the picture is almost unique as a perfect conception perfectly executed."*

Do you know that in 38 days the British and Empire troops advanced 350 miles and captured 75,000 prisoners, yet they only suffered less than 5,000 casualties. True they were fighting demoralised Turkish troops but nevertheless the enemy had the German Liman von Sanders and Mustafa Kamel as leaders.' He stood there gazing out along the valley before returning to the subject. 'Sam, you're a military man - as well as several other things - how do you rate Megiddo as a campaign?'

And for the next hour they were deep in military discussion and appraisal, looking at maps with Sam giving details of the terrain.

'Well this is a fascinating visit, it's good to have a guide who knows his war history and really appreciates what's involved in a campaign. By the way how far are we from Tel Aviv?'

'About 60 km, Mark, why do you want to know?'

'I was just thinking about what would have happened here if the thing had gone off.'

'I'm not sure. If I remember rightly Moshe's figures were for an aerial explosion 5,000 metres up. That would have put *Har-Megiddo*, the Hill of Megiddo within the severe blast damage area - 65% fatalities and 30% of the rest injured. But from a ground level blast with the Carmel Range in the way, I just don't know. And fortunately it's academic, though interesting! But it seems a long time ago that Moshe was scaring the pants off some of us with the details.'

And it also seemed such a long time since Sam had last stood at Megiddo with Erik Blum and seen the normally staid Swiss transformed by contemplation of the final battle - Armageddon. Then they had looked back 3,000 years or more to another battle, the defeat Sisera's mighty force of 900 iron chariots by Deborah and Barak, after the Almighty's intervention with a downpour to render the high-tech Iron Age chariots unusable.

While they had been discussing Allenby's triumph Erik had wandered off on his own, as on his previous visit he was deep in eschatological thought.

Sam's reflections were broken by Mark, 'Well, I suppose we ought to be on our way, your Elizabeth will be wondering what's become of us. But you'll take me out into the Golan and talk me through some of the tank battles of the Six Days War and the *Yom Kippur War* won't you?'

'Certainly, I'd enjoy that, Mark. As for Elizabeth, I called her while you were looking at Solomon's Stables - or whatever they really were - and said we'd be home within a couple of hours. Let's go, you might want to stop off somewhere else on the way. We'll have a short break in Tiberias so you can see Kinneret. Elizabeth's been packing some of the things we won't be leaving at Katzrin when we move to Tel Aviv. And that's another thought, Mark, if the Germans and their Turkish allies had had mobile 'phones in 1918 Allenby would have had a far harder task - it wouldn't have been any use cutting the enemy's telegraph wires! That's what it's all about in the field, movement, intelligence and communication.'

Erik had finished his reflection and was waiting for them by the car, he had been more interested in the Biblical significance of the site than in the events of World War I. Sam followed through a line of thought that had been started off by the reference to mobile 'phones: in 1918, *three thousand years on* from the battle of 1000 BCE, there had still been reliance on horses for transport. Now, less than a hundred years later, things had changed radically and were, even now, changing at an accelerating pace. The means and ways of bringing life to an apocalyptic end were readily to hand as he had lately experienced at very close quarters.

Sam unlocked the car, 'Well, Erik, Armageddon averted?'

Blum smiled and replied quietly, 'Armageddon postponed, perhaps. And when the real thing comes I don't expect that any of Mossad, British Intelligence or Swiss Security will have very much influence on the course of events!'

***

Tanya had just succeeded in balancing the restaurant's books for the previous month, they were doing pretty well, Pierre's changes seemed to be working. Her mobile signalled a message. It was from Michael. She had been wondering how the operation had gone, he had previously told her more than he ought and she had been worried that it might have failed, though nothing apocalyptic had been in the news.

> *'Operation Account successful. Device defused. Thank you for your assistance. Over and out for the last time. All the best with Pierre and your restaurant. M.'*

She had replied to him:

> *'Glad to have been of use but glad to be retired. T.'*

Then she had wiped both messages. Farewell to Mossad! Another phase in her life completed ... though she wondered how Michael knew about the restaurant. She was determined not to do them any favours in future. Life with Pierre was as good as it came and she was glad, very glad that they had sent her to his café.

Life was very interesting and this was very different from her past experiences in Russia's academic world, in the Tel Aviv brothel and as the bait in Mossad's honey traps. Being regularly with the same partner and in love was something new. As near as she had come to this in the past was with Teddy, a Tel Aviv financier who had persuaded her to spend the night with him once a week at his up-market apartment. She'd liked him, he'd been gentle and caring but unwilling to commit himself, preferring a commercial relationship. Once when she'd referred to herself as his “regular call-girl” he'd objected to the term and suggested "salaried girl friend" which indeed had appealed to her, after all they regularly ate out at posh restaurants and attended concerts together. Her salary had always been there waiting on the hall table of his apartment when she called – there'd very often been more money than her fee, perhaps a bonus for being good in the girl friend rôle, and sometimes a generous voucher for one of the women's-wear shops in the Dizengoff Center. But life with Pierre was totally different – they were committed to one another and were partners both in business and in their home. Again she was grateful to Mossad for her very last assignment. She went down to the restaurant to report to Pierre on the state of the finances and to tell him, once again, how much she loved him.

Chapter 38

Monday 19th November 2001

The wind was beginning to strengthen, its gusts causing the fabric of the black tent to shudder. ' ... I'd heard nothing from Jakob for so long - for almost three months – 16th September had passed without anything happening in Palestine - though as you well know much had happened elsewhere - so I decided that I must find out what had become of him.' The other nodded his assent.

'First I went to Frankfurt, to that tiny apartment of his - I have a key to the place - and there? Nothing to help. There was almost nothing at all there, you would have thought it was up for sale, the refrigerator empty, switched off and with the door open. A few cans of food in a cupboard as well as some tea and a jar of coffee. There was nothing in the trash bin apart from packaging from a pain killer. His library was still there but there were no personal papers in his desk, no bank accounts or anything like that. Of course there could have been something tucked away in one of his books but I hadn't long enough to search. I went late in the evening and, as I've said, I was quick but *that* didn't stop someone from following me. No, he didn't trouble me for long - a quick blow to the back of his head and he lost interest in the pursuit, temporarily at any rate. They were obviously short of personnel that late in the evening. I expect they'd have fielded a full team if I'd obliged by calling there between nine and five the next day! Clearly the German Security had been through the place and that might account for the absence of any papers, but I don't think so. It looked to me as though, when he left the apartment, Jakob knew he was leaving it for the last time - I mean that he had made up his mind to clear out.' Again the other nodded his assent.

'So Jakob was gone. Then I followed a hunch. Do you

remember the woman psychiatrist he was involved with, the one who had worked with kids in the camps?' Another nod. 'I decided to look her up, I couldn't think of any other idea. I remembered that she worked in a hospital in Mulhouse - that's in eastern France - and it wasn't difficult to get her address and telephone number. So once again I called. Or rather I reached the door and found a faded wreath of flowers propped up against it, clearly an indication of death. A neighbour told me that the woman and the man who had been there with her had died early in September, it seems there had been a suicide pact ... after all Jakob was in the late stages of cancer.

'The house was up for sale and I managed to get inside and get rid of the clerk who came with me. I told him that I'd heard of the violent deaths in the house and wanted to be sure that the atmosphere of the place wouldn't affect me, to make sure it wouldn't be an unquiet house - the French are an amazingly superstitious people, given to horoscopes and fortune tellers, so he swallowed it. I found nothing there, they'd already cleared out all the woman's papers, probably they'd gone to some university or medical department. The neighbour who told me of the deaths said that a Swiss woman psychiatrist had spoken on the local television news and announced a memorial fund for the woman to support work among Palestinian kids. Some mysterious donor it seems.'

'Our money?'

'Yes, possibly. Maybe not all of it, I wouldn't be surprised if the Ukrainians hadn't taken him for a ride, parted him from the money and given nothing in return. They wouldn't have dared to try that with us! Failure could have been another motive for the suicide pact, disillusion as well as impending death.'

'Have *you* any illusions?'

'None that I know of!'

'Keep it that way then!'

'Do you want me to investigate the Swiss woman

psychiatrist.'

'No, if the money's going to be used for the benefit of our people she's unlikely to have been involved in plundering the funds. What's been lost?'

'Probably $10 million. As well as Mustafa Malik ... lost overboard from that ludicrously named yacht of his, the *Viagra,* if the French authorities are to be believed. The theory is that he got drunk and fell overboard. But we would have had to dispose of him in any case, he had become even more decadent than the average Westerner and too much of a risk.'

The wind had strengthened and sand was beating on the sides of the black tent. It was a potent reminder of how far removed they were from the West and its dangerous culture. Here it was almost possible to feel sorry for Westerners! For them life was so complex, so cluttered: here it was wondrously, exhilaratingly, pure, simple, unadorned and unadulterated.

Chapter 39

Friday 25 January 2002

Sam Kagan sat at breakfast in a Mossad safe house situated in a road just off Knightsbridge, London, not far from Harrods. That morning's edition of *The Times* lay open at the obituary page. The day would be spent renewing contacts with old acquaintances from the CIA's London station and the weekend with one of them in the Buckinghamshire countryside. He suspected that these relaxed encounters would be of considerably more value than Monday's formal meeting with the Brits and Americans at Grosvenor Square. He poured himself a second coffee and turned back to the paper:

"Elie Hobeika

Pro-Israel Lebanese warlord who was accused of the Sabra and Chatila massacres but later reinvented himself and co-operated with Syria

Even in the grisly annals of civil strife in the Lebanon in the 1970s and 1980s, the career of the Maronite Christian warlord Elie Hobeika stands out as one of particular notoriety. At his door are laid the massacres of Palestinian refugees in the Sabra and Chatila camps in September 1982, and though he always denied involvement the evidence against him is overwhelming ...

By 1975, when full-scale civil war erupted between Christians and Muslims in Lebanon, Hobeika already had, although barely 18, a fearsome reputation in the Maronite League's military faction known as the

Tanzim. On December 6, 1975, as a member of the crack militia unit known as the "Begin group", he was one of the participants in the first major massacre of the civil war, when forty Muslims were killed in retaliation for the deaths of four Christians.

As fighting intensified throughout the 1970s, Hobeika gained a reputation for his ruthlessness. One of his young subordinates, Robert Maroun Hatem, who later wrote the book *From Israel to Damascus*, attested to his mesmerising personality and the infectious power of his anti-Syrian invective. The union of the various Maronite militias in 1976 to form what was styled the Lebanese Forces (LF) gave the rising commander more influence on military issues.

By 1978 Hobeika was at the head of the LF's 3rd Division, which he organised into three rapid intervention units. His sobriquet "HK", by which he was known throughout the Phalangist ranks, arose from the Heckler and Koch sub-machinegun he always carried. Hobeika led special Phalangist units which had received training in Israel in all the fiercest fighting of the period 1978-81, which saw the Israeli invasion of southern Lebanon, soon after to be followed by their withdrawal and the establishment of a buffer zone controlled by Christian militias friendly to Israel.

In June 1982 the Israelis were back in the Lebanon, this time with the avowed aim of eliminating the Palestinian Liberation Organisation's threat to their northern border once and for all. In September that year, with

Israeli forces pushing into West Beirut and trapping more than 6,000 Palestinian fighters there, Hobeika and his unit were guarding 2,000 refugees who had crowded into two camps at Sabra and Chatila in the western sector of the city.

An Israeli commission, the Kahan Commission, which reported on subsequent events the following year concluded that Hobeika was directly responsible for what followed, an opinion echoed by Hatem's account in *From Israel to Damascus*.

On September 15, Hobeika informed his subordinates that the 2,000 fugitives were mainly terrorists and that he had been charged with clearing them out of the camp and handing them over to Israeli troops. According to Hatem, Ariel Sharon, then Israel's Defence Minister, had expressly ordered Hobeika to be on the watch for any irregular behaviour by his men.

On September 16 Hobeika ordered the extermination of the occupants of the camps. Late that afternoon his troops, many of whom were high on cocaine and heroin, passed through the Israeli lines surrounding the camps and began a systematic butchery of men, women and children as well as foreign nurses and doctors. At one point during the massacre, which went on throughout the night, Hobeika was called on his radio by one of his subordinates and asked what should be done with a group of women and children. Hobeika replied: "That is the last time you will ask me that question. You know exactly what to do."

By the time Sharon - himself criticised as

having had indirect responsibility by the Kahan Commission - realised that something was amiss at Sabra and Chatila, the slaughter was complete. Sharon ordered flares to be fired to illuminate the camps and prevent any further "misunderstandings". But the light from the flares revealed only the extent of the horror.

The events of September 1982 did not, however, prevent Hobeika from playing a continuing role in the political process that eventually brought peace to Lebanon. By 1985 he had turned his back on his sponsors the Israelis and was dutifully declaring for Syrian ears that Lebanon was "Arab" and that Syria had a "major role" to play in the country's destiny ...

After benefiting from a parliamentary amnesty for war crimes committed during the civil war, Hobeika was appointed head of a government office for the resettlement of more than one million Lebanese displaced by the years of conflict. In 1992 and 1996 he was elected to parliament, and in 1998 he served as Minister for Water. In some quarters he was even seen as a presidential candidate, but he was defeated in the parliamentary elections of 2000.

Elie Hobeika, Lebanese militia leader and politician, was born in 1957. He died in a bomb explosion on January 23, 2002, aged 44."

Sam's eyes were drawn back to the words "a systematic butchery of men, women and children as well as foreign nurses and doctors." And one of those nurses had been Jakob Schmidt's fiancée. Her loss had led to

Schmidt sustaining for 19 years his festering desire to avenge the evil done to her, her colleagues and the Palestinian refugees for whom they were caring. Only a week before, as part of the final tidying up of the Basel Account file, he had looked at a list of the victims of the Sabra and Shatila atrocity and wondered which one of the European women it was who would have married Jakob Schmidt had she lived. Somehow Sam had found it a profound relief to be aware of the rationale underlying Schmidt's actions. He had always needed to know what was in people's minds, to have some idea of their thoughts and motives. Irrational and random violence was far harder to anticipate or counter.

Sam had recently read up on the events of 16th to 18th September 1982 and one fact had jumped out at him: the knock-on effect of violence. In 1976 Hobeika's family and fiancée had been murdered by Palestinian militiamen and their Lebanese allies, that massacre had been in response to one, earlier that year, of Palestinians and Lebanese Muslims by Christian militants. Atrocity, revenge and yet further revenge. An escalating cycle of violence which in 2001 had almost reached the ultimate catastrophe. For a moment he regretted that Schmidt had died before Hobeika and without the knowledge that justice had at last come to the perpetrator of his fiancée's murder.

For their recent deliverance Rabbi Sam Kagan, now a member of Mossad's top leadership (he disliked the word management) gave hearty thanks to the Almighty.

The thought of the savagery unleashed on the occupants of the camps sickened him. And now someone had dealt with the chief perpetrator of the outrage. What was the quote? Yes that was it, appropriately from the Christian scriptures, it was something like, "All they that take the sword shall perish by the sword." How sad it was that so much of the history of the Mid-East was written, and continued to be written, with gun, bomb and rocket.

And this obituary would be treated by historians as a footnote to the account of the events of September 1982 in the Lebanon. He wondered whether there were any more such footnotes to come. The Protective Security Department of *Shin Bet* would certainly be on the alert. But Schmidt's bomb, had it detonated, would have been far more than a footnote to September 1982, it would have been an unparalleled atrocity on such a scale that millions would have had neither obituary nor grave. It had indeed been a deliverance - and by such a slender margin. They had escaped by the skin of their teeth like long-suffering Job of old. Now that was an interesting Biblical expression! And the rabbi in Sam Kagan found time to ponder the words for a while.

There was so much to be done. Sam had asked for a substantial job and Mossad had given him a huge one. The grim shadow of Schmidt's bomb had gone but the conflict in Israel and the Territories seemed only to be intensifying. If anyone had fresh thoughts on resolving the situation Sam would be only too pleased to listen and then take them back home to Arik Sharon and the other politicians whose promises of increased security were so far from fulfilment. How incredible it was that a few suicide bombers should pose a greater threat to Israel than a host of Arab armies with tanks! And, if the Americans were to attack Iraq, Israel would, once more, be the prime target of Iraqi rockets, this time loaded with chemical or biological payloads. Some would argue that it was time, once again, for a pre-emptive strike on Iraq by the Israeli Air Force - as they had done to the Daura nuclear reactor on the banks of the River Tigris in 1981. Sam would be listening to all sides of the argument and would have his own contribution to make.

He folded the newspaper and cleared the table. Then, after a telephone call to Elizabeth in Tel Aviv, he set off with his bodyguard into a wet English morning heading for Grosvenor Square and the day's work.

Glossary of Terms

These are not authoritative definitions but a guide to the meaning of various terms.

Chabad-Lubavitch – One of the most dynamic Chassidic groups with headquarters in Brooklyn, New York. Founded 250 years ago it was based for many years in a Russian town which gave it the name Lubavitch, "the city of brotherly love". Its last Rebbe (see below) died in 1994 and there has been no successor though the group continues to be very active.

Chassidism – a Jewish religious movement, divided into numerous separate groups There are at least 30 larger groups. It was founded in 18th-century Eastern Europe by Rabbi Israel Baal Shem Tov as a reaction against what was perceived by some as excessively legalistic Judaism. It may be said to emphasise a felt faith rather than a cerebral one.

Halakha – Jewish law.

Jupette – miniskirt from the French *jupe* = skirt. The 12 women in the first government of Alain Juppé (17th May to 7th November 1995) were known as ***Juppettes*** (or *Jupettes*) a term considered sexist and condescending.

***Kibbutz** (plural Kibbutzim)* **-** an economically and socially independent society founded on principles of communal ownership of property, social justice, and equality, often (though not always) agricultural.

Kibbutznik – a member of a kibbutz.

***Moshav** (plural Moshavim)* – similar to a kibbutz but farms in a Moshav are owned individually rather than communally and are of equal size, the owner being entitled to keep his own profits. Equipment is shared and sometimes labour is pooled.

Rebbe – the leader of a Chassidic group, a sort of super-rabbi.

Shabbat – Sabbath, the Jewish day of rest and worship.

Shalom – Hebrew for peace, harmony, wholeness, prosperity, welfare and tranquility. Commonly used to say both hello and goodbye.

Shabbat Shalom – the Sabbath greeting.

The Institute - *HaMossad leModi'in uleTafkidim Meyuhadim* (The Institute for Intelligence and Special Operations or simply *Mossad*) is Israel's national intelligence agency.

About the Author

Born 21 August 1939, Plymouth, Devon, UK. Secondary education at Plymouth College.

Working life with HM Customs and Excise (on purchase tax in north and west London and at a distillery in Dagenham) and then with the Inland Revenue, including five years at the Special Investigations Section, dealing with tax avoidance and also tax evasion cases, followed by spells as a Senior Inspector in charge of tax offices in Willesden (north-west London), Dalston (north-east London) and finally Paignton, Devon.

From 1960 to 1962 did National Service in the RAF, servicing V-bomber navigation and bombing radar equipment, mainly at Marham, Norfolk.

Married to Jennifer with a son (in Australia) and a daughter (in the UK) and five very sporty grandsons.

Interests: politics, music, history, theology (Christian and Jewish), travel, railways and photography (which two often combine).

Published in 2015 *The Basel Formula (Part 1 of The Basel Trilogy) and in 2016 The Basel Exodus (Part 2).* Both are available from Amazon on Kindle and in Paperback.

Now published, in late 2016, Part 3, *The Basel Account.*

Also in the pipeline, an unconnected novel: *O Château, O Seasons!* a romance set in the Ardèche region of France south of Lyon.

Apart from Moscow he has visited all the locations featured in these novels.

His book of railway photographs, *Plymouth Steam 1954 to 1963* was published in 1984 and he has contributed photographs to several railway magazines. Another book of railway photographs is planned which will cover the Southern Region of British Railways from Padstow through to Dover during the 1950s and early 1960s.

His website is at www.baseltrilogy.co.uk

98185062R00235

Made in the USA
Columbia, SC
22 June 2018